RETURNED

D1160817

REIGN
RETURNED

The Felserpent Chronicles

KATIE KERIDAN

Published by SparkPress, a BookSparks imprint,
A division of SparkPoint Studio, LLC
Phoenix, Arizona, USA, 85007
www.gosparkpress.com

Published 2022
Printed in the United States of America
Print ISBN: 978-1-68463-155-1
E-ISBN: 978-1-68463-156-8
Library of Congress Control Number: 2022904956

Book design by Stacey Aaronson

REIGN
RETURNED

PROLOGUE

The spells surrounding the castle wouldn't hold much longer. Blow after blow rained down against the outer walls, and through the window, Schatten caught a glimpse of blue sparks ricocheting off grey stone. He felt the assault in his own body, as if unseen hands were pummeling his chest.

The image of a four-footed serpent appeared on the wide gold bracelets he wore on each wrist, and his wife's voice filled his mind.

I don't think the spells will last much longer, Kareth said.

She was right. When the protective enchantments fell, so too would their kingdom. And that would be the end—the end of everything they had worked for, the end of a thousand-year-old monarchy that had withstood every other change and challenge.

Where are you? he asked Kareth, tightening the straps of his scabbard and securing his sword between his shoulder blades.

In the library, she replied.

I'll be right there.

Schatten hurried down the marble stairs two at a time. The military-trained part of him was pleased to have an objective, even as the rest of him was all too aware each footstep carried him closer to decisions he didn't relish making.

Suddenly, the walls on either side of him trembled, causing the heavy tapestries to sway as paintings shook in their gilded frames. The bombardments were becoming stronger. Clenching his jaw, he lengthened his stride.

Reaching the bottom of the stairs, Schatten turned down a hallway and ducked into a set of open double doors. Kareth was there, dressed for traveling in loose breeches, an oversized tunic, and her cloak. She was holding her crown and staring at it as if trying to memorize every detail of the delicate gold and silver headpiece. Schatten pulled the doors shut behind him, causing his wife to look up. Her red-rimmed eyes were filled with sadness, and his chest constricted again, only this time, it wasn't from an attack on the castle. He quickly gathered Kareth into his arms and rested his cheek against the top of her head.

"Where did we go wrong?" she asked softly, her voice muffled against his shirt. "Every other time someone attempted a coup, we were able to stop it."

"This time our enemy was different," he replied. "There were traitors on both sides." So many lives had been lost as the result of vicious, careful planning that had caught everyone unawares. Inhaling deeply, he forced down the heartbroken rage threatening to overwhelm him. He would be strong in his final moments as king.

Kareth pulled away and looked up at him, her gaze serious.

"I don't want to leave, Schatten. Running away and leaving everyone to fend for themselves is wrong."

"I don't want to leave either," he agreed, "but we can't protect them anymore. I wish we could, but . . ." He fell silent, then continued. "We gave them permission to do as they think best, whether that means leaving or staying to try their luck under the new regime. Right now, they're better off on their own. We're the ones he's after."

He swallowed hard.

"Besides, we have to get the sword to safety. We can't risk it falling into the wrong hands."

Kareth's mouth quivered, but she gave a quick nod. Setting her crown down gently on a nearby chair, she ran her fingers over it one last time. She then picked up a knapsack from the floor and slipped it over her shoulders. Meeting Schatten's gaze, a soft smile tugged at the corners of her mouth. "I packed the—"

Before she could finish, an explosion rang out nearby, and the castle swayed as if it had been picked up by a churning ocean wave and hurled forward. Stone screeched, glass shattered, and wooden beams groaned as dust sifted down from the ceiling.

Schatten's breath caught mid-inhale, and he instinctively widened his stance and flexed his fingers, ready to reach for his sword. Kareth covered her mouth as she turned towards him, eyes filling with tears.

The protective spells had broken.

Shouts of delight from the insurgents mingled with shrieks from the few castle staff who remained, but both were quickly drowned out by the ear-piercing din of buckling metal and splintering wood.

"The front gate," said Schatten hoarsely.

Kareth nodded, placing a hand on his arm.

Abruptly, the library doors flung open, and Farent, captain of the castle guard and one of Schatten's most trusted advisors, stumbled into the room. His torso heaved, and the front of his shirt was spattered with blood.

"Your majesties!" he gasped, sounding as if the words were costing him his very life. "You must leave, now!"

All at once, his body straightened, as if someone had jerked him upright, and his face contorted into a painful grimace. Kareth shouted and tried to dart forward but Schatten shoved her behind him. Farent's eyes widened as he rose into the air. All was still for a moment, and then dark purple flames burst from the captain's body. They twined around his arms and legs, spilling from his nose and mouth, filling the air with the acrid stench of burned flesh. A moment later, the captain's body fell to the floor in a blackened heap.

Schatten turned around just in time to see his wife close her eyes as her fingers reached for the beads of her *sana* bracelet.

"No!" he yelled, shaking Kareth hard enough to make her open her eyes. "If it's not his time, you can find him later. But we have to leave!"

As he spoke, a figure moved through the veil of smoke filling the entryway, and Schatten extended a hand towards the doorframe. Red fire flowed from his fingers and melted the wood and stone, creating a temporary impasse. The figure on the other side screamed something unintelligible but didn't advance further.

Schatten caught Kareth's gaze, the spell for opening the portal on the end of his tongue.

"Have you got the Chronicles?"

Gulping back tears, she nodded.

"Fosgail!" said Schatten, and the air before them shimmered, then ripped apart with a loud hiss, scattering broken lines of light in all directions. As the portal expanded, the figure in the doorway leapt into the library, but Schatten didn't wait to see his face. He didn't need to. He shoved Kareth through the portal, then darted in after her as a shout cut through the crackling flames:

"I'll find you! *Both* of you!"

Schatten stepped out onto the shrub-covered mountainside and snapped his fingers, closing the portal. Kareth pressed against him, sobbing into his chest so hard her entire body shook. Tears filled his own eyes, and his breathing was ragged. Farent had been a gifted soldier and an unflinchingly loyal presence in the castle, but, more than that, he had been a friend.

"I'm so sorry, darling." Kareth's voice was thick with grief. After a moment, she turned to gaze at their beloved home. "Do you think they'll save it or let it be destroyed?"

Far in the valley below, smoke streamed out the castle windows, forming billowing ash clouds that spread swiftly across a reddening sky.

Schatten exhaled slowly. "I can't imagine they'd let it burn, but it would certainly send a message, if they did."He paused. Ridiculous as it was, he couldn't help himself. "All those books . . ."

He couldn't finish the sentence. If he allowed his grief over one loss to surface, the sorrow of all their losses would wash over him, rendering him useless. He couldn't afford that.

Kareth stretched up onto her tiptoes and kissed his jaw. "I know nothing will replace them, but we will build a magnificent library again. I promise."

Schatten gazed down at her, one side of his mouth lifting as he tucked her long black hair behind her ear before cupping his wife's cheek.

"Thank you. At least we made it out with the Chronicles."

She nodded and patted the straps of her knapsack. The book recounted everything important in their history—the constant wars between golden-blooded Astrals and silver-blooded Daevals; how Schatten, a Daevalic warrior, had been chosen to wed Kareth, an Astral healer, ending the violence by establishing the Felserpent monarchy; as well as the details of the Blood Treaty, the agreement that founded a kingdom where all citizens, regardless of their blood, could live peaceably. Without this book, such events could be forgotten, and that could never be allowed to happen.

The hillside suddenly rolled, and Schatten swayed on his feet, steadying Kareth with one hand and pressing the other to his chest.

"We haven't had earthquakes since we assumed responsibility for the realm!" he exclaimed. "What was that?"

Kareth winced, then bent down and placed her palm on the ground, closing her eyes for a moment before inhaling sharply.

Schatten reached down and jerked her to her feet, worried she might somehow sink into the rock below, then reached over his shoulder and withdrew the large gold and silver sword from his scabbard.

"What's happening?" he asked, fear sharpening his tone.

Kareth blinked in shock. "They're using the *Fragmen Incanta* . . . the Breaking Incantation." Her voice fell to little more than a whisper. "They're going to divide Aeles-Nocens. That's why members of both sides were willing to work together to overthrow us. Astrals and Daevals will each have their own realm."

Schatten was truly and utterly astounded. A few beats passed, and then Kareth slipped her hand into his, refocusing his thoughts.

As long as he had her, he could face anything else that befell him. Squaring his shoulders, he forced himself to begin walking, keeping a firm grasp on his wife's hand; then, he was struck by a thought so terrifying he came to an abrupt stop, causing Kareth to do the same. Looking down at her, he asked, "Do you think the breaking of the realm will end our immortality?"

The fire that filled his veins by virtue of his pyromancy surged through his chest, stealing the air from his lungs and for a moment, he couldn't breathe. He had never imagined a life without Kareth, never once envisioned some arbitrary end to their time together.

The anguish in his wife's eyes confirmed his fear.

"That is *not* what I agreed to!" he snapped angrily. "I will never be without you!"

An expression he couldn't quite decipher flickered across Kareth's face.

"I . . . well," she said, "you should know the Chronicles wasn't the only thing I saved from the library. I also brought the Pelagian Scroll."

Schatten stared at her, mystified. "Why?"

A blush of pride colored his wife's cheeks.

"I finished deciphering it. With Bartholomew's help, of course. It contains spells I've never heard of before, for all sorts of things." Her eyes glowed a deep, cerulean blue, and Schatten immediately recognized the determined set of her jaw. "There's even a spell for binding the shades of two lovers together."

"While that sounds wonderful, my dear," he said, "I fail to see what good it would do."

Kareth's face lit up with a fierce joy. "What if we could ensure we would be together, *forever*? Perhaps not in one continuous lifetime, like we had assumed, but what if we returned and were able to find one another? And, what if we could save the realm when we did? Not now, but . . . someday?"

Schatten's heart nearly stopped beating. Carefully, he replaced his sword in the scabbard, then ran a hand through his hair, pushing it back off his forehead. One of the benefits of his crown had been keeping his hair in place, and he already missed it.

"Is such a thing possible?" he finally asked.

Kareth nodded.

"I believe it is. We'll need Laycus's help, but . . . I have no doubt we can find each another again."

1

KYRA

I pressed down harder on the pestle, grinding the herbs in the small bowl until they were crushed into a fine paste. Scooping out the mixture, I spread it on a damp cloth and handed it to my father. He smiled his approval, and I grinned, pleased I'd remembered the fever-reducing properties of elderflowers and yarrow without being reminded.

Leaning forward, my father gently placed the cloth on the forehead of the woman lying before us. She coughed, a rattling sound that shook her entire torso, then slowly opened her eyes.

"Arakiss?" she rasped. Letting go of the bedsheet she'd been clenching, she reached out her hand, as if she needed to touch my father to believe he was truly there.

My father uncurled her gnarled fingers and took her hand in his own, giving it a firm squeeze.

"I'm here, Marta," he assured her.

"I hope you didn't come all this way . . . just for me," Marta wheezed, her breathing labored. The pneumonia had advanced since the village healer had contacted my father a few days ago and shared his concerns about the elderly woman's health. My father was the *Princeps Shaman* of Aeles, the highest-ranking healer in our realm, and his expertise was sought when local healers were unable to cure an illness.

"Of course I didn't come here just for you," my father replied as I fought down a smile. I had known Marta for as long as I could remember. Thinking she had inconvenienced someone—especially someone as important as my father—would only upset the feisty woman who clung stubbornly to the belief she didn't require help from anyone.

My father gestured towards me.

"Kyra's home for a few days before her internship starts in Celenia, and she wanted to do some traveling. We happened to be in Aravost and when we heard you weren't feeling well, we decided to stop by."

Marta chuckled, but her laughter quickly dissolved into a fit of coughing. She was silent for a moment, then asked, "Which *Donec* did you decide on for internship, Kyra?"

A kettle began to whistle from the fireplace across the room, and my father moved to attend to it. I stepped closer to the bed to make it easier for Marta to hear me.

"I don't find out where I matched for a few more days," I said. "I hope I'll be at the *Donec Medicinae*, but it's a very competitive placement. They're only taking one intern this year."

Marta waved a hand as if swatting away my worries.

"Nonsense! They'd be lucky to have you. In fact, if they don't take you, I'll lodge a formal complaint with—"

The woman began coughing again, and her Cypher, a dark grey squirrel named Nimkins, flicked her tail unhappily from her watchful post on the brass headboard.

I helped Marta sit up a little more, smoothing her long grey hair before patting her shoulder.

"Right now, your health needs more attention than my internship placement," I admonished her.

She rolled her jade eyes, but her lips twitched upwards ever so slightly.

"You sound just like your father." She watched as my father poured water from the kettle into a teacup filled with willow bark, which he placed on her nightstand. "You've trained her well, Arakiss."

My father looked at me with a pride that made me feel as if I could do anything, even though I was certain he overestimated my skills.

"Kyra is a natural healer," he said. "She's already better than I ever dreamed of being at her age."

A warmth spread over my cheeks, and for the thousandth time, I resented how easily my face gave away my feelings.

"Now," continued my father, coming around the bed to stand next to me. "Let's get Marta back on her feet so she will be ready to draft her complaint to the Council, should you be placed somewhere other than the *Donec Medicinae*." He dipped his head towards me. "Why don't you take the lead?"

I nodded and let out a slow exhale, concentrating. I could feel my *alera*, the basis of life that formed my connection with the rest of the world, swirling inside me. Everyone used their *alera* in different ways, sharing whatever special talent they'd been granted by the Gifters, and my gift involved healing sickness and injury.

A soft yellow light began to shine at my fingertips, moving up my fingers and encircling my wrists. Leaning forward, I gently placed one hand against Marta's chest, just below her collarbone, while placing my other hand against her neck. And then, I waited. At first, I could only hear the sounds in the bedroom—the crackling fire, the creaking hardwood floor beneath my boots, the squeak of the brass bed as Marta shifted beneath the blankets. But the background noises soon faded, and all I was aware of were the sounds and images filling my mind from Marta's body.

I could hear the fluid sloshing in her chest. I could see where air that should have flowed freely was blocked, obstructed by a small mass in her right lung. Focusing on it, I guided my *alera* to surround it, envisioning the light unmaking the mass piece by piece, similar to undoing a carpet on a loom by removing one thread of yarn at a time. As I took the mass apart, I let my *alera* absorb the poison that rushed to fill Marta's body, neutralizing it to flow harmlessly through her bloodstream.

"Humor excoqatur est," I said once the mass was gone, using the combination of a spell and my *alera* to dry up the remaining fluid and heal the infection.

As I lifted my hands and drew the *alera* back inside my body, Marta cautiously took a deep breath. When she didn't cough, she smiled and let out a pleased exhale, sinking deeper into the bed. Nimkins scurried down and curled up in the crook of Marta's neck, rubbing her head against the elderly woman's cheek.

"Well done," said my father. He then pointed to the *sana* bracelet on my left wrist. He had given it to me five years ago as a present for my thirteenth birth anniversary, and it was one of my most cherished possessions.

"Even though you are the one doing the work, the process of healing is still effortful for the patient's body," he explained. "I always like to use Saund to ease the process and make whoever you've healed as comfortable as possible."

I nodded, fingering the pearl known as the Soother, the second smallest of the seven beads on my bracelet. *"Huius vocis salicti,"* I replied, rubbing the bead as I said the incantation. Saund was always eager to be of service, and as the bead softly but determinedly let out a comforting note, the room was bathed with a peacefulness I couldn't help but enjoy myself.

"Excellent," nodded my father, his eyes crinkling with happiness as he watched the easy rise and fall of Marta's chest. "Our work here is done."

He patted Marta's hand, then pointed to Nimkins. "Make sure she drinks that tea," he instructed.

"Oh, she will," replied the squirrel, even as Marta made an unhappy noise. I hugged the woman goodbye, careful not to disturb her Cypher, and she gave my back a rough pat.

"You let me know if I need to file that complaint," she said. "I'm a living testament to your healing skills."

I assured her I would, and my father and I made our way to the living room, where Marta's children and many of her grandchildren waited. When my father told them of her recovery, there were tears and hugs and prayers of gratitude to the Medela, the Gifter of Healing.

Marta's eldest daughter, Henlynn, stepped forward and presented a scarf to my father. It appeared to be handmade, knit from yarn dyed various shades of blue—light aquamarine, cheerful teal, and dark cobalt. Since my father was paid for his work by the Astral government, he never charged his patients; however, I knew from traveling with him that families still wanted to express their gratitude, and he had long ago given up trying to refuse such gifts. As a result, his office in Aeles was overflowing with tokens of appreciation. Occasionally, some of them made their way into our house, prompting my mother to complain they clashed with the décor as she nevertheless found places to display them.

Rather than accept the scarf, though, my father smiled and gestured towards me.

"Kyra is the one who healed Marta," he said. "She deserves your thanks."

Henlynn turned towards me, and I tried to appear dignified, as if I did this sort of thing every day, even as my mouth went dry and my heart began to pound. It had never crossed my mind that I might receive such an honor, since my father had been with me the entire time, ready to answer questions or lend his expertise. But, I supposed he was right—I *had* done the actual healing by myself. Taking a deep breath, I tilted my head forward and allowed Henlynn to settle the scarf over my neck.

"It's beautiful," I said, untucking my long black hair and fingering the soft wool. "Thank you so much."

Henlynn grinned.

"It's no match for those blue eyes of yours," she said. "But it does highlight them nicely. Nothing wrong with drawing a little attention to ourselves now and then. After all, how else does one start a courtship?" She raised her eyebrows meaningfully and then winked at me.

For some reason I would never understand, my relationship status was a topic of endless interest to the folks my father and I helped. Here I had successfully healed a very sick woman, but rather than focusing on how I had done it or how to keep Marta healthy moving forward, we were discussing my *courtship*, or lack thereof! I clenched my jaw then quickly loosened it, trying to keep my annoyance from reaching my face. Henlynn didn't mean any harm; she, like so many women in so many villages we visited, simply seemed to think the greatest accomplishment of my life would be accepting an offer of marriage.

Henlynn's daughter, Adeline, raised a finger, and I drew a long breath, bracing myself for what the professional matchmaker would say.

"Just because Kyra *can* attract the eye of any man she wishes doesn't mean she ought to. Given your position, Arakiss, as well as your family's standing in the realm, there are things that must be considered." She pointed a plump finger at my father. "You could do very well allying yourself with certain political families, you know."

I shot my father a pleading look, silently begging him to end the conversation, and he gave me a smile that was both apologetic and amused before responding to Adeline.

"Kyra's focus right now is on extending her training and establishing her career, and her mother and I fully support her."

While that was true, I also knew nothing in the realm would please my mother more than the day my betrothal was announced. While she'd never done more than drop less-than-subtle hints about the possibility of potential suitors, I suspected that was because my father acted as a sort of buffer, absorbing or deflecting her matrimonial dreams for my future and leaving me free to pursue my own interests.

Gesturing towards the front door, my father suggested we take our leave. I thanked Henlynn again for the scarf and suffered through Adeline patting my check and encouraging me to meet with her when my "priorities" changed. Forcing a smile to my face and waving a goodbye that was far cheerier than I felt, I quickly followed my father outside.

2

KYRA

*T*he warm breeze ruffled the ivy climbing up the nearby grey stone wall, infusing the air with the sweet aroma of honeysuckle. My father and I had stopped at a tavern for lunch and were sitting on the outdoor patio. The sun shone through the trees, which provided a leafy green canopy overhead, and water bubbled cheerfully in a nearby brook.

I sliced off a piece of fresh-baked bread and spread a thick layer of honey over it. The four provinces that made up Aeles were all known for something, and Aravost was renowned for its smooth, sweet honey.

"Something on your mind?"

I glanced up at my father and grimaced, searching for the words to begin a conversation I wasn't certain I wanted to have.

Thankfully, my response was postponed by the arrival of my Cypher, Aurelius, materializing next to me. The lynx rested his furry jowls on the wrought-iron arm of my chair, and I reached over to pet him, letting the sensation of silky fur gliding through my fingers comfort me. As a child, when I'd woken after a nightmare, I had fallen back asleep with one hand buried in the creature's white and grey coat, and touching him never failed to make me feel better.

Aurelius's appearance was followed by the arrival of my father's Cypher, an intimidating timber wolf named Flavius. I nodded a welcome to him, then looked down into Aurelius's cerulean eyes, the same color as my own.

You'll feel better if you talk about it, he said, speaking directly into my mind rather than out loud. There was no point in trying to pretend I didn't know what he meant—Aurelius could hear all my thoughts as intimately as his own, even though he gave me privacy when I asked for it. Such a connection had caused more than a few embarrassing situations between us over the fourteen years we'd been together, having been paired at my fourth birth anniversary, but for the most part, I was glad of our bond and appreciated the lynx almost as much as I loved him.

I swallowed hard and lifted my head, meeting my father's increasingly concerned gaze.

"Today was . . . challenging," I began hesitantly.

My father fished a ribbon out of his pocket and tied back his hair. I wasn't sure whose was longer now, mine or his, but I loved that I had inherited both his dark hair and his tawny skin. I wouldn't have minded having his high cheekbones, too, as my round cheeks sometimes made me resemble a hoarding chipmunk. I could thank my mother for the shape of my face, though, as well as for the freckles scattered across my nose.

I sighed, and something about the act served to release the words I'd been holding back. "I don't understand why everyone was more concerned about me being in a relationship than about me healing Marta." I hadn't meant to sound bitter, but there was an unmistakable edge to my voice, and my father cocked his head to one side.

"Do you feel as if you weren't appropriately thanked or appreciated?" he asked. There was no judgment in his tone, but I quickly shook my head, not wanting him to think I was capable of such pettiness.

"No," I said, patting the scarf, "I know everyone was appreciative. And even if they hadn't been, it wouldn't have mattered. We don't heal others for accolades or gifts. I helped Marta because she needed something, and I had the ability to give it to her."

My father nodded, then reached for the copper kettle in the middle of the table and poured tea into two delicate porcelain cups. He carefully slid one towards me, and the sharp scents of ginger and licorice tickled my nose.

"I love healing," I continued, watching the steam rise from the cup. "I couldn't have been happier when I realized I had the same gift as you, even though I know most children don't inherit the same abilities or choose the same careers as their parents. Being a healer is what I want . . . what I've always wanted. I want to intern at the *Donec Medicinae* and learn everything I can about *alera* and sickness and medicine, and someday when you retire, I want to be the *Princeps Shaman* of Aeles. I *want* to help others and when I do, *that's* what I want them to focus on. I want them to see me for what I've done, not just as a woman who is or isn't courting someone!"

A passing cloud cast a shadow over the table, and noting my father's continued silence, I scowled, worried none of what I'd said had made sense.

"Just because I heal someone doesn't mean they know me or have any right to comment on my life," I grumbled.

My father chuckled.

"While that is certainly true," he said, "it's also never been my experience . . . for two reasons, I think. Healing is an intimate process, and our patients feel connected to us, even if it's a closeness born of circumstance. They feel invested in us and our lives. Remember, while we may have hundreds of patients, most citizens only work with one, perhaps two, healers. But more than that," he settled deeper into his chair, "the *Princeps Shaman* is a public position. Being the embodiment of healing to the entire realm can't help but invite curiosity and speculation."

"Perhaps I should consider a private healing practice, then," I sighed, even though I didn't really mean it, and my father knew it.

"Somewhere in Rynstyn?" he asked with an arched eyebrow before taking a sip of his tea.

A smile sprang to my face. My father traveled extensively for work and once I'd begun assisting him, I had been permitted to join him when school allowed. On one trip to heal a patient injured in a rockslide, my father had taught me to ski in the Gettrent mountains of Rynstyn. I had loved the exhilaration of flying across the snow and ice, and we returned there as often as we could.

"I certainly wouldn't mind living in Rynstyn," I admitted, "although I intend to travel as much as possible before I settle down in one place." We were silent for a moment, and I enjoyed another mouthful of bread and honey, then said, "So, you're saying part of being the *Princeps Shaman* means accepting that others are going to scrutinize me and comment on my choices, whether I ask for their opinions or not?"

"Yes," replied my father.

Much as I disliked his answer, I appreciated his honesty. He'd always been honest with me, never pretending things were anything other than exactly what they were, and trusting me to handle the resulting knowledge. I worked hard to live up to his faith in me, even though I still sometimes fell into wishful thinking.

"Well," I said glumly, tracing my fingertip along the rim of the teacup, "I might not be chosen for the *Donec Medicinae* internship, and then none of this will matter because I won't even be considered for your position."

"You'll get the internship," he assured me.

"You don't know that," I argued, worry fluttering in my stomach. "You weren't allowed to read any of the applications or cast a vote. There might be someone out there more suited for it."

"You'll get it," he replied, his tone more forceful than before as his eyes sought mine. "You are the most gifted healer I've ever known, Kyra. When I was your age, I couldn't perform a fraction of the spells you've already mastered. Sometimes I feel as if I'm simply helping you uncover things you already know rather than actually teaching you. It won't be long before you surpass my skills, and when you do, all of Aeles will benefit."

I smiled at him, a little embarrassed but also grateful for his unshakable confidence in me.

"The downside of such a gift is that others *are* going to speculate about you," he continued. "They'll discuss what you wear and what you look like, where you go on vacation, where you live, and whom you may or may not be courting. And more times than not, they'll tell you exactly what they think about your choices. Today won't be the last time some aspect of your life is deemed more remarkable than your healing work. I wish I could protect you from it, but I can't . . . all I can do is help you learn, as I did, that your worth doesn't lie in what others think of you and your choices. Your value is determined by who you are and what you decide to do with the gifts you've been given."

I was about to respond when the ground beneath my chair suddenly rolled, tilting me sideways, and I gasped as a loud rumbling sound filled the air.

"What's happening?" I shouted, leaning forward to steady my rattling teacup. Before I could reach it, though, the ground rolled again, and my chair pitched wildly. The cup tipped over, rolled off the edge of the table, and shattered on the ceramic tile below, followed quickly by the teapot.

"It's an earthquake!" replied my father, jumping to his feet and lunging towards me. I grabbed his outstretched hand as the ground shook again, so hard it rattled my teeth. All around us, Astrals were running, shouting for their children, leaving push-carts and packages in the street as they sought shelter wherever they could. The ground gave a violent shudder, and dust rose in the distance as a building swayed, then collapsed in on itself.

Flavius gave a loud bark.

"There is a root cellar on the other side of the tavern!" he said. "Follow me!"

My father nodded, and I clutched his hand, but we'd only taken a few steps when the ground before us exploded upwards, throwing us off balance as dirt, grass, and bits of broken tile shot into the air. We ducked, crouching so low our foreheads pressed against our knees. When it became clear the shaking wasn't going to stop anytime soon, my father rose and tugged me to my feet. I swayed as I stood, the muscles in my legs burning from bracing to steady myself.

"What do we do?" I shouted. And then the ground beneath us ruptured, ripped apart in opposite directions, one side rising as the other fell, and I was thrown backwards, crying out as my hand slipped from my father's.

3

KYRA

Covering my face with my arms, I found myself rolling down a newly formed hill, crashing into things I couldn't identify. I tucked my knees into my chest and did my best to protect my head, making my body as small as possible until I slowed enough to stop myself.

Struggling onto my hands and knees, I coughed and looked around, blinking through the dirt covering my eyes. My ears rang, overflowing with the sounds of breaking stone, crashing lumber, and the screams of those caught between.

Aurelius immediately appeared at my side, but I spoke before he could.

"I'm fine," I panted. "Where's Father?"

"Still at the tavern," said the lynx.

I looked up at the tavern, or what was left of it—half of it had fallen in on itself, and the other half looked as if the slightest gust of wind would blow it over. Through the dust and debris, I could just make out the uppermost part of the ivy wall we'd been sitting by, the bright green leaves still waving happily, undisturbed by the devastation below.

Getting to my feet, I took a few uneasy steps, then forced my legs into a jog. Reaching the earthen embankment that hadn't existed only moments before, I crawled upwards as fast as I could, and as my head crested the rise, I caught a glimpse of my father. He was propped up against what was left of the ivy-covered wall, one leg splayed outwards at an odd angle, his mouth clenched in pain.

"Father!" I shouted.

He lifted his head and smiled, his straight white teeth bright against the dust and leaves covering his face.

"Thank the Gifters!" he said.

And then, everything around me began to tremble, as if someone had picked up the village and started shaking it. The few trees that still stood waved their limbs, even though there was no wind, and I watched in horror as a great oak fell forward, its roots ripped from the earth as it crashed into the tavern.

"No!" I screamed, leaping to my feet and breaking into a run, tripping over wooden planks and stumbling over rocks, until I stood where I had last seen my father. The stone wall behind him had collapsed under the weight of the tree, and I rubbed my eyes, although it did nothing to clear the detritus swirling through the air. Flavius was standing on top of a mound, digging feverishly at a scrap of fabric peeking through the rubble.

"He's here, Kyra! Help me!" the wolf shouted.

I ran to him and began tugging on stones, tossing those I could lift behind me and pushing the heavier ones away. My father groaned, and as I managed to clear away branches, rocks, and roof tiles, I could finally make out his shoulders and head. I placed a hand against his neck, relieved when I felt the flutter of a pulse against my fingertips. Slowly, he opened his eyes, squinting as he did.

"Kyra?" he whispered.

"You're going to be fine," I assured him. There was blood on his face, but the cuts didn't appear deep. It was a good sign he knew who I was and was able to speak. He no doubt had some broken bones, but those could easily be mended. He winced, and it was only then that I looked down at the rest of his body.

As I did, everything inside of me froze.

A heavy wooden beam had broken in two, and one half was lodged in my father's side, poking out through his chest. The sharp tips of the splintered wood glinted a lovely golden color—coated in my father's blood.

My father swallowed, and the effort it cost him was obvious.

"I thought I had more time . . . to tell you things," he said, but I shook my head, only vaguely aware of the hot tears streaming down my cheeks.

"We'll have plenty of time after I heal you," I said. "Lie still!"

One side of his mouth lifted in a sad smile.

"I'm afraid we are beyond that. Flavius will give my messages to your mother and siblings. But I want . . . you to know . . ." He inhaled sharply and grimaced, gritting his teeth before forcing his next words out, "I love you and . . . I could not be prouder of you. I . . . wish I could . . . see . . . the amazing things . . . you're going . . . to do."

He held up a hand, and I clutched it between both of mine, sobbing as I pressed my forehead against his knuckles before bringing my eyes back to his. His eyelids drooped, but he blinked them open, and his gaze was unwavering.

"Trust yourself, Kyra . . . regardless of what anyone else thinks. Use your gifts to do what you know is right."

With that, his eyes closed, and his breathing slowed.

I gently released his hand, inhaled deeply, and summoned my *alera*. The yellow light flowed out of my fingertips, and I pressed my hands against my father's chest, identifying the holes in his punctured lungs, as well as where other internal organs had been damaged into stillness. The wounds were serious, but they were only injuries. I healed injuries.

My father wasn't going to die. I wouldn't let him.

Pulling my father's torso forward, I managed to free him from the wooden beam, then carefully laid him back on a pile of rocks before administering the most powerful healing spells I knew. While the spells quickly repaired his visible wounds, as well as his internal injuries, unfortunately, they weren't restoring my father's health. Gulping back tears, I stared at his face. His eyes didn't move beneath his closed lids, and his lips were parted and still.

Staring at him, lying there so helpless, whatever had frozen inside me before suddenly snapped, and without knowing why, I reached for my *sana* bracelet. I ran a finger over Tawazun, The Balancer, and a perfectly balanced note of contentment rang out from the sapphire bead. At the same time, I ran a second finger over Rheolath, The Controller, tensing at the commanding sound that sprang from the dark red carnelian stone. This wasn't a bead combination I recalled learning, but something about it felt so right I didn't stop. A spell began to take shape in my mind, and I suddenly shouted, *"Bidh mi a 'dol a-steach!"*

Aurelius's panicked voice filled my mind. *Kyra, what are you—*

His words were cut off by a rushing sound that drowned out everything else. It reminded me of the time I'd been caught in an ocean current off the coast of Iscre. The salt-filled waves had crashed over my head, tossing me end over end, crushing me with their weight. I dropped my hand from the *sana* bracelet, over-whelmed by dizziness and the sensation of spinning. My father and Aurelius winked out of sight, and everything went black, leaving me unable to tell which way was up and which was down. I might have been screaming, but aside from feeling as if my mouth was open, I couldn't tell. Pitching forward, I landed on my hands and knees as something wet splashed against my face.

Thankfully, the blackness enveloping me quickly faded, allowing me to see more of my surroundings. The wetness I'd felt was water. I scrambled to get my feet underneath me, but in my haste, I slipped and sat down hard, nearly falling over backwards. Thankfully, my head and shoulders remained above the water-line, and I ran a hand over my face as I worked to slow my breath-ing. The rushing sound had stopped and there were no other noises, which made my movements seem especially loud. Judging by the current flowing calmly past me, I was in a creek or shallow river.

Pushing my hair behind my ears, I peered through the ten-drils of fog hanging lazily in the air and partially obscuring an overcast sky. I could just make out land on either side of the wa-ter, forming twin slices of shoreline, but beyond that there was nothing besides great jagged rocks, reminding me of an oversized fence marking a boundary of some sort.

Shivering, I rose to my feet, squeezing the wetness from my clothes as best I could. The water wasn't particularly cold, but it wasn't warm, either, and something about it felt unnatural . . . as if it was tugging me forwards, each drop like a lodestone, pulling me closer to something.

Aurelius! Can you hear me?

Kyra, thank the Gifters! Where are you?

I don't know, I replied, relieved I could still communicate with my lynx but concerned he was nowhere to be seen. Why hadn't he found me and joined me? *Are you still with Father?*

Yes, but I've never seen anything like this! One moment you were here, talking, and the next, you just slumped over. I thought you'd fainted. Where are you? I can't establish your location, and if I can't locate you, I can't come to you!

The hair pricked on the back of my neck, and a coldness slipped down my spine before spreading out to my arms and legs.

There was only one place Astrals could go where Cyphers, being immortal creatures, couldn't follow.

Vaneklus. The realm of the dead.

Am I . . . dead? I asked weakly.

We wouldn't be communicating if you were dead, snapped Aurelius, although I knew his irritation came from fear, not anger. *Our bond would have been severed, and I would be presenting myself for reassignment to another Astral. However*—he took a deep breath— *as I cannot come to you, and there is only one place my kind cannot venture, we must consider the possibility that you have somehow ended up in Vaneklus, even though you are very much alive.*

How is that possible? I asked as Aurelius sifted through my thoughts, seeing what I had seen of my environment and searching for clues. *How long can I be here without being dead? And how do I get back to you and Father?*

A splash rang out ahead of me, and I whipped my head towards it, wrenching something in my neck. For the first time in my life, I wished I carried a sword or some type of weapon. Astrals were peaceful, and I'd never felt the slightest bit threatened, not walking on my own at night in Celenia or out in the remote villages my father and I often visited. But right now . . . it would have been nice to know I could protect myself.

I heard more splashing, but this time it was measured and rhythmic—a splash, then a pause, a splash, then a pause—like oars dipping into the water and rising up again. Oars meant a boat, and a boat likely meant company, but whether that boded well or ill remained to be seen.

Should I try to run? I asked Aurelius.

Where would you run to? he replied. *You'll find no safe place in the realm of the dead. You managed to get yourself there, somehow, so we simply have to hope you will be able get yourself out as well.*

While his words were meant to be encouraging, I didn't miss the uncertainty in his voice.

The prow of a wooden boat soon broke through the fog that had shifted to form a curtain in front of me. A cloaked figure stood at the front, but a black hood hid his or her face. The boat was propelled by the oars I'd heard before, but they must have been enchanted, since no one was holding them. At some silent command, they slid deeper into the water, bringing the boat to a stop just a few feet from me. The head of the cloaked figure rose, and as the hood fell away, I staggered backwards in fear.

Merciful Gifters, whispered Aurelius, following my thoughts so closely it was almost as if he was seeing through my eyes. *The Shade Transporter!*

The man's face was little more than a skull, covered in skin as thin as parchment, an almost translucent shade of pale. Ruby-red eyes flashed so bright, I raised my arms to shield my face. I had grown up hearing stories of the Shade Transporter, tasked with greeting the shades of Astrals when they died and ferrying them onwards to rest or rebirth. But while I'd always half-heartedly believed in his existence, I had never contemplated what meeting the guardian of the realm of the dead would be like.

The Shade Transporter spoke, and his voice was both painfully grating and strangely soothing, making some part of me feel drawn to it, while the rest of me shuddered in revulsion.

"And so, another Recovrancer makes her way into my waters," he said, sounding unhappy and bored at the same time. "I'm not certain why you're here *now*, though, since it was clearly that shade's appointed time." The man's voice darkened. "Even you are bound by the natural laws—you cannot recover what is rightfully mine!"

No, whispered my lynx, sounding more terrified than I had ever heard him.

Slowly, I lowered my arms from my face.

The Shade Transporter inhaled sharply, then gaped at me. "But . . . it cannot be! What are *you* doing here?"

"I don't know!" I said. "My father was badly injured, and I was trying to heal him and somehow brought myself here. Please, can you send me back? He needs me!"

The Shade Transporter leaned so far forward over the edge of the boat, it was a wonder he didn't fall into the water. Frowning, he squinted at me.

"Can it be you truly do not know who you are?"

He reached out a hand, and the current in the water suddenly became stronger, carrying me towards him. Driven by some instinct I hadn't known I possessed, I pressed my fingers against Tawazun and Rheoleth on my *sana* bracelet again and said, *"Bidh mi gad fhàgail!"*

The rushing sound I'd heard before filled my ears, and I crouched into a ball, pushing my face against my thighs and shielding the back of my head with my hands. The Shade Transporter shouted something, but I couldn't make out his words, and I was aware of things moving around me, even though I knew I was standing still. Then, the rushing sound abruptly stopped, and I raised my head, swaying where I sat, only to be knocked over by Aurelius launching himself at me. His sandpaper tongue was rough against my face.

Oh, I was so worried! he wailed. *Thank all that's good you're back!*

I hugged the lynx, shocked to discover my clothes were wet, and water sloshed inside my boots. Peering around Aurelius, I let out a trembling exhale and relaxed against him, relieved to see Flavius standing next to my father's body. If the wolf was still here, that meant there was still a chance I could save my father.

But, as Flavius's yellow eyes met mine, they filled with a sadness that instantly turned my stomach.

"I'm so sorry, Kyra," he said. And then he vanished.

"*No!*" I cried, reaching for him, but it was too late—the Cypher was gone. Tears slid down my face, and Aurelius pressed himself against me.

"No," I whimpered, shaking my head as I struggled to breathe, dimly aware I was fighting a losing battle against the great hiccupping sobs seeking to shake my entire torso. Flavius couldn't be gone. For him to leave now meant his bond with my father had broken and he'd been summoned to Celenia for reassignment to another Astral . . . another *living* Astral.

"I'm so sorry, Kyra," said Aurelius.

"This can't be happening," I said. "Not now! Father, please! Come back! I need to talk to you about what just happened to me!"

Aurelius gently nudged my shoulder with his head, and I dropped my face into my hands.

I couldn't save him! I cried. *Why couldn't I save him? Why?*

When Aurelius had no answer, I crawled forward and curled into a ball near my father, my body shaking with each fresh sob. The pain in my chest was so unbearable, I was certain each tear streaming down my face was made of golden blood pulsing straight from my broken heart. It was simply too much to bear— losing my father, going into Vaneklus, talking to the Shade Transporter—and I closed my eyes, desperately wishing things would be different when I opened them.

4

KYRA

I didn't tell anyone about my accidental foray into Vaneklus. The days immediately after my father's death were so busy that when I finally fell into bed at night, I passed out into an exhausted, dreamless sleep. The entire realm of Aeles was in mourning. On the day of my father's funeral, even the sky arranged itself for the occasion: normally a dazzling blue, it was instead covered in overlapping grey clouds that hid the sun.

The funeral took place in Celenia, the capital of the realm, and was so well attended, it seemed as if everyone my father had ever healed was there. Tenebris Rex, one of the senators who represented my home province of Montem, stood behind an ornately carved white quartz podium and spoke eloquently of what a loss we had suffered. He then looked at me and smiled as he spoke of "the hope that sustains us and will always be our greatest asset."

Tears filled my eyes. How would I ever become the healer I wanted to be without my father's guidance? Thankfully, I was saved from drowning in my feelings of inadequacy by the pressure of my best friend's hand. Demitri's fingers were interlaced with my own, and I squeezed back, mustering what I could of a smile as another government official stood up to speak.

At home later that evening, after a seemingly endless stream of visitors had finally gone, I was at last alone with my family. Demitri was still there, but he was family, even though we weren't actually related. As an only child, he'd practically grown up at my house, happily wrapped up in the pandemonium that came with my three siblings and their Cyphers. My parents had always encouraged our friendship, although I suspected my mother hoped we would someday become *more* than friends.

My fifteen-year-old sister Seren pulled out the pins keeping her cornsilk blonde hair in an ornate updo and gave her head a shake, letting her hair fall down her back.

"Did you see the hat Senator Brandt's wife was wearing?" she asked with a laugh. "It looked like she enchanted a chicken and ordered it to sit on her head!"

While the observation wasn't particularly nice, I smiled anyway. Seren could always lighten the mood; in fact, my mother maintained she had been born into our family for the specific purpose of making us laugh. Her Cypher, a black and white sea snake named Sappho, normally would have admonished my little sister for such an unkind comment, as character development was part of the lifelong guidance Cyphers were assigned to provide. But in this instance, even she gave a hissing chuckle.

My mother leaned her head against the back of the sofa and rubbed her eyes, her auburn curls falling down to frame her face. Demitri, ever attentive, leaned forward.

"Skandhar, can I get you something to drink?" he asked.

My mother smiled and shook her head. "No, I'm fine, thank you. Just tired."

The doorbell rang, and Seren and I groaned as my mother shushed us.

"Folks wish to pay their respects, and we will not begrudge them their desire to honor your father!" she scolded.

"I'll get it!" hollered my twelve-year-old brother Enif, jumping up from the blue velvet ottoman he'd been sitting on and dashing towards the foyer. His Cypher, a dwarf owl named Tiberius, flapped his wings and screeched as he tried to maintain his balance on Enif's shoulder.

There was a pause as the door opened, and I heard Enif grunt as if he was lifting something heavy. He returned to the family room, and in his arms was an enormous glass vase filled with the oddest flowers I'd ever seen. Inky black roses towered over dark purple peonies, and calla lilies the color of coal bowed their dark fluted heads over soot-colored tulips. Strands of onyx-colored vines were laced around the flowers' stems, their pointed thorns glittering like black jewels.

My mother's face went so pale her freckles stood out in stark relief, and she jumped up from the sofa, displacing my seven-year-old brother Deneb, who had fallen asleep against her. Snatching the note accompanying the flowers, she quickly read it, then grabbed the vase from my brother.

"Enif, open the door!" she commanded. My brother was quick to obey, and the two of them rushed outside as Demitri, Seren, and I followed. My mother trotted down the front porch steps and placed the vase on the lawn. At her command, a hole began to form, grass and soil moving aside as if they were being vigorously shoveled by some invisible hand. When the hole was deep enough to hold the entire vase, the dirt began to pile back on top of the bouquet, burying it until every last flower and thorn was hidden from view. After a moment, the yard looked as if it had never been disturbed, and my mother wiped her hands on her dress before striding back into the house, waving for us to join her.

"What's wrong?" I asked, thoroughly confused.

My mother locked the front door, then leaned back against it. Her hands were shaking as she opened the note again and read it silently to herself.

"Well?" prodded Seren, hands on her hips.

My mother finally cleared her throat.

"It says, 'To the Valorian family—please allow me to express my deepest condolences over the loss of Arakiss. I had the privilege of being healed by him when the healers in my own realm proved less than effective. I never forget a kindness. Should you ever need anything, I am in your debt. Most sincerely, Caz Dekarai.'"

"The healers in my own realm?" I repeated, and then it dawned on me why my mother hadn't wanted the flowers in the house. "Were those flowers from . . . *Nocens?*"

My mother gave a barely perceptible nod.

I looked at Demitri in shock. Nocens was the realm of the Daevals, vicious beings with silver blood who hated my kind. If the note with the flowers was to be believed, not only had my father interacted with a Daeval, he had healed one. My mind raced to process a thing I'd never even imagined—had my father gone to Nocens? He'd never mentioned it to me . . . but then again, where else would he have encountered a Daeval? Those with silver blood were forbidden from entering our realm, and spells throughout Aeles would cause the Blood Alarm to go off if one somehow managed to get in.

"How would you even get flowers from Nocens into Aeles?" asked Demitri.

Enif's dark brown eyes were wide. "They were just sitting on the porch when I opened the door. I don't know who delivered them."

"I don't know how they got here," said my mother, "and the less we think about it, the better. Whoever this Caz is, he expressed his thanks, and we can leave it at that."

"He'd probably be mad to know his thanks ended up buried in our front yard," observed Seren.

"He'll never know," I pointed out before turning back to my mother. "But when did Father meet a Daeval? He never mentioned anything to me about healing one, or even speaking with one!"

"I don't know," replied my mother. "Perhaps it was a confidential part of his work."

I scowled, disliking the answer even as I begrudgingly admitted to myself it might be true.

"I don't understand why a Daeval would go to so much trouble to express his thanks to us, though," I said. "They hate our kind."

"It seems your father's kindness overcame such prejudices," replied my mother softly.

I wasn't so certain, but Aurelius interrupted my thoughts.

Flavius is taking a well-deserved respite before reassignment, said the lynx, *but I can contact him in a few days to see what he knows of this Caz Dekarai. In the meantime, you have much more pressing things to worry about—such as what will happen to you if anyone learns you managed to enter the realm of the dead!*

I nodded at my Cypher's words as I returned to the living room, mentally reviewing what I knew of Astral history, hoping my family would assume I was simply overwhelmed by recent events rather than guessing the real direction of my thoughts.

At one time, a few rare Astrals, known as Recovrancers, had been able to go in and out of Vaneklus as they wished; however, this ability had been deemed too dangerous, even with government oversight, and as a result, recovrancy had been outlawed. Those who were able to wield the power had been forbidden from doing so, sent into exile, or worse, and eventually, the ability had ceased to exist. That meant there *had* to be another explanation for my going into Vaneklus . . . if for no other reason than the alternative was too terrible to consider.

5

SEBASTIAN

*T*he hot wind stung my eyes, and I squinted, adjusting the oversized black hood to cover more of my face. There was a reason I avoided contracts that required me to go to Jaasfar—I despised this part of Nocens. The sun beat down mercilessly and burned every inch of skin I didn't keep covered. Sand worked its way inside my boots and rubbed blisters on my feet. The light played tricks on the dunes, making me see things that weren't there and disguising things I was looking for. It wasn't an ideal place for an assassin, which made it a perfect place for someone looking to hide from one.

This time, though, my target hadn't even tried to cover his tracks. He must have assumed word of his thievery hadn't yet reached his employer, although I couldn't fathom why he would make such an assumption. Then again, not everyone expected the worst and planned accordingly, as I did. And, to be fair, more caution wouldn't have kept him alive—it would only have delayed the inevitable.

I stared ahead at where the tracks ended near a group of palm trees. *"Fosgail,"* I whispered, and a portal the size of a door shimmered into view. I stepped through and emerged beneath the palm trees, grateful for the shade. The tracks continued into the oasis, and I slipped between the peeling grey trunks, using their shadows for concealment.

My target was crouched in front of a small pond ringed with clumps of orange moss and bright green papyrus reeds. Pushing aside a large, flat stone, he pulled out a canvas pouch, which he tucked inside his tunic before replacing the stone. Well, at least he'd saved himself from an interrogation, as that pouch was the reason I'd been sent to kill him. It wasn't enough to simply retrieve the rubies he'd stolen from his employer—I was to make an example of what happened to those foolish enough to steal from Dunston Dekarai in the first place.

As the man rose and turned around, I summoned the fire inside my blood and directed it to the upper half of my face. I could feel the skin around my eyes blackening into scales, and red flames rose to fill the spaces in between. The mask provided anonymity, which was necessary in my line of work, but it also made quite the impression.

The man before me gasped, and his dark brown face blanched two shades lighter. His eyes darted about, but he must have realized the futility of trying to escape because he quickly pulled the canvas pouch from his tunic and tossed it at my feet.

"Here, take it!" he squeaked.

I held out my hand towards him.

"Bywta," I said, and flames leaped from my fingertips, settling hungrily on the man's clothes before licking against his skin. He screamed, tearing at his tunic as the scents of burning cloth and then burning flesh filled the air. I let the flames rage for a few heartbeats before pulling them back inside myself. The man fell to the ground and lay still, burned almost beyond recognition. I strode towards him and ran my sword through his chest to ensure he was dead before letting the mask fall from my face.

Drawing a length of rope from my side, I looped one end around his neck. I then tossed the other end over a sturdy palm frond and hoisted the still-smoking body into the air. This oasis was a frequent stop for Daevals and the deceased thief would be discovered soon.

Using my *alera*, I attached a message to the trunk of the palm tree. The *aleric* tag would flare to life when someone drew near, allowing them to read the words I left: "For daring to steal from Dunston Dekarai." I picked up the rubies, brushed the sand from the bag, and slipped it into a pocket of the weapons belt slung around my waist. Surveying my handiwork one final time, I nodded, then conjured a portal to Vartox.

As the capital of the entire realm, Vartox was always busy, but today the city seemed especially congested. I stepped out onto the dark green marble landing of Dunston's office building, startling a few Daevals with my unexpected appearance. Portaling was a rare ability, and I was lucky to have it. It had undoubtedly contributed to my success as an assassin, and a twinge of pride flickered behind my sternum as I pulled open a heavy glass door.

Walking inside, I pushed back my hood and dipped my head towards the security officers standing inside the building. Dunston was my oldest customer and the most frequent purchaser of my services, and while he hadn't informed his security of the exact nature of our relationship, they knew I was never to be stopped for questioning or searched for weapons.

Stepping onto the platinum intersector leading directly to Dunston's office, I quickly found myself standing before an imposing pair of mahogany doors. I rapped my knuckles sharply against the wood, then busied myself brushing away the few remaining grains of sand clinging insistently to my breeches.

The doors opened, and I bowed my head at the Daeval before me. Those I respected were few and far between, but Dunston had earned my regard. His beady eyes shone as he clapped his hands together, causing the numerous rings he wore to clink softly. Dimples were hidden in the folds of his cheeks on either side of his nose. They appeared every time he smiled, which meant they were almost permanently on display.

"Sebastian!" he thundered happily, ushering me inside. Everything about the office was extravagant, from the plush black carpet to the twin crystal chandeliers suspended from the high ceiling. The walls were covered in black onyx tiles, and a mosaic ran across them, creating a repetitive circular pattern formed by pieces of gold, red beryl, and ivory.

"So, *so* good to see you!" Dunston continued. "I trust things went well in Jaasfar?"

I nodded and handed him the bag of precious stones.

His grin turned malicious. "Excellent. Let's hope this discourages any of my other employees from trying something similar."

Officially, Dunston worked for the Daeval government in the Trades and Tariffs *Adran*, but that was simply to keep him familiar with laws regarding commerce. His real employment, or at least his most profitable, was the import/export business he ran with his brother and sister. When it came to transporting goods across the realm, the Dekarais had the market not only cornered, but surrounded.

Speaking of Dunston's brother, I watched as he rose from an overstuffed red leather armchair near Dunston's enormous desk. His name was Norman Casablanca Dekarai, but everyone, friends and enemies alike, knew him as Caz. He and Dunston shared the same pasty skin and oversized gut, the result of excessive living, but Caz was younger by a few years and projected more innocence than his brother. That didn't mean he was any less brutal, but he enjoyed being underestimated.

"Sebastian! Our family's favorite weapon!" said Caz gleefully.

He was so focused on hurrying towards me that he didn't see Dunston's Cypher, a large Komodo dragon, materialize in front of his feet. He stumbled over the creature and grabbed onto an amethyst sculpture decorated with ribbons of twisted silver to right himself.

"Burning realm fires, Wayah!" he shouted, as the lizard let out a throaty chuckle. "One of these days I'll turn you into a pair of pants!"

Dunston laughed heartily as the Cypher ambled over to a window, used his tail to pull back the curtains, and stretched out in the late afternoon sunlight that streamed inside.

Caz ran a hand through his unruly brown hair and scowled. "One of these days I'm going to hire Sebastian to eliminate you *and* that menace!" he snapped at his brother.

He frequently made such a threat, even though he knew I would never do such a thing—the only way I had agreed to work with the three Dekarai siblings was to make them promise they wouldn't use me to kill one other. They continued to abide by their pact, fully aware of the *aleric* consequences that resulted from breaking promises, although it hadn't escaped my attention that their sister, Minerva, had taken the oath with obvious reluctance.

I extended my hand and let Caz pump it up and down with his usual vigor.

"It's nice to see you, Caz," I said. "What kind of trouble are you stirring up today?"

Caz beamed as if I couldn't have given him a better compliment. "No trouble today, unfortunately. I was just following up with my brother about a flower delivery I sent to Aeles."

I raised my eyebrows. My kind were forbidden from entering the hateful Astral realm, but if anyone could get a delivery inside, it would certainly be Dunston.

Caz laughed at my expression. "I know what you're thinking,

and while it's true I have enjoyed many lovers over the years, these particular flowers were not sent with an amorous intent."

His smile disappeared, and his expression became serious.

"Months ago, I had a particular problem our healers were unable to address. I happened to meet the head Astral healer—their *Princeps Shaman*—Arakiss Valorian. He did what our healers couldn't, and I never forgot him." Caz sighed. "I received news he died earlier this week—in an earthquake of all things—so I sent my condolences to his family and told them I was in their debt."

That was certainly unexpected. Caz didn't offer favors—he collected them, with a friendly smile, a calculated gleam in his eyes, and a casual, "Now you owe me." I often suspected he did certain things *just* so others would be indebted to him. This was peculiar, even for him.

He shook his head and continued.

"Anyway, now the Astral government will begin the process of selecting Arakiss's replacement. Rumor has it his daughter is the most obvious candidate, but she's also quite young. I expect they'll choose someone to temporarily fill the position for a few years until she's ready." His eyes twinkled with interest. "If she's as gifted as I hear, I should very much like to meet her."

I couldn't have cared less about the workings of the Astral government, but there was no need for my best customers to know that. Caz and Dunston frequently interacted with the golden bloods, and it made sense they'd be well-informed. Rather than share my opinion, I simply said, "Well, perhaps your paths will cross one day."

Dunston sank down into the chair behind his ebony desk with a grunt and tapped his fingers against the armrests. "Do you have plans for dinner tonight?" he asked me. "You're welcome to join us. Eslee was just saying she hasn't seen you since Summer Solstice."

I'd known the Dekarais for as long as I could remember, having gone to school with Dunston's children, Devlin and Eslee. It was true I sometimes had dinner with the family, but I couldn't this evening.

"Thank you," I said, "but I have other plans tonight."

Dunston's mouth turned down, making him look like a hound dog that had just lost the scent of something he'd been eagerly tracking.

"Are you sure?" he asked. His voice softened. "I just thought, given what day it is . . ." His voice trailed off, and he swallowed hard, then cleared his throat.

I should have known better than to hope he'd forgotten the importance of this specific date. The fire in my veins stirred, even as I forced my expression to remain calm. Had it been *anyone* other than Dunston edging close to this particular topic of conversation, I would have pinned their tongue to their chin with a knife.

"I appreciate the offer," I said, "but I have some things to attend to."

I glanced at Caz. He crossed his arms, making his already ill-fitting jacket bunch around his waist, and gave his brother a look that veered between annoyance and understanding. Dunston pulled out a white silk handkerchief, dabbed his eyes, and then nodded.

"I understand. But let's make plans for you to come for dinner sometime soon."

I told him we would, excused myself, and hurried outside. While his offer had been kind, I would honor the anniversary of my mother's death as I always did—alone.

6

SEBASTIAN

J paused in front of the squat wood and plaster building.
The burgundy paint was faded, and the trimming buckled
around the windows, which were covered in a layer of grime so
thick, it was almost impossible to see inside. The lettered sign out
front was crooked, and the open door leaned to one side, as if
straining to escape its hinges. Aside from where I lived, this was
my favorite place in all of Nocens—LeBehr's Bookstore.

I stepped carefully over the black cat sprawled across the entryway, and to my relief, she blinked her mismatched green and
yellow eyes and hissed loudly at me. LeBehr always said it was a
bad sign if her Cypher, Mischief, didn't hiss at a customer, since
refusing to even acknowledge someone was the worst insult a cat
could give. I'd actually seen LeBehr insist a Daeval leave her store
immediately if the cat ignored their arrival, and while I didn't
understand her reasoning, I didn't need to, so long as Mischief
continued to yowl at me.

The store was empty except for the Cypher and LeBehr, a
rotund woman with short, thick white hair that never appeared
to have encountered a brush. She had a booming voice and favored wearing corsets over dresses, and dresses over breeches.
She almost always had a scarf or shawl draped over her shoulders,
although I suspected that was more to do with a sense of theatri-
cality than any practical use. I also suspected the woman never

slept. Given my line of work, I was frequently out at all hours of the night, and regardless of the time, LeBehr's door was always open, with Mischief guarding the entrance.

"Well, if it isn't the man who single-handedly ensures book printing will never go out of business!" said LeBehr, striding out from around a teetering pile of books. Books were everywhere, lining the numerous shelves, filling the hanging baskets that could be raised or lowered as needed, and forming towers taller than my head. Yet despite the lack of an obvious cataloguing system, LeBehr always knew exactly where a particular book could be found.

I nodded at her, not disputing her greeting, since there was at least some truth to it, instead letting my eyes drift over the nearest shelf. Some might think it odd to honor my mother by coming to a bookstore, but this had been our second home in Nocens. In LeBehr's store, books came alive, and we had spent hours here, laughing when volumes tried to catch LeBehr's fingers between their covers, watching the store owner coax shy books to open their pages, and listening to her talk about her grand travels to save rare editions from certain oblivion.

I'd lost my mother thirteen years ago, at the age of seven, but time hadn't dulled the pain; if anything, it had kept the pain alive, feeding it, shaping it so perfectly to the contours of my shade it was now a part of me, a burden I would never be free of. Not that I was complaining . . . I deserved nothing less, given the circumstances surrounding her death.

Not wanting to dwell on memories I would no doubt revisit later in my dreams, I grasped the spine of a green and red clothbound volume. Although I pulled hard, the book clung stubbornly to the shelf. I tugged harder, but it refused to come free.

I looked at LeBehr, whose broad shoulders somehow managed a graceful shrug.

"Obviously, that is not the book for you," she said. "I'm not surprised, considering you have already purchased three books on the Calliope War from me. I doubt this one wants to compete with them or risk being bought but never read." She combed her fingers through her hair so it stood straight up as she considered something, then snapped her fingers and exclaimed, "I have just the book for you!"

She disappeared behind a sagging shelf of maps, ducking to avoid hitting her head on a basket filled with small leather books. I sighed and brushed my hair back from my forehead. Perhaps coming here had been a mistake.

The mistake was in going there without me! my Cypher snapped, his voice grating in my mind like a dull saw against metal. The bat never accompanied me when I completed contracts, but he also never passed up an opportunity to offer his unwanted opinion. I half-expected him to appear in the bookstore any moment, black eyes bulging, the yellow fur around his neck stained with the remains of whatever he'd been eating.

My eyes do not bulge, and my fur is clean, he sniffed. *Well, mostly clean. Shall I join you so you can see for yourself?* His nasal voice was filled with the delusional hope of a creature who would never learn.

No! I snarled at him. *I want to be alone.*

He groaned. *How am I supposed to offer guidance or comfort if you always insist on being alone?*

You can offer guidance when you have something to say that's worth listening to. And I don't need comforting.

LeBehr reappeared, and I turned my attention to her. I could never completely shut out the bat, but I could sometimes ignore him to the point of missing most of what he said.

The bookshop owner handed me a slim blue book, and I ran

my fingers over the worn leather cover. The book fluttered its pages with a happy sigh, and I read the title printed on the first sheet of parchment: *"The Book of Recovrancy."*

For a moment, my lungs forgot how to breathe.

"Where did you get this?" I finally asked, my voice the slightest bit hoarse.

LeBehr smiled broadly, clearly pleased with herself. "From a Daeval who was gifted it by his sister. She bought a chest of drawers at one of Minerva Dekarai's auctions, where it seems some of the items *may* once have been part of an Astral estate . . . you never know with such things. The book was inside the furniture." She studied the book appreciatively. "There's a spell in there I've only come across a handful of times in my illustrious career. What you and I are able to read isn't actually all that's written . . . the book chooses what to reveal, based on the reader. Given the topic, I assume you'd have to be a Recovrancer to see everything, but, I thought it would still be of interest to you."

I nodded, not even bothering to pretend otherwise.

LeBehr's green and yellow eyes danced. "Perhaps one day you will find Rhannu, after all."

Every Daeval knew the story of Rhannu, the infamous sword that had toppled kingdoms, slayed monsters, and made whoever wielded it invincible. As I child, I had been obsessed with stories of the sword's exploits, stories from books my mother and I had bought at LeBehr's. I had also been devastated to learn—in this very shop—that the sword had been stolen millennia ago by Astrals, who had used their Recovrancer to hide it in the realm of the dead. Since only Astrals had the gift of recovrancy, they had effectively ensured no Daeval would be able to retrieve the sword. And since they had then outlawed recovrancy and killed everyone born with the gift, it seemed impossible the sword would ever be reclaimed at all.

That hadn't squelched my interest, though, and I continued to read everything I could find about the weapon. I looked at LeBehr, suspicions winding through my mind. Was she simply providing me with another book on a topic she knew I enjoyed, or was this her way of acknowledging our shared past and lamenting the passage of another year without my mother?

Fortunately, the shop owner's eyes held no trace of pity, and I was pleased she charged me for the volume rather than offering it as a gift. She grinned as she rang up the purchase.

"If I ever come across a book on how to revive long-lost Astral abilities, I'll be sure to set it aside for you," she chuckled. "Then all you'll need is an Astral to go after that sword."

My top lip curled upwards in disgust. The possibility of retrieving Rhannu was the *only* reason I would ever interact with an Astral.

"You do that," I replied, then added the only thing I could think of even more outrageous than LeBehr finding the book she'd just described. "And if I ever meet a Recovrancer, I promise to bring them here and introduce you."

LeBehr laughed so hard she had to readjust the shawl sliding off her shoulders, and I said goodbye before heading out into the warm night air, careful not to step on Mischief. Conjuring a portal, I stepped onto the familiar grey stone floor of my cave, ready to clean the sand from inside my boots and delve into my new book.

My Cypher was standing on the kitchen table, and his eyes narrowed as he wrapped his wings around himself. "I see you did not bring me anything to read," he said unhappily. "I suppose I will have to ask Mischief to send me something." His nose began to drip, and he rubbed a wing under it, sniffling loudly and complaining about his allergies.

I ignored him and crossed the cavern to the alcove that

housed my bed. I hadn't grown up with the intention of someday living in a cave, but after I'd stumbled upon it roughly a decade ago, I'd realized there were enormous benefits to living somewhere accessible only by portal.

I set the book on my nightstand, then, glancing around to make sure the bat hadn't materialized nearby, I quietly opened a drawer of the small table and pulled out a captum. I stared at the glass lens for a moment, then positioned it in front of one eye. The copper rim was cool against my skin, and I gently pressed the small lever on the side, starting the series of moving pictures.

Dunston had captured the images, and I watched my five-year-old self standing on top of a dining table, wearing a silk sheet as a cape, shoving a tilting paper crown back onto my head as I pointed a wooden sword at Dunston's son, Devlin. A door swung open, and my mother entered the room. She waved at the captum, her brown eyes beaming as her blonde hair brushed the tops of her shoulders. Sweeping me into her arms, she spun me around in a tight circle, making my childhood self squeal with delight as I clutched my crown against my head. My mother's Cypher, a hummingbird named Verbena, darted around her head as we spun, and Batty clapped his wings while hanging upside down from the ornate light fixture. My mother slowed her spin until we swayed to a stop, and she pressed a kiss to the top of my head as Dunston invited us to stay for dinner.

The pictures stopped, and I swallowed against the tightness in my throat. Replacing the captum in the drawer, I ran a hand through my hair. It was a darker blonde than my mother's had been, but the resemblance was still there. She would be surprised to see how tall I'd grown, though, as I'd been quite small as a child.

"She would be surprised about a lot of things," said the bat dryly.

Turning around, I glared at where he'd materialized on the footboard of my bed.

"There is nothing wrong with remembering your mother," he chided. "Or missing her."

Refusing to respond, I rose to my feet, stalked past him, and snatched fresh clothes from my dresser. The past was past, and there was nothing I could do about it. Instead, I would clean up, read my book, and stop reliving happier times that ultimately only reminded me of how much I'd lost.

7

KYRA

*T*he doorbell rang, a deep, melodious chime that sounded a bit like Glir, one of the larger stones on my *sana* bracelet. The diamond bead was associated with clarity, which was exactly what I hoped to find today. I tugged on my other well-worn boot and glanced at myself in the full-length mirror opposite my bed. At school, I often wore dresses, but when I was home on break, I favored breeches and tunics, and today I'd paired rust-colored pants with a soft sunflower yellow shirt embroidered with silver leaves.

I hurried downstairs, hoping to beat my mother to the door, but she was already there, chatting happily with Demitri and his Cypher, a red-tailed hawk named Halo. I shouldn't have begrudged her any happiness after what she'd been through, but I was anxious to get going. Normally, Demitri worked in the *Donec Auctoritas*, a government department responsible for the dispersal of information throughout the realm, but given his closeness to my family, he'd been given a few days leave to be with us. I'd asked him to accompany me to the Aelian Archives today, where I planned to do some research into recovrancy. On the way there, awkward as it would be, I was going to tell him about my experience in Vaneklus. It was too important for me to keep to myself, and there was no one better in the realm at keeping secrets than Demitri.

My mother turned and smiled at me as I reached the door. Her blue-grey eyes were brighter than I'd seen them in days.

"Demitri was just telling me you two are headed off to the Archives," she said. "I hope you're also planning on doing something fun while you're in Celenia; after all, you *are* on break, Kyra. You should at least get lunch or see a play or go shopping."

Or get betrothed, added Aurelius, materializing next to me. He shared a look with my mother's Cypher, Dova, a large brown hare, who chuckled before running a paw over one of her long ears.

I dropped my gaze to the floor, hoping to hide the heat rising to my cheeks. It was true nothing would delight my mother more than Demitri and me declaring our love for one another, but it was simply never going to happen. The problem was, I couldn't tell my mother *why* it would never happen without revealing Demitri's secret—that he was more interested in having a romantic relationship with a man than a woman. It was partly my mother's reaction to such a revelation that worried me, but there was also the unavoidable fact that same-sex relationships had been outlawed in Aeles for centuries.

Thankfully, Demitri saved me from having to respond.

"I'm happy to make sure Kyra doesn't spend all day in the Archives. In fact, I've been meaning to try a new eatery my mother told me about, Ralex's, in the Estes Market. She said it was the perfect spot to see and be seen."

My mother nodded eagerly and asked Demitri something else, but I wasn't paying attention. Demitri's mother, a powerful Astral in charge of litigation between provinces, never missed a chance to be in the public eye. If she had recommended the eatery, that meant it would be filled with well-meaning but intrusive Astrals wanting to know if or when I was going to assume my father's position as *Princeps Shaman.* I glanced at Aurelius, who smiled sympathetically.

One problem at a time, he said gently.

I gave my mother a hug, then followed Demitri down the front porch to the intersector. My family lived in Montem, and the Archives were located in Celenia, the government seat that was separate from the four provinces. I held the image of where I wanted to go in my mind, stepped onto the platinum plate, and soon found myself standing outside the Archives, an imposing columned building of white marble situated along a bustling street.

Stepping off the intersector, I looked around, taking in my second home. I couldn't help but feel proud whenever I returned to Celenia, even if I hadn't been gone long. The city was immaculate, every surface polished until it shone, pearl and glass and gold shimmering in the sunlight. The buildings stood tall and straight, elegant and unshakeable. Silver birch trees softened the spaces between structures, and water flowed everywhere—from bubbling fountains to shallow pools to gently frothing waterfalls, their loud roars tempered to a soft hum with the use of spells. The boulevards were lined with life-like statues of the Gifters, and banners bearing the crests of government *Donecs* fluttered in the breeze. Well-dressed Astrals laughed and called out to one another as a wind harp sang out nearby.

Today, though, such familiar loveliness also served as a painful reminder—my father was gone. My chest constricted, and I wrapped my arms around myself. I would never again meet him for lunch or surprise him with his favorite lemon-blueberry scones between classes or watch him deliver an address to the Senate, advocating for his patients and pushing for further research into *aleric* healing. The surrounding buildings wavered as tears filled my eyes. Aurelius materialized and gazed up at me with concern as Demitri appeared on the intersector with Halo on his shoulder.

"I can't go to Ralex's," I said hoarsely, my words coming out faster than I'd intended. "I don't want to see and be seen."

Understanding flashed across Demitri's crystal-blue eyes, and he nodded. Looping his arm through mine, he led us to a café across the street, and I blinked away my tears as I sat down at a table beneath a blue-and-gold striped awning. Demitri disappeared inside and soon returned with two cups of steaming drinking chocolate. Placing them on the table, he sat down across from me, brushing his stylishly layered brown hair out of his eyes with his fingertips.

"I don't suppose you've found out anything about your internship, have you?" he asked.

I shook my head. "As far as I know, positions will still be announced next week."

Demitri sighed. "You'd think they could make an exception, given the circumstances. Although, really, they ought to let you skip internship and just name you *Princeps Shaman*."

"I'm not ready," I said. "I still have so much to learn. And even if I get the internship, without my father . . . I'm not sure I'll ever be ready." I bit the inside of my cheek for a moment. "I spoke with Senator Rex briefly, at my father's funeral." I doubted I would ever mention my father's funeral without a searing pain slashing across my chest. "He said they have to name someone to take my father's place, even if it's just a temporary assignment. The realm can't be without a *Princeps Shaman*."

Demitri considered that as he took a sip of chocolate. "Any idea who they might choose?"

I shrugged. "Most likely whoever has the strongest healing skills at the *Donec Medicinae*, but I'm not certain who that would be. It was always my father."

We sat in silence for a few moments, listening to the happy conversations of passing Astrals mixed with the patter of water from a nearby fountain.

"You know, Senator Rex is becoming quite popular," said

Demitri, "especially considering he's relatively new to politics and just celebrated his twenty-eighth birth anniversary. He's managed to impress my mother."

"What does your father say?"

Demitri's father was a celebrated author and lecturer with a seemingly endless knowledge of plants and flowers. When he wasn't speaking to packed auditoriums, he preferred being in his garden to socializing, but my father had always said he was an excellent judge of character.

Demitri chuckled.

"Apparently Senator Rex has an interest in some rare climbing orchid and asked my father's advice on growing them. If it was a calculated move to get on my father's good side, it was a smart one, because my father's said nothing but nice things about him . . . when he says anything to me at all, of course."

A frown marred my best friend's handsome face, and I reached over and squeezed his hand. I had no doubt Demitri's parents loved him, but they didn't always show it in ways that were meaningful to him; while they favored grand gestures and expensive presents, he would have been satisfied with an uninterrupted conversation over a cup of tea. He'd never felt comfortable telling them he wasn't interested in courting women, and while I hated that for him, I also didn't blame him.

He took a moment to collect himself, then said, "So, what are we looking for in the Archives?"

I took a deep breath. The air was tinged with sweetness, as it always was in Celenia, and across the street, a little girl set a bouquet of lilacs at the base of an enormous statue depicting Acies, the Gifter of Wisdom. Saying a silent prayer for her assistance, I told Demitri everything that had happened when I'd tried to save my father.

His eyes grew wide as I spoke, and his jaw went so slack at

one point I worried about it unhinging and dropping from his face. When I finished, he ran his hands through his hair, giving himself an uncharacteristically disheveled appearance.

"Well," he finally said, "at least I'm not the only one at risk of breaking Astral law. Perhaps we can share a cell at Tor'Ex."

I winced. Tor'Ex was the prison hidden deep in the mountains of Rynstyn, a supposedly terrifying place where the rare Astrals who committed crimes were sent for rehabilitation.

"Kyra will not be going to Tor'Ex," snapped Aurelius, flattening his black tufted ears against his head. "What happened was simply a mistake, one we shall soon rectify."

I smiled at him, appreciating his devotion.

Demitri looked at the Cyphers. "Were either of you alive the last time there was a Recovrancer in Aeles?"

Like all other creatures, Cyphers were born, but unlike other creatures, they could become immortal by dedicating their lives to serving others. According to our shared history, the promise of such immortality had prompted them to make an agreement with my kind—a Cypher was paired with an Astral to provide lifelong guidance and instruction. When the Astral died, the creature appeared before the Cypher Commission to choose between being reassigned or taking a temporary rest, although too long of a rest would result in the Cypher becoming mortal again.

Halo stopped running his curved beak through his dark red feathers and cocked his head thoughtfully.

"I believe the last Recovrancer lived approximately five hundred years ago, although we'd have to check the official records to be sure." He fluttered his wings. "I was hatched 327 years ago, so it was before my time."

The three of us looked at Aurelius, who licked an oversized paw and ran it over one ear.

"That sounds right. I remember hearing something about

it . . . although the Astral I was paired with at the time lived so deep in the Wystern Mountains, we rarely had news of the rest of Aeles. He preferred his privacy."

Aurelius was 812 years old, which never ceased to amaze me. I couldn't imagine what it would be like to live for so long, to accumulate experiences and gain practically endless knowledge . . . but also, as Aurelius had pointed out, to watch those you cared about die while you lived on.

"Well," said Demitri, "we can find out for certain in the Archives. Speaking of, have you thought about what we're going to tell the Archivists—you know, to explain why we're researching something outlawed by the government and never mentioned in polite society?"

I nodded.

"I thought we'd tell them I was studying recovrancy as part of my training . . . with my father." My voice faltered, but I continued. "I can say we were trying to understand if going into Vaneklus affected the health of Recovrancers. From what I learned in school, it seems like being in the realm of the dead didn't make them ill, but no one knows why. Perhaps there's knowledge to be gained from their experiences that could help healers prolong life, or even stop death completely."

It was a bit of a stretch, but I assumed, given my father's recent death, others would be feeling especially charitable towards me. Part of me hated using his passing for such a purpose, but I couldn't think of a better way to get the information I needed.

Demitri considered that, then gave a decisive nod and raised his ceramic mug.

"To getting answers," he said with a cheerful smile.

I nodded, clinking my mug against his, and we finished our chocolate before making our way to the Archives. The white and grey granite street gleamed beneath our feet, and sunlight glinted off the hanging gold lanterns that would flare to life when darkness fell. Climbing the wide stone steps, we wound our way between rows of towering columns. I'd always loved how small the Archives made me feel, like a single speck of salt in an immense ocean of knowledge.

The air inside the building smelled of ink and parchment, and hushed tones mixed with the whispers of turning pages. We stopped at the Archivists' desk, where a woman with smooth olive skin and cinnamon-colored eyes was working. A long brown braid hung down nearly to her waist, and she tossed it over her shoulder as she greeted us. I knew her from the hours I'd spent here, which I hoped was a good sign. Her name was Veris, and she smiled, then bowed her head and offered her condolences on the passing of my father.

"Thank you," I said as Demitri wrapped an arm around my shoulder and gave me a squeeze. He was a wonderful actor, even though I knew his skills had been born of necessity, developed to hide parts of himself others deemed unacceptable.

Looking at the Archivist, I managed a weak smile. "It's actually partly because of my father that I'm here."

Veris stood up a little straighter and nodded, clearly eager to help.

I told her the story Demitri and I had agreed on at the café. When I first mentioned Recovrancers, Veris's eyes narrowed, and she appeared ready to interrupt me, but by the time I'd finished, she was nodding again, and her expression had turned thoughtful.

"We don't have much on that particular subject," she explained, gesturing for us to follow her. "Most documents pertaining to Recovrancers were taken centuries ago by the government and placed into safekeeping. But we do have a few things."

We walked through aisle after aisle of documents, each shelf filled to bursting with books, parchments, scrolls, folios, and maps. Halo rode on Demitri's shoulder, since flying in the Archives was forbidden—the wind generated by flapping wings didn't mix well with the loose papers lying about—and Aurelius padded silently next to me, occasionally nodding to other Cyphers he knew. Finally, after numerous twists and turns, we reached a section slightly darker and cooler than those we'd passed through.

"Some of the texts here are very old," explained Veris, "and need to be kept in special environments, so please don't take them past that line." She pointed to where the shadows ended, and the light was noticeably brighter. Demitri and I agreed to keep the texts well within the spelled air, and moving with practiced efficiency, Veris retrieved two rolled scrolls, which she handed to me.

"Anything we have about recovrancy will be in those documents," she said. "I'm not certain how helpful they'll be, but good luck." She paused, then added, "Your father healed my older brother once. I'm so pleased to see you following in his footsteps." She squeezed my shoulder, then excused herself.

I carefully unrolled one of the scrolls as Demitri pulled a captum from his pocket. He positioned it in front of one eye, then touched the tiny lever on the side and recorded an image of the text:

The term 'Recovrancer' was developed to describe those individuals capable of entering the realm of the dead. Those possessing this strange skill were able to recover the shades of those who had died and restore them to their physical bodies, bringing them back to life. While the ability to overcome death was initially welcomed, it was soon seen for what it really was—a perversion of the blessing of life bestowed by the Gifters. Someone who could enter Vaneklus and restore life at will possessed immense power, too much power for any one individual. A Recovrancer could demand any price for bringing back a shade, as most citizens would give all they owned for the chance to be reunited with a loved one. There was also the possibility a Recovrancer might create an army formed of those who had died, offering shades the chance to live again in exchange for their service. Even with government oversight, the potential for chaos was deemed too high, and as such, recovrancy was outlawed.

I sighed, disappointment settling in my stomach. It was simply the Astral decree outlining why recovrancy was dangerous and banning the practice. We'd studied this in school.

I rolled up the scroll, placed it back on the shelf, then turned to the other parchment. In some places the ink had faded, but I could make out four names, which appeared to be the names of past Recovrancers. Beside each name were two dates, which I assumed to be those of birth and death, as well as a few hastily jotted notes.

The first Recovrancer mentioned was a woman named Jaesian. There was no way of knowing if she was the first Recovrancer in Astral history, or simply the first one chronicled in this scroll. She'd lived almost a thousand years ago and beside her name was written, "silver tuning fork—broken." The second Recovrancer was a woman named Lochlyn, and she had lived approximately eight hundred years ago. Next to her name was written, "bells— melted." The third Recovrancer was named Fazeera, and she had died roughly six hundred years ago; next to her name it said "voice —silenced." And the fourth Recovrancer, who, as Halo suspected, had lived around five hundred years ago, was named Yerpa. Next to her name were the words, "wind flute—burned."

Demitri clicked the captum lever, then placed the device back in his pocket.

"It's interesting everyone mentioned here is a woman," he said softly. "Do you suppose men can't use recovrancy? I've never heard of abilities being exclusive."

"I don't know," I said, careful to keep my voice equally low. "The things mentioned here—a tuning fork, bells, a voice, and a wind flute—don't have anything in common. It doesn't make sense why they'd be recorded."

We stared at the words a little longer, but neither of us had any additional insights. After replacing the scroll, we stopped by the Archivists' desk to thank Veris for her help, then headed outside. I continued to mentally review the listed items, trying to find a connection between them and the realm of the dead. What was so important about them to warrant listing them after the Recovrancer they'd belonged to? I reached over and ran my finger across Glir, letting the bead clarify my thoughts. An idea suddenly came to me, and I stopped, grabbing Demitri's arm and turning him to face me.

"What if that's how they went in and out of Vaneklus?" I asked. Demitri squinted, not understanding.

"I was using my *sana* bracelet when I went in and out of Vaneklus," I reminded him. "What if the items listed on the scroll were how Recovrancers did the same thing?" My heartbeat sped up at the possibility of having discovered something important. "I touched Tawazun and Rheolath, beads for balancing and controlling. You could make those same notes with a tuning fork, with bells, with a wind flute . . . or with your voice, if you were a good singer."

Demitri crossed his arms and drummed his fingers soundlessly against the sleeves of his white cable sweater.

"Perhaps that's why the fate of each instrument was

recorded," he mused, "to make it clear they didn't work anymore, so no one else would try to find and use them. The tuning fork was *broken*, the bells were *melted*, and the wind flute was *burned*." His sandy eyebrows scrunched towards one another. "But the one named Fazeera . . . if she used her voice, that's not something you can destroy . . . at least not like the other instruments."

I glanced at Aurelius, pride over my discovery transforming into a queasy apprehension. "On the contrary," said the lynx quietly, glancing from Demitri to me. "The scroll was very clear about what happened to Fazeera's instrument—it was *silenced*."

8

SEBASTIAN

I stared over the ledge at the water churning below, letting the roar of the underground river form a cocoon around me, filling my ears with a dull background noise that heightened my other senses and helped me focus. I had finished *The Book of Recovrancy* a few hours ago, and although most of the pages had remained blank, since the book recognized I wasn't a Recovrancer, what I had been able to read had left me too excited to sleep. I'd paced around my living area for a while, then come here to the furthest reaches of my cavern, where I often retreated to think.

Pulling the book from my pocket, I ran my fingers over the cover. It had confirmed much I'd either suspected or read elsewhere, but it had also mentioned things I'd never heard before. I flipped to a page I'd marked and read the text again:

Recovrancers possess both the right and the power to recover a shade that has entered Vaneklus before its appointed time, and no payment is required for such a recovery. However, should a Recovrancer wish to remove an item that is not a shade from the realm of the dead, payment must be made to the Shade Transporter. The type of payment is commensurate with the importance of the item being sought. To begin the process of retrieving Rhannu, for instance, whoever wishes to remove the sword must obtain a unicorn horn. The horn must be given freely by the unicorn, and afterwards, it can be offered as payment to the Shade Transporter.

My mind reeled. What other types of things besides Rhannu were hidden in Vaneklus? What would happen if a Recovrancer tried to take something without having the requisite payment? And more importantly, how was I going to find a unicorn and convince the creature to freely give me its horn?

I rose to my feet and headed to my weapons vault. The room was well lit, thanks to the lanterns I'd connected to the veins of turmaxinase gas snaking throughout the cave. I could have used spelled lighting, but sometimes I preferred building things for the sheer pleasure of creating with my own two hands. I pulled a stack of parchment from a tall metal cabinet and carried it to my workbench. Moving aside the arrows I'd been fletching, I spread the papers out and sifted through them until I found my map of Aeles. The golden bloods worked hard to ensure nothing related to their realm found its way into Nocens, but I'd learned a long time ago almost anything could be had for the right price.

I skimmed the map until I found what I was looking for—the Astral unicorn sanctuary. At one time, unicorns had freely roamed both realms, but, unfortunately, they'd been hunted to extinction in Nocens, prized for their powerful horns. Left intact, the horns amplified spells; ground up, they cured a variety of ailments and were important ingredients in certain potions. I'd never understood why my kind had killed off the creatures— they shed their horns seasonally, like stags, and the horns could have been retrieved during the shedding period without eliminating the source of the supply. Now, only a few unicorns remained, and they lived in a sanctuary in the Aelian province of Rynstyn.

Rynstyn.

Just seeing that name made the flames inside me surge, begging to be let out. I clenched my hands into fists and took a deep breath, then exhaled slowly. I shouldn't be so affected by a name. Every time I let something about Aeles or Astrals bother me, I allowed my past to seep into my present, and I was stronger than that.

"Refusing to think about something is not the same as being strong," scolded my Cypher, materializing on the workbench and nearly upsetting a bottle of ink. "After what you survived, it is only natural you would be affected by the name of the place where you—"

I hissed and swatted at the creature, who vanished, only to appear on the back of a nearby chair, where he blinked up at me.

"Why don't you have Dunston or Caz find you a horn?"

I rolled my eyes. "You know what the book said—whoever wishes to remove Rhannu from Vaneklus has to obtain the horn."

The bat made a face. "Technically, those are instructions for how an *Astral* can work with a Recovrancer to retrieve the sword. You are not an Astral."

"Well, it wouldn't exactly say, 'If you're a Daeval seeking to reclaim what was stolen from your kind, here's how you do it,'" I snapped. "Whoever wrote the book would assume only Astrals would be working with Recovrancers."

"I suppose that is true," conceded the bat. "Well, if we cannot have a horn brought to us, we must go to the unicorns and get one ourselves." He looked at the map and giggled. "This is going to be *quite* the adventure!"

For once, he wasn't wrong. My kind had been outlawed in Aeles for centuries. The entire realm was spelled so an alarm would sound the instant it detected Daevalic blood, which meant I would need to trick it into thinking my silver blood was gold. I'd never heard of such a thing, but if anyone had, it was the Dekarais.

I pulled my peerin from my pocket, clicked open the coral-colored device that had always reminded me of a clam, and said Dunston's name into the chormorite lens. Thankfully, I didn't have to wait long before he answered, his face filling the disc. Usually, he reached out to me, so my contacting him was unusual enough to warrant his immediate attention.

"It's nice to hear from you so soon!" he said with a crooked grin. "Ready to tell me when you're coming over for dinner?"

"Actually," I said, "I'm in the market for something, but I'm not sure it exists. I need to disguise my blood so I can get into Aeles."

His grin disappeared, and he let out a low whistle.

"Did someone hire you to take out an Astral? I don't mean to insult you, Sebastian, but that's dangerous, even for you."

"I can handle dangerous," I said. "How do I get into Aeles?"

He ran a hand over his face and was silent for a few beats.

"We both know it's possible," I reminded him.

He cringed, but didn't deny it, then said, "This is a conversation better had face to face. Can you meet me at Caz's Diomhair Way office in an hour?"

A frisson of excitement raced through my limbs, and I quickly agreed. For Dunston to want to meet at that particular location meant he had at least some idea of how to get into Aeles. I busied myself cleaning weapons until it was time to leave, then slipped on my scabbard and favorite sword. Opening a portal, I made my way to a dilapidated brick structure that looked more like an abandoned row house than a meeting place for one of the most powerful Daevals in Nocens . . . which was just how Caz wanted it, of course.

I rapped the brass knocker against the front door, and Dunston quickly ushered me inside. I followed him to an inner room where Caz was standing next to a table, untying the knotted strings of a small burlap sack. I hadn't known whether he'd be in attendance or not, but having him here seemed like a good sign.

Dunston shot a decidedly unhappy glance at the burlap sack before stopping near a wingback chair and crossing his arms over his chest. "Before we begin," he said, "I want to say no one understands the value of privacy more than I do, Sebastian . . . you know this. But, in order to help you, I need some information."

I'd expected as much, and while I knew Dunston and Caz would never reveal something shared in confidence, I also didn't want to tell them about the unicorn horn and why I needed it. Regardless of my personal beliefs involving Recovrancers, Vaneklus, and Rhannu, I didn't want to risk my best customers thinking I was, at best, utterly ridiculous, and at worst, completely deranged.

"What specifically do you need to know?" I asked.

"Why are you trying to get into Aeles?" The question was so direct and unlike Dunston, I was momentarily taken aback by his bluntness; thankfully, my instincts kicked in and rather than blurting out an answer, I merely blinked in response.

Dunston shot me a mischievous grin. "Well, it was worth a try. Alright, in all seriousness—what can you tell me about why you need to sneak into Aeles?"

"I'm not going there for work," I said, addressing his earlier concern. "I just need to grab something, and, to the best of my knowledge, it's not locked up. It should be readily available for the taking."

"Well, that should make it easier," Dunston muttered, rubbing the back of his neck. He glanced at Caz before turning his gaze back to me. "Are you *sure* you want to do this?"

That was odd—Dunston never questioned my decisions. He also never gave away information for free, but based on the question he'd just asked, he had indirectly admitted he knew how to get me into Aeles.

"Are you worried I'll balk at what this is going to cost me?" I asked, even though I sensed that wasn't the source of Dunston's concern.

"No," he said, "it's not that. I know you're good for it. I just . . . this could go really bad, really fast . . . you going to Aeles."

"All of the jobs I've completed for you over the past five years could have gone really bad, really fast," I reminded him. "But I'm still here." I didn't like feeling as if I had to convince Dunston I could do this. He, more than anyone, knew what I was capable of, so why was he suddenly acting as if he needed to protect me?

"Sebastian makes a good a point," interjected Caz, leaning back and drumming his fingers against the lip of the desk.

Dunston's shoulders sagged beneath his well-tailored jacket, and eventually, he nodded. "You're right," he agreed. "When it comes to anything involving Astrals, I'm probably just overly cautious. If they catch one of our kind in their realm—" he shook his head "—the repercussions won't be pretty." I didn't miss the worry flitting through his eyes even as he looked at me and added, "But, if anyone stands a chance of getting in and out of there without being caught, I suppose it's you."

I dipped my head in agreement, and Dunston gestured tiredly at Caz, who smiled, pushed himself off the desk, and crossed the room, stopping before a bamboo screen decorated with colorful paintings of waterfowl.

"You already know Dunston and I conduct frequent business transactions with Astrals," he began, pushing up the overly long sleeves of his garish turquoise robe. "Some of those transactions are government-sanctioned, while others are related to the family business. What you may not know, however, is many of my interactions have taken place *in* Aeles."

He moved aside the bamboo screen and there, embedded in the floor, was an intersector.

"This intersector," Caz continued, "is one of a very, very few that does not track and report comings and goings to the Nocenian bureaucracy, the way normal intersectors do. It's untraceable. It was their concession to me after I helped them with some other things."

I nodded my understanding, impressed if not entirely surprised. Caz's device would allow me to travel without alerting anyone in my own realm, which was useful, but there was still one glaring problem.

"What about the Blood Alarm?" I asked. "Does your intersector also disguise silver blood?"

"No," Caz grimaced, and his expression turned apologetic, as if he knew I might not like what he was about to say. "Every time I go to Aeles, I'm greeted by someone who immediately pins a medallion to my shirt. They prick their finger and press a tiny bit of golden blood onto the medallion, and something about the combination of the two disguises my blood. I've never been able to smuggle one back with me—I'm not allowed to bring my Cypher, otherwise I'd have her steal one—but . . . I assume you're familiar with the concept."

I nodded tersely, all too familiar with that particular method of disguising silver blood. "But if there's time to pin a medallion on you, that means the Blood Alarm doesn't go off right away. If I used your intersector to get in, how long do you think I'd have?"

"An excellent question, and something I wondered myself," said Caz. "During one visit, I made it a point to extend a lengthy personal greeting to every member of the delegation sent to welcome me. I then pretended to trip over one of them—an exceptionally attractive one of them, I might add—which resulted in the two of us falling down. We were just starting to untangle our limbs when the alarm went off, so by my estimation, there's a roughly three-minute lag before silver blood is detected. Certainly no more than five minutes."

I supposed it was theoretically possible to find a unicorn horn in that amount of time, but it was also highly unlikely, and I didn't like odds so blatantly stacked against me. "So, you're saying in order to get into Aeles, I need a medallion not even you've been able to acquire, as well as a vial of Astral blood." I raised my eyebrows. "Did you have any other ideas?"

Caz nodded and pointed to the burlap sack on his desk. Reaching inside, I pulled out a small but heavy green bottle. The frosted glass was cool to my touch, and heavy copper wire held a cork stopper firmly in place.

"What is it?" I asked, uneasiness trickling into my stomach.

Caz clasped his hands behind his back. "Do you remember a few years ago, there was a big to-do about a potion master who lost her position at *Uchaf* Academy for being too adventurous with her concoctions?"

"Vaguely," I said, trying to recall the incident. "Wasn't there also something about her using subjects in experiments without fully obtaining their consent?"

Dunston groaned, but Caz nodded vigorously. "That's the one! Rosaria Lemquist. She disappeared from Vartox before the government could bring her in for questioning and hasn't been heard from since. Lucky for us, she's still in the potions business; she simply moved to the far reaches of Nocens—to Brengwen, of all places—and changed her name." Caz's eyes twinkled. "And *especially* lucky for us, she owed me a favor."

I ran my thumb over the copper wiring. "How does it work?"

"We don't even know if it *will* work!" exclaimed Dunston. "For all we know, it'll paralyze you or make you blind or worse, *kill you* the second you swallow it!"

Caz rolled his eyes. "Rosaria wouldn't give me something deadly. She knows how I'd respond. Plus, while she may be exiled, she's still passionate about her potions, and no one wants to know how this works more than she does. I told her in exchange for her cooperation, I would provide her with a full report of the effects."

"Sebastian isn't just some experiment for you to observe and report on!" snapped Dunston.

While I agreed with Dunston, I directed my question to Caz. "What did she tell you about it?"

"She said if everything works as planned, you'll have half an hour, but that's *at most*, and your time will likely be shorter."

Dunston began twisting one of the large rings he was wearing, a sure sign he was agitated. "You don't have to do this," he said. "We can find another way."

I knew he was worried, but I didn't need protecting—I took better care of myself than anyone else ever had or would.

"It's the best option I have," I replied in a tone that said I'd made up my mind.

Dunston's nostrils flared, and he shook his head before pulling out a red silk handkerchief and running it over his face.

"Do you have the coordinates for where you wish to go?" asked Caz.

I nodded, having memorized them from the map of the unicorn sanctuary. I also pressed a hand against my pocket, just to make sure *The Book of Recovrancy* was still there. I couldn't explain why I'd brought it, since I likely wouldn't have time to use it as a reference . . . but it had felt wrong to leave it behind. If nothing else, perhaps it would function as a talisman for good fortune.

Meeting Caz's gaze, I took a deep breath. "I'm ready," I said.

Whatever the risk, it was worth it to be one step closer to Rhannu.

9

※

KYRA

*I*t was the sort of autumn morning perfectly crafted for being outdoors. The warmth of the sun provided a nice contrast to the cool wind arriving in fits and spurts. Red and orange leaves stood out against the greenery of the forest, and the shrill warble of a bird sounded nearby.

It was especially nice to be out in the forest alone, as I had only *just* managed to leave the house without Seren or my brothers tagging along. Normally, I would have enjoyed their company, but today I needed some time by myself.

Summoning my *alera*, I ran my fingers over my *sana* bracelet, touching Tawazun and Rheolath at the same time. Closing my eyes, I tried to remember the words I'd said to enter the realm of the dead, but nothing came to me.

"Why can't I remember?" I asked Aurelius. "And how did I know to say a spell I'd never heard before?"

"I have no idea," replied the lynx. "You were very motivated. You were also very emotional. Perhaps those are factors that must be considered, as well as the beads and the spell."

"Well, perhaps one of my remaining family members will be crushed under a building soon, and I can try again!" I snapped, slapping aside a tree branch that had done nothing to deserve such treatment.

Aurelius paused and twitched his ears, waiting for me to share what was really bothering me.

"I just want to understand what happened," I sighed. "You know me, Aurelius . . . I can handle almost anything as long as I know *why* it's happening. If I don't know why this happened, how will I keep it from happening again?"

I rested my palm against the rough bark of a fir tree, enjoying the feeling of something solid against my skin.

"I need answers, and there's no one who can help me and—" my throat constricted. "I didn't mean to do anything wrong. I don't want to get in trouble with the government, especially now. I'm supposed to be working for them soon, and I need to take care of my family after—" I forced down the sobs that sought to escape my throat "—after losing Father."

I ran my flannel sleeve under my nose and let the tears pooling in my eyes fall silently to the forest floor.

Aurelius hopped onto a tree stump so we were eye level with one another. His cerulean eyes were bright, and while his expression was firm, it was also kind. Sensing the lynx preparing what was likely to be a lengthy speech, I stifled a groan. I knew he was simply fulfilling his assigned role, offering guidance and pointing out things I might not have considered, but part of me wished he would tell me everything was going to be fine and there was no need to worry about what going into Vaneklus might mean.

"My dear, I don't know why this happened," he began. "We may never know. Some parts of life, we enjoy; other parts, we endure. You cannot cross the mountains without going through the valleys. You are not a child anymore, and part of being an adult is learning to accept things as they are—not as you wish them to be. Wishing things were different will not change them. And we *must* change them, Kyra."

His thick silver whiskers drooped.

"What if you're healing someone and you disappear into Vaneklus again? And what if another Astral sees it happen? Your well-being is my utmost priority, so right now, I am less concerned with why's, what-if's, and hypothetical conjectures and more focused on the *facts* of what actually happened. That is where we must start in order to fix this."

"I still think knowing *why* it happened is important," I maintained, "but perhaps starting with the facts will lead us there."

Aurelius gave a satisfied nod as he hopped down from the stump, and we continued walking, ducking under low-hanging evergreen boughs and jumping over large rocks to cross a swiftly flowing creek.

"We can't do anything about how I entered Vaneklus until I remember the spell," I said. "So, if we're going to deal with facts, let's start with what happened once I got there. What do you know about the Shade Transporter?"

Aurelius flicked his short tail. "One of the downfalls of being immortal is that I know very little about the realm of the dead."

I let out an exasperated sigh.

"Well, what I know about the Shade Transporter only relates to what he *does* . . . he greets shades when they cross over from the realm of the living and ferries them down the river. He either takes them to Karnis, where they prepare for rebirth in a new body, or to Ceelum, where they can rest. But I don't know anything about who he *is*."

I walked across a fallen tree forming a bridge over a small chasm, extending my arms for balance as Aurelius dematerialized and then reappeared on the opposite side.

"I always assumed the Shade Transporter existed without beginning or end, like the Gifters, but is that true?" I asked, jumping down from the tree. "Have there been different Shade

Transporters throughout history? Could someone else take his place? Is it always a *him?*"

"I truly do not know," replied Aurelius. "As a Cypher, I've never had a reason to look into such things, seeing as how they're primarily Astral concerns."

"None of the other Astrals you were paired with ever asked questions like this?"

The lynx shook his head, causing the furry mane below his jowls to sway. "Most Astrals are content to believe what they're told or what they can see with their own two eyes. You experienced something unique, and as a result, your perspective has changed. You're seeking answers to questions most of your kind would never think to ask."

I leaned back against a large boulder, careful not to bump the delicate brown and orange mushrooms growing out of a crack.

"Is that bad?" I asked, hesitantly.

"Knowledge can be a burden," Aurelius replied with a shrug. "However, you and I are alike in that we value it above almost everything else."

I smiled, a quiet pride at my lynx's words warming my insides. Was it merely chance we were similar in certain regards, or had the assigners at the Cypher Commission somehow known we would turn out to be a good match? Cypher assignment took place on an Astral's fourth birth anniversary, since gifts were fully manifested by that age, but before the assignment, every child underwent a series of tests designed to showcase his or her special ability. I wasn't certain if the results were shared with available Cyphers, who then selected a partner of their choice, or if the Commission chose a particular Cypher based off the test data. I'd asked Aurelius, of course, but he'd simply said he wasn't at liberty to discuss it. Regardless of how the pairing had happened, though, I couldn't imagine my life without him.

I feel the same way about you, said Aurelius, and I ran a hand over his back. We continued deeper into the forest until we reached the place I loved most—a secluded glen ringed with evergreens and filled with late-blooming roses. There was an intersector near the roses, but I'd never seen anyone use it in all the years I'd been coming here; the plate was so overgrown with weeds, I might be the only one who even knew of its existence. Lowering myself down to the soft grass, I tilted my face upwards, savoring the peacefulness.

Aurelius dropped down next to me and stretched out on his side, basking in the sunlight.

"When I met the Shade Transporter," I said, returning to our original discussion, "he said, 'And so another Recovrancer makes her way into my waters.' Do you think I reminded him of a past Recovrancer?"

"I doubt it," replied Aurelius. "He likely assumed you were a Recovrancer because you managed to be both alive and in Vaneklus at the same time."

That made sense. It was probably best if I didn't resemble Astrals who had come to be considered dangerous enemies of my realm, anyway.

I leaned back against my palms.

"He said he didn't know why I was there, since it was *that shade's* appointed time." I replayed the Shade Transporter's next words in my head: *"Even you are bound by the natural laws—you cannot recover what is rightfully mine."*

"Do you think Recovrancers could only recover certain shades?" I asked. "I wonder why they could bring back some and not others."

I tapped my fingers against the ground, thinking.

"The Shade Transporter made it sound like I—someone he thought was a Recovrancer—had appeared because a shade had appeared . . . but I couldn't recover it because the shade was there at an appointed time. But that would mean someone had died at an appointed time. Deaths aren't appointed."

My stomach suddenly tightened, and I felt as if I was on the verge of discovering something important, about to answer a question I hadn't fully formed. I was missing something . . . but what? I reconsidered the timing of events. My father had been badly injured when I'd taken myself into Vaneklus. When I'd returned, he had passed. That meant his shade must have entered the realm of the dead while—

"No," I said abruptly.

Aurelius shifted into a sitting position, watching me carefully.

I felt so many things at once, it was like a cyclone had formed in my chest and was struggling to break free of my body. My hands shook, and the whirling sensation behind my ribs expanded outwards, pushing against my lungs until I could barely breathe.

"*That shade* the Transporter was referring to . . . that was my father?"

Aurelius nodded, his tufted ears wilting. "I believe so."

I shoved myself to my feet and wrapped my arms around myself as I began pacing about the clearing. My father and I had been in Vaneklus at the same time. I could have spoken to him, told him I loved him one last time, apologized for failing to heal him . . . or tried to recover him.

"No, you could not have done *that*," said Aurelius, following my thoughts.

"Why not?" I cried. "Because I'm not actually a Recovrancer? Or because of what the Shade Transporter said about it being my father's time?"

My heart slammed against my sternum with every beat, pulsing so vigorously it reverberated inside my bones. I glared at my Cypher.

"The Shade Transporter was wrong! It couldn't have been my father's time. He died in an earthquake! We hardly ever have earthquakes. It was a completely unpredictable accident."

"What do the Gifters say about death?" asked the lynx in a much-too-calm voice.

I gritted my teeth and continued pacing as Aurelius answered his own question: "Life is a gift because it is not without end; cherish your days, because they are numbered."

I spun and faced him. "Don't talk to me about days being numbered! You're immortal! And besides, do you *honestly* believe the Gifters assign a certain number of days to each Astral when they're born and when those days are done, that's it? You die?"

"I was merely quoting what your deities have said," replied Aurelius. "I was not—"

"I *know* what the Gifters said!" I practically shouted. "But if the Shade Transporter was wrong, then for all I know, the Gifters are wrong, too! It couldn't have been my father's time. I'll prove it. I'll find a way back into Vaneklus, and I'll find my father's shade and—"

A shrill whistle cut through the glen, causing me to stop pacing. A loud *crack* rang out, followed by the sound of something sizzling and the grinding of rusted gears. What in the realm was happening? Why did everything in my life—my lovely, happy, *predictable* life—suddenly seem to be spinning out of my control? I darted towards Aurelius, then skidded to a stop as a light began to shine upwards from the intersector.

10

KYRA

*H*ave *you ever seen one do that before?* I asked the lynx.

No, he replied, *which means we should be leaving* now.

Before we could move, however, a man suddenly appeared on the silver plate. He was wearing a black tunic and black breeches and clutching his stomach. His blonde hair glinted in the sunlight, and he took an unsteady step forward before falling to the ground with a groan.

I started to run towards him, but Aurelius grabbed the back of my shirt with his teeth, pulling me to a halt.

Kyra, something is wrong, he said. *I can't put my paw on what, exactly, but—*

What's wrong is that he's ill, I insisted. *I can heal him. I need to heal him.*

I needed to do something familiar, something that came easily to me . . . something that would allow me to have even a moment where things made sense again.

The lynx begrudgingly let go of my tunic, and I hurried forward, kneeling down beside the man.

"It's alright," I said, "I'm going to help you." Sliding my hands beneath his shoulders, I gently rolled him onto his back, careful to avoid the large sword strapped into a leather scabbard.

As I better situated him, the man's face suddenly transformed.

Shiny black scales spread across his forehead and the top of his cheeks, and red flames flickered between them. Before I could back away or even shout, the fiery mask disappeared, leaving a smooth face with high cheekbones and thin lips that immediately contorted into a grimace of pain. I'd never heard of a substance capable of making someone so ill it changed their appearance.

The man clutched his stomach again.

"Is this . . . Rynstyn?" he gasped through clenched teeth.

"No," I said, "this is Montem. The Tryllet Forest, to be exact."

The man groaned, then rolled to his side, curling his head and knees in towards one another. I leaned forward and pressed my hand against his neck, sending out an exploratory pulse of *alera* to find the cause of his illness.

There's something wrong with his blood, I said to Aurelius. *It's not anything I recognize, but I need to clean it.*

I tried to wrap my *alera* around a single drop of blood, so I could identify the poison and create an antidote that would spread naturally throughout the man's body. For some reason, though, I struggled to maintain a steady mental grasp—the man's blood was twisting and writhing in his veins, almost as if it was angry at my scrutiny and determined to stay just beyond my reach.

I changed course and sent more *alera* into the stranger's body, letting it coat his blood from head to toe, purifying it from any foreign substances. Sounds and images tried to force their way into my mind, a side effect of being a healer having prolonged contact with someone, but I didn't have time to learn about the man's past injuries, so I kept my focus on his blood until slowly, I felt the poison disappear. The man's groans softened, and he began to breathe easier. Uncurling from his fetal position, he rolled onto his back, and a hint of color returned to his pale face. I let out a deep sigh of relief, grateful I'd been able to help him.

"You're going to be fine," I assured him. "You might feel tired, but a little rest will fix that."

He blinked a few times and gazed up at me. I'd never seen him before and yet, as I stared down into eyes the color of rich chocolate, I felt an inexplicable sense of familiarity. Caught in the intensity of his gaze, it was as if I'd tumbled over the edge of a canyon and was falling with no end in sight. I couldn't breathe, I couldn't think, and I couldn't look away. I also discovered I didn't *want* to look away.

And then, the loudest alarm I'd ever heard in my life began to wail.

It's the Blood Alarm! shouted Aurelius. *Merciful Gifters, Kyra, that's what's wrong—he's a* Daeval! *Run!*

I could sense it now, the silver blood filling the intruder's veins. How had I missed it before? More importantly, how had the wards surrounding Aeles missed it and allowed him to enter the realm?

He must have hidden it somehow, said Aurelius, agitatedly hopping from one paw to another. *And when you healed him, you removed the disguise!*

I scrambled to my feet, all the terrible stories I'd heard about Daevals flooding my mind. Here I was, alone in the forest, with the most dangerous creature in existence. Should I run? Would the intruder chase me? Daevals were supposedly preternaturally fast. Had the Astral military heard the Alarm? Would they send soldiers?

While I weighed my options, the man rose clumsily to his feet, and as he did, a book slipped from the folds of his tunic. I only caught a glimpse of the title, but that was all I needed, since the words veritably branded themselves onto my eyes.

The Book of Recovrancy.

Everything inside of me stilled. I couldn't hear Aurelius, and I wasn't even aware of the alarm blaring anymore.

"Where did you get that?" I said, looking from the book to the Daeval, my voice half-accusing, half-pleading.

The man reached down, snatched up the book, and shoved it back into his pocket.

"Wait!" I shouted, extending a hand and lunging forward. Before I could reach him, though, he grabbed me and spun me around so my arms were pinned behind my back.

"Listen—" he began, but whatever he was going to say was cut off by the sound of a portal snapping open. Across the meadow, a dozen Astral soldiers in military blue poured through the doorway, fanning out to form a semicircle in front of us. One tall soldier moved ahead of the rest and raised his hand into a fist that began to glow a deep orange. He moved towards us cautiously, then paused, assessing the situation. His wavy mahogany hair fell over the tops of his shoulders, and his wide mouth pulled into a frown. I would know Adonis Prior anywhere, and as his eyes met mine, they instantly widened.

"*Kyra?*" Adonis shouted incredulously. "Falling stars, what— did he hurt you?"

I shook my head. "No, I'm fine."

Adonis turned his attention towards the Daeval behind me. The soldier whispered something, and the light surrounding his hand changed from orange to blue as he crooked his fingers into a spell-casting position.

"Let her go," he commanded, his sea-green eyes narrowing.

The Daeval let go of my arms, then suddenly raised a hand and shot a ball of fire at one of the soldiers, engulfing her in flames. Adonis dashed towards his colleague and, knowing he was a strong healer, I glanced back at the Daeval, desperate to ask him more about the book. Before I could speak, though, a second portal suddenly sprang open directly behind him, crackling loudly as a swath of darkness snapped into existence. For a moment, I thought it might be more members of the Astral military, but when none arrived, I realized why—the Daeval had opened the portal! The intruder stepped back towards his planned escape route, and Adonis, having healed the burned soldier, darted forward.

"Kyra, move aside!" he shouted, and the rest of his squadron immediately assumed spell-casting positions or fixed their weapons on the silver-blooded man behind me.

I have to know where he got that book, I said to Aurelius, my need for information swelling stronger than my fear. *If Adonis takes him in for questioning, I'll never see him again.*

Kyra, no! yowled the lynx, but I'd already made up my mind. I stepped forward, as if I was going to join Adonis, then spun around and threw myself against the Daeval. While I wasn't especially strong, he was still weak from whatever had been in his blood. He also wasn't expecting me to crash into him, and he shouted and fell backwards into the portal, arms grasping at the empty air, unable to regain his balance.

I pitched forward after the Daeval, aware of Adonis and the other soldiers shouting over the still-droning Blood Alarm. Aurelius wrapped his front paws around my leg out of devotion, terror, or some combination of the two.

And with that, the three of us crashed through the portal.

11

⚜

SEBASTIAN

*M*y back smacked against the cave floor, causing the scabbard to dig painfully between my shoulder blades. I hadn't been certain I'd be able to open a portal, but it seemed getting out of Aeles was much easier than getting in. I'd considered trying to reach the intersector to return to Caz's office, but there was a good chance I would have been shot or spelled while attempting to do so, so I'd gone with the portal instead. Unfortunately, portals were incredibly temperamental, and while I'd been distracted by the presence of Astral soldiers, apparently mine had shifted position, relocating itself roughly six feet *above* the floor of my cave. I groaned, every inch of my body aching, then gasped as something landed on top of me and knocked the air from my lungs.

My head was still reeling, and my stomach felt as if someone had forced me to swallow flaming iron barbs, but I managed to close the portal, and it winked out of existence, throwing the cavern into complete darkness. Then, inhaling as best I could, I let my instincts take over, giving me the strength to roll over and pin the Astral intruder beneath me. She screamed and struggled, but I quickly wrapped one hand around her throat and used the other to pin her arms over her head.

"What in the burning realm is *wrong* with you?" I growled. "Why did you do that?"

No one had ever attempted to follow me through a portal before, much less shove me into one. The woman made some sort of rasping noise I couldn't understand, so I loosened my grip around her throat.

"I knew if the soldiers . . . took you away . . . I'd never see you again," she choked. "And . . . I need . . . your book."

Of all the things for her to say . . . did she honestly expect me to believe she'd followed me for a *book?*

The darkness surrounding us was slowly punctured with solitary points of light, leapfrogging over one another in rapid succession. I glanced over my shoulder to see my Cypher standing next to a lantern, turning the knob to adjust the brightness.

Now that I wasn't ill or worried about an Astral soldier putting a spell on me, I studied the woman beneath me more closely. I didn't remember much about her from the forest, aside from her eyes . . . when she'd gazed down at me, I'd felt as if I was drowning in her unnaturally blue gaze, unable to get my head above water as she'd stared straight through my defenses and into my secrets. It had felt oddly familiar, which made no sense, as I'd never seen her before.

She was small, but there was nothing frail about her. Long black hair fanned outwards on the stone floor around an oval face, and a few freckles were scattered across her nose. I could sense the golden blood thrumming beneath her dark brown skin. She was younger than I was, perhaps seventeen or eighteen, but there was a depth to her eyes that made her actual age difficult to pinpoint—it was as if she'd seen things that had aged some parts of her without affecting others.

She blinked up at me, and tears filled her eyes. I could feel her body shaking beneath me.

"Please don't hurt me," she begged. "I just want to talk to you."

Batty materialized closer, on a rocky ledge a few feet away. *She did heal you,* he said. *It seems only fair you listen to what she has to say.*

I didn't care about the bat's definition of fairness, but I did care about getting my own questions answered. Everything the woman had done since I'd arrived in the glen had been the exact opposite of how I would have expected someone with golden blood to act. I didn't like when things defied the categories I placed them in, especially when it related to Astrals. While my silver blood urged me to simply run a sword through the filth and be done with her, I wasn't a mindless killer, and this woman was currently more valuable alive than dead.

"If this is a trick," I warned the woman, "and you're some-how working with those soldiers, you're going to be very sorry."

She shook her head as best she could with my hand still around her throat.

"I'm not working with them. I recognized one of them, the one who spoke to you, because we went to school together, but I don't have anything to do with the Astral military. I just hap-pened to be in the forest when you appeared."

"Before I let you go," I said, "you should know the only way in or out of this cave is by portal. There's no point in trying to run."

"I won't," she assured me.

I dropped my hands and rose to my feet, allowing the woman to push herself up off the ground. As she stood, she stroked the head of her Cypher, a large white and grey lynx with black spots scattered across his haunches. If I hadn't known that Cyphers, by virtue of the role they assumed, were forbidden from fighting or causing injury, I might have been more worried about the impos-ing creature. After a few beats, the Astral woman drew herself up straight and took a shaky breath.

"I'm Kyra," she offered hesitantly. I blinked in response, not about to reveal my name.

"He is Sebastian," piped up the bat, making me clench my jaw. "And, as my full name is too long for everyday use, I am pleased to be Batty, your humble host. It is so nice to make your acquaintance!"

Kyra glanced at him and smoothed the front of her red and black plaid flannel tunic with trembling hands.

"Um, thank you. This is Aurelius," she said, gesturing to the lynx, who shook his head and turned away, refusing to look at the bat.

Kyra was about to speak again, when Batty pulled a pouch from one of the innumerable pockets in his wings and offered it to her.

"Would you like a caramel?" he grinned. "They are freshly spun from Dal Mar."

A surprised smile spread across Kyra's face, but she shook her head.

"No, thank you," she said, watching as the bat popped a sugared candy into his mouth before tucking away the pouch. She then turned her attention to me.

"I'm sorry for pushing you," she said, her smile disappearing, "but I've never seen a book about recovrancy. May I ask where you got it?"

"Why do you care?" I asked. "Your kind outlawed recovrancy ages ago."

She nodded. "That's why we don't have any books about it. There are exactly two scrolls mentioning Recovrancers in the entire Aelian Archives, and I know because I've read them both. Everything else ever written about recovrancy was taken by the government and locked away somewhere."

Why had she done so much delving into recovrancy? And

since when was an Astral interested in something forbidden by their government? I'd always believed the golden bloods respected laws above everything else, following rules without question and mindlessly doing whatever they were told.

She gestured towards my pocket, which still held the book. "Did you steal that from Celenia?"

To my surprise, she sounded more curious than judgmental. I shook my head. "I bought it."

Kyra's eyes widened, and her mouth opened slightly. "Where did you buy a book about Recovrancers? Do they have more?"

She was making her interest far too obvious, which significantly weakened her bargaining power, but oddly enough, she didn't seem to care. Clearly, she wasn't used to negotiating for what she wanted . . . judging by her tailored clothes and glossy hair, she was well-off and used to being given whatever she desired.

"Why are you so interested in recovrancy?" I asked.

Several things flashed across her eyes—pain, fear, anger, and something else that passed before I could decipher it—and she swallowed and scuffed the heel of her boot against the stone floor.

"It's complicated," she finally said, her voice soft.

"It seems to me," interjected Aurelius with a disdainful sneer, "there is a far more fascinating question to be asked—why is a *Daeval* so interested in something that cannot even be performed by his kind?"

"I like to know everything I can about my enemies," I replied, ignoring his petty insult, "particularly the parts of their history Astrals prefer to keep hidden."

"It's true," added my bat. "He has been interested in recovrancy since he was just a small boy."

The lynx's eyes narrowed with suspicion, and I lashed out telepathically at my Cypher.

If you say one more word about my interest in this, I will destroy every stockpile of sweets you've hidden around the cave!

The bat crossed his wings and made an unhappy noise but refrained from further comment.

Kyra's eyes roamed the toffee-colored walls, as if a solution might suddenly appear on the stone. "Can I buy that book from you?" she offered.

"No."

The corners of her mouth turned down in frustration, and she looked at her lynx before bringing her gaze back to mine. "I can't tell you why I'm interested in recovrancy. If one of my kind ever found out . . ." She shook her head. "I would be in a great deal of trouble, which is something I can't afford. My family needs me."

I hadn't expected that, and my inability to predict her explanation annoyed me. It took a lot to catch me off guard, given everything I'd seen and done, but this woman had managed to do so.

And that made her dangerous in a way I hadn't anticipated.

Reevaluating my first impression of the golden blood standing before me, I considered my next move. I'd become quite good at predicting the most effective way to elicit information from a given target, and while I had no issue with drawing my sword and threatening Kyra, violence wasn't always the fastest way to get results, especially when the target would speak freely with the right encouragement.

"I go out of my way to avoid Astrals," I assured Kyra. I sensed, deep down, she actually wanted to talk about recovrancy, which meant verbal, rather than physical, persuasion was the place to start. "Especially those who work for your government. I have no interest in telling your kind anything."

Kyra looked down at her lynx as he vigorously shook his head. Like most folks, she seemed to take her Cypher's advice seriously, but it was clear they weren't in agreement about how to proceed. The lynx stamped an oversized paw angrily on the stone floor, and Kyra groaned, then rubbed her temples with her fingertips before looking at me again.

"I'm trying to learn about Recovrancers . . . because . . . I know someone who went into Vaneklus."

I felt like I was falling backwards through the portal again. I stared at her, waiting for her to laugh and say she was only teasing, but she simply stared back at me.

"What did you just say?" I asked quietly, afraid speaking too loudly might shatter the moment and prove I was somehow dreaming.

Kyra grimaced, but her gaze didn't waver from mine.

"I said, I know someone who went into Vaneklus. It was an accident, but . . . there might be a Recovrancer in Aeles again. I need information, though, before I can know for sure."

I glanced at Batty, who raised his wings and shrugged. By virtue of my profession, I'd become quite skilled at reading body language and knowing when folks were lying. Kyra wasn't lying, but how could what she was telling me *possibly* be true?

There was one way to know for certain.

"Come on," I said, grabbing her arm and steering her towards a passageway.

She stumbled, then righted herself as her legs pumped to keep up with the pace I'd set.

"Where are we going?" she asked, eyes widening with fear.

"To find out the truth," I said.

12

KYRA

I hurried to keep up in the wake of Sebastian's ground-eating strides as he half-guided, half-pulled me forward. Before we disappeared into the tunnel, I caught a glimpse of a table situated beneath a large iron chandelier fitted with delicate amethyst lamps. Behind it, partially separated from the rest of the cavern by tall stalagmites rising out of the stone floor, was a bed covered in blue and grey blankets. There was also a dresser and a wardrobe, both of which looked to be made of smooth planks of driftwood.

Do you think Sebastian lives here? I asked Aurelius, shocked at such a possibility. *Do most Daevals live in caves? I never really thought about their homes before, but—*

Their homes.

I inhaled sharply and twisted my neck to look up at Sebastian.

"We're in Nocens, aren't we?" I asked, my heartbeat speeding up. Of course we would be . . . it only made sense a portal opened by a Daeval would lead to Nocens. Even faced with such logic, however, I hoped Sebastian would correct me. The stories I'd heard about the Daevalic realm had likely been too outrageous to be true, but they'd made me want to stay far away, all the same.

I blinked up at the stone-faced Daeval, wishing he'd loosen his grip on my arm. "Don't your kind have wards or a Blood Alarm to keep my kind out?"

"Unlike your kind, we don't barricade ourselves behind enchantments," replied Sebastian. "We don't have to—Astrals know better than to come here."

I shivered at the cruel edge to his voice. I also took the opportunity to look at him again, now that I wasn't solely focused on healing him or getting out from underneath him. While I hadn't necessarily believed Daevals possessed the horns and tails depicted in my childhood nursery rhyme books, I still hadn't expected someone with silver blood to look so much like one of my kind. He was tall, but not remarkably so and although he had a slender build, he seemed quite strong, at least judging by his grip on my arm. His dark eyes were deep-set beneath a proud browbone, and his movements were tight and controlled.

He glanced over, and I quickly dropped my gaze to Aurelius, trotting along beside me. The fur on his neck was raised, and anger rolled off him in waves so thick, I could almost see them.

I'm sorry, I said to him.

Sorry will not keep that monster from whatever vile plans he has for you! retorted the lynx. *I know you want answers, Kyra, but was this really the* best *way to get them? And what if he figures out you are actually the Astral who went into Vaneklus?*

I focused on my boots, ashamed at upsetting Aurelius. There were few things worse than feeling like I'd let him down, especially when I knew he was only trying to look out for me. But at the same time, this was the closest I'd come to learning something useful about what had happened to me.

I had to give him some reason why I wanted information about Recovrancers, I said. *And of course pushing a Daeval through a portal to ask about a book wasn't the best way to get answers—but, right now, it seems like the only way. Remember, Father used to say sometimes we must go to war and ask the Gifter of Victory to meet us there,* I added, quoting a well-known Astral proverb.

Aurelius's whiskers twitched, but he remained silent.

The tunnel ended in an enormous cavern, much larger than the one I'd been in before. Sebastian pulled a lever on the wall, and the space was flooded with light from a system of interconnected lanterns. The cavern was filled with tall rocks jutting up from the ground, resembling stone fingers clawing their way towards the surface, and sharp pink and orange stalactites stretched down menacingly from the towering ceiling. A waterfall spilled from a jagged crack high overhead as colorful gems winked at me from the slick rock walls. Sebastian released his grasp, and I stopped at the mouth of the passageway, rubbing my hand against my arm to counteract the numbing effects of his grip.

Sebastian, however, continued forward and strode out onto a sliver of rock extending over a wide canyon. He then whistled a short series of notes. Batty materialized nearby on a cluster of petrified wood and gave me what seemed to be an encouraging smile. I tried to swallow my rising fear but couldn't manage much more than a half-hearted grimace in return.

Soft clinking sounds began to rise from the canyon, becoming louder, until it sounded like a hundred crystal chandeliers clanging against each other during a violent storm. I stared in shock as a dragon suddenly lifted his massive head from the chasm as coins, gemstones, and other treasures dripped from his scales.

Aurelius, LOOK! I didn't think they existed anymore!

Merciful Gifters of the Realm, gasped the lynx.

The beast stood out in stark relief against the pink quartz walls. His scales shimmered a liquid black, and wicked-looking horns the size of trees sprouted from his head. Flaps of leathery skin hung below his mouth, and the underside of his neck was a rich crimson that, unfortunately, reminded me of blood. I had never seen anything more beautiful or more terrifying in my entire life.

The dragon blinked sleepily and yawned, his sharp teeth glinting in the lantern light.

"Is it the first of the month already?" The beast flicked a forked red python-sized tongue into the air. "I feel as if I couldn't have been sleeping for more than two weeks."

Sebastian shook his head.

"This is something else," he said in a tight voice, gesturing towards me.

The dragon slowly turned his head in the direction of Sebastian's hand. As he realized Sebastian wasn't alone, his drooping eyelids lifted in surprise, revealing yellow eyes the size of boulders.

"Oh, my!" His voice boomed off the walls, causing the pebbles at my feet to rattle.

My arms and legs began to quiver.

The dragon extended his sinewy neck, bringing his head near Sebastian, and in a voice only marginally softer than a thunderclap, asked, "Who is she?"

"A problem that needs solving," replied Sebastian before turning to face me. "Dragons have the ability to know when someone is lying," he explained. "This one's going to ask you some questions to get to know you; then, *I'll* ask some questions. If you tell the truth, no harm will come to you. If you lie, he'll eat you."

I gulped and glanced at Aurelius. I certainly didn't want Sebastian to know I had gone into Vaneklus, but I wasn't about to lie and risk being a dragon's dinner. My stomach churned anxiously, but I forced myself to nod to show I understood.

The dragon blew a puff of smoke from his nostrils and narrowed his eyes at Sebastian. "This is all very untoward," he frowned. "Since it has never happened before, I suppose I can overlook the fact that you did not actually *ask* for my assistance and instead, I shall offer it. But if this happens again, you will not have to bring my next meal to me . . . I shall come and find it." He lowered his head ever so slightly. "Do we have an understanding?"

"Yes," Sebastian quickly assured him. "And thank you for your assistance."

I shuddered, horrified at whatever feeding arrangement Sebastian appeared to have with the creature. It was, however, nice to see even a Daeval didn't want to be on the wrong side of a dragon.

The dragon swiveled his neck to face me.

"Welcome, my dear." His sonorous voice belied just how truly awe-inspiring he was. "I am so sorry, but my eyes are not what they used to be, and it's *awfully* difficult to see you back there. Would it be a terrible imposition for you to come just a tiny bit closer?"

If I didn't comply, Sebastian would likely drag me the rest of the way, and I much preferred walking on my own. Stepping cautiously across the pebbles littering the ground, Aurelius and I made our way to the edge of the chasm. Taking a deep breath, I lifted my eyes and met the dragon's inquisitive gaze.

The nostrils on either side of his broad nose flared.

"Oh, my dear," he breathed. "Can it be? You look *exactly* like—"

Batty suddenly screeched and leaped into the air, flapping his wings wildly. Sebastian, the dragon, Aurelius, and I all turned to look at him, and he lowered himself to the cavern floor with an apologetic smile.

"I thought I saw a rock worm," he said. "I am so sorry, please continue."

The dragon appeared startled, and it took him a moment to collect himself.

"Well, I was saying . . . that is . . ." He turned back to me. "You look exactly like I remember your kind, although I admit it has been some years since I spoke with an Astral. I am Nerudian. And what may I have the pleasure of calling you?"

"My name is Kyra," I replied, pleased my voice sounded stronger than I currently felt. "This is my Cypher, Aurelius."

Nerudian slowly rose up onto his back legs. Dipping his head, he extended his magnificent wings to their full length. They were tinted with the same crimson as the underside of his throat and shimmered as he bowed.

"Welcome to you and your Cypher," he said. Aurelius and I returned the bow as the dragon settled himself back into the canyon.

"Now," he said, "I should like to know where you are visiting us from. If all the creatures there are as lovely as you, I simply *must* stop by!"

Warmth spread across my cheeks. "I live in Montem," I said. "That's where I met Sebastian . . . in the Tryllet Forest."

The dragon looked at Sebastian in surprise. "How did you manage to get into Aeles without setting off their Blood Alarm?"

Sebastian scowled and shoved his hands into the back pockets of his breeches.

"I didn't," he replied. "I used a potion to disguise my blood, but I still set off the alarm."

"Whatever he took made him incredibly sick," I offered. "He fell off the intersector as soon as he arrived. I thought he'd been poisoned, so I cleansed the poison from his blood, but what I removed was actually the potion. That's when the alarm went off."

The dragon raised a bony ridge over one eye and considered me with a newfound respect.

"Impressive," he said. "You must have some training in heal-ing. But how did you end up *here?*"

"Sebastian dropped a book in the forest," I explained, "and I wanted to ask him about it, but Astral soldiers appeared when the Blood Alarm went off. I was worried they would take Sebast-ian away and I'd never see him again, so, when he made a portal, I shoved him through it and came after him."

Sebastian pulled the book from his tunic, and my heart leapt at the sight of it. If he would just allow me to read it, even once, there was no telling what I could learn!

Nerudian squinted at the title, then dipped his head towards Sebastian. I took this to mean the dragon now understood me well enough to know if I lied, and Sebastian was free to begin his questioning.

The Daeval crossed his arms over his chest. "Do you really know someone who went into Vaneklus?" he demanded.

"Yes," I said.

Sebastian's dark eyes glinted in the bright lantern light. "Who?" His voice was hoarse, and there was an eager, almost desperate, edge to his question.

I hesitated, but my fear over what Sebastian might do with such information was quickly replaced by the terrifying alterna-tive of what would happen if I lied.

"Me," I said softly. "I went into Vaneklus." Taking a deep breath, I then told Nerudian and Sebastian everything about my experience in the realm of the dead.

When I finished, Sebastian looked as if the slightest breeze would knock him over. He seemed to have a naturally fair com-plexion, but after hearing my story, he was so pale I wouldn't have been surprised to see his silver blood zipping below his skin. Batty was shoveling caramels in his mouth and looking between Sebastian and the dragon, and, for once, Aurelius had nothing to say. Nerudian alternated between gaping at me and gaping at the bat until, finally, he gave his head a slow shake and broke the silence.

"So," he rumbled, "once again, there is a Recovrancer in Aeles."

"Then, it's true?" I asked, still not quite believing it. "I'm a Recovrancer?"

"You are, indeed," nodded the dragon. "This will not be welcomed by those who rule your realm."

"I know," I said. "That's why I'm trying to learn more about it, so I can stop it or make it go away or—"

"You can't make it go away!" interrupted Sebastian.

I looked at him, surprised by the urgency in his voice.

"That is, based on what I've read, it's a permanent change," he clarified. "It's debatable whether you're born a Recovrancer or if you acquire the gift at a certain age, but regardless, once the ability manifests, you can't change it. It's part of you."

"There has to be a way to change it!" I argued. "I'm a healer. I'm starting internship soon, and eventually I'm supposed to become the *Princeps Shaman*! I can't be a Recovrancer and end up locked away in Tor'Ex or worse!"

Sebastian shrugged. "I'll let you read what I have on the subject, and we'll see if you interpret it differently," he said.

Relief flooded through me.

"Thank you!" I said. "I can't tell you how much that means to me!"

Sebastian gave a curt nod and thanked Nerudian for his assistance.

The dragon grinned and nudged Sebastian affectionately with his head, almost knocking the Daeval over. He then glanced at Batty before turning to me.

"I should very much like to give you something to remember

our meeting by," Nerudian said, and I didn't miss the way Sebastian's frown deepened. In the stories I'd read as a child, dragons were notoriously possessive of their treasure, so perhaps he was surprised Nerudian was offering me something.

The dragon rummaged around in his canyon for a moment, then held a plum-colored foot over the ledge. As he uncurled his talons, I could see a small pile of fabric in his palm. He grinned at me, so I stepped forward and gently picked up the cloth; holding it at arm's length, I marveled at what turned out to be a cloak. The dark blue velvet was covered in swirls of indigo, purple, and pink, and silver flecks were strewn liberally across the fabric, making it seem as if the cloak were dotted with galaxies and sprinkled with stardust.

"It's beautiful," I said, stroking the soft fabric. The material shivered beneath my hand, then stilled, releasing what sounded like a contented sigh.

"This is a shifter cloak," said Nerudian. "It establishes a touch bond with whoever owns it, which will allow you to change the pattern or colors at will. Try it," he encouraged.

I placed my hand against the cloak and thought of the ocean I loved so much—the blue-grey water just before a storm, darkened by the shadows of low-hanging clouds and dotted with rising and falling whitecaps. The fabric stirred and then transformed into the exact color I'd been imagining. If I hadn't known better, I would have thought I was holding part of the ocean in my hands.

I slipped the cloak on and smiled at the dragon as I fastened it around my shoulders. "I don't need anything to remember meeting you, but thank you so much!"

He beamed in response, then offered me a toothy grin. "You never know when being able to blend into your surroundings will be useful, Recovrancer."

A nervous excitement swirled through me, and after thanking the dragon again, I turned and followed Sebastian back into the tunnel, ready to read every scrap of information he had acquired about my outlawed ability.

13

SEBASTIAN

*I*nstead of returning to my living area, I led Kyra to my weapons vault. Her eyes lingered anxiously on the weapons lining the walls, and she and her lynx walked so close together they were almost on top of one another. I stopped near my workbench, still not entirely believing what had happened in Nerudian's cavern. I felt confused, excited, and apprehensive all at the same time—with one revelation, my entire life had changed, and it seemed wrong for everything around me to still be the same. There should be fanfare, fireworks, a parade, *something* to mark the occasion.

Batty suddenly appeared on my shoulder holding a pair of cymbals, which he banged together in a manner lacking even the slightest rhythm.

We can have our own parade! he squealed gleefully in my head. I swatted at him, but he disappeared before I could grab either him or the cymbals. Reappearing a few feet away, well beyond my reach, he laughed as he hung upside down from a rope I used to hold training dummies.

Kyra watched our interaction with far too much interest, which annoyed me, since I doubted her lynx ever engaged in such ridiculousness. I didn't make it a habit to feel jealous, but she had no idea how lucky she was to have been paired with such a respectable Cypher.

Kyra then turned her attention to the shelves around the table, which held casters, miniature smelters, mixing bowls, and spelled stirring rods. There were also numerous vials of different shapes and sizes, fitted with glass or lead stoppers.

"Don't touch any of those," I said. "Some of them contain poisons that would kill you on contact."

Her eyes widened, and she gave a quick nod. If she was wondering why I had a cavern full of weapons and deadly toxins, she wisely didn't ask.

I leaned back against the table and crossed my arms over my chest. I wasn't used to the Fates favoring me, and while I appreciated the change, I also wasn't going to deviate from my usual method of operating. I would approach this as carefully as I would any assassination contract.

At first glance, it seemed simple—I needed a Recovrancer to retrieve Rhannu for me. Kyra was a Recovrancer. She wanted to learn more about her powers, and I had books that could help her do so.

In my experience, though, things that seemed too good to be true usually were, and the ease of recent events concerned me. It was so unlikely it should have been impossible—I'd been headed to Rynstyn, yet I'd somehow ended up in another part of Aeles, and the very first Astral I encountered just happened to be the first Recovrancer her realm had seen in ages. I didn't trust things I hadn't worked for, as they could too easily be lost or taken away. I especially didn't like including anyone else in my plans, much less depending on them to perform certain tasks, but, to my immense discomfort, there was no way around it. Rather than simply giving Kyra everything I'd gathered on recovrancy, however, I would use her interest as leverage, increasing the likelihood of her participation and reducing my risk to the absolute smallest amount.

"Before I show you what I have about recovrancy, what do you know about Rhannu?" I asked her.

She squinted, then shook her head. "I've never heard of a Rhannu . . . is he or she a Daeval?"

"Rhannu is the name of a sword," I said, grabbing a book from a shelf. I was surprised she'd never heard of it, given how much Astrals enjoyed besting my kind; I'd always assumed they had a national holiday to commemorate their thievery of the weapon. Then again, the story involved recovrancy, which Astrals had worked hard to distance themselves from.

I flipped open the book to a picture, and without meaning to, flexed the fingers of my left hand, almost able to feel the leather-wrapped hilt against my palm. I never failed to be impressed by the power contained in the gold and silver weapon, even in a simple drawing.

"This sword," I continued, "is one the most famous weapons in Daeval history. Centuries ago, it was stolen from us by your kind. The Astrals who took it had their Recovrancer hide the sword in Vaneklus."

I stared directly into Kyra's eyes.

"I want Rhannu back," I said. "I want you to go into the realm of the dead and recover it for me."

Kyra gazed helplessly at me, then ran her hands over her face before lowering them to her sides. "But I don't even know how to go back to the realm of the dead . . . much less, how to find a sword!"

"I'll help you," I assured her. "I'll give you all the information I have about Recovrancers, so you can learn how to be one. In return, you recover Rhannu for me. Do we have a deal?"

If she agreed, I would tell her about the obstacles she'd have to overcome in order to retrieve the sword, but that could come later. Kyra looked down at Aurelius, who growled and shook his head and appeared on the verge of foaming at the mouth. I was used to ignoring anything my Cypher said, but she obviously had a different relationship with hers. I was confident she would agree to my terms, since there was no other way for her to learn about her powers, but I also recognized exactly how unheard of such a business relationship would be.

Finally, Kyra directed her gaze back to me.

"I want to know about being a Recovrancer more than anything," she said. "None of my own kind can help me . . . but, this seems like a terrible idea. Aurelius says it won't work, and I'm inclined to agree with him. Can't I just buy the books from you or offer you some sort of trade?"

"You can trade recovering the sword for the books," I replied, irked she hadn't immediately agreed to my terms.

She hesitated and ran a finger over a large diamond bead on the bracelet she wore. A clear, cheerful note sounding of truth and revelation rang out, and I immediately stood up straighter, feeling my focus sharpen and my senses enhance.

"What are you doing?" I demanded. I didn't like feeling as if I wasn't in complete control of myself, especially in my own cave.

Kyra dropped her hand from the bracelet. "It's a *sana* bracelet," she said, as if that explained everything. When I simply blinked at her, she correctly interpreted I had no idea what she was talking about and added, "It's a tool I use in healing . . . to help focus my *alera*."

She pointed to the largest stone on the left side of her wrist, a bead of black onyx. "This is Mwyaf, The Forgetful. He's used to erase memories." Her finger moved to the next slightly smaller bead, the diamond she'd just been touching. "This is Glir, The Clarifier. He brings clarity and focus and helps those who hear him make wise decisions." The third bead was a dark blue sapphire. "This is Tawazun," Kyra said, "The Balancer. She finds equilibrium in all things." Her finger moved towards the next bead, a grey agate, but I noticed she refrained from touching this one. "This is Zerstoren," she said quietly, "The Destroyer." She quickly moved to the fifth bead, a small, bright red carnelian. "This is Rheolath, The Controller. She can take charge of living or inanimate objects and make them do her bidding . . . well, *my* bidding, I suppose." Tilting her wrist slightly, Kyra pointed to the sixth bead, which was actually a pearl. "This is Saund," she said, a smile pulling her mouth upwards, "The Soother. She brings peace and calmness to all who hear her. I use her a lot." She then gently touched the seventh, and smallest bead, a citrine stone that glowed like a miniature sun against her skin. "And this is Lleiaf, The Rememberer. She helps folks recall events that happened long ago or things they can't remember on their own."

I nodded, more fascinated than I wanted to admit. I'd never seen such a bracelet. Could anyone wield it, or did it require training to use?

As if somehow guessing my thoughts, Kyra cupped her hand over the bracelet, hiding it from view, and cocked her head at me. "Why, exactly, do you want Rhannu?" she asked, returning to our original topic of conversation. "I understand it's a historical artifact that belongs to your kind, but . . . why do *you* want it? Are you planning on donating it to an artifact preservation center?"

"I'm not answering any questions unless you agree to my deal," I said. "You're not the only one who could get into serious trouble over this."

"Who would you get into trouble with?" She appeared genuinely confused. "Don't Daevals just do whatever they want?"

Her naiveté was astounding, although I shouldn't have expected anything less.

"There are laws in Nocens," I snapped. "And if you break them, you get into trouble. Simply because we define right and wrong differently than your kind doesn't mean we've done away with the concepts entirely!"

The rounded edges of her cheeks reddened.

"I'm sorry," she said. "I wasn't trying to be rude. I know almost nothing about your realm." She sighed, and her previous concern seemed to be diminishing. "If I agree to help you, you'll answer my questions?"

"I'll give you the information you need to use your recovrancy powers, go into Vaneklus, and retrieve the sword," I replied.

Kyra pressed her lips together. I shifted my weight from one leg to the other, then forced myself to be still, not wanting to broadcast my impatience or my rising concern the Astral might not accept my terms.

"I don't want to assume you're going to do something bad with this sword," she finally said, "but you *are* trying to find what sounds like a very powerful weapon. I'm a healer. I don't want others to get hurt because I decided to help you."

Her expression was hopeful I would divulge something about my plans for Rhannu, but I simply gazed back at her. After a few beats, Kyra sighed and turned to her lynx. The longer they telepathically conversed, the more distraught she appeared, and I couldn't decide if she was moving closer to accepting or rejecting my offer. The flames simmered beneath my skin, and I shoved my hands into the back pockets of my breeches, trying hard to appear unconcerned as I awaited the Astral's decision.

14

SEBASTIAN

"Well," Kyra finally said with an unhappy frown, "it seems neither of us can get what we want without the other's help." She squared her shoulders and took a deep breath. "Alright, Sebastian, I agree to your deal—you help me learn about recovrancy, and I promise I'll do my best to retrieve Rhannu for you."

I held out my hand, and as our palms touched, I suddenly felt as though someone had struck a tuning fork inside my skull. My vision blurred, and my bones vibrated. It was most likely a response to touching someone with golden blood, but it was thoroughly unnerving, and I quickly let go of Kyra's hand, although not before noticing how soft her skin was. Mine was callused from years of fighting and wielding weapons, but hers felt like the finest silk milled from mulberry worms in Jaasfar.

Touching someone with silver blood must have been equally uncomfortable for her, because her cheeks flushed and she ducked her head so her hair partially obscured her face.

I pulled *The Book of Recovrancy* from my tunic, and it didn't escape my notice her eyes rose to follow my every move. I read her the part about the unicorn horn, then placed the book on the table.

"That's why I was in Aeles," I said. "I was trying to get into the unicorn sanctuary. For some reason—possibly the potion, I'm not sure—I ended up in the forest where you were, even though I directed the intersector to Rynstyn."

"Have you ever had trouble directing intersectors before?" she asked.

"No, which is why I think the potion played some sort of a role," I said. From the corner of my eye, I saw Batty observing the conversation with more than his usual degree of interest. I glared at him, and he quickly picked up a brown and white feather and began dancing with it, humming softly to himself.

Kyra tucked her hair behind an ear. "I'm surprised you knew the sanctuary was in Rynstyn," she admitted. "Since the potion didn't work, what are you going to try next to avoid the Blood Alarm?"

I crossed my arms. "Next time I'll use something made by your kind—something you're going to get for me."

Her eyes widened. "What do you mean?"

"There are devices that allow someone with silver blood to be in your realm without setting off the Blood Alarm," I explained. "And you're going to find one and give it to me."

Kyra let out a disbelieving laugh. "Why would something like that even exist?" she asked incredulously. "That would defeat the entire purpose of the Blood Alarm. Think about it—why would Astrals create an alarm to stop Daevals from entering our realm if there was some other way they could come in unnoticed? It doesn't make sense."

"Regardless," I replied, "it's possible."

"How?" she demanded.

"It just is," I replied firmly. Even if I hadn't heard about the medallions from Caz, I had firsthand knowledge of their effectiveness, having lived in Rynstyn for two years as a child, part of an experiment at a prison my Astral captors had referred to as a "rehabilitation center." They had tried to change me and others like me, working to transform my blood from silver to gold . . . in effect, trying to turn me into an Astral.

It hadn't worked, and I'd eventually escaped, but not once during my time there had the Blood Alarm gone off. After careful observation, I'd decided it had something to do with the metal collars they'd forced me and the other Daeval children to wear. The band had been fitted around my throat, just tight enough to be an ever-present discomfort, and a small gold medallion the size of a coin had hung from it. Every seven days, some Astral would prick their finger and brush a bead of blood against the medallion, somehow suppressing my blood from the sensors. For a moment, I wished I'd kept the hateful contraption, but I'd burned it off my neck shortly after escaping and melted it into an unrecognizable lump I'd thrown deep into a river.

Of course, I couldn't tell Kyra any of that . . . for one thing, she would never believe anything I said that cast her kind in such an unfavorable light. And second, the rehabilitation program had been highly covert and most likely long since shut down, making it impossible to prove I was telling the truth. At least it sounded like the medallion Caz wore when visiting Aeles worked in a similar fashion, and who better to find one than the woman poised to assume a government position as the *Princeps Shaman* who also possessed golden blood?

Kyra ran her hands through her hair, worry filling her eyes as she exhaled loudly. "I'm going to need a lot more information, but before we delve into the specifics, is there anything else I'm going to have to do?"

"Figure out how to get a unicorn to freely give up its horn."

"Oh," she said, "that's easy—you ask them for it."

I rolled my eyes, about to tell her to stop being ridiculous, but she shook her head.

"No, I'm serious. Unicorns shed their horns seasonally, like elk and stags, but from having the sanctuary, my kind learned they can also shed their horns whenever they choose. According to Astral history, one day one of the sanctuary founders was upset because his sister was ill, and the only potion that would heal her required a unicorn horn. He went to the unicorns and told them about his sister, and after hearing his story, one of the unicorns shed their horn and gave it to him. His sister was healed."

She traced her fingers over the clasp of her cloak. I hadn't noticed it before, but the silver had been shaped into the image of a four-legged serpent. "Of course," she added, "there are strict regulations about who's supposed to ask for a horn and what it can be used for, but it's definitely possible."

"So, you're saying if I can get into the sanctuary, all I have to do is ask a unicorn and it'll just give me its horn?"

"No," she corrected, "you explain what you need the horn for and ask politely for it, and the unicorn will decide whether or not your request is a worthy one."

I stared across the cavern. It was highly unlikely a unicorn would believe recovering a Daeval sword was a worthy request for a horn . . . then again, I didn't have any other options, which meant all I could do was try.

Kyra sighed loudly and scowled at me. "In exchange for everything I'm going to do, how *exactly* are you going to help me learn to be a Recovrancer?"

"I have three books about recovrancy—two actual books and one folio of documents I've compiled myself," I replied. "I'll give you one book now, because you need to start learning about what you are. After you acquire the device to get me into the unicorn sanctuary and I find a horn, I'll give you the other two."

She nodded, twisting her fingers into the edges of her cloak as if she could almost feel the books in her hands. In case she was searching for loopholes, like I would have done, I added, "Of course, you *could* always help me get a horn, take the books, and then refuse to retrieve the sword. But if you did," I paused, "your government would receive an anonymous tip about you being a Recovrancer."

She already said she would help you! the bat grumbled. *There is no need to threaten her!*

Kyra's eyes darkened. "I'll help you because it's what I agreed to do," she said. "I'm not someone who goes back on her word."

Clearly, she'd been more insulted than threatened by my words, but as long as she held up her end of the agreement, the reason behind her motivation didn't matter. I handed her the blue recovrancy book, and she snatched it from my hand and clasped it to her chest as if she'd never held anything more precious.

"Before we leave," I said, "tell me what you see on the first page of that book." Kyra looked up in confusion, so I told her what LeBehr had said. "Since you're a Recovancer, perhaps the book will reveal more of itself to you. When I read it, only the title was printed on the first page."

Kyra opened the book, and I moved to stand next to her. There was the title, exactly as I'd seen it before, but then, slowly, black ink began to rise to the surface of the parchment, revealing words written in a sweeping hand:

Welcome, Recovrancer. In your hands, you hold the summation of all knowledge involving the art of recovrancy. Refer to this volume often, for while some pages will remain the same, others will change to suit your particular needs, as well as your unique experiences. In some instances, you will forget what you have read until after a specific event comes to pass, at which time you will remember the necessary information. This is a kindness, as much of what is contained herein is too great to bear during every waking moment. Every Recovrancer is encouraged to add her own observations to this volume, and, on behalf of those who have come before, we wish you every success in your fight to preserve life.

Kyra looked up at me, her eyes sparkling as a smile spread across her face. "I've heard of books like this before, but I never imagined I'd read one that applied to *me!*"

I didn't like being excluded from something that directly affected me getting Rhannu, and Kyra must have realized I wasn't sharing her enthusiasm, because her excitement quickly dimmed.

"Well, then," she said in a business-like tone, "I suppose we should focus on getting me back to Aeles. You also need to tell me more about this blood-disguising device I'm supposed to find for you."

I ran a hand along my jaw. I needed Caz's intersector, but I doubted he'd let me use his prized possession for free, and I already owed him for using it once, as well as for the potion he'd gotten me. The biggest problem with Caz was that he didn't always equate payment with money . . . he frequently preferred to let others remain indebted to him before calling in the accumulated favors when it suited him. I hated being in anyone's debt for anything.

"Is something wrong?" Kyra asked, studying my face.

"No," I scowled, "But getting you out of here may turn out to be more expensive than I'd planned."

"I can pay you back," she offered. "Or—and I'm sure this is a long shot—do you know a Daeval named Caz Dekarai? He owes my family a favor and might be able to help."

15

KYRA

S ebastian took a step towards me.

"How do you know that name?" he demanded.

I gulped and leaned as far back as I could without actually stepping away from him.

"My father healed him once, and he sent flowers to my family after . . . after my father died . . . and said if we ever needed anything, he was in our debt."

Sebastian visibly startled and something flashed in his eyes. "Your father was the *Princeps Shaman*," he said. "Ara—something."

"Arakiss," I said softly.

Sebastian nodded. "I heard Caz mention him." He paused. "He mentioned you too . . . not by name, but he said you were supposedly a gifted healer, like your father."

Tears filled my eyes, and I quickly brushed them away.

"Then, you know Caz," I said, my voice tight.

"Yes." Sebastian turned to his bat. "Contact Alistair. Say I'm with Arakiss's daughter, and she's ready to collect on the debt Caz owes her family."

Batty gave a smart salute and dematerialized.

I busied myself thumbing through the recovrancy book and thankfully, Sebastian walked over to inspect some weapons and didn't ask me any more questions. Aurelius gave himself a hard shake and muttered something about sterilizing his fur from nose to tail when we returned home. It was obvious he was simply looking for a target at which to direct his annoyance, though, as I hadn't seen a speck of dust in the entire cavern. Did Sebastian clean frequently, or had he spelled the stone to repel dirt? In Aeles, we often used the phrase "dirtier than a Daeval" to refer to someone or something especially filthy. Either Sebastian was an exception to this or whoever had coined the phrase had been wrong about the cleanliness of those with silver blood.

Batty suddenly reappeared on the table, tripped over a feather, and skidded across the wood until he ran snout-first into an open book. Lifting his head and not seeming the least bit bothered, he grinned at Sebastian. "Caz would like for you and Kyra to visit him at his Diomhair Way office."

Sebastian gave a satisfied nod, then opened a portal and waved me over.

"Wait!" I said, slipping the recovrancy book into a pocket of my cloak.

The expression on Sebastian's face made it clear he wasn't happy about the delay.

"You're the only Daeval I've ever met," I said. I hadn't expected to be nervous about leaving an underground cave inhabited by a dragon, but my immediate surroundings were the only thing I knew of this realm. "Is Caz . . . is he . . . is he like you?"

Sebastian raised his eyebrows, and I hurried to clarify my question.

"What I mean is, is he safe?"

"Do you think *I'm* safe?" asked Sebastian in a low voice, indicating he found such a description applied to himself terribly insulting.

"I, um . . ." I hedged, trying to avoid upsetting him.

Sebastian angled to face me, and I gasped as the fiery mask

I'd seen in the forest spread across the upper part of his face. His top lip curled upwards as the black scales shimmered, red flames pulsing brightly between them. I half-expected to smell charred flesh, but the fire obviously wasn't burning him.

"Don't make the mistake of thinking we're friends," Sebastian said, his voice gusting over me like an icy wind and making me shiver beneath the cloak. "We're not. You would be hard-pressed to find someone who despises your kind more than I do . . . however, I'm willing to overlook your golden blood because of what you can do for me. We're business partners until you recover the sword, and then we'll go our separate ways. Do you understand?"

I nodded, feeling as frightened as when Sebastian had pinned me to the ground earlier. His fiery mask vanished, and I found myself suddenly anxious to meet Caz and put a realm's worth of distance between Sebastian and myself.

"Try not to draw too much attention," Sebastian instructed. "Caz's office and the area around it are sealed to portals, so we can't go directly there, which means we'll have to walk a little."

I quickly pulled the hood of the cloak over my head. Hopefully we wouldn't have to walk far. In one of my history classes, we'd read an essay written by an Astral who had visited Nocens as part of a government delegation a few years ago. He had described the Daeval realm as being in almost constant darkness, cursed with extreme temperatures, and ravaged by disease. But if the only way to go home was to go through such a place, I would do it.

Batty informed us he would meet us at Caz's office and disappeared. Taking a deep breath and saying a quick prayer to Praesidio, the Gifter of Protection, I followed Sebastian through the waiting portal.

If my feet hadn't assured me the ground below was solid, I would have thought I was standing on the back of an immense black and gold python. I had never seen such an incredible side-walk before—miniscule tiles were arranged to form geometric patterns that looked exactly like the skin of a snake. Casting my eyes as far ahead as I could see, the sidewalk appeared to undulate beneath the streetlights, rippling like a boa constrictor slowly coiling and uncoiling its body. I'd always liked snakes, and while the effect was slightly dizzying, it was also beautiful.

We had come out in a space between two large buildings near a fairly busy intersection. To my immense surprise, stars shone brightly overhead, twinkling against the black backdrop of a clear night sky.

I turned in a slow circle, trying to take in everything around me.

"All the stories I heard growing up . . . and in school . . ." My voice trailed off. What I was seeing couldn't have been more dif-ferent than what I'd been taught.

Everything was so clean . . . there were no putrid, disease-car-rying rivers or streets filled with reeking garbage. In fact, the air was scented with wood smoke and spices and smelled delicious. The buildings around me weren't dilapidated hovels caving in on themselves; they were well-built and gave the impression of pos-sessing an aged solidness, as if they'd already stood the test of time many times over and would stoically continue to do so.

Everything was also incredibly, shockingly, opulent. Precious metals and stones were used with wanton abandon, as if there were no concern quantities might someday diminish. Palladium lampposts rose every few yards, resembling slim trees with reflec-tive silver trunks, spreading their leafless branches out over the sidewalk. Instead of lamps, though, large chandeliers hung from the posts, tiers of alternating black and white crystals glowing with spelled lighting.

I felt as if I'd fallen into the middle of Nerudian's treasure trove, surrounded by gorgeous, glittering things everywhere I looked.

Sebastian took off walking, and I hurried to keep up with him, even as my eyes clung greedily to the shops we passed. There was a jewelry store with brightly lit windows, advertising breathtaking tiaras, necklaces, and cufflinks. This was next to a shop that specialized in cutting-edge enchanted or mechanical illumination fixtures. A women's clothing boutique was adjacent to a men's personal grooming establishment and both sat, much to my chagrin, directly across from the garish storefront of a furrier. A building that could have been a bank was hunkered down in a manner that reminded me of a fat blue marbled toad.

The majority of the traffic around us was on foot, walking along one of two sidewalks separated by a wide black stone street. The architects of the Daevalic city must have found walking in straight lines abhorrent, because all the routes were gently curved, bending in a slight arc in one direction before sinuously winding back the other way.

"Where exactly are we?" I asked.

"Vartox," Sebastian replied. "The capital of Nocens."

"What time is it? It seems late, but it's still so busy," I observed.

"Nocens runs twelve hours ahead of Aeles," he explained. "It's a little after midnight."

I was surprised to see so many folks out, shopping, laughing, and moving in groups from one tavern or eatery to another. I was even more surprised at how much the Daevals I saw resembled my kind—based purely on outward appearances, I wouldn't have been able to tell them apart. I could sense the difference in our blood, of course, and the awareness of being in a virtual sea of silver caused a slight pressure to tingle at the base of my skull. Did Daevals sense golden blood the same way I sensed silver?

Sebastian said my kind never came here, so hopefully if anyone we passed felt a similar internal alert, we'd be long gone by the time they thought to look for an Astral.

As we rounded a curve, I found myself gasping as the city fell away to reveal a group of enormous castle-like buildings. They were set below where we were walking, in a bowl-shaped depression of land, such that the sidewalk formed a perfect half-circle around them. While the five buildings were all physically separate, they were also linked together by enclosed skybridges several stories off the ground.

Behind the buildings, lava gushed out of an open crevice in a rock wall. It formed a glowing red waterfall that eventually became a river, winding its slow way around each of the buildings; not surprisingly, the grey stone of the castles was scorched along the bases and corners. Adorned with numerous statues and spires, the massive configuration easily took up the equivalent of several Aelian blocks.

"What's that?" I asked.

"The Territorial *Adran*," Sebastian replied without stopping.

"What does that mean?" I pressed.

Sebastian sighed, not even trying to hide his irritation over my questions, which was rude. "In the Nocenian government, we have *Adrans*, which, loosely translated, means departments."

"What happens there?"

"Whatever is required to maintain cooperation between the Daevalic territories. There are five of them—Dal Mar, Doldarian, Oexiss, Jaasfar, and Eisig—so there's always a dispute about something."

"In Aeles, we have four provinces," I offered. "Rynstyn, Montem, Aravost, and Iscre. We have *Donecs* in Celenia, but they aren't unique to any one province. They oversee things that affect the entire realm."

"Such as?" prompted Sebastian, apparently fine with questions so long as he was the one asking them.

Kyra, I cannot think of any reason why this hellion needs to know more about Aeles than he already does, cautioned Aurelius.

He's telling me about Nocens, so it's only fair I share something about Aeles, I pointed out before answering Sebastian.

"There are seven *Donecs*—*Donec Legibus* deals with drafting and amending laws. *Donec Auctoritas* oversees the distribution of information throughout the realm. *Donec Doctrina* is responsible for all Astral education, and *Donec Pactum* handles diplomacy between the provinces. *Donec Economia* deals with finances and the economy. *Donec Proelium* is the military branch. And *Donec Medicinae* is in charge of medicine and healing."

Sebastian nodded as if he was carefully filing the information away in some corner of his mind . . . which, Aurelius assured me, he most likely was. After a few more feet, Sebastian turned off the main road and led us down a side street filled with less ostentatious buildings, until we came to a stop in front of a faded red-brick structure that looked more like a house than an office. Black shutters were sorely in need of fresh paint. The granite stairs leading up to the stoop were cracked and chipped in places, and one of the iron handrails leaned too far to one side.

"This is Caz's office?" I asked, doubt swirling in my stomach. How could the owner of the most run-down place I'd seen in Nocens help me get home?

"It's his second office," replied Sebastian. "Only a few folks know about it. Some deals require more privacy than others."

I wasn't certain what he meant, but I was distracted by the sight of the front door opening. A woman stepped out onto the landing, and to say she was beautiful only explained part of the impression she made. She had presence, one of those rare folks who acted like a planet, immediately drawing anyone who came close enough into her orbit.

Her skin looked as if someone had spent hours polishing bronze before shaping it into long limbs and perfectly proportioned curves. She had a shoulder-length mane of chestnut-brown hair, and her strategically placed blonde highlights glinted beneath the spelled overhead lighting. But it was her eyes that were particularly arresting—they were the color of melted butterscotch and appeared lit from within, offset by dark, slitted pupils slightly feline in appearance.

She wore a short red tunic, fitted black breeches, and black and grey snakeskin boots that had cost the lives of who knew how many snakes. Her red-stained lips curled into a mischievous smile as she walked down the stairs towards us, eyes fixed on Sebastian. A furry brown mink suddenly materialized on her shoulder.

"Uncle Caz said you'd be coming by," she said, reaching up to stroke her Cypher. "I was going to take him to the gallery to see a piece I just finished—to make him buy it, of course—but he told me I had to leave because you were coming over. When I tried to get more details, all he said was, 'Eslee, some days you're the mongoose, other days, you're the cobra.'"

"Was he saying today you're the cobra?" frowned Sebastian.

The woman—Eslee—raised and then dropped the shoulder not supporting her Cypher.

"Who knows? But *clearly* you're here about something important—it's not every day we have a golden blood in Vartox," she said, turning her gaze to me. I felt small, mousy, and terribly disheveled under her scrutiny, but she flashed me a broad smile as I lowered the hood of my cloak.

"I'm Eslee," she said, before gesturing to the mink. "And this is Sasha. Caz is my uncle, in case that wasn't clear. Sebastian and

I went to school together. He's the son my father always wanted . . . unlike my actual brother, Devlin, who's picking me up." She nodded her head towards a carriage pulling to a stop where the street we were on joined the broader road. There were no horses pulling it, so I assumed it was enchanted.

"I'm Kyra," I said. "It's—

"We don't have all night," interrupted Sebastian, striding past me up the stone stairs.

Eslee rolled her eyes and gave her head an apologetic shake.

"He's always focused on business. Don't take it personally. You know, I've never met an Astral before," she said, an eager light glowing in her eyes. "I've only heard about them from Daddy and Uncle Caz. If you ever come back to Nocens, look me up. Eslee Dekarai. I'd love to ask you some questions about your realm, and I'd be happy to show you around Vartox."

"That would be nice," I said with a tentative smile. Part of me did think it would be nice, but I was careful to avoid actually making a promise, since I doubted I would be able to fulfill it any time soon . . . if ever. As Aurelius and I followed Sebastian up the stairs, I glanced back at the carriage just in time to see Eslee's brother climb out, and I managed to catch a glimpse of broad shoulders, messy brown hair, and black leather breeches before I stepped into Caz's office. Sebastian closed the door behind me, and I suddenly found myself engulfed in a pair of arms, my face pressed against scratchy maroon fabric that smelled a little like sour red wine as someone said, "My dear, *dear* Miss Valorian . . . I cannot tell you what an absolute pleasure it is to make your acquaintance!"

16

KYRA

*M*y response was unintelligible, smashed as I was against the stranger's chest, but thankfully he gave me another squeeze and then lowered his arms. I took a quick step back and shot a glance at Sebastian, who appeared completely unfazed.

"This is Caz," he said, as if that explained the man's odd behavior.

I turned back to the Daeval, who bowed and extended his hand. I cautiously offered him mine, and he quickly pressed it to his lips, grinning roguishly before releasing me and tucking his thumbs under the lapels of his smoking jacket. The dark red material strained across his stomach and was embroidered with purple roses that matched the flowing purple silk pants he wore.

I rearranged my cloak and attempted to regain my composure.

"It's . . . nice to meet you, too," I said. Caz was shorter than Sebastian and appeared to be middle-aged, but then again, I had no idea if Daevals aged the same way my kind did, living to around a century or so and gaining more wrinkles and whiter hair the older they got. Caz had quite a few wrinkles around his eyes, but while his brown hair was thinning on top, it was still thick and unruly above his ears.

He held a hand over his heart, and his violet-tinged blue eyes burned fervently.

"I was so sorry to hear of your father's passing. Arakiss was truly one of a kind, and he shall be deeply missed."

"Thank you for the flowers you sent," I said. "I'm glad my father was able to help you." I wanted to ask what he'd healed Caz from, but if it was a sensitive topic, it wouldn't do me any good to embarrass the one Daeval who might be able to help me get home.

Caz gave a solemn nod then fixed a searching gaze on me. "From what I hear, you are similarly gifted in the healing arts," he said. "Now, I don't require an answer to this, because I am the one in your debt, but do I have the honor of speaking with the future *Princeps Shaman* of Aeles?"

His question caught me completely off-guard, and I glanced at Aurelius for guidance. Caz chuckled at my surprise.

"My dear, regardless of the realm, one thing remains the same . . . knowledge is power. Brute strength has its place—" he grinned at Sebastian "—and tangible goods and physical comforts certainly make life enjoyable. But information . . . *that* is what makes us rise or fall, whether we be an individual, a government, or an entire civilization."

I drew a shaky breath before offering a careful reply.

"I'm still waiting to see where I'll be placed for internship," I said. "A lot depends on that. There was still so much I needed to learn from my father . . . but, I hope to have the position, one day."

Of course, I'd never imagined assuming the position while also being a Recovrancer, and I had no idea how I would manage to hide such an unacceptable secret while holding one of the most public positions in Aeles. But that was a problem for another day, as right now, I simply needed to get home.

Caz rubbed his hands together.

"Excellent," he purred. "Thank you, Kyra . . . if I may call you that?"

I nodded.

"Now, then," he puffed out his chest, making the shiny buttons on the front of his jacket strain with the effort of staying closed. "How can I repay the debt I owe your family?"

Sebastian spoke before I could.

"She needs to return to Aeles without drawing unwanted attention," he said, then quickly explained how I'd come to be in Nocens in the first place. He left out numerous details—such as his recovrancy books, the fact that I was a Recovrancer, and his desire to reclaim Rhannu—and while it was clear Caz noticed the omissions, he didn't ask any questions. He simply nodded a few times, then rocked back on his heels.

"Well, that explains why you didn't return the same way you left," he said. "Dunston was so irate, I thought he was going to attack me with his bare hands, but, thankfully, your Cypher sent word once you were back in Nocens, saying you were alive and would contact us when you could."

Waving us further into his wood-paneled office, Caz crossed the room and moved aside an ornately painted bamboo screen. A large porcupine sat there, languidly peeling the bark off a tree branch and slowly stuffing the strands into its mouth.

"Go away, Alistair!" shouted Caz, making me jump. "There was no reason for your behavior earlier, no reason at all, and I told you I didn't want to see you for the rest of the night!"

The porcupine, which I took to be Caz's Cypher, responded by biting off the end of the branch with a loud *crunch.*

Clenching his fists, Caz turned to us.

"She ruined a deal for me earlier—materialized in my chair *just* as I was sitting down!" He shook his head. "Made me look like a lunatic, jumping up and screaming and grabbing myself. It's a wonder I'm not pulling quills out of my backside!"

"It was a bad deal," intoned the porcupine. "I had to get your attention."

"You could have tried telling me!" retorted Caz.

The porcupine shrugged and took another bite of the tree branch, making her cheek bulge. "You were willing to overlook things because you thought he was handsome. You're too easily swayed by a pretty face." She gave Caz a considering look. "Your business would be better if I shoved my quills in your eyes and blinded you."

I shuddered, hoping the creature was merely trying to make a point. The Cyphers paired with my kind would never harm someone, but for all I knew, Daeval Cyphers behaved differently.

Caz gave an injured sniff.

"My business is fine, thank you very much," he said, "and if I'm occasionally distracted by the urges of the flesh, well, that is a burden I shall simply have to bear as best I can."

The porcupine grunted and dematerialized. Near where she'd been sitting, a platinum intersector was embedded in the floor.

Caz held up a hand. "Now, I know what you're thinking, Kyra, and for the most part, intersectors here function exactly like those in your realm, recording comings and goings and reporting them to some government bureau or another. *This* one, however, does not, so we needn't fear anyone else in Nocens learning of your visit."

I nodded, trying to pretend as if I had indeed been concerned about such a thing when really, my mind was racing. I'd never heard of intersectors tracking travel before, although to be fair, I'd never given them much thought, simply using them to go where I wished. Why would the Aelian government care who went where, when? And how did Caz know anything about my realm?

I glanced at Sebastian, piecing together what must have transpired before he'd appeared in the forest. "That's how you entered Aeles . . . you used this intersector so there wouldn't be a record of where you went. But intersectors can't disguise blood, so that's why you took the potion."

He gave a curt nod, and Caz spoke again.

"Since you have golden blood, though, there should be no impediment to you using the intersector to return to Aeles," he said with a reassuring smile, and while that was helpful to know, my mind was elsewhere.

Do you think that's a thriving business in Nocens? I asked Aurelius, *making potions to disguise silver blood so Daevals can sneak into Aeles?*

Oh, I'm certain of it, he replied grimly.

That was a terrifying thought, and I wasn't sure how to handle having such important information. Should I tell someone in my government? But then I'd have to explain how I'd acquired the knowledge, and Sebastian had already threatened to expose me as a Recovrancer if I didn't go along with our agreed-upon plan.

"Before you leave," Sebastian's voice interrupted my thoughts, "I need to tell you about the device you're going to retrieve." He glanced at Caz. "Feel free to add any details that might be helpful." Caz scratched his head but nodded anyway.

"You're going to be looking for a small gold medallion," explained Sebastian. "It will resemble a medal or military pendant, and it's designed to be pinned to your clothes."

Caz chuckled, suggesting he understood Sebastian now. "On the medallion," he added, "will be an eight-sided star, the symbol of Aeles."

"What does the medallion do?" I asked, even though part of me didn't want to know.

Sebastian shifted his stance ever so slightly. "When you apply a drop of Astral blood to the medallion, it works as a suppressor, disguising the fact that whoever is wearing it has silver blood."

"I thought you were making that up," I said, and Caz quickly shook his head.

"Oh, no, my dear . . . I can assure you they're very real."

"How do you know?" I asked, a shiver speeding down my spine.

"I've seen them," he replied.

While he didn't elaborate, I suspected he'd worn them, as well. Was that how he'd met my father? Perhaps my father hadn't gone to Nocens after all . . . perhaps Caz had come to Aeles, but if that was the case, it meant someone in my realm had knowingly used this suppressor medallion to allow a Daeval into our realm. Who would do such a thing?

Perhaps the more important question is, why would someone do such a thing? asked Aurelius.

I nodded at him, again forced to sit with possessing valuable information while having no way to share it. Clearly Aeles wasn't as safe as I'd been taught to believe, but unfortunately, there was nothing I could do about it.

Instead, I made my way to the intersector.

"Thank y—" I started to say, but Sebastian interrupted.

"She's going to need to come back," he said to Caz. "As part of settling your debt with her family, will you allow her to use your intersector again? At a date and time convenient for you, of course."

An impish grin spread across Caz's mouth.

"Well, well, it's nice to see you interested in something outside of work for a change." He turned to me. "You may use the intersector whenever you wish. Simply have your Cypher send word to mine, and we'll arrange it."

"My Cypher can communicate telepathically with yours?" I

asked, dumbfounded. I'd known Aurelius could speak to other Astral Cyphers, but I'd never considered whether he could communicate with those paired with Daevals. I looked at the lynx, who shrugged his white and grey shoulders.

"I never had a reason to communicate with a Cypher paired with a Daeval," he sniffed. "But I don't see why I couldn't, if I chose to."

Caz tilted his head to one side, a bemused expression on his face.

"What *do* they teach in Aeles these days? Cyphers are all the same creatures, regardless of which realm they're born in; the blood of whomever they're paired with doesn't affect their abilities." He shook his head. "Astrals are so determined to maintain their separateness from us, one day future generations will think Daevals were just a myth concocted by their grandparents to scare them!"

He sighed, then gave a slight bow.

"I must excuse myself to check on something. Kyra, I look forward to seeing you again soon. You are always welcome here."

"Thank you," I said, returning the bow, then turning towards Sebastian as Caz disappeared into the front of his office.

"Thank you for finding a way to get me home," I said, even though he wasn't helping me out of a desire to be kind. Careful to keep my voice low, I added, "Once I've found a medallion, I'll have Aurelius reach out to Batty. It might take a little while, but I'll hurry."

Sebastian nodded, and I took a step towards the intersector, then stopped, suddenly struck by the sheer magnitude of what had taken place since I'd left my house that morning. What would it be like when I returned home? Would it be obvious where I'd been? Would my family suddenly be able to tell I was a Recovrancer?

Sebastian misread my hesitation. "Are you thinking about backing out of our deal?" he asked, and although he spoke quietly, I didn't miss the warning in his voice.

"No," I assured him, "I was thinking about what it'll be like when I go back. So much has happened since this morning. My family's probably worried sick about me."

"What are you going to tell them?" he asked.

I considered that. "I think I'll go back to the forest and then walk home, rather than taking the intersector directly to my house. That way I can say after I fell through the portal, you managed to reopen it and returned me to the woods."

He raised an eyebrow. "And they'll believe that?"

"They won't be expecting me to lie, so yes, I think they will," I said, my insides knotting at the thought of intentionally lying to my family. "Hopefully they'll be so happy to see me they won't ask too many questions. And it's believable, since I'm the only one who saw you come in on the intersector; everyone else saw you leave by portal. I just . . ." I tucked my hair behind my ear. "You can't tell I've been to Nocens just by looking at me, can you? Or that I'm a Recovrancer?"

Sebastian rolled his eyes. "You look exactly the same as when I first met you. You were already a Recovrancer then, even if you didn't know it. And being around Daevals isn't going to change you—you're not going to grow fangs or start sacrificing children under the full moon or whatever else it is Astrals think we do."

I didn't appreciate his snide tone, but at the same time, I was glad to know nothing about me would alert anyone to where I'd been or what I'd been doing. I pulled the recovrancy book from my cloak and looked at Aurelius.

"Can you put this somewhere safe?" I asked him. "I don't want to risk my family seeing it." Holding the book gingerly between his teeth, as if it tasted bad, the Cypher dematerialized, saying he would hide the book in the furthest reaches of my large, poorly organized closet.

I slipped the cloak from my shoulders and ran a hand over it before offering it to Sebastian.

"If I go back wearing this, it'll only raise more questions for me to answer," I said, deeply saddened to part with the gift. "Would you mind keeping it until I come back?"

He nodded, and I appreciated how carefully he folded the cloak into a pouch hanging from his belt.

Stepping onto the intersector, I closed my eyes, picturing the platinum plate near the cluster of wild roses in the Tryllet Forest. Then, as my body tensed for transport, I suddenly felt something cold press against my left wrist. Glancing down, I was surprised to see Batty, who had materialized out of nowhere and snapped a wide gold bracelet on me. He giggled, but before I could question him, Caz's office blinked out of sight and I found myself whisked out of Nocens.

17

SEBASTIAN

I stared ahead, not believing what I was seeing, as Kyra disappeared on the intersector wearing a gold bracelet put on her arm by my Cypher. Suddenly, I felt metal pressing against my right wrist, and Batty grinned up at me as he clicked an identical bracelet into place.

"What are you *doing?*" I shouted, jerking my hand away, but it was too late. He waved a wing and dematerialized.

"Is everything alright?" asked Caz, jogging over from another room. Even though he'd only trotted a few yards, he was wheezing loudly and quickly came to a stop, resting his hands on his knees to catch his breath.

I pulled my sleeve down to cover the bracelet.

"It was just my Cypher," I explained, "being his usual imbecilic self. It's nothing."

I thanked Caz for his assistance, and he gave me a wicked grin.

"May I ask what you plan to do with the suppressor medallion once you have no further need of it? Are you planning on keeping it and expanding the territory you cover for work?"

I had no interest in assassinating Astrals, and once I'd retrieved the unicorn horn, I wanted to be as far away from such a painful reminder of my past as possible. Of course, there was no reason I couldn't profit from such a powerful device, and even though I was distracted by the bracelet on my wrist, I managed a nonchalant shrug. "I'm open to discussing some kind of an arrangement."

For a moment, I thought Caz might attempt to pull me into a hug, but he settled for rubbing his hands together and smiling broadly. Excusing myself, I left his office and walked down the street until I could no longer sense the antiportal wards he kept in place. I then conjured a portal and returned to the cave, my mind racing for an explanation of the bat's actions.

I tried to pull the bracelet over my wrist, but it was too tight. Wherever the clasp had been, it had vanished after the bat had clicked it into place. My only remaining option seemed to be melting the jewelry from my arm.

I placed my hand against the bracelet, summoned the fire within me, and let the flames flow through my fingers. A small black dragon suddenly appeared on the bracelet's surface. It reminded me of Nerudian, but perhaps that was simply due to the color. Unfortunately, no matter how much heat I poured into the jewelry, it didn't melt . . . it just continued to absorb the flames.

"Take this off!" I shouted into the stillness.

Batty materialized into view, hanging upside-down from the chandelier over my kitchen table.

"Gold is a very good color on you, if I do say so myself," he said with a smile.

I stormed over to him and raised my arm. "Take this off *now!*"

He sighed. "Alas, I cannot."

"You can, and you will."

He shook his head. "No, you see, the bracelets must be together—physically near one another—in order for them to come off."

I ground my teeth, then said in the calmest tone I could muster, "So, when Kyra returns, you'll take them off?"

The bat let go of the chandelier, extended his wings, and floated down to the table. Scratching one of his ears, he gazed at me.

"Even when she returns, I cannot take them off, no."

"But you said—"

"I said the bracelets must be near one another to be removed. I never said *I* knew how to remove them," he clarified.

I felt like one of the volcanoes off the coast of Dal Mar, emitting smoke in preparation of spewing molten lava. "How do you know the bracelets need to be together to be removed?"

The bat examined one of his feet before replying, "I was told they function as a single unit."

"Who told you that?"

"A friend.

"Which friend?"

The bat wiggled his nose. "The one who gave me the bracelets."

Now we were getting somewhere. "*Who* gave you the bracelets?"

Batty scratched the golden mantle of fur around his neck. "I am not certain I should say."

There was one other thing I could do before I spent an absurd amount of time trying to get more information from the bat. Concentrating, I placed my hand against the bracelet. If I heated metal to just the right temperature, I could learn the history of the material. I let the flames flow against the gold with less intensity this time and watched as scenes began to take shape before my eyes.

I saw the bat slapping the bracelet around my wrist, then around Kyra's. There was the bat removing the two bracelets from a wooden box lined with blue velvet. The images were playing in reverse order, beginning with what had happened most recently. The wooden chest sat in the dark . . . it was cold . . . ages seemed to pass, and then I was in a meadow.

A man was on his knees, hugging the lifeless body of a woman to his chest. He was sobbing so hard his entire torso shook. One of the woman's limp arms rolled to the ground, and a golden bracelet gleamed as lightning tore across the sky. . . . I was in a grove, surrounded by trees, and a tall woman was fastening two golden cuffs around the wrists of a man with shoulder-length blonde hair. His black and grey cloak gleamed in the moonlight. . . . I was outside on a terrace. It was nighttime, and a small wooden chest was placed next to a figure reclining on a sofa. Thin curtains fluttered in a breeze, and a woman gasped as the chest was opened, revealing two golden bracelets. . . . I was in a dry valley dotted with oversized rocks, and a hot wind scorched my face. A black dragon blew flames at a lump of gold, which slowly began to melt. As the flames died down, I was able to see the dragon's face, and I inhaled sharply.

The bracelets had been forged by Nerudian.

I dropped my hand from the bracelet and stared at the bat, who beamed at me.

"That was very clever," he said, sounding as if he was proud of me.

Had he purposefully refused to answer my questions so I would be forced to see the history of the bracelets for myself? Why would he do such a thing? Was he even intelligent enough to do such a thing? Puzzling over such thoughts, I sprinted towards the passageway leading to Nerudian's chamber and didn't stop running until I reached his cavern, turning on the lights and whistling the notes to summon the dragon. Soon, I heard a sleepy yawn echoing up from the canyon below me. This was followed by the sound of shifting treasure, and a moment later, Nerudian's head rose into view.

He blinked a few times. "I can't recall the last time you visited me so frequently."

I pulled up the sleeve of my tunic and held out my arm. "Explain yourself, Nerudian."

"That's quite a tone to take when you have interrupted my sleep," he scowled.

"Tell me why you gave this to my Cypher!"

The dragon shrugged, and the scales on his shoulder rippled as if someone had skipped a stone over dark water. "He asked me for it. Very politely, too, I might add."

"What is it? And how do I get it off?"

The bat materialized a few feet away. He and Nerudian exchanged a long look that did nothing to calm my anger, but eventually, the dragon spoke.

"To answer your questions . . . it is a very old bracelet. And in order to remove it . . . well, both bracelets must be near one another, and then they can be removed by the same dragon's breath in which they were forged."

His careful response wasn't as helpful as I'd hoped it would be.

"They can be removed by *your* breath, because you were the dragon who forged them. I saw their history," I said. "So, you're saying once Kyra returns, you can remove the bracelets, and we can be done with this?"

He nodded. "Yes, but rather than focusing on having them removed, you might consider what you and Kyra are able to do while wearing them."

That caught my attention. "What do you mean?"

"Well, Kyra's Cypher can reach out when she is ready to return, but wouldn't it be nice to communicate with her while she is back in Aeles? To find out what sort of progress she is making on getting you into the unicorn sanctuary?"

I hadn't shared my need for a unicorn horn with Nerudian

when Kyra and I had visited him before, which meant my bat had told him. I turned to chastise him, but the dragon continued.

"The bracelets will allow you to speak with Kyra the same way you speak with your Cypher . . . in your head, whenever you wish." His yellow eyes dimmed with concern. "You really don't remember?"

"Remember what?" I asked, now more confused than upset.

"You don't remember . . . ah . . . you don't remember I once mentioned enchanted objects that allowed for such communication?" asked the dragon, shifting uneasily in his treasure. "Hmm, well, perhaps I only thought about mentioning them to you."

"I believe you told me instead," offered the bat. "That is how I knew to ask you for them."

"Indeed!" said Nerudian. A wide grin spread across his face, and he nodded his head so vigorously, it was a wonder it didn't snap off his neck. "Yes, that makes sense, because that is exactly how it happened!"

I studied the bracelet, then looked up at Nerudian. "Why did you forge enchanted objects allowing the wearers to communicate like Cyphers?"

The dragon blew a puff of smoke from his nostrils, and one side of his enormous mouth rose in a wistful smile. "I was asked to make them, many, many ages ago, as presents for a king and queen."

I was about to ask another question, but the dragon yawned.

"That is enough for now," he said. "Simply touch the bracelet, wait for the dragon to appear, and then speak as you would to your Cypher. Kyra will hear you and be able to do the same. Oh, and you might consider thanking your bat . . . after all, he *did* acquire the bracelets to help you."

Nerudian's expression made it clear he wasn't returning to sleep until I'd expressed some form of appreciation to the bat. I sighed and looked down at Batty, who grinned and clasped his wings behind him before rocking slowly back and forth.

"Thank you," I muttered.

Nerudian winked at me, then disappeared into the canyon, and Batty flew up and settled on my shoulder.

"I promised her I would look out for you," he said, patting my cheek with a wing. "And I don't intend on stopping any time soon."

I assumed he was referring to a promise he'd made to my mother, but he chose that moment to sneeze, and I was too busy running my sleeve over my face to think more about his words.

18

~~❦~~

KYRA

I squinted up at the light streaming down through the trees, surprised to see the sun out, since it had been the middle of the night in Vartox. It was odd to see trees and shrubs after the extravagant buildings of the city, and I glanced down at the dried leaves crunching beneath my boots, picturing the sinuous black and gold sidewalk from the Nocenian capital. While it certainly felt good to be back amidst familiar surroundings, I had to admit part of me had enjoyed seeing the Daeval realm. For the sake of accuracy, I was tempted to write a paper outlining all the errors my kind had made about Nocens. I would never do such a thing, of course, but I didn't like knowing Astrals were being misinformed and believing things that weren't true.

Making my way through the forest, I could soon see part of my house, the white stucco and light brown wood gleaming brightly beneath a cheery red tile roof. The coziness of my childhood home sent an unexpected jolt through my limbs, and I cringed, hoping Sebastian was right and I wasn't somehow tainted with an unseen evil after being around those with silver blood. How in the realm was I going to keep being a Recovrancer a secret from my family . . . much less a Recovrancer who had made a deal with a Daeval to retrieve an ancient sword in exchange for forbidden books?

I gave the golden bracelet another tug, but it refused to slide over my wrist, so I pulled my tunic sleeve down farther to hide it. Aurelius had examined the bracelet back in the meadow but hadn't come to any conclusions about what it did or why Batty might have put it on me. At least it didn't seem to be dangerous, which meant I could deal with it after assuring my family I was safe.

Hurrying up the front steps of the house, I crossed the porch and rushed inside. "Mother?" I called. "Hello? I'm home!"

My family emerged from various parts of the house—Enif and Demitri from the kitchen, Seren and my mother from upstairs, and Deneb from his bedroom. Soon we were all entangled with one another, a hugging mass of tears, questions, Cyphers, and prayers of gratitude to the Gifters.

My mother wiped her eyes and pressed a kiss to the top of my head. Even though I'd only been gone a few hours, she had to have been terrified having me go missing so soon after my father's death. My siblings and Demitri clamored to know what had happened, but my mother raised her hands for silence.

"I know we all want to hear details, but first, we need to let the proper authorities know Kyra has returned." She squeezed my shoulder and smiled. "I suspect someone will want to come over and ask you some questions about your experience, so perhaps you'd like a moment to freshen up."

Icy dread rushed over me, as if someone had tipped a bucket of cold water over my head. While I understood the need to tell members of the military I'd returned safely, since they'd seen me disappear through the portal, the last thing I wanted was to have government officials in the house, asking me questions I couldn't, and wouldn't, answer.

"I don't really think that's necessary," I began, but my mother had already disappeared around the corner, likely to retrieve her peerin. There was no swaying her once she'd made up her mind, so, I darted upstairs to the bathroom Seren and I shared as everyone else settled into the formal living room.

I splashed cold water on my face, then ran a towel over my skin and studied my reflection in the mirror. Sebastian was right —I looked exactly the same as I had before going to Nocens. That seemed wrong, although I couldn't say why. Perhaps I simply wanted proof of my unexpected adventure, or for the changes I'd felt taking place inside of me to be visible on the outside.

As you always say, Aurelius, I said, pulling open a drawer and searching for my brush, *knowledge changes you. You can never go back to who you were before you knew something.*

The lynx materialized on the plush white rug near the claw-footed bathtub.

And in most instances, I still believe that's a good thing, he said. *Although I have no idea how you gaining firsthand knowledge of Nocens will ever be more than a liability, much less something good.*

Having found my brush, I ran it through my tangled hair, grimacing at the knots, when the gold bracelet around my wrist suddenly vibrated. I gasped, and Aurelius raised his ears.

The bracelet vibrated again, more insistently this time. I set down my brush and pressed my fingers against the jewelry, willing it to stop. A small black dragon appeared on the surface, and something about the graceful curve of its neck brought Nerudian to mind. The dragon zipped around my wrist, and then I heard something I had *never* imagined hearing.

Kyra? Are you there?

It was Sebastian's voice . . . inside my head.

I spun towards Aurelius, holding my arm as far away from my body as I could. The lynx's eyes were wide, and his fur stood on end.

"What's wrong?" he asked, speaking out loud as I clutched my head with the hand not wearing the bracelet.

"I . . . I just heard Sebastian . . . in my head," I whispered.

Kyra? There he was again! *It's Sebastian. If you can hear me, think a response, like you would to your Cypher.*

"Can't you hear him too?" I asked Aurelius, panic tightening my voice.

"I cannot," he said, more mystified than I'd ever seen him. "Try responding to him, and perhaps I'll hear that."

Are you still there? I asked tentatively, some part of me hoping there would be no response. I looked at Aurelius, but he shook his head. Why couldn't he hear this conversation when he overheard all my other thoughts?

I'm here, said Sebastian, and I grabbed the edge of the cream-colored vanity to steady myself.

How is this possible? I asked, fighting the disorientation coursing through me. *What did these bracelets do to us?*

They allow us to communicate like Cyphers, Sebastian explained. *Nerudian made them, apparently, centuries ago, for some king and queen. Batty thought it would be helpful if we could communicate while you're back in Aeles, so he put them on us.*

Well, he might have told us that and at least asked if we wanted to wear them! I retorted, simultaneously irritated at Batty's actions and relieved to know the bracelets weren't dangerous. *And speaking of Cyphers, mine can't hear my thoughts when I'm speaking to you like this. I didn't know that was possible!*

Really? asked Sebastian with something approaching enthusiasm in his voice. I didn't understand why he'd be excited to keep things from his Cypher, but then again, he clearly had a different relationship with Batty than I had with Aurelius.

I dropped down to a gold tufted stool and rested my elbows

against the top of the vanity, careful not to bump the numerous pots of lotions, creams, and cosmetics scattered across the surface. On the one hand, I was relieved to know I wasn't hallucinating or suffering the effects of some illness I'd caught in Nocens. On the other, I wasn't certain it was a good idea to walk around maintaining a telepathic connection to a Daeval. If anyone ever found out—

A knock on the door made me jump and nearly fall back against the glass-enclosed shower.

"Kyra?" came Demitri's voice from the hallway. "Your mother just spoke with Adonis. He and Senator Rex are on their way over. Do you need anything?"

"No, thank you, I'm almost done," I assured him. "I'll be down in just a minute."

As Demitri's footsteps faded, I turned my attention back to Sebastian.

I don't mean to be rude, I said, *but I have to go. One of the soldiers who saw us in the forest is on his way to my house with a member of the Aelian Senate. They want to hear about my encounter with a Daeval. But don't worry, I won't tell them anything about you.*

I could feel his suspicions crawling through his mind, like vines climbing a trellis. It was jarring how easily I could sense his emotions, and how comfortable conversing with him like this was. It felt . . . familiar. Then again, I'd communicated with Aurelius in such a manner for almost my entire life, so of course telepathically conversing with Sebastian would seem instinctive.

Leave the connection open so I can hear your thoughts, he said. *That's the only way I'll know you aren't setting me up to be chased down by your government.*

First of all, I replied, *I am not about to speak with a senator and a soldier with you in my head. It would be too nerve-wracking. And sec-*

ond, even if I hadn't promised to work with you—which I have—it's in my best interest to keep my kind away from you because you still have two recovrancy books I want.

My logic must have made a stronger impression than re-minders of my promise to help him, because he gave a resigned sigh. *Fine. But let me know how it goes. And then start looking for a suppressor medallion.*

Sebastian explained how to activate the connection using the bracelets. He wasn't certain how to end our conversation, but when I pressed my fingertips against the gold metal again, the dragon disappeared, and I could no longer feel the Daeval in my head.

Aurelius shook his head. *Yet another problem to add to our ever-growing list,* he groaned.

And with that, we stepped out into the hall and headed downstairs.

19

✺

KYRA

*A*s I descended the lucite staircase, the doorbell rang, and my mother hurried to welcome the visitors. Adonis stepped inside first, the gold buttons on his dark blue military jacket shining almost as bright as his ear-to-ear grin. I looked down at Demitri, whom I could see sitting on the sofa below. Judging by the rise and fall of his chest, he was focused on taking deep, evenly spaced breaths. He'd harbored feelings for Adonis for years, and I knew seeing the man brought up an abundance of emotions for him.

Adonis crossed the blue slate floor and stopped at the bottom of the stairs, gazing up at me. "Of all the Astrals to encounter a Daeval in their own backyard!" he said, kindness filling his green eyes as his grin widened. "I'm so glad to see you're home safe, Kyra."

I stepped off the stairs and gave him a hug. At twenty, he was two years older than I was, and while we'd never been especially close as children, he'd started spending more time with me and Demitri over the last few years. At first, I'd been worried he might be developing romantic feelings towards me, which would have been excruciating for Demitri and awkward for me, as I'd never been attracted to the soldier. Thankfully, though, while Adonis had always been kind, he'd never treated me as anything other than a friend.

As I turned towards the second Astral who'd entered the house, a bubble of nervousness floated across my stomach. Even though my father had held a government position, it wasn't every day we had a senator in our home. Each Aelian province had two senators, one senior and one junior. Our senior senator was an elderly woman named Duartha Barmly, and our junior was Tenebris Rex, currently standing in my foyer.

He dipped his head towards me, and I bowed mine in return, then straightened to meet his gaze. His eyes were pale glacier blue, reminding me of the ice floes in the furthest reaches of Rynstyn. His curly reddish-blonde hair was cropped short and brushed back as if he wasn't particularly concerned with styling it, and his angular face tapered down to a softly pointed chin. He cleared his throat, and his eyes moved slightly, as if he was reading from a piece of parchment only he could see.

"On behalf of the Senate, the four provinces represented therein, the seven *Donecs*, and the entire Aelian government, may I say how relieved we are you've returned," he said. "Should you need to speak with someone about your experience, I will happily connect you with a counselor. Should you need anything else, simply name it, and I'll see it done."

I thanked him, and by extension, the government and the realm, for their concern. His stiff posture quickly relaxed, and he glanced back and forth between me and Adonis as an embarrassed smile skittered across his face.

"I don't suppose anyone knows what I'm supposed to do next, do they?" His expression turned apologetic. "I volunteered to accompany Adonis in place of Senator Barmly because I wanted to help, but now, I'm not certain what to do."

Such an admission from anyone else could have made them seem untrustworthy or inexperienced, but coming from Senator Rex, it only made him seem approachable and even endearing.

No wonder he was gaining notoriety in politics . . . it was impossible to dislike him.

"Colonel Vonyas would like a recounting of Kyra's experiences," said Adonis. "He'd like to know what happened before and especially *after* she went through the portal." The soldier gestured into the living area. "There's no protocol saying we have to stand while we speak, though."

We spread out over the chairs and sofas not already occupied by my siblings, and I sat down next to Demitri, directly across from Adonis and Senator Rex. My heart thudded as Adonis pulled a captum from his pocket and settled it in front of his eye, ready to record my story for his commander. I had never felt nervous around my own kind. I'd never even thought of them as *my* kind until I'd encountered a Daeval and had something to compare them to.

Demitri shifted beside me, glanced at Adonis, then pursed his lips and forced his gaze back to the floor. Senator Rex leaned forward and nodded encouragingly.

"Well," I began, choosing my words carefully, "Aurelius and I were out in the forest when, all of a sudden, a portal opened. I thought it was an odd place for someone to portal to, but I wasn't immediately concerned. Then, a man fell out of the portal, and it seemed like he was ill. He wanted to know where he was, so I said Montem, and that's when the Blood Alarm went off."

I glanced at Aurelius, sitting on his haunches near the large plate glass windows overlooking the front porch and lawn. His whiskers turned down disapprovingly, since he hated when I lied, but he remained silent.

"It was such a relief to see you, Adonis," I said, redirecting my gaze to the solider. "And the other soldiers. I was so scared, I didn't know what to do. I was afraid if I ran towards you, the Daeval might chase me. I wanted to catch him off guard, so I decided to run the last way he'd expect—right in front of him—but what you probably couldn't tell was that I tripped. I landed on the Daeval and accidentally knocked him through the portal and then fell in after him."

I swallowed and quickly arranged my next words.

"The portal led to a room that looked like it was used mostly for storage. I remember there being a lot of boxes and crates. The Daeval was furious I'd come through with him, and he told me not to move, then left for a long time. When he came back, he looked sick again, but he opened another portal and told me to leave, so . . . we did. Aurelius and I came out back in the meadow and made our way home as fast as we could."

I desperately hoped my story sounded plausible. I wasn't skilled at lying, but the upside was no one listening expected me to be dishonest. I didn't like making use of their trust in such a manner, but I also didn't see any other alternatives.

"May I ask you some questions?" asked Senator Rex. I nodded, and he continued. "Are you saying you were not kidnapped by a Daeval?"

"That's correct," I said. "It was just a poor choice on my part."

"Fear can lead anyone to make poor choices—you are certainly not the first, nor to be blamed," assured Senator Rex. "While you were trapped, the Daeval didn't harm you in any way?"

I gave my head an emphatic shake. "Thank the Gifter of Protection, no. He seemed as ready for me to leave as I was."

Senator Rex and Adonis asked me a few other questions and, thankfully, I was able to answer without too much fabrication.

"So, we still don't know why a silver blood opened a portal to Aeles . . . or how he was able to," mused Adonis. "There's likely a connection between him being so ill and being able to enter our realm. Perhaps he did something to himself . . . temporarily altered his blood or something."

I sat incredibly still and focused on appearing calmer than I felt, pressing my teeth against one another as if the truth might pry open my mouth and force its way out.

Senator Rex nodded solemnly, resting his elbows on his knees and steepling his long fingers. "This incident has made it clear we're not as safe from Daevals as we'd previously believed." He faced me. "Do you think the boxes and crates you saw could have contained weapons? I wouldn't have expected Daevals to attempt an invasion, but they're clearly testing our borders." His eyes bored deeply into mine. "Do you think you would recognize the Daeval if you saw him again, should we be able to capture him and bring him to Aeles for questioning?"

I shuddered and Demitri, mistaking my response, put his arm around me and gave me a comforting squeeze.

"I'll come with you," he said. "If you have to face him again."

"Thank you," I said, then, noticing Adonis was watching our interaction closely, I directed my next words to him and Senator Rex. "I want to help, but I don't think I would recognize him. I've mostly tried to put what happened from my mind, and I didn't actually see him for very long. There really wasn't anything memorable about him, either."

As soon as I spoke, my mind was filled with the image of Sebastian lying on the ground after falling off the intersector, and how I'd lost all sense of myself staring down into his dark eyes. I quickly shoved the thought aside.

"I understand," nodded Senator Rex. "Thank you for what you've told us. If nothing else, we now know Daevals are actively trying to enter Aeles. We won't be caught unawares again. Additional precautions have been added to strengthen the wards, and nothing originating in Nocens will be coming through again any time soon."

The conviction in his voice made the hair on the back of my

neck stand up. Then, something else occurred to me. "What is the government telling everyone about what happened?" The last thing I wanted was to draw any more attention to myself and the secrets I was trying so hard to keep. "Does everyone know I was the one who went through the portal?"

"The official statement is that we were conducting a test of the Blood Alarm," said Senator Rex. "Those who needed to know the truth, in the government and in the military, were given more specific information, and of those, only a handful were made aware of your involvement. They won't be discussing it with you or anyone else, though, as this is highly classified."

"Thank you," I said, letting out a relieved breath.

Senator Rex nodded, then a smile spread across his mouth and his eyes lit up.

"On a happier note," he said, "you were going to find this out next week, but given everything that's happened, my colleagues and I thought it would be nice to tell you sooner . . . you've been matched with the *Donec Medicinae* for internship."

My mother gasped and clapped her hands, and Demitri shouted with excitement and pulled me into a hug as Adonis and my siblings offered their congratulations. My vision blurred, tears filling my eyes, as Aurelius trotted over to stand before me.

Your father would be so proud, he said, *as am I.*

I reached down and hugged him tightly, letting my tears fall into his silken fur. For the briefest moment, I imagined my father's face upon hearing the news—his smile would have outshone the sun, and his amber eyes would have beamed with a mixture of pride and happiness. After *everything* that had occurred in my life since his death, it was a blessed relief to know good things could still happen. It felt wonderful knowing there were still a few things I could count on, like hard work paying off and dedication being rewarded.

Lifting my head, I wiped my face and smiled at Senator Rex. "Thank you," I said hoarsely. "I can't believe it. I wanted it so much."

"You'll be reporting to Healer Omnurion," continued Senator Rex. "While she will be your direct supervisor, I hope you don't mind I've taken the liberty of becoming involved in your training as well." He grinned and brushed an imaginary speck of dirt off the sleeve of his tailored gold and white jacket. "One of these days, I'll be expected to have an intern or two of my own. I'd love the chance to learn how to guide them from a supervisor as experienced as Healer Omnurion. And while there's absolutely nothing I can teach you about healing or medicine, perhaps my knowledge of the government may prove helpful . . . should you find yourself in a government position one of these days."

I thanked him profusely, taken aback at his kindness.

Something shifted in the senator's gaze, and his eyes held mine so intently I wasn't sure I could have looked away, even if I'd wanted to.

"We both have the chance to do great things for Aeles, Kyra. To guide it in the direction it ought to go, to make it safe from disease, safe from Daevals . . . safe in a way it has never been before. I look forward to doing that with you."

Yesterday, I would have agreed wholeheartedly with the senator's view on Daevals. But that was before I'd been to Nocens and interacted with them for myself. I certainly didn't think anyone with silver blood ought to immediately and indiscriminately be allowed into Aeles, but I also wasn't certain they were all as vile as I'd grown up believing. I thought of Eslee and how friendly she'd been and the nice things Caz had said about my father. Whatever Daevals were, they weren't mindless, unfeeling beasts. Also, given my partnership with Sebastian, I couldn't in good conscience openly champion the worthiness of keeping my kind separate from theirs.

I was about to make some sort of a reply when Seren's Cypher, Sappho, suddenly materialized near my feet and slithered across the floor. Demitri shouted and jerked his legs up, then blushed a furious shade of red and muttered an apology. He'd always been terrified of snakes, and it had taken concerted effort on his part over the years to be near Sappho when he was expecting to see her, even more so when she appeared without warning.

"I didn't know you were afraid of snakes," said Adonis, cocking an eyebrow. "All these years, you've been keeping secrets from me."

Demitri made a noise between snorting and choking, then tossed his head, reclaiming some of his usual confidence. "I am an open book to those who know how to read me."

I frowned at Seren, but she shook her head, meaning the sea snake had acted of her own accord. I glanced at Aurelius, but he shrugged as if to say you never could tell with Cyphers, and so I rose with Adonis and Senator Rex and escorted them to the intersector on the porch. Demitri decided to leave as well, since I was home safe, but promised to call later to see how I was doing.

After bidding them goodbye, I turned my attention to the conundrum of sneaking the very Daeval who had sparked such a government uproar back into my realm. I *hated* keeping secrets from those I loved, but the faster I helped Sebastian get his sword, the faster I could learn about being a Recovrancer . . . and how to keep my secret from impacting my internship and ruining my future.

20

Schatten blinked against the torchlight reflecting off the tunnel walls, stone worn slick from years of being rubbed by serpentine scales. He turned, then gasped as an enormous pair of orange eyes flecked with gold appeared in the darkness.

Slipping on the smooth stone, he caught himself with his free hand, managing to keep the torch in the air. Straightening to his full height, he stared at the serpent before him. The creature had the stocky legs of a dragon combined with the tubular body of a snake, albeit one the width of a giant spruce tree. He had to be at least thirty feet long, and every inch of him was covered with undulating black and grey scales.

Schatten bowed low, his heart thudding loudly. "It is an honor, Great Serpent."

The serpent bowed the upper part of his muscular body.

"I have waited long for the appearance of a worthy successor," he said, his deep voice punctuated with a slight hiss.

"I hope I shall be a worthy successor," Schatten replied. "In order to obtain peace between my kind and Astrals, my authority must be absolute and unquestionable."

The serpent nodded.

"The reign of the beasts is ending. More of my kind leave every day for the Fertile Grounds." He sighed. "The reign of your kind is only beginning."

"I have never faced such an admirable opponent before," said Schatten regretfully. "I do not relish what I must do." As skilled a warrior as he was, he never took life unless it was absolutely necessary. "If there was another way . . ." his voice trailed off.

The beast smiled.

"Perhaps there is."

Lowering his face until his enormous fanged jowls were level with Schatten's eyes, the serpent let out a long, slow breath. Schatten felt himself becoming warmer, as if the serpent's breath had kindled a fire inside of him. The heat began to increase, spreading from his torso to wind through his arms and legs. He started sweating, grimacing in pain, but the heat was still rising. Was he going to be cooked from the inside out?

Unable to stand it any longer, he dropped the torch and bent forward, shouting as a furnace raged beneath his skin. Then, just before the burning became unbearable and everything inside him melted, flames sprang from his hands. He stared in shock as they danced across his palms without so much as singeing his skin.

He gaped at the serpent, who grinned, looking pleased with himself.

"The ability to wield fire is part of accepting my title," explained the creature. "I also have no doubt it will contribute to your reputation as a formidable king. To summon the flames, simply envision them. When you are finished, imagine pulling them back inside your body."

Schatten followed the instructions, amazed at how the fire responded to his will.

"Thank you," he said, and the serpent nodded.

"Now," the creature said with a flick of his tongue, "all I ask is for you to present my departure as more fearsome than it will actually be. Craft a tale that will delight future generations with the story of our battle. In the meantime, summon the flames and place your hands against my head."

Schatten did as he was told and, as his hands touched either side of the serpent's face, the fire from his fingers quickly spread. Within a few heartbeats, the entire beast was covered in roiling red flames.

"Take what I am leaving you to your Uchel Doeth," the Great Serpent said as his scales began dropping to the ground below. "Serve well, Felserpent King!"

And with that, he vanished. The only sounds in the tunnel were those of the torch, still burning in the sand, and Schatten's own breathing. Picking up the torch, he walked towards the pile of scales, and when he reached out to touch them, he found they had somehow joined together to form a single sheet. Carefully picking it up, he made his way out of the tunnel, wondering what the Uchel Doeth would do with them.

A dull roar became steadily louder as he neared the entrance to the cavern, and he stepped out onto a sandy beach strewn with driftwood and broken shells. The sun was just peeking over the mountains in the distance, and he squinted as the light struck the ocean before him. The tunnel was one of many dotting the sharp cliffs, hollowed out ages before when the sea had been higher.

Extinguishing the torch in the water, he found a sharp clam shell and used it to make shallow cuts along his arms. He spread the blood from the cuts over himself, making it appear as if he had endured a fierce battle, as he crafted a tale wherein he had only just managed to defeat the Great Serpent and emerge victorious. He then tossed the shell into the ocean and made his way towards his village.

The sun had crested the mountains and was shining warmly when he finally arrived home. He was soon surrounded by Daevals of all ages, clapping and cheering and thanking the Fates as they welcomed his return. Embarrassed by the attention, he made his way towards an elderly man leaning against a tall staff. Schatten inclined his head and handed him the snakeskin. A smile spread across the older man's face, and he tucked the scales into a bag at his side. He then struck the ground three times with his staff, and everyone fell silent.

"Today marks the beginning of a new era," exclaimed the Uchel Doeth. "With Schatten's victory over the Great Serpent, we can now begin to build the civilization we have dreamed of for so long."

The crowd cheered, and Schatten dropped his gaze to his feet. He was far more comfortable facing an adversary than receiving accolades. Yet another thing he would have to become used to in his new position.

The Uchel Doeth gestured for silence.

"By his actions, Schatten has proven himself worthy of commanding not only our military, but also our community and our realm. The authority and responsibility to lead are now his, and we welcome the establishment of a new rule."

The man crooked the first two fingers of his right hand so they resembled the fangs of a snake. Striking them against his chest, he shouted, "Hail the Felserpent King!"

"Hail the Felserpent King!" shouted the crowd. Schatten's heart beat faster as every man, woman, and child made similar motions, striking their fingers against their chests as they repeated the chant. Of course, he'd known this was coming—assuming the Great Serpent's authority was the first step to establishing a brand-new monarchy in the realm of Aeles-Nocens. But to see those he knew, who knew him, referring to him as "King" was going to take some getting used to.

As the cries died down, the Uchel Doeth made a gesture with his hand, and a solider stepped forward holding a large silver and gold sword. Schatten's left hand twitched, eager to feel the hilt against his palm again. Every Daeval knew this sword . . . Rhannu was carried by the military commander during battle and made whoever used it invincible, protected from even the slightest injury. Since becoming commander two years ago, Schatten had brandished the sword numerous times.

Would he now have to bequeath the weapon to someone else, since he was to be king?

As if reading his mind, the Uchel Doeth smiled at him.

"Rhannu belongs to you," he said. "From this day forward, it shall be the sword of the King."

Schatten closed his eyes, offering a silent prayer of thanks to whichever Fate had brought this about, then stepped forward and accepted the proffered sword. Turning to face the crowd, he raised the weapon high above his head, prompting another chorus of cheers.

The Uchel Doeth struck the ground again with his staff, and when the din had died down, he said, "Now, we shall feast and celebrate your victory. And then tonight, you shall secure the peace we have so long sought through your marriage to the Astral healer."

Nervous anticipation unfurled in Schatten's chest. He would do whatever it took to protect his kind, and if that meant marriage rather than war, he would face it with the same determination. Tightening his grip on the sword, he drew strength from the weapon, hearing the Great Serpent's final words: "Serve well, Felserpent King."

21

SEBASTIAN

J blinked my eyes open and sat up in bed, running a hand across my face to erase any remaining traces of sleep. What in the burning realm sort of dream had that been? It wasn't one of my usual nightmares, which was nice, but clearly my mind was so fixated on finding Rhannu, I was thinking about it even while sleeping. It made sense, I supposed—I'd been obsessed with the sword since childhood and that was before I'd met a Recovrancer and had a real chance of owning it.

I glanced at the spelled mechanical clock on my nightstand. It was nighttime in Aeles, which meant Kyra was finished with her questioning. How had the meeting with the Astral delegation gone? And more importantly, had she started searching for a suppressor medallion?

I kicked aside the dark blue covers and swung my legs over the edge of the bed. I would check my peerin and see if there were any interesting open contracts, since there was no reason not to go about my usual routines until I heard from Kyra. After work, I would stop by LeBehr's and see if she had any books about enchanting jewelry to disguise one's blood. By then, hopefully Kyra would have a lead and I'd find myself another step closer to owning Rhannu for *real* and not just in my dreams.

22

KYRA

I rubbed the palms of my hands against my eyes, pressing my head further into the pillow. The *last* thing I wanted to dream about was Sebastian, or someone who looked like him! This was obviously a terrible downside of the deal I'd made with him. While I probably deserved as much, I didn't like feeling as if I'd brought any part of the Daeval back to Aeles with me. I rolled to my side, careful not to bump Aurelius where he lay by my feet, and looked out the large windows I loved to leave uncovered at night.

A single falling star blazed against the black sky before it, too, surrendered and joined the darkness. After a few moments, unable to return to sleep, I pushed myself up, turned on my bed-side light, and pulled *The Book of Recovrancy* from beneath my pillow.

I'd gone to bed early with apologies of being exhausted from the events of the day, then stayed up and read the book through three times. As if it sensed my utter lack of even basic informa-tion, the book wasn't currently very long and hadn't changed during each reading. Much of what it mentioned only provoked more questions, but at least I'd learned a few things.

According to the book, Recovrancers had existed long be-fore those chronicled in the scroll I'd found in the Aelian

Archives. No one knew who the first one had been, but eventually my kind had started keeping records about them. It seemed Recovrancers were always women, although no one knew why, and they often also possessed the gift of healing. Unlike other Astral gifts that manifested in early childhood, a girl might not be aware of her ability to enter the realm of the dead until she was quite a bit older. Sometimes her first trip into Vaneklus was a calm affair, occurring while she slept; other times, the trip was prompted by some event, often of a traumatic nature, such as almost dying herself or losing a loved one.

I could certainly relate to that.

Flipping through a few of the thick pages, I reread a particularly interesting part:

Given the rarity of their ability, Recovrancers tend to work alone; however, prior to retiring, a senior Recovrancer will select a protégé to train in the art of recovrancy. She will instruct the girl in the ways of Vaneklus, provide a proper introduction to the Shade Transporter, and eventually permit her student to perform shade recoveries.

If only there was another Recovrancer who could train me! It would be wonderful to not feel so alone, capable of doing things I couldn't even talk to others about, much less expect them to understand. The book didn't include spells for recovering shades, but it did include the spells I'd said to take myself in and out of Vaneklus. I still questioned how I'd known to say them, but perhaps that was simply part of being a Recovrancer—the ability came with an innate knowledge of a few, select things.

Sliding the book back beneath my pillow, I turned off the light and settled down between the covers. Aurelius's feet twitched in his sleep, and I wondered if the normally dignified creature was dreaming of chasing a mouse, like a normal housecat. I smiled at the idea and closed my eyes, eventually drifting back to sleep.

꧁꧂

Hours later, I sighed, letting my gaze roam around the library. Light from the afternoon sun was shining through the curtained bay windows of the upstairs room, my favorite in the house next to my bedroom. Aurelius was sprawled on the window seat, pleased my task at least allowed us to stay indoors. I'd spent the morning with my family before coming here to search for ideas on how I might find a suppressor medallion.

Unfortunately, I wasn't having any luck.

I stretched my arms over my head and yawned, then considered which of the floor-to-ceiling shelves to tackle next. Thanks to my entire family's love of reading, we had amassed an impressive home library. In fact, we'd had to knock down a wall and requisition the guest bedroom next door to expand our ever-growing collection. Books were generally grouped by genre, although we also had a section of rare first editions featuring a variety of titles. If only we had a section labeled, "Ways to Disguise Daevalic Blood."

Where do you think I should start? I asked Aurelius, limiting my conversation to telepathy, as I didn't want anyone overhearing me discussing this particular subject.

The lynx rolled over onto his back, kicking aside a tasseled pillow and sticking his paws in the air. *Perhaps we drain every drop of silver blood from the fiend, then pump him full of donated golden blood?* he suggested.

I rolled my eyes. *I meant, where should I start trying to find information about that medallion?* I couldn't imagine the havoc trying to introduce a different type of blood would wreak on Sebastian's body. *Also, his name is Sebastian, not fiend.*

Aurelius grunted in response, then continued. *Perhaps you*

should start with spells, he suggested. *Spells involving invisibility and blood, in particular, and how they might be linked to an inanimate object.* He batted at the air with an oversize paw. *Although I must say, any incantation involving blood gives me pause, as it's certainly not a typical ingredient in Astral spells.*

I don't like the idea, either, I agreed, striding to the nearest bookshelf. *But that's as good a place to start as any.*

As Aurelius had suspected, there were very few spells involving blood in any of the books I searched, and I was already familiar with most of them from my healing work, such as how to detect and stop internal bleeding or how to remove various poisons from the bloodstream. After exhausting that line of research, I turned to reading about spells designed to alter the appearance of an object, alive or inanimate. I read about cloaking spells, transfiguration spells, invisibility spells, spells to make an object appear to change shape when viewed through certain glasses, spells to make objects change color, and spells to enchant jewelry, making the wearer seem more intelligent or witty. There were spells for temporarily changing hair or eye color, making someone appear taller or thinner, or making a ghostly apparition blink in and out of view. Hours later, after following countless leads, each of which ultimately proved useless, I leaned back in the chair and rubbed at the knots forming in my neck, frustration simmering in my chest.

This is hopeless, I moaned. *How am I going to find something when there's no record of it even existing?*

Didn't your father keep a few books in his bedroom? suggested Aurelius. *They might be worth checking before we decide whether a trip to the Archives is in order.*

I suppose, I agreed sullenly. My mother was downstairs reading to Deneb, but she readily gave her permission for me to retrieve books from the bedroom she and Father had shared.

Stepping into my parents' room, I was immediately taken back to being a little girl, snuggling between my mother and father in the large four-poster bed while we took turns reading, telling stories, or projecting moving images stored on captums onto the ceiling. My throat tightened, picturing my mother sleeping in the large bed by herself, and even though it was no longer needed, I was glad to see she'd kept my father's pillow, neatly arranged next to hers against the dark wood headboard.

Aurelius rubbed his head against my knee, and I turned my attention to my father's nightstand. A few books were stacked there, next to a picture of the whole family taken just last month and a surprisingly good portrait of Flavius that Seren had painted years ago. Unfortunately, all the books were meant for pleasure reading and didn't contain any information about spells. I was just about to return to the library when I noticed my father's black cork satchel on top of the dresser. He'd mostly used it for transporting things to and from his office in Celenia, as he had another bag with specialized compartments for herbs and powders he carried when visiting patients. I'd definitely known him to stick a book or two in the satchel, though, just in case he found himself with unexpected time between meetings.

Walking over, I carefully flipped up the brass closure and opened the bag; sure enough, there was a well-read book inside, and I smiled, even though it turned out to be a simple reference guide on the medicinal uses of flowers. Rummaging around, in case there was a smaller book further down, my fingers grazed an iron key ring strung with different sized keys, most of which I assumed opened cabinets in my father's office. There were a few loose pieces of quartz, useful for their healing properties, as well as some bandages and pieces of parchment, and a silver scalpel was safely contained in a padded sheath. Pushing aside everything I'd already seen, I plunged my hand in deeper, and my searching fingertips suddenly grazed something hard. I turned the satchel to better catch the available light and peered inside, not seeing anything besides the smooth maroon inner lining, but when I scratched at it with my nail, I could definitely feel something hard . . . *behind* the lining.

Inhaling deeply, I ran my fingers along the inside edges of the satchel, searching for a loose flap of material or something that might lead to a hidden compartment. My finger unexpectedly pressed a bump almost completely hidden beneath a seam, and I heard a soft *click*. I ran my fingers over the lining again, prodding at the tight stitching in the corners, and this time I discovered I could pull the lining away from the outer shell, revealing a hidden pocket between the two. Slipping my hand inside, I closed my fingers around something cold and hard that felt like a large coin. Withdrawing the hidden object, I quickly opened my fist.

No, I said to Aurelius, refusing to believe my eyes. *That's impossible. It can't be.*

But there it was, in the palm of my hand . . . a small gold medallion. I stared in horror at the raised eight-pointed star embossed on the shiny background, then turned the item over, careful to avoid the sharp pin used to attach it to clothing.

I looked down at Aurelius, struggling to hear myself think over my thudding heart.

Perhaps he found it and wanted to study it, I said, and Aurelius nodded, even though neither of us believed my attempt at an explanation.

Slipping the medallion into my pocket, I closed my father's satchel and retreated to the safety of my own bedroom. I needed to think.

I can't tell Sebastian where I found this, I said to Aurelius as I closed my door behind us. *I can't. Not until I have more information.*

The lynx flicked his short tail. *I doubt he'll care where it came from. And now—*

I care! I interrupted, louder than I'd intended. *Falling stars, Aurelius, do you know what this means? It means my father might have been involved in bringing Daevals into Aeles! That he knew it was possible for them to come here and he ... he ... helped them do it.*

Tears pricked my eyes as anger and confusion swirled through my chest, making it difficult to breathe. Why would my father—my gentle father devoted to healing those with golden blood—knowingly endanger our realm?

Aurelius gazed up at me, then eventually nodded. *We'll need to develop a believable story,* he said. *But your father did work for the government, and you'll be interning at the* Donec Medicinae, *so it's at least plausible for you to have gained access to where such a thing would be stored . . . you might have even seen it simply laying around and picked it up.*

Thank you, I whispered. As much as I wasn't ready to know the answer, I also couldn't help wondering—what exactly had my father been involved in?

23

❧

SEBASTIAN

J slipped through the narrow alley, the cross-hatched soles of my boots silent against the cobblestone street. The air still held the coolness of night, even though dawn was fast approaching, and the dusky scents of honeysuckle and gardenia tickled my nose. I could identify most flowers quickly, what with my mother growing them the way she had.

A few vendors were slowly making their way to their carts, licking the remains of breakfast from their fingers or yawning and patting their furry-eared donkeys. I kept close to the wall, using the cover provided by the ever-changing shadows. Shadows were most prevalent just before dawn and just after sunset, making those my two preferred times to work. During those brief periods, folks were more apt to believe their eyes were playing tricks on them, and less inclined to investigate what they might have seen.

Given that I couldn't do anything to speed along Kyra's research on tricking the Astral Blood Alarm, I'd accepted a contract in Falmayne, a village in Doldarian, the same territory as my cave. I might as well stay busy and add to my bank account while she figured out how to get me into the unicorn sanctuary.

Somewhere in the distance, a hen clucked. I ducked under a low archway and came out on the edge of a large square that would soon be a teeming market. Two women worked to arrange a checkered green and brown awning to provide shade near their fruit stall. Across from them, a man lit a fire in a grate and began roasting nuts. The air was soon filled with the scent of hickory-smoked almonds, but thankfully, I'd eaten before leaving my cave. In my line of work, a growling stomach could give away my hiding place or distract me just long enough for someone to slip past me.

A tall woman with her hair woven into twin braids gathered at the nape of her neck stepped into the square, waving at folks she knew as she made her way to her stall. She was carrying a pouch close to her chest, and her eyes darted back and forth, watching those around her, even as she smiled and offered pleasantries. Ya'nark was a jeweler and guarded her merchandise closely. Normally she wouldn't be found without her wife, Lenara, at her side, as the two of them were practically inseparable—except for at the full moon market when she rose early to set up the jewelry display and her wife arrived a while later with a hot breakfast.

My informant had been right. I'd stood in this same spot last month, where I'd watched things play out exactly as the former household servant had recalled. Judging by my previous surveillance, I had roughly an hour before Lenara appeared with food. Giving Ya'nark a final look, I retreated back through the low doorway, then made my way down several side streets, across a foul-smelling stream, down a steep embankment, around an overturned pushcart, before finally stopping outside a two-story stone and stucco building.

Supposedly the lower windows of the house were always kept closed, but those on the second floor were usually left open or at least unlocked. Flexing my fingers inside my gloves, I grabbed the low-hanging eaves and hauled myself onto the roof.

Crouching down, I made my way to the wood-trimmed window and tugged on the edge. It opened without protest, although rough orange curtains obscured the room from view. Pulling them aside long enough to see the layout, I slipped inside, rolled forward, and landed on the balls of my feet, hands on the hilts of the knives strapped to my calves. The room was empty, but I could hear noise through the open doorway leading further into the house. Pulling out one of the knives, I made my way across the bedroom, coming out in a wide hallway ending in a set of stairs. Summoning the fiery mask to my face, I crept down the stairs, arriving in a living area with an open view into the kitchen.

Lenara's back was towards me as she stood at the sink and scrubbed something. Music played softly, and she hummed along with it. I inhaled slowly through my nose, calming my mind and steadying my nerves. There was no room for error on this as-signment, as prior to marrying Ya'Nark, Lenara had worked as a bodyguard for a wealthy Daeval in Larmoxx, a large city in Oexiss. By all accounts from others whose word I believed, she had been very good at her work and was skilled in hand-to-hand combat. When it came to fighting, most folks assumed size was all that mattered, and while size could certainly be an advantage, it could also be a hindrance, as smaller opponents were often faster.

Just as I was about to take a step forward, the bracelet on my wrist began to vibrate. I immediately pressed it against one side of my face, since it seemed to respond to skin contact and my gloves prevented me from using my hands. Hopefully, Lenara hadn't heard the sound over the music. Kyra's voice filled my head, and I flinched, worried my target might somehow hear her.

I think I found what we were looking for, she said.

I can't talk right now, I snapped.

Oh, I'm sorry, she replied, but I wasn't paying attention—the water in the kitchen was no longer running. I tightened my grip on the dagger just as Lenara sprang through the doorway, brandishing a large carving knife in each hand.

I brushed away one of the blades with my own knife, then stepped backwards, trying to size up my opponent. If I'd planned on engaging her in combat, I would have paid closer attention to the layout of the room, but since I'd intended to slit her throat before she knew I was there, I hadn't bothered. I attempted a quick look around but found myself needing to devote all my attention to the woman before me.

"Who sent you?" Lenara demanded, slicing up with one knife and down with the other, causing me to duck and twist sideways.

What are you doing? asked Kyra. I wasn't certain if she could hear any of my specific thoughts or if our connection simply kept her attuned to my changing emotions. I grabbed the second dagger from my other calf and charged towards Lenara, steel clashing and clanging as our knives met.

I'm working, I grunted to Kyra, wishing I had a moment to touch the bracelet and sever our connection. One of Lenara's blades slipped past mine, and she managed to make contact with my shoulder, but thankfully, even though I didn't have armor on, I never went after a target without wearing something spelled to stop at least a few thrusts or swipes.

"How *dare* you come into my home!" Lenara spat angrily. I kicked out, catching her in the stomach and sending her skidding backwards, but she simply rolled over and was almost immediately back on her feet. She threw a blade at me, which I responded to by throwing one of mine, hitting hers midair and sending both weapons spinning across the room. Lenara rushed at me with the other knife, so I swept my leg out, hit her shins, and caused her to stumble. As she fell, I sliced at her wrist and cut her deeply enough that she winced and dropped her blade. I dropped mine as well and lunged for her, grabbing both of her hands and grunt-ing in my efforts to subdue her.

Are you alright? Kyra asked, doubt filling her voice. *You sound upset or, like you're running or—*

I told you, I can't talk now! I snarled, craning my neck to one side as Lenara tried to smash her head against my jaw. At the same time, she kicked up with her leg and very nearly hit the back of my head. Growling, I finally managed to force her to the ground. There, I snapped her left wrist, and as she cried out, dis-tracted by the pain, I reached across her, grabbed my fallen knife, and brought it smoothly across her throat. Her eyes widened, and her mouth fell open as blood pooled down her neck, covering the ornate silver necklace she wore.

I let out a loud exhale, then reached into my weapons belt and pulled out Caz's note. Placing it where it wouldn't become covered in blood, I skimmed the words written in his sweeping handwriting one last time: "I hope your wife enjoyed the silver."

Ya'nark oversaw exportation of one of Caz's silver mines, and after metal counts had started coming up short, Caz had sus-pected the woman of stealing. I'd followed her and confirmed as much; she used the stolen silver to create jewelry, some of which she sold and some of which she used to fashion pieces she gave to her wife.

When I'd first started in the assassination business, I had assumed every Daeval should pay for their own crimes, but I'd soon come to see that lessons involving others—specifically, loved ones—made the most lasting impression. When Caz had asked which woman should pay the price for the silver thievery, I hadn't hesitated to name Lenara.

Rising to my feet, I retrieved my other dagger, unhappy with the mess I was leaving behind. I could feel Kyra still lurking in my mind, waves of uncertainty radiating outwards from her.

I'll contact you when I'm done, I said, pressing the bracelet against my cheek. Thankfully, she didn't attempt to reach back out to me, and I turned to leave when I heard a soft squeak from the kitchen. Walking into the room, I looked around and there, near the oven, was a cushion with a small grey and white kitten curled up on it. The miniscule creature gazed up at me, then cried again, louder this time.

Was it hungry? Wouldn't Lenara have fed it already? I couldn't very well leave it crying for a meal, as it might be a while before Ya'nark returned, so I grabbed a bowl and filled it with milk from a bottle beside the sink. The kitten stumbled clumsily off the cushion, then trotted over and began lapping up the milk. I ran a hand over its back before standing up, shaking the cat hair off my glove, and turned off the stove. I'd always liked animals, and at least now this one would be safe until its remaining owner returned.

My work done, I conjured a portal, then blinked in surprise as it flickered before stabilizing. I'd never seen it do that before. Frowning, I stepped through and quickly closed the doorway behind me, glad to leave the village of Falmayne behind.

In my weapons vault, I ignored Batty, who was sitting on the table, and he crossed his wings as I strode past. I then pressed my fingers against the gold bracelet and immediately felt myself connected to Kyra.

What were you saying earlier? I asked, skipping the pleasantries the Astral likely expected that were nothing more than a waste of time.

I was saying, I think I found a suppressor medallion, she replied.

My heart nearly leapt out of my chest. *Are you certain?* I demanded.

I'm positive, replied Kyra, although her voice was more subdued than excited. Now that I was paying attention to her, I sensed tension emanating from the Astral, an agitated mixture of anger, worry, and fear. It was odd to sense her emotions so intensely; obviously, I knew such a thing was possible from the bond with my Cypher, but I tried to avoid any awareness of his mood or feelings. Perhaps Kyra was simply upset over whatever methods she'd been forced to employ to obtain the medallion. To be honest, I hadn't expected her to acquire one so quickly, and while I wanted this to be a welcome discovery, being suspicious was second nature to me. Had she told someone about working with me, leading them to give her the medallion in exchange for information? She might have even promised to tell them when we visited the unicorn sanctuary so they could attempt to capture me.

Did you tell anyone about me? I demanded.

Of course not! she replied indignantly. *Why do you keep thinking I'm going to tell someone about you when I've repeatedly said I won't?*

How did you find a medallion so quickly? I persisted.

I . . . she sighed. *It's complicated.*

I remained silent and, perhaps sensing I wasn't going to drop the issue until I'd received a satisfactory explanation, she eventually continued.

There's a lot of change happening in Celenia right now—remember when I told you about Donecs? Well, every Donec is partially staffed by interns, and right now old interns are moving out, new interns are moving in, and everyone's relocating before the government returns to session in a couple of weeks. I was assigned to move some boxes to storage, and one of them fell open while I was trying to get it on a shelf. She swallowed hard. *Most of what fell out seemed like junk, but I repacked it anyway, and as I was cleaning up, I found the medallion. It was going into storage, so I didn't see any harm in taking it, but . . . I was just surprised.* Her tone hardened, and the pain flashing through her was too real to be made up. *I know him, Sebastian . . . the Astral who had the boxes containing the medallion. At least, I thought I knew him.*

Clearly my initial impression of the Astral had been correct—for her to just now realize those she trusted carried secrets and were capable of disappointing, or even betraying, her revealed how sheltered she was. I'd known others would let you down to the point of completely failing you well before my tenth birthday.

Shaking my head, I grabbed a rag and started cleaning one of my blood-stained knives while quoting a Daevalic maxim: *The higher the pedestal of adoration, the longer the fall to disillusionment.*

To my surprise, Kyra let out a soft laugh. I wasn't sure why, as I hadn't meant to be funny; I'd meant to make a point she obviously hadn't learned yet. As someone who had been teased frequently as a child, I detested being made fun of or laughed at and I was about to say as much when she spoke again.

Aurelius says that to me sometimes, she explained. *I wonder if all Cyphers say the same things, whether they're paired with an Astral or a Daeval.*

I didn't want her incorrectly thinking Batty had shared such wisdom with me—I'd actually come across it in a book about the Fates—but before I could clarify, Kyra added, *I've never been able to find out much about the training Cyphers go through before they're bonded . . . it's supposed to be fairly rigorous, but unless you're involved with it, it's kept very quiet.*

I couldn't imagine Batty undergoing anything even approaching rigorous training. I could imagine, however, LeBehr having at least one or two books on the topic of Cypher training and pairing . . . but there was no point in sharing that with Kyra. We were working together for a specific reason, and that reason didn't involve a trip to the bookstore.

So, I said, changing the subject, *when can you come back so we can go after the horn?*

Well, she said, *once we reach the unicorn sanctuary, I don't know how quickly we'll find a horn. We may need to be there a while or even make multiple trips. My mother's planning on us leaving tomorrow to visit my cousins in Iscre for a few days, and I think it makes the most sense if I stay home. I can pretend to be sick, but . . .* she paused, then added, *I don't like lying to my family. Especially since I lied to everyone about what happened when I went through your portal.*

She told me what she'd shared during her questioning, and while I would have torn a similar story to shreds during an investigation, apparently the golden bloods had accepted it without hesitation.

I wouldn't worry about it, I assured her. *Lying is one of those things that gets easier the more you do it.*

But I don't want it to get easier, she said, as if I'd missed something she found completely obvious. *That's my point. Hopefully I won't have to do it much more.*

I rolled my eyes, then ran a whetstone against the newly clean knife blade. I abhorred dull weapons almost as much as I despised those who thought they should always have a choice in how they behaved . . . folks who'd never had to do whatever it took simply to survive. Clearly, Kyra thought herself above such things.

Sometimes there isn't an easier or "better" option, I said. *You act, and you get through it. After you recover Rhannu, you can go back to only doing things that make you happy.*

She was silent, but I could feel her anger rising, building like rain-filled clouds coming together before a storm. Finally, she spoke.

I didn't want to find a way to break the law and sneak you into

Aeles . . . but I did. I didn't want to make a deal with a Daeval to learn about being a Recovrancer . . . but I did. I didn't want to watch my father die in my arms . . . but I did. Her voice was a maelstrom of pain and fury. *Have you ever had to tell one of your parents their spouse died, and there was nothing you could do to stop it? Because until you have, don't talk to me about doing things I don't want to do!*

Her voice caught, as if she was barely managing to hold back a sob.

No, I replied, my voice steady. *I've never had to tell one of my parents the other died.*

And why would I? My father had been there the night my mother had died—he had driven the dagger into her heart with his own hand as my seven-year-old self had screamed and pleaded and begged for him to let her go. My father himself died a few years later, killed in a business dispute, and the only thing I'd felt at the news of his death was relief and a profound sense of regret I hadn't been the one to kill him.

I ground my teeth against the sadness trying to escape the corner of my mind where I relegated it, but it moved quickly, slipping past my usual defenses to wake the shame I felt at not protecting my mother.

Burning realm fires, I didn't need such distractions! I hurried to get myself in hand, but unfortunately, Kyra sensed the shift in my mood.

Are you alright? she asked hesitantly. *I thought I felt . . . I don't know how to explain it, but I—*

It's nothing, I interrupted. *So, when exactly is your family leaving?*

Tomorrow evening.

That would be early morning Nocenian time, but I didn't care. I often worked odd hours, and I would give up a lot more than sleep in exchange for a unicorn horn.

I should probably tell Demitri what I'm doing, Kyra added distractedly, as if she'd forgotten she was talking to someone other than herself. *I doubt my peerin will work in Nocens and if my family can't reach me, they'll contact him to see why I'm not answering. I mean, we shouldn't be gone too long, but still . . .*

Who's Demitri? I asked. The more Astrals who knew about Kyra being in Nocens, the more likely we would be caught.

Oh, he's my best friend and practically my brother, she explained. *He already knows about me being a Recovrancer, so I can't imagine this will be too shocking.* She didn't sound quite as certain as she was trying to seem, which was worrisome, but there wasn't anything I could do about it.

I'll contact Caz, I said, *and make sure we can use his intersector. Do you need the coordinates?*

Yes, she said, and I had her repeat them until I was satisfied she'd memorized them, then ended our connection. I cleaned the other dagger I'd dirtied while working, removed the sheaths from my calves, and returned the weapons to their proper spot on the wall. Then, running both hands through my hair, I paced the length of my weapons vault. Try as I did, I couldn't stop thinking about my mother's death and my father's role in it and other things I had no desire to remember.

"Kyra *is* a Recovrancer," offered the bat. "Perhaps she recovers other things, in addition to shades . . . you know, memories you have tried to destroy or feelings you have left for dead."

"That's ridiculous!" I spat. "I've never read anything about Recovrancers doing that!"

"While you are the resident expert on recovrancy, even experts do not know everything," replied the bat. "They simply know more than everyone else."

If such a thing was true, then it was yet another reason to

recover Rhannu as quickly as possible and put a realm of distance between myself and that insufferable golden-blooded Recovrancer.

24

SEBASTIAN

I stood inside Caz's office, glancing at the intersector every few seconds, as Batty shoved a piece of roasted pineapple into his mouth. Nearby, Alistair used a quill she'd pulled from her back to spear another chunk of the bright yellow fruit. I summoned flames into my hand and let them flicker beneath the pineapple, which Alistair slowly turned until all sides were nicely toasted.

"Thank you," she said, before popping the fruit into her mouth.

I nodded, retracting the flames. I didn't usually perform what I viewed as party tricks with my fire, but if Caz's Cypher was willing to meet me before dawn so Kyra could use the intersector, I was fine to roast some fruit for the porcupine. She had shared it with Batty, too, who, of course, had gotten as much on his fur as in his mouth.

Suddenly, Aurelius materialized next to the intersector and a second later, Kyra appeared. She let out a relieved breath and stepped forward, breaking into a smile as Batty jumped off the desk, landed on the floor, and scurried towards her. He waved a wing, which he somehow managed to trip on, and I watched the lynx roll his eyes as Kyra gasped and worried over the bat. My Cypher was fine, of course, and, after hugging the Astral, he flew over to perch on the back of a chair.

Kyra rose to her feet and smoothed the front of her shirt. I was glad to see she'd chosen clothing meant for stealth—she was wearing a green tunic with gold embroidery on the sleeves and russet-colored breeches tucked into tall boots, none of which would hinder her movements or attract unwanted attention. Her gaze met mine, and she looked nervous even as she nodded a greeting. Considering what we were about to attempt, I couldn't fault her apprehension.

Reaching into a pouch on my weapon's belt, I pulled out her shifter cloak and handed it to her. Her eyes lit up and a smile spread across her face, erasing the worry and making her look more like how she probably did on any given day. She seemed like someone who was naturally cheerful and, speaking solely on the arrangement of her physical features, she was quite pretty. Then again, even in my limited experience, I'd never seen an un-attractive Astral; also, their outward appearance was the best thing about them.

"Thank you for remembering!" she said, settling the cloak around her shoulders.

"It belongs to you," I replied brusquely. I hadn't wanted Nerudian to think I was trying to keep his gift for myself, so it made sense to return it to Kyra as quickly as I could.

Alistair reinserted her quill, then waved Kyra over to where she was sitting on top of a small table.

"Caz would like to congratulate you on your internship placement," the Cypher said, "and asks that you accept this as a token of his esteem." She snapped a clawed paw, and a black box appeared, wrapped in a red satin ribbon. Kyra's eyes widened, and she glanced at me.

"You might as well open it," I said, confused at the porcu-pine's words and annoyed by my confusion.

Kyra did, and I shifted my stance to get a better view of the present, which turned out to be a large lightning ridge opal set in gold and fashioned into a brooch. The stone was streaked with blues and greens, each fleck of color flashing like a miniature lightning bolt where the light caught it.

"It's beautiful!" exclaimed Kyra. "But I'm not sure I can accept it . . ." her voice trailed off, and she looked at Aurelius before turning back to Alistair. "How did Caz know about my internship placement? There hasn't even been a formal announcement." Concern settled into the corners of her eyes.

Alistair grinned. "Caz makes it a practice to keep up with what interests him. And you most *certainly* fall in that category."

Kyra looked as if she didn't know whether to be flattered or troubled.

"I don't know if I'll be able to take it home with me, since it was made in Nocens," she said, "but I don't think there's any harm in wearing it while I'm here." She pinned the brooch near the clasp of her cloak, and asked Alistair to thank Caz for her. The porcupine agreed, and I began walking towards the front door. Now that we had a suppressor medallion, I could open a portal directly to Rynstyn, meaning we wouldn't need to use Caz's intersector.

"Oh!" said Alistair, as she escorted us to the door. "Sebastian, Caz wanted me to tell you Ya'nark resigned her position after her *shocking loss*, so we don't have to worry about the silver export from Eisig, at least for the time being."

I nodded, having received all the thanks I needed in the form of gold in my bank account. It was nice to know my client was pleased, though. As Kyra and I walked to where I could open a portal, I debated between asking her about her internship placement, which I didn't particularly want to do, and remaining ignorant of the reason behind Caz's gift, which I also didn't want to do. My desire for information finally won out.

"What was that back there, about your internship place-ment?" I asked.

"In Aeles, after graduation and depending on your career, you complete an internship at a *Donec*," she explained. "You ap-ply to the positions that interest you and hope you match with at least one."

Aurelius leaned around Kyra's legs to give me a smug smile.

"The entire process is very selective and highly competitive," he said. "Kyra was matched with her top choice, and the *Donec Medicinae* is very lucky to have her."

Kyra's cheeks reddened, and she reached down and stroked the lynx's head.

"It will give me the best chance to follow in my father's foot-steps," she said quietly. "He did the same internship when he was around my age."

Given how incredibly hard I worked to be nothing like my father, I found it interesting, if completely unrelatable, how much Kyra had looked up to hers.

Kyra straightened and turned her attention to me.

"Was your schooling anything like mine?" she asked. One side of her mouth quirked upwards. "Nocenian education isn't exactly something I've studied in great detail."

"We attend *Alempi* Academy, or Lower Academy, for six years and then *Uchaf*, Upper, Academy for six more," I said. Of course, I'd missed nearly two years of *Alempi* Academy when I'd been imprisoned in Rynstyn, but she didn't need to know that. "After graduation, you accept a position or do apprenticeships to prepare for a specific career."

Kyra nodded, and by this time we were far enough from Caz's office for me to open a portal. I said the spell under my breath, but nothing happened. I blinked, then tried again. Slowly, the portal shimmered into view.

That is the second time your portals have been temperamental lately,
observed Batty as we arrived at my cave. *You really ought to take Kyra
to meet LeBehr and fulfill your promise before you can't open one at all.*

What are you talking about? I asked, thinking over the last few
times I'd been at the bookstore, and then, suddenly, I remembered—I had promised LeBehr if I ever met a Recovrancer, I
would introduce them to her. At the time, such a thing had
seemed preposterous, but now, I was experiencing the consequences of being able to fulfill my promise without having done
so. Consequences for failing to keep a promise could range from
small inconveniences, such as diminished spell-casting abilities,
to all-out sickness to the complete inability to use *alera*. In my
case, it seemed my portals were being affected.

I rubbed the back of my neck as I stepped into my living area,
but before I could broach what promised to be a *very* uncomfortable conversation with Kyra, she spoke.

"Yesterday, when I contacted you, you said you were working . . . are you still completing apprenticeships or have you already accepted a position somewhere?"

This wasn't information Kyra needed to know in order to
retrieve the sword, and I didn't share personal information without a reason. However, the more she spoke about Aeles, the more
I learned; I couldn't very well stay silent and expect her to keep
divulging things. On the other hand, I could only *imagine* what
someone like her would think about what I did for a living.

"I have my own business," I finally replied.

Kyra mulled that over, and from the corner of my eye, I saw
Aurelius shake his head, clearly not happy with whatever she was
planning. Regardless, she straightened herself to her full height,
which meant the top of her head just reached my chin. Fixing her
eyes on mine, she asked, "What do you do . . . for work?"

I held her gaze. "Do you have some idea about what you think I do?"

She swallowed hard, and I thought she might drop the subject, but instead she said, "When I contacted you yesterday, you sounded like you were in the middle of a fight. When Alistair thanked you just now, she mentioned someone resigning because of their *shocking loss*."

Kyra caught her bottom lip between her teeth, looked around nervously, then said, "I think . . . you've worn weapons every time I've seen you. You have an entire cavern dedicated to swords and daggers and bows and poisons. I think . . . I think you might hurt others for a living."

Her expression was both hopeful I would contradict her and resigned she had arrived at the correct answer.

"I'm an assassin," I said. If we were going to do this, we might as well get it over with.

Kyra's face paled, and she took a step away from me.

"I'm not going to hurt you," I snapped. "Believe me, I've had plenty of chances, and I haven't."

Kyra covered her face with her hands, shoulders rising and falling rapidly as she struggled to process my occupation. She finally lowered her arms to her side, and her eyes blazed above her flushed cheeks.

"How can you do that?" she asked, her voice shaking. "How can you just decide to end someone's life? What gives you the right?"

"I suppose because I'm willing and able to do it," I said.

Kyra glared at me. "Did you just wake up one day and decide you wanted to spend the rest of your life *killing*?"

I glared back at her and said in my coldest voice, "I imagine everyone gravitates to the things they're best at."

"Being the best at hurting others isn't something to be proud of!" she shouted. "That's despicable! I can't . . ." she shook her head as if trying to shake my words from her ears. "And this is an actual business in your realm? You get paid to kill?"

"Very well," I assured her, and she blanched, looking like she might be ill.

"Who, exactly, do you kill?" she asked.

"Whoever I'm hired to," I replied. "Not that it's any of your business, but I don't just fling my weapons around at random. All the targets I'm hired to eliminate have done something even you would probably consider bad. They've lied, stolen, harmed someone . . . they deserve to be punished."

"By society, perhaps," she countered. "Not by an individual, and certainly not just because whomever they slighted can afford to hire *you*."

"That's your opinion, Astral," I reminded her.

Clenching her jaw, she wrapped her arms around herself. "I heal others, Sebastian. I use my gifts to ease suffering and restore health. How can I—"

"That's your choice," I interrupted. "You could just as easily use your powers to hurt as to heal."

Kyra recoiled as if I'd struck her. "What are you talking about? I would never do that!"

"But you could. It's all about the direction you choose to work in," I said. "You choose to start with an injury and progress towards healing. You could just as easily start with a healthy body and progress towards it being injured."

Kyra's mouth fell open. "Is that what Daevals with healing abilities do in Nocens?" she asked.

"Not all of them . . . obviously we need healers, and they're well compensated, but those with healing abilities often choose to enter the information acquisition business rather than engaging in more traditional medicine."

"The information acquisi—you mean, *torture?* Injuring others on purpose?" Kyra's chest was rising and falling so quickly I decided there was a real chance she might faint from lack of air. Her eyes flashed as she clenched her hands into fists and slammed them against her thighs. "That's it—our deal is off! I can't work with someone who thinks the way you do, and I'm certainly not going to help an *assassin* retrieve a *sword!* If I'd known what you did before we made our deal, I *never* would have agreed to help you!"

"But you did agree," I reminded her. "And I told you what would happen if you changed your mind."

"If you tell my government I'm a Recovrancer, I'll tell Adonis and Senator Rex everything I know about you," she retorted. "Your name, how you live in a cave, about Nerudian, *and* what you do for a living. They'll find you," she assured me, "and lock you up in Tor'Ex where you belong!"

"Then I suppose it will be a question of who the Astral government thinks is a bigger threat," I replied, narrowing my eyes. "I'm sure they'd come for me, eventually, but I suspect they would start with you, seeing as how they already know where you live and where you'll be doing internship . . . and where to find your family."

Kyra's nostrils flared and some of the redness left her cheeks. Her eyes flickered anxiously around the cavern, and slowly she unclenched her hands, eventually dropping her gaze to the floor.

"You're right," she said softly. "They'd come for me first. And then I'd never become the *Princeps Shaman* or understand being a Recovrancer . . . not to mention what they might do to my family." A tear ran down her face, and she brushed it away. "The last thing my father said to me was, 'Use your gifts to do what you know is right.' I can't make a difference if I'm locked away."

Slowly, the fury drained from her eyes, replaced by an unhappy acceptance. After a few moments, she seemed to have gotten herself in hand. "Alright, then," she said. "Let's try to get into the unicorn sanctuary."

25

SEBASTIAN

"Where's the medallion?" I asked. Even though I knew it was necessary, I was far from comfortable being around such a deplorable part of my past.

Reaching into a pocket of her breeches, she carefully withdrew the gold pendant and handed it to me. Just seeing that hateful star was enough to make a cold sweat break out on the back of my neck.

"I wish we could practice before using it for real," fretted Kyra. "What if it lets you into the sanctuary but then you get ill or burst into flames or—"

I held up a hand and let the flames flow across my palm.

"I'm a Pyromancer," I reminded her. "Fire is the least of my worries."

She cringed as I retracted the flames.

"Alright, we don't have to worry about fire," she agreed, "but it goes against every healing instinct I have to just pin a piece of jewelry on you, head into Aeles, and see what happens. I didn't even know these medallions existed until a few days ago, and I don't want us to be too hasty."

I snorted at such ridiculousness, and Kyra scowled. "I'm serious," she insisted. "Falling stars, Sebastian, you're not just some experiment, and—"

"Oh, that's rich coming from your kind!" I sneered, closing my fist around the medallion as I fought the urge to burn it to ash. My chest was rising and falling faster than usual, and it was taking a great deal of effort to keep my voice at a reasonable level. Without meaning to, I felt myself redistribute my weight, balancing on the balls of my feet in preparation of either fighting or fleeing.

Kyra glanced at Aurelius before turning her gaze back to me.

"Is there something you're not telling me?" she asked, softening her tone.

I barked out a harsh laugh. "No!" The toffee-colored walls wavered around me, and I inhaled the sterile, lemon-scented air as I heard footsteps slapping against the cold, slick floor, footsteps coming to take me one of two places—the medical unit, where I would be hooked up to countless tubes and wires, or the teaching unit, where I would be asked questions and tortured. I took a step back and raised a hand, ready to summon the fire and protect myself as best I could.

The bracelet around my wrist vibrated, and I grabbed at it, trying to tug it off, before I realized Kyra was speaking to me.

It's all right, she said. *Nothing bad is happening. Everything's fine. I'm not going to hurt you.*

A pleasant, comforting sound filled the air, and I felt myself relaxing, as if I'd been shivering with frostbite and someone had wrapped a blanket around me. I was in my cave. I was free. I was safe.

After a few beats, I fixed my attention back on Kyra and watched as she continued to run her finger over the pearl-colored bead on her *sana* bracelet. She raised her wrist without letting go of the bead.

"Saund," she said. "The Soother."

I nodded and drew a shuddering inhale before running a hand over my face. I couldn't remember the last time I'd come so undone . . . probably when I'd passed out on Dunston's doorstep following my escape from Rynstyn, then woken up in the office of a healer he'd taken me to who had tried, unsuccessfully, to examine me.

"I . . . " I hesitated, uncertain what to say. It didn't feel right to apologize for my reaction, but I also didn't want Kyra thinking I was losing my mind. "I've had . . . bad experiences . . . with something similar to the medallion," I finally said.

Confusion swept over Kyra's face, but she nodded, nevertheless.

"Do you want me to pin it on you?" she asked, gesturing towards where my closed fist was still wrapped around the medallion. Uncurling my fingers, I nodded, not trusting myself to have a steady hand.

Kyra stepped forward and took the pendant. Tilting her head back, she studied the upper part of my chest, and while I assumed she was simply deciding where to place the medallion, it was unnerving to be the object of her scrutiny. Lifting a hand, she gently pinched the fabric of my tunic before pulling it away from my chest.

"So I don't accidentally stick you," she explained, and I nodded, too distracted by how close she was to offer a better response. I usually only stood so close to someone when I was about to end their life, not because I was allowing them to touch me, or at least, touch my clothing.

You know, offered Batty, *if she is indeed destined to be the next Princeps Shaman, she is going to be a very powerful figure. Perhaps you ought to tell her what happened in Rynstyn so she can ensure it never happens again. If any Astral would believe you, it would be her.*

I doubt that program is even active anymore, I countered. *There's no need for her to know about something that happened thirteen years ago and doesn't affect anyone now.*

It still affects you, said the bat pointedly, *and if there are other Daevals who—*

Enough! I interrupted him, as Kyra slipped the pin through my tunic and locked it closed with a slight *click.* Looking up at me, she swallowed hard as a flush crept over her cheeks.

"I need to put my blood on the medallion," she said. "Do you have a knife?"

Reaching down to the holster near my boot, I withdrew a dagger, then straightened and summoned the fire to my free hand. Holding the dagger over the flames, I made sure it was sterilized before offering the handle to Kyra. If anyone had told me I would one day be standing in my cave with an Astral and freely offering them a weapon, I would have pitied their idiocy . . . yet here I was. LeBehr always said truth was stranger than fiction.

You can tell her she was right when you take Kyra to meet her, said the bat, but I couldn't think about that now.

Kyra eyed the dagger as if it might attack her of its own volition before gingerly grasping the handle. Holding the blade upright, she pressed the thumbpad of her right hand against the sharp metal, wincing as a bead of golden blood rose to the surface. She quickly smeared the blood over the medallion, and for a moment I couldn't breathe. It was a familiar situation, to be sure, having an Astral spread their blood over a suppressor medallion I was wearing, but more than that, there was something intimate about the situation I didn't like. I felt vulnerable, as if Kyra might accidentally see inside my shade or worse, into my memories.

As Kyra stepped back and healed her thumb, I cast about for something to focus on other than my own discomfort.

"How long have you had your *sana* bracelet?" I asked. Trying to distract myself by voluntarily engaging in conversation was a mark of exactly how uneasy I was.

"Five years," replied Kyra, inspecting her healed thumb. "It was a present for my thirteenth birth anniversary."

"Could anyone use it?"

Kyra made a face. "They could try, but I doubt it would end well. The stones are very temperamental. Some of them are always trying to get their own way, and using them without training can backfire, making you cast a spell on yourself, or worse." Smoothing the edge of her shifter cloak, her gaze met mine. "Is there anything else we need to do before we go to the unicorn sanctuary?"

I walked over to my wardrobe and slipped on my favorite leather jacket, then grabbed the sword hanging from the foot of my bed and buckled the harness across my chest. The familiar weight of the weapon in its leather sheath against my back felt good, and I told myself this was no different from preparing for one of my usual jobs.

Walking back towards Kyra, I watched as her gaze settled unhappily on the straps crossing my torso.

"I'm not going to hurt the unicorns," I assured her. "The sword is for our protection."

She grimaced and shook her head.

"No, I was just . . ." she sighed loudly. "Astrals are planterians, meaning we don't eat animals and . . . we don't wear them, either."

I glanced down at my jacket. It had been one of the first expensive pieces of clothing I'd bought myself after I started making money, and it was broken in to where it was supple and moved with me like a second skin.

"If the animal this came from was used for food, wouldn't it have been wasteful to not use its hide for something too?" I asked.

Kyra's mouth turned down as her shoulders slumped. "It's just sad an animal had to die in the first place," she replied.

I rolled my eyes, not about to get drawn into a discussion on the ethics of animal welfare with an Astral, and Kyra turned towards Batty, who was sitting on the table, shoving pieces of dried apricot into his mouth.

"What about your Cypher?" she asked. "I don't know how to keep him from setting off the Blood Alarm."

"I'd just as soon leave our Cyphers here," I said.

"Absolutely not!" cried Aurelius. "Kyra's not going anywhere without me!"

Kyra cast an affectionate smile at the lynx, who hadn't even bothered to confine his remarks to telepathy, but Batty simply shook his head.

"I will not set off the alarm. Cyphers do not have gold or silver blood; we are made differently."

"Does it matter you were born in Nocens, though?" asked Kyra. "Senator Rex said the wards had been strengthened so nothing originating in Nocens could come through."

Batty chuckled and tossed a piece of fruit into the air, intending to catch it, but he opened his mouth too late. The apricot hit his nose and landed by his feet, and he was forced to lean forward to grab it.

"I was born so long ago, the realm might not even have been called Nocens at the time. I will be fine, I assure you," he smiled.

Kyra nodded, but I wasn't so easily swayed.

"Just how old are you?" I demanded, even though some part of me knew it was futile. The creature had always been annoyingly vague about his age.

Batty blinked up at me, more serious than I was used to seeing him.

"I remember Nerudian when he was just an egg waiting to be

hatched; his mother thought he would *never* come out. I remember when Cyphers weren't bonded with Astrals or Daevals. I remember when Astrals and Daevals didn't speak the same language. I *also* remember when it was considered impolite to ask someone how old they were!" He threw a piece of dried fruit at me, then fell backwards, wrapping his wings around his sides and giggling as if he had truly outdone himself.

"Just ignore him," I instructed Kyra. While the bat's words had a ring of truth to them, he was simply playing me for a fool; Nerudian was well over a thousand years old, and it was unfathomable for Batty to have been around even close to that long.

I held the coordinates for the sanctuary in my mind, having gotten them from my map, then summoned the portal. *"Fosgail,"* I said, and to my relief, the portal opened, even though it took longer than usual to stabilize.

"Well, that's a good sign!" said Kyra, and Aurelius scowled, obviously displeased with the entire proceedings. I hadn't expected him to support Kyra even when he disagreed with her, but aside from making his unhappiness known, he made no attempt to interfere.

"I'll go through first," I said, apprehension jangling through me as I took a deep breath, then stepped through the rippling doorway.

26

KYRA

J followed Sebastian through the portal, letting my eyes adjust to the twilight in the sanctuary. With the autumn days getting shorter, a full moon was already rising, making it easier to see my surroundings. In the distance, a range of mountains cut a jagged outline across the darkened sky. Stars glimmered overhead, so close I imagined reaching out my hand and brushing my fingers over them. Tall grasses shivered in the chilly wind blowing down from snow-capped peaks, and I inhaled deeply, my lungs burning in response to the crisp air, taking in the smell of damp grass, fir trees, and ice. When I exhaled, I could see my breath in front of me, a soft puff of white against the midnight blue of the sky. But most important was what was missing—the hair-raising wail of the Blood Alarm.

I stood still, feeling like a coiled spring pulled taut, ready to snap back in on itself at any moment. Batty flew past me and perched on Sebastian's shoulder as Aurelius took a cautious look around. I swept my eyes across the open field again, half expecting soldiers to appear any moment. Was the medallion really working? Had we truly confounded the sensors and snuck a Daeval into Aeles without anyone being the wiser?

My *sana* bracelet glinted in the moonlight, and I glanced at the beads. If we were caught, perhaps I could use Mwyaf to induce forgetting in whoever discovered us. Erasing memories wasn't something to be undertaken lightly, and I'd only done it a handful of times under the supervision of my father, but it was certainly preferable to being caught and dragged before the Senate.

Sebastian took one step forward, then another, and still I didn't hear anything besides the wind and my own heartbeat. My pulse finally began to slow, and the fear tightening my chest gave way to relief.

The combination of the medallion and my golden blood was working.

Sebastian waved a hand and caught my eye, then pointed to the bracelet.

I nodded and touched the jewelry. *The medallion seems to be working!* I noted. *It looks like you and Caz were right.*

Sebastian nodded, but didn't dwell on our success. *We should probably start looking for a horn. I don't want to be here any longer than absolutely necessary.*

I didn't disagree. *From what I know of them, unicorns like to feel safe at night and tend to gather where there are trees or some other form of protection.*

Sebastian gestured towards the nearest cluster of trees. *Let's start there.*

We made our way towards the grove, Batty flying a few feet ahead, and although I continued to look around, there was no sign of movement on the flat land around us.

When was the last time you were here? Sebastian asked.

I've only been here once, on a school trip when I was fifteen, I said. *Astrals try to leave the unicorns alone as much as possible, which means limiting the number of visitors. You couldn't get close to them, but, even from far away, they were beautiful.*

Sebastian nodded in acknowledgment, then asked, *Do you have any idea what kind of security to expect?*

The sanctuary's enclosed by a fence, and there are guards, but they're mostly near the entrance. I remember seeing one walking around every now and then, but they're really more focused on keeping curious Astrals out than on keeping the unicorns in. I glanced at Sebastian. What will you do if we see a guard?

He remained quiet, which I took to mean he'd already decided on a course of action, so I stepped in front of him, forcing him to stop.

Astrals will try to find the least violent way to deal with intruders, I explained. You won't have to fight. You can just make a portal, and we'll leave. There won't be any need to . . . hurt someone.

Let's just hope we don't see any guards, he replied. I'm not as convinced your kind's first response won't involve violence.

He stepped around me and continued walking, and I frowned at his back, annoyed he didn't believe me about my own kind. As I fell into step behind the assassin, I sent up a quick prayer to the Gifter of Protection, asking him to keep us away from any sanctuary guards.

We continued into the grove in silence. The close-growing trees were so tall, I had to tilt my head back to see the stars. A softly gurgling creek flowed nearby, a ribbon of silver beneath the moonlight, and the grass beneath my boots was as thick as the finest Montemian carpet. A fox peeked out from behind a bush, its red fur providing luxurious insulation against the dropping temperature. It blinked at us, then darted out of sight.

Listen, Sebastian said, pausing, and I did the same.

At first, I could only hear the general nighttime cacophony. But I soon began to differentiate the noises around me—wind gently rustling through the tops of the trees, snow breaking and sliding off rocks, and a soft nicker, followed by the sound of a hoof stamping firmly against the ground.

Sebastian started walking again, quickening his pace as he veered slightly to the left, slipping between the brown and grey tree trunks. I hurried after him and didn't realize he'd come to a stop until I ran into him, bumping my chest against his scabbard and only just managing to stifle a gasp.

Look, Sebastian said, dropping his voice to a whisper even though we were speaking through the bracelets.

Rubbing my sternum, I moved beside him, then immediately lowered my hand to my side, the pain in my chest forgotten.

Standing before us were three white unicorns.

Power radiated from their sleek, muscular bodies as the creatures studied us, caution mixing with curiosity in their luminous eyes. The one closest to us bobbed her head lightly, and not knowing what else to do, I bowed, lowering my eyes in deference to show I meant no harm. From the corner of my eye, I saw Sebastian do the same, which surprised me; I hadn't expected him to be so respectful of the animals.

After a moment, Sebastian straightened, but kept his gaze on the unicorns as if he was trying to memorize everything about them. There was something different about him as he studied the creatures—he seemed less guarded, more approachable, and his jaw was relaxed, softening his perpetual frown. In fact, his scowl softened so much that the corners of his mouth turned upwards ever so slightly.

On anyone else, it wouldn't have been considered noteworthy, but from what I'd seen of Sebastian's facial expressions, it might as well have been an ear-to-ear grin. Come to think of it, I hadn't paid a great deal of attention to what Sebastian looked like, as there'd always been more pressing things to focus on whenever we'd been together, but now . . . I couldn't help noticing he was actually quite handsome.

He glanced at me, and his dark eyes shone with a mixture of

awe and sadness. *We don't have unicorns in Nocens anymore,* he offered, as if he needed a reason to marvel at the creatures.

I nodded, then, realizing I'd been unabashedly staring at the
Daeval, I quickly turned my gaze to the unicorns, ignoring the
unhappy noise Aurelius made in the back of my mind.

Thankfully, Sebastian didn't appear to have noticed my scrutiny, and he ran a hand through his hair as he drew a deep breath.
So, now I just choose one and walk up and explain why I need a horn?

Yes, I replied, wishing I knew something else to tell him. I'd
gotten Sebastian into the sanctuary, but now it was up to him to
get a horn.

27

SEBASTIAN

Taking a deep breath, I stepped forward. As I did, I was startled by a sudden noise to my right, the crunch of hooves snapping apart twigs strewn on the leaf-covered forest floor. Peering into the trees, I backed away as another unicorn emerged from the shadows to join the group. This one was different, though. I had never seen a black unicorn before, not even in pictures, and the creature's dark coat glistened like polished ebony. Her mane and tail glowed a lovely, pale silver in the moonlight, and her purple-hued eyes shone brightly from beneath long white lashes.

She stopped so near me I could have reached out and touched her if I'd wanted to, but I stood still and let her examine me.

Do I need to speak out loud, or can they hear my thoughts? I asked Kyra.

I've never heard of them reading minds, she said, *so I'd try speaking out loud.*

I calmed my racing heart as best I could and bowed deeply to the black unicorn. Still on my shoulder, Batty gripped my tunic with his clawed feet and bowed, as well. Standing up straight, I kept my voice low, partly to avoid scaring the creatures, but also because I didn't want my words to carry. How was I going to be as vague as possible while still convincing the unicorn of the worthiness of my request?

"I have need of a horn," I began, "to retrieve something very valuable to me."

The unicorn merely blinked, so I tried again, this time phrasing my request as a question and offering additional information.

"May I have a horn to recover a sword that was stolen centuries ago? Please?"

The unicorn tossed her head, rippling her long mane, and pawed at the ground. I didn't know what such behavior meant, but then Kyra spoke, momentarily distracting me from the panic dancing at the edges of my thoughts.

You know how Nerudian can tell if someone's lying? she said. *Perhaps unicorns are similar. Maybe they won't voluntarily shed their horn unless you voluntarily tell them the truth.*

I fixed my gaze on the unicorn, who dipped her head and flicked her ears, waiting. I didn't like the idea of telling the whole truth to anyone about anything, preferring to parcel it out as needed, but when would I ever have the chance to stand before a unicorn again?

"I'm a Daeval," I said, before gesturing to Kyra. "She found a medallion to disguise my blood, so I could trick the Blood Alarm and sneak into your sanctuary. She's a Recovrancer, and I want her to recover a sword for me, Rhannu, that Astrals stole from my kind ages ago. In order to recover the sword, we have to give the Shade Transporter a freely offered unicorn horn. I don't have any noble purpose for wanting the sword . . . I just want it. I've always wanted it and, for reasons I can't explain, I've always felt like it should belong to me. Sometimes I dream about it, and . . . when I think about it, it feels like I'm missing something that ought to be mine."

I paused, uncertain whether to say more or if I'd said too

much. The unicorn extended her neck and sniffed my face, the breath from her wide nostrils stirring my hair. She sniffed Batty too, and the creatures shared a long look with one another. Nothing else happened, and after a moment, my shoulders sagged, hope rushing out of me. This would never work . . . no unicorn would give up a horn to someone with such a selfish desire. It wasn't as if I was trying to heal a loved one or do something similarly virtuous.

I was about to turn away when the unicorn lowered her head. She was still for a moment, then grunted and gave her entire body a rough shake. Her horn began to glow with a faint light, and I watched in amazement as it slid off her head and landed with a soft thump on the grass next to my feet.

As the unicorn raised her head, a new horn appeared, growing out from between her ears and parting her silver forelock. She gave a satisfied nicker and then ambled away, followed by the other unicorns, as if this sort of thing happened every day.

Pulling a long, thin box from the side of my scabbard, I bent down and carefully picked up the horn. The ivory was cool against my hand, and each curving spiral glistened where it was struck by moonlight. I carefully placed it inside the box, which I'd lined with felt for additional protection, then slipped it back into my scabbard and rose to my feet before turning to face Kyra.

Her eyes were wide, and her mouth was slightly open. *I can't believe that really happened,* she whispered. *You got a horn.*

I can't believe it either, I agreed. Hooking my fingers under the shoulder straps of the scabbard, I flexed my shoulders. *Well, it looks like you earned my other two recovrancy books.*

Kyra shot a grin at Aurelius before turning back to me.

As much as I'm looking forward to collecting my prizes, she said, *do you know how long the suppressor medallion disguises your blood?*

We could walk around a little, if we have time. If we get really lucky, we might see a foal!

My rational mind said we'd fulfilled the purpose of our visit and ought to leave while we could. The part of me that knew I would never have the chance to see a unicorn again, however, immediately overrode all rational thoughts. Not wanting to say more about my personal experience with the medallion, I kept my response vague. *We can stay a little while longer.*

We continued further into the forest, which soon opened up to a grass-covered field that stretched out towards the mountains I'd seen earlier. A large frozen pond glowed like a flattened pearl before us, and an owl hooted nearby.

Kyra pulled the hood of her cloak over her head and peered out hesitantly at me.

You'll probably want me to go after Rhannu as soon as we get back to your cave, she said, *but I'm going to need some time to read through the other books and make sure I understand everything I can about going into Vaneklus.*

I nodded. *We have the horn, and it's not going anywhere. We'll move forward when you're ready.*

She smiled at me, which caught me completely off-guard. She'd smiled at me before, of course, but something about *this* smile felt different. It was shy, not as broad, and appeared to have less to do with an accomplishment than simply sharing something . . . with me.

What are you thinking? she asked, her eyes dropping from mine to move across my face. *I can sense when your feelings change, and I can pinpoint something specific if it's really clear—like how happy and surprised you were when the unicorn shed her horn—but it's not as easy as understanding my Cypher. Probably because I've been connected to him longer.*

I couldn't very well tell her I was thinking about her smile, so I stumbled about for something else to say.

I was thinking that . . . working with you has actually been better than I expected, I said.

She chuckled dryly. *I can only imagine what you expected. Hopefully I've disproved at least* some *of the myths your kind have about mine.*

I stared out at the mountains, wondering if they housed the clandestine rehabilitation facility, and considered what Batty had said earlier. This would be a perfect opportunity to tell Kyra about my experiences with Astrals. I could explain what I'd been through and ask her to look into it, if she did indeed become the next *Princeps Shaman.* But that would mean divulging things I'd never told anyone besides Dunston or Caz, and they'd known me my entire life.

She will believe you, said Batty confidently. *If you could keep even one other Daeval from enduring what you were forced to, wouldn't sharing your past be worth it?*

I wasn't so sure, as I'd never been especially motivated by the idea of helping others. While I was unwaveringly loyal to the few Daevals I cared about, I wasn't particularly interested in the greater good or helping those I didn't know. But I *did* want revenge on the Astrals who had hurt me, and ensuring that their project was shut down would be the second-best form of revenge. In a perfect realm, I would go back and kill more of my captors than I had when I'd left, but since that wasn't possible, involving Kyra was probably the next best option. Taking a deep breath, I turned towards her, but before I could speak, another voice broke the silence.

"And just what do you two think you're doing?"

Kyra and I whirled around as an Astral guard strode out of

the trees on the other side of the pond. I quickly drew my sword and stepped in front of Kyra. The guard's eyes narrowed.

"How did you get in here?" he demanded.

"I walked," I replied calmly. I considered summoning the mask to my face but decided against it since the Blood Alarm remained blessedly silent.

The guard walked closer until I could make out his name plate, which read, "Lt. Coran." He attempted to get a better look at Kyra, but I stayed in front of her, doing my best to keep her from view.

"You can't just come in here whenever you want," the soldier snapped as the breeze ruffled his ash blonde hair. "You know the rules. You two need to come with me."

"No, I think we'll be leaving now," I replied. I started to summon the portal but to my surprise, I found myself blocked, similar to when I tried to make one near Caz's Diomhair Way office. This wasn't just my portals being temperamental . . . this was something else. I glared at the guard, and he pulled a small device from his pocket. I didn't recognize it, but I could guess its purpose.

"After a Daeval escaped being captured by opening a portal, every soldier was issued one of these. It's like a ward, but portable," he explained. "We're calling it a portal disrupter."

I couldn't begin to fathom how expensive such spelled equipment was, but then again, it made sense—the Astral military would be heavily invested in keeping unwanted visitors out of Rynstyn, home to not only the unicorns but also Tor'Ex. I should have expected as much.

Scowling at my lack of foresight, as well as the guard, I twirled my sword in a slow circle.

"Why don't you walk away while you still have the chance, and let us leave?" I suggested. "Otherwise, you're going to be sorry."

"You're the one who'll be sorry!" he snapped, his grey eyes

narrowing as he drew his sword from the scabbard on his back and pointed it at me.

You don't need to see this, I said to Kyra without taking my eyes off Lieutenant Coran. *Wait for me in the trees, and I'll find you when I'm done.*

No! she said. *You can't—*

I will never be an Astral prisoner again, I cut her off as my heart began to beat with the unique mixture of excitement and anticipation I only experienced before a fight.

Aurelius used his head to shove Kyra back towards the tree line, but I was only partly paying attention. The guard drew closer, and while he was shorter than I was, judging by the way he held his sword, he'd had at least some training with weapons.

"Adonis Prior said the Daeval he saw in the Tryllet Forest had blonde hair and was about your height," remarked the guard. "You just couldn't stay away, could you?"

I brought my blade against his so hard he had to raise his other hand to steady his sword.

Within three moves, I'd disarmed him and sent his sword flying above the pond where it fell onto the ice with a loud clang. Glaring at me, the guard darted out and picked it up, then began sketching marks in the air, casting a spell to bind me in place. I extended a hand and sent a ball of fire directly at him. He shouted and dropped his sword, slapping at where the flames had caught his dark blue uniform.

While he was otherwise occupied, I ran towards him, my boots maintaining a good grip even on the ice. When I neared the guard, rather than swinging my sword or attacking with a spell, as he likely expected, I crouched down and swept my leg out, hooking my foot behind his calves and pulling his feet out from under him. Yelping loudly, he crashed onto his back, but unfortunately, the fall didn't knock him out.

As he tried to get up, I spun around and drove my fist into his face. He screamed in pain and fell backwards, clutching his broken nose, and I pointed the tip of my blade at his throat before reaching down into his pocket. Grabbing the disruptor, I summoned the flames to my hand, letting them burn the device until it was no more than a lump of metal, which I tossed aside. I probably could have sold it to Caz or Dunston for an exorbitant profit, but the satisfaction of destroying the device was more than worth the financial loss.

Turning my attention back to the guard, I raised my sword to run him through. As I lifted my weapon, however, I suddenly heard, "Sebastian, *please*, don't!"

I looked towards the edge of the pond, as did the guard, and there was Kyra, who had somehow managed to get away from Aurelius, staring beseechingly at me as her cloak fluttered behind her. Lieutenant Coran took advantage of the distraction to grab his sword, then said something in a language I didn't know before striking the ice with the hilt of the weapon. As the ice groaned beneath my feet, he said a spell that threw him backwards and deposited him unceremoniously on the grass beside the pond, where he lay still.

I stared down as spidery cracks streaked outwards beneath my boots. Holding my breath, I brought my gaze back to Kyra's. Before I could speak, the ice groaned loudly . . . then, it broke, snapping into pieces and collapsing underneath me, and I shouted as I fell into the freezing water below.

28

KYRA

"NO!" I screamed as Sebastian fell into the pond with a loud splash. From the corner of my eye, I saw the guard slowly start to push himself up. Batty suddenly materialized on my shoulder.

"If you can get to Sebastian, I can take us back to the cave!" he said.

"Alright!" I said, running out onto the ice without a second thought as Batty disappeared. Sebastian was grasping for a handhold, but he kept sliding back into the pond, and it was no wonder—the sanctuary guard had used the old Astral language of Praxum to enchant the water, ordering it to drag Sebastian down and drown him.

After only a few feet, I could sense the ice becoming thinner, and my boots threatened to slide out from under me, but I refused to slow down. When the ice finally creaked and began cracking in protest, I threw myself forward, using the momentum I'd gathered to slide into the hole Sebastian had made.

Crashing through the opening, I broke off chunks of ice as I fell. The water was so cold I shrieked in pain, earning myself a mouthful of water I quickly tried to spit back out. As I sank below the surface, the water lapped hungrily at me, twisting around my legs and trying to force its way into my nose and throat. It must have recognized my golden blood, however, because it quickly fell still, and soon the only movement beneath the ice was the result of my kicking and floundering.

Steeling my nerves before sinking deeper into the water, I moved my arms in widening arcs. Thankfully, one of my hands soon made contact with Sebastian's leather jacket, which I never thought I'd be happy to feel. Tugging him closer, I managed to wrap my hand around his wrist. As I kicked my way upwards, dragging Sebastian behind me, sounds and images suddenly filled my mind, likely the ones that had tried to present themselves back when I'd cleansed the potion from Sebastian's blood —a whip snaked through the air, slapping against pale skin as someone screamed; distant snow-capped mountains stood outside a high window; tubes hummed loudly as they were connected to a buzzing machine; and a bead of golden blood glinted on a medallion hanging from a collar around a small boy's neck . . . a small blonde boy.

Kicking with all my might, I managed to get my nose and mouth above the waterline. "I've got him, Batty!" I shouted, before dropping back below the surface. I would revisit what I'd learned from Sebastian's body later; right now, we just needed to get back to his cave.

The water surrounding me began to churn, and I felt myself rocked from side to side. Pressure built, squeezing me in on all sides until I couldn't move. I gripped Sebastian with every bit of strength I possessed, worried about breaking his wrist but more worried about being separated from him. I'd gotten him into the sanctuary, and I couldn't help feeling responsible for him. And even if he hadn't possessed two recovrancy books I very much wanted and I hadn't promised to help him recover Rhannu, I couldn't leave him to die, unconscious in an icy pond.

Suddenly, I had the discombobulating sense of being hurtled through space, moving so fast it was like being thrown forward by a powerful explosion. I felt dizzy and disoriented, unsure which way was up and which was down. Thrashing with my free arm, I soon noticed something—the temperature of the water had changed. When I looked up, I no longer saw ice or water or even the night sky; instead, I saw beautiful, shining gemstones.

Straining, I pushed myself upwards, fighting for the surface, sputtering as my head emerged from the water . . . the *hot* water, I suddenly realized.

"Where are we?" I gasped to Batty, letting go of Sebastian's wrist and grasping the front of his jacket with both hands, pulling his head above the water as I tried to get my bearings.

"Back in the cave, in a heated pool," replied the bat, perched on a rock ledge. Aurelius materialized next to him, and both Cyphers stared worriedly at Sebastian.

Recruiting most of the physical strength I possessed, I dragged Sebastian to one side of the small pool and leaned him back against the rocks. He was so much bigger than I was and the fact that he was unconscious made it even more difficult to move him.

When I finally gained a good look at his face, I felt as if I had been plunged right back into the frozen pond—his eyes were closed, and his lips were tinged blue.

A search for his pulse proved horribly disappointing, and his chest was perfectly still.

I jerked off my water-logged cloak so I could move more easily, then unbuckled the strap crossing Sebastian's chest. Tugging awkwardly on different parts of the holster, I was able to slide the scabbard down his arms. Yanking it free, I tossed it on the ledge before peeling off his leather jacket one arm at a time.

I then pulled Sebastian towards me, desperate to warm him up, and wrapped my arms around him before rubbing my hands against where his grey tunic clung to his back.

"Come on, Sebastian," I muttered in a low voice.

He didn't reply, and not a single muscle so much as twitched.
I gave him a hard shake and splashed warm water over him.
His eyes didn't even flutter, and the water ran down his cheeks
before dripping off his jaw.

"Sebastian, wake up!"

Putting my hand against his forehead, I winced at how cold
he still felt. Hugging him tightly, I pulled him as close to myself as
possible, fervently hoping my body heat, combined with the hot
water, might help revive him.

"Wake *up!*" I pleaded, spelling my hands to increase their
warmth before pressing them against his back again, trying to
innervate frozen tissue. "You have to wake up, Sebastian!"

I pulled back from him a little, searching for the faintest hint
of color somewhere on his face. He had always been pale, but
now he appeared pallid and, much as I didn't want to think it,
corpse-like.

"Sebastian, please! We're safe, we're back in your cave! Just
open your eyes, that's all you have to do, and you can see for
yourself!"

He remained silent, and I pressed the palms of my hands
against my eyes as tears began to flow. This couldn't be happening! Not *again!* I was a healer! I was supposed to be the most gifted
healer my realm had seen in ages. I was next in line to be named
the *Princeps Shaman!* The same sense of helplessness that had
filled me in Aravost when I'd struggled to save my father wound
its way through my limbs, wrapping around my lungs until it finally pierced my heart, making me keel forward with a scream of
fury. Hadn't it been enough to watch my father die? What good
was my gift if I couldn't use it when I needed it most?

My dear, I am so sorry. Aurelius's voice was as soft and comforting as perhaps it had ever been. *Knowing when to let go is just as important for a healer as knowing when to keep fighting. You did everything*

you could. Healing does not only come through ensuring survival and prolonging life . . . healing also comes through the cessation of suffering.

The lynx was right, but I didn't care. Something inside me stirred, a power pressing me to turn it loose, a voice telling me this wasn't the end because I wasn't *just* a healer—I was also a Recovrancer.

Clenching my fists, I made my decision.

I'm going to bring him back, Aurelius.

But he's an assassin, and a Daeval, in addition to who knows what else! argued the Cypher. *Both realms, his own included, are likely much better off without him!*

He said he would never be imprisoned by Astrals again, I countered. *He's had prior experiences with something like that suppressor medallion. And we haven't even discussed what I learned from his body when I was holding onto him in the pond! If Astrals are experimenting on Daevals, we have to do something! There's more to him than he's told us, and if anything would make someone reconsider their choices, it's a second chance at life!*

And with that, I closed my eyes, and let the cyclone forming inside my chest explode outwards. *Alera* pooled at the tips of my fingers before streaming all the way out to the ends of my hair. Leaning forward, I placed my left hand on Sebastian's still chest. I then summoned every bit of courage I possessed as I pressed the fingers of my right hand against my *sana* bracelet, touching Tawazun and Rheolath at the same time.

"Bidh mi a 'dol a-steach!" I said. Once again, everything around me was drowned out by a rushing sound that filled my ears and shook my body all the way to my bones. When I felt myself falling forward, this time I leaned back and, rather than landing on my hands and knees, I found myself sitting upright in the mist-grey waters of Vaneklus.

29

KYRA

It was eerily silent, except for the water dripping off me as I rose to my feet. Fog slipped over the riverbank, moving like outstretched fingers reaching eagerly for me and twining around my limbs. Cautiously, shuffling my feet, I took a few steps forward. The riverbed seemed to be a mixture of rock and sand beneath my boots; hopefully I wouldn't encounter any unexpectedly deep areas.

"Sebastian!" I shouted, having no idea how to seek out a particular shade in the realm of the dead. "Can you hear me?"

All was quiet, until I heard the splash of oars dipping into the water. I had attracted the attention of the Shade Transporter, but I couldn't tell which direction he was coming from. Trying to move faster, I trudged forward, splashing noisily as I recalled everything I'd read about shades in *The Book of Recovrancy*. A bank of fog ahead of me suddenly parted, and I could see a well-worn dock jutting out into the river. And there, standing on the end of the dock, running his hand through his hair and looking around with wide, frightened eyes, was Sebastian. I didn't know if shades always took on the appearance of the last body they'd resided in, but I was thankful Sebastian's had.

I found him! I said to Aurelius. *Now I just have to figure out how to bring him back.*

May the Gifter of Wisdom guide you! fretted the lynx. *Oh, I wish I was there with you!*

A loud splash caused me to turn around so quickly I almost fell face-first into the bow of the Shade Transporter's boat. Heaving my torso back, I managed to stay upright and forced my eyes to meet the bright red gaze studying me intently.

"So," the Shade Transporter said, his voice a mixture of annoyance and bemusement, "you cannot seem to stay away, can you, Recovrancer? Your father is no longer here."

I felt as if someone had slammed a fist into my stomach, and my breath, along with much of my courage, immediately left me. Of course my father wouldn't still be here, but hearing it said so plainly made me ache.

"I haven't come for my father," I said, pushing aside the pain. "My name is Kyra Valorian, and I have come to recover that shade." I pointed to where Sebastian stood, frozen, on the dock. I didn't know if he could hear us or not, but at least he could see I was here.

"My name is Laycus," said the Shade Transporter, "and I hate to inform you, but you will not be recovering that shade. He is a special favorite of mine, and I'm quite looking forward to having him back." He studied me, curiosity flitting across his face. "You're different than the last time you were here."

"I know what I am now," I said, "and as a Recovrancer, I have the right to recover shades that die before their time." Something about the Shade Transporter's name tickled the back of my mind, but I couldn't imagine why, as I'd never heard the name Laycus before.

"You know *what* you are, but not *who* you are, it would seem," mused Laycus. "And what makes you so certain it was not that shade's time to die?"

"I don't know," I admitted, "but his death feels wrong."

"Would you know if it felt right?" asked Laycus.

I was silent for a few beats, then finally admitted, "I haven't read about that yet." At the baffled expression on the Shade Transporter's face, I explained how I had agreed to help Sebastian with "something" in exchange for his recovrancy books, which were the only way I could learn about my powers.

Laycus leaned against his staff and considered me, then gestured towards Sebastian.

"Why *that* shade? What interest can you possibly have in him? If he's dead, you can take his recovrancy books and not have to worry about whatever you promised to do for him. Besides," he leaned forward as if he was about to share a secret, "do you know about his past? The things he's done?"

"I'm sure he's done terrible things, but he's kept his end of our agreement," I replied staunchly. "Perhaps with a second chance, he'll make better choices and not be so quick to end lives simply because he can. And, regardless of his past, he has information about my realm and my kind I desperately need."

"I see," said the Shade Transporter. He suddenly grinned at me, and the expression made the cheekbones of his skull-like face even more pronounced. "I must admit, Kyra, I've missed having someone to talk to."

"Did you use to talk to Recovrancers?" I asked.

He nodded, and there was something sad about the action. "We mostly argued about shades, but sometimes we simply talked . . . I would tell them interesting news I'd learned from the shades I ferried, and they would tell me about life in the realm of the living."

"If I agreed to come back and talk to you, would you let Sebastian go?" I asked.

Laycus shook his head inside his cowl.

"You are brave to offer, but it doesn't work that way." He

drummed his fingers against his staff and exhaled loudly. "You are right about it not being Sebastian's time. You don't know *why* you are right, but you are. Hopefully you'll come to that part in one of your books so you don't barge in here again demanding something you don't actually have the right to claim."

"I'm sorry," I said. "This is all so confusing. I'm just doing the best I can."

He nodded, his gaze falling on the gold bracelet around my wrist. Before I could back away, he leaned forward, pulled my arm up to his face, and exhaled softly over the gold.

"Well, perhaps there is hope for you after all!" he said with a slight smile as he watched the dragon swim around the cuff.

I wanted to know what he meant, but he dropped my arm and made a dismissive wave towards Sebastian.

"Take him away before I decide to try and send him on . . . or do something else with him. I trust I will see you again?"

I nodded, relief coursing through me and making my legs wobble, even though I tried to appear as if I'd expected such an answer all along. "Thank you. And yes, I'll be back. I'll have read all the recovrancy books by then, but I'm certain I'll still have questions."

He chuckled. "If you like, you may ask me one question before you leave."

My breath caught somewhere between my nose and my chest. A multitude of possible questions raced through my mind, but there was really only one that mattered. "If I had known what I am . . . before . . . could I have recovered my father?"

"No," replied Laycus.

"You mean . . . it was his time?" Tears burned the backs of my eyes, and I swayed where I stood, overcome by alternating pangs of regret and relief.

The Shade Transporter nodded. "When it is a shade's appointed time, it does not matter how fast you are—you cannot recover them."

"But when it's not their time—like Sebastian—how long do I have to recover them before you take them onwards?" I pressed.

Laycus gave me a wicked grin.

"That is a question for another time, should you not find the answer in those books of yours. In the meantime, know I shall very much be looking forward to seeing you again."

And with that, the oars dipped back into the water, and the wooden boat was soon hidden behind a fast-moving cloud of fog.

Kyra, every Gifter of the realm must have been looking out for you today, said Aurelius weakly. I couldn't disagree and said a hastily constructed prayer of thanks dedicated to every Gifter who came to mind. Then, turning back towards Sebastian, I made my way through the water until I reached the rocky shore, carefully picking my way over sand and stones towards the wooden dock. Sebastian was hurrying towards me with ground-eating strides, and seeing the fear in his eyes, something inside me softened towards the assassin. I held out my hand as we reached one another.

"Come on," I said, "we're going home. It's not your time."

He let out such an exhale that his broad shoulders lowered a good inch. Rather than taking my hand, though, he turned and cast a longing look towards the river, his eyes tracing its path until it disappeared from sight.

Unsure what else to do, I lowered my hand to my side. "Don't you want to go back?" I asked, not understanding.

Sebastian looked at me with more anguish than anyone, alive or dead, ought to feel, and when he spoke, his voice was hoarse.

"Can you recover a shade whose physical body died a long time ago? I'm positive it wasn't her time."

"Whose time?" I asked softly.

Sebastian swallowed hard. "My mother's. She was killed thirteen years ago."

"I'm so sorry," I said, my mind reeling at Sebastian's unexpected disclosure. Not knowing what else to do, I quickly explained what I'd learned about my abilities from my conversation with the Shade Transporter. "The next time I speak with him, I'll ask about your mother," I assured Sebastian.

He nodded, dropping his eyes to his boots before bringing them up to meet mine.

"Why did you come after me?" he asked, and for once, his voice was more curious than sharp.

"I didn't think it was your time to die," I said, struggling to put my exact reasons into words. "I wasn't able to save my father, so if there was a chance I could save you . . ." my voice tightened, and I cleared my throat before continuing. "It would allow something good to come from me being what I am. And, I gave you my word I'd recover Rhannu for you. In order for me to keep my promise, you need to be alive."

Sebastian stepped forward and tentatively extended his hand. I shook it, immediately feeling the same internal jolt I'd experienced the first time we'd shaken hands, back when we'd agreed to work together. It was like stirring a singing bowl, chanting, and rubbing Glir for clarity all at the same time, causing everything inside me to vibrate at the same frequency. I'd thought it might simply be my body's response to touching someone with silver blood, but I hadn't experienced anything remotely similar when touching Caz. What was it about Sebastian that provoked such a response?

Rather than immediately letting go, he surprised me by giving my fingers a gentle squeeze.

"Thank you," he said.

I nodded, most of my attention on how well my hand fit

against his. Apparently, it was possible to blush even in the realm of the dead, which was ridiculous—there was nothing romantic about being in the realm of the dead with Sebastian. I would have done this for anyone. "It's too bad we don't have the unicorn horn," I said, trying to appear as if standing in Vaneklus holding hands with a Daeval was just an ordinary day for me. "We could go after the sword right now."

"I've had enough of this place for a while," said Sebastian dryly. "Besides, I have a feeling we're going to need all our wits about us when we go after the sword."

I nodded and tightened my grip on Sebastian's hand. I then took a deep breath, and as if I'd said them a thousand times before, the words for leaving Vaneklus leapt off the tip of my tongue, *"Bidh mi gad fhàgail!"*

The rushing sound again filled my ears, and I squeezed Sebastian's hand harder. I felt myself thrown forward, and then I was aware of warm water swirling around me as I blinked open my eyes. I was sitting next to Sebastian on the rocky ledge of the heated pool, and he stirred as I drew a long breath. Looking down, I was surprised to see we were still holding hands in the aquamarine water.

"Welcome back!" squealed Batty, leaping off the ledge and throwing his wings around Sebastian's neck.

Grimacing as he craned his head away from the bat, Sebastian must have noticed our interlocked hands as well, because he quickly let go of me, then raised his hand to touch the medallion as if reassuring himself it was still pinned to his tunic.

I looked over at Aurelius, who scowled at me from a crouched position at the edge of the pool. Water dripped from his fur and whiskers, and he appeared as miserable as I'd ever seen him.

"What happened to you?" I asked, pushing my wet hair off my face.

"When you went into Vaneklus, your physical body collapsed, and you sank down under the water," he replied. "I jumped in and positioned you so *you* wouldn't drown too." His whiskers twitched unhappily as water ran down his furry jowls. "We shall have to be more careful in the future."

Batty let go of Sebastian and hopped onto my shoulder, pressing his snout against my cheek and giving me a loud kiss before flying over to Aurelius.

"Your lynx did not even hesitate," he said admiringly. "He did very well for someone who despises water."

Not even caring I was soaking wet, I pushed myself up onto my knees and threw my arms around Aurelius. He purred softly and rubbed his head against mine.

"Thank you," I said.

He nodded, then pulled back to look at me. I expected him to launch into a lecture on why I shouldn't have saved Sebastian, but to my surprise, his eyes were glowing with pride.

You did it, Kyra, he said. *You brought him back. You recovered a shade from Vaneklus.*

I suppose I did, I said, a disbelieving smile tugging my mouth upwards.

I glanced over at Sebastian, who ran a hand over his face, then smoothed his wet hair back from where it stuck to his forehead. His dark eyes studied me, a mixture of uncertainty and interest combined with a begrudging respect. I wanted to ask him more about his mother, but I suddenly found myself so exhausted I doubted I could even form a coherent sentence. Aurelius sensed my tiredness and quickly jumped into action.

"Kyra needs rest," he said to Batty, who nodded. The lynx's eyes flickered to Sebastian, and he added, almost kindly, "I imagine they both do."

"I will prepare the sofa," said Batty before dematerializing.

Pushing myself out of the water onto the surrounding rocks,

I grunted as I tugged off first one boot, then the other. Tipping them over the heated pool, I let the water drain out, wiggling my toes uncomfortably in my wet socks. It was awkward moving with my clothes plastered to me, but I eventually got to my feet as Sebastian followed my lead and climbed out of the pool. Water pattered from our wet clothes onto the stone floor, and I was relieved to see I wasn't alone in my dishevelment—Sebastian's tunic and breeches stuck to his torso and limbs, and his boots squeaked as he walked over to retrieve his scabbard and jacket from where I'd flung them.

I gathered my water-logged cloak and followed him up a flight of uneven stone steps, worn smooth by time or use, then along a moonstone-lit tunnel back into the living area. A fire was crackling cheerfully in a hollowed-out stone column, and a pillow and thick quilt had been placed on the dark brown sofa. Batty appeared on the back of the sofa and patted it with a wing. I smiled gratefully at him, then was surprised to hear Sebastian say, "I have dry clothes . . . if you want to borrow something."

I hadn't expected such a considerate offer, but I wasn't about to pass it up. "I would love that!"

Following him first to the weapons vault to lock up the scabbard, still containing the unicorn horn, then to his dresser, I waited as he pulled out a black tunic and a pair of dark blue flannel pants.

"These are the smallest things I have," he said. Opening another drawer, he pulled out a belt, which he placed on top of the clothes before handing the pile to me.

"They're perfect," I assured him, eager to change into something dry and lose myself in a deep sleep. "Um, where should I change?"

"Batty can take you down one of the tunnels," he said, leaning tiredly against his dresser, "or you can change here. I'll turn away."

I'd never changed clothes in the presence of a man who wasn't Demitri, and looking at Sebastian, I was suddenly reminded he wasn't just a Daeval, but also a man. At the same time, though, I had serious doubts about my exhausted body's ability to walk more than a few steps.

Thankfully, Aurelius was aware of my fatigue and made the decision for me.

"Go ahead, Kyra," he said, facing Sebastian and sitting down on his haunches. "I shall keep watch."

Sebastian rolled his eyes, but turned away, and I quickly changed into the dry clothes. Pulling Sebastian's tunic over my head, I couldn't help but notice how nice it smelled—cool and clean, like the first snow of winter, with a hint of juniper that reminded me of the forest.

"I'm done," I called out. "Do you want me to turn around so you can change, too?"

"Alright," he replied gruffly, and I turned to face the fireplace, extending my hands towards the warmth flowing out and filling the cavern. The sound of wet clothes falling heavily to the ground inexplicably caused my heart to speed up. I'd never seen a man unclothed, outside of anatomy textbooks, and while that wasn't about to change, knowing Sebastian was undressing just a few yards away made me feel something in the pit of my stomach right where nervousness and excitement overlapped.

While intimate relationships were encouraged in Aeles, I'd always been rather shy about the subject, letting my imagination outpace my actual actions. I certainly hadn't imagined my first time alone in a room with a man in various states of undress would be in a cave in Nocens with a Daeval.

Aurelius gave a loud cough. *I trust after we leave, this will not cross your mind again.*

"You can turn around now," called Sebastian, and I focused on spreading my wet clothes in front of the fireplace to dry. I then made my way to the couch and watched as Sebastian climbed into the bed in the nearby alcove. Pulling the quilt over me, I rolled to one side, making space for Aurelius near my feet. He tucked himself into a tight ball and let out a long sigh as Batty smoothed the quilt under my chin. I smiled at him, then, powerless to keep my eyes open, I sank into the sofa and fell asleep.

30

areth sighed and looked down at the book in her lap. She'd read the same page at least three times and still couldn't remember what had happened. That was completely unlike her, as normally she lost herself in books and required an obvious interruption—a shout, a snap, or having something tossed at her—to redirect her attention. She set the book aside, dimmed the nearby lantern, and lay back on the reclining sofa. It wasn't yet morning; dawn was still little more than a possibility that would eventually be realized, but she hadn't been able to sleep. Perhaps that was only normal so close to one's wedding.

Water sluiced down a sheet of granite behind her, and the curtains surrounding the sofa billowed in the cool night air. Crickets chirped in the shadows of the terrace, and a night heron cawed overhead. Looking up, she traced the familiar constellations with her eyes, imagining lines of moonlight connecting the twinkling orbs. Did her intended husband know the stories behind the stars? She would be glad to teach him, if he cared to learn. It was also possible he knew stories of constellations she had never heard of before, and the thought brought a hopeful smile to her face.

Tucking her long black hair behind an ear, Kareth considered the little she knew of the man she was to marry. His name was Schatten, and he was a gifted military strategist and soldier. He was to be the other half of the newly established Felserpent monarchy, assuming responsibil-

ity for the land and everyone in it after the passing of the Great Serpent. Schatten was also a Daeval, his veins filled with silver blood as hers ran with gold.

A Daeval . . . at any other time in Astral history, merely speaking *to one would have been unthinkable, much less marrying one. Kareth pursed her lips, remembering the numerous soldiers she'd healed, injured during one of the seemingly endless battles against Daevals. She'd grown up in a realm at war and for years she'd offered to travel with the military, providing immediate healing to those who were wounded. To her disappointment, she'd always been told she was "too important" for such dangerous work, given her recovrancy abilities. She'd done what she could from the safety of the capital, recovering the shades of soldiers who had died before their time, but there had still been far too many legitimately claimed by Laycus and taken further into Vaneklus. She'd felt each loss keenly, and not just because of the loss to the realm—every death had been a reminder her brother could be called upon at any time to join the Astral military.*

Looking out into the darkness, Kareth gently ran a fingertip over her sana bracelet, lingering on Lleiaf. The smallest of the seven beads was a bright citrine stone known as The Rememberer. Rubbing it, she recalled the fear that had been with her for as long as she could remember, a constant tension in the back of her mind, the knowledge she might one day return home and find Donovan gone, sent off to fight in the far reaches of Aeles-Nocens. When she'd been given the chance to stop the blood feud once and for all, she hadn't hesitated . . . while she'd wanted to save the realm, she'd first and foremost wanted to protect her brother.

A healer and a warrior . . . would she and Schatten have anything in common? As a soldier, Schatten was trained to kill; as a Recovrancer, she worked to restore life. Sometimes she felt as if she spent more time in Vaneklus than in her own realm . . . although, admittedly, she sometimes visited the realm of the dead solely to see Laycus, taking him news of the living in exchange for hearing what he'd learned from the shades he'd ferried.

She ran a hand across her forehead, worry creasing her brow. Everyone had such high hopes for this marriage. She wouldn't disappoint them, no matter how difficult being partnered with a Daeval might be. She barely knew anything about their kind, but her healing mentor, the Princeps Shaman, had dispelled many of the myths she'd grown up with and assured her no harm would come to her as a result of her marriage. That was a relief, at least. Unlike many of her friends, Kareth hadn't spent her childhood dreaming of her wedding; in fact, she hadn't been certain she would marry at all. If she wasn't destined to wed for love, then doing so to protect her kind was certainly the next best reason, a noble one, even if it wasn't nearly as romantic.

The sound of sandals slapping lightly against stone reached her ears, and she watched as a willowy figure made her way up the stairs of the outdoor terrace. It was Gathalia, the Princeps Shaman. Streaks of white were dispersed liberally throughout her auburn hair, long and held in place by a slim copper circlet that rested against her forehead. The circlet was inlaid with a large moonstone, and Kareth had often wondered what it would be like to wear the headpiece. Alone in her room or out in the forest, she had imagined one day holding the esteemed position herself.

As if reading her thoughts, Gathalia smiled as she drew near. "Soon you shall wear a different crown, but one no less important."

Kareth moved to swing her legs over the sofa in order to rise and offer the proper respect, but Gathalia shook her head.

"Stay," she said. "I have a gift for you."

She set down a small wooden chest, and with a word, the light in the nearby lantern burned brighter. Kareth leaned forward, curiosity shining in her eyes. She'd already received so many presents from friends and family—jewelry, ornate gowns, new books to establish a royal library, as well as paintings, sculptures, and other works of art to decorate the castle that would be her new home.

Gathalia raised the lid of the chest, and Kareth gasped. Inside, nestled among folds of blue velvet, lay two gleaming, golden bracelets.

"They're beautiful," she said reverently.

Gathalia smiled, the expression of a teacher who has one final lesson to impart to her student.

"I hope under my tutelage you have learned the function of a thing is always more important than the appearance," she said. "Function reveals, whereas appearance too often conceals."

Kareth blushed. "Of course," she said. "I simply assumed the bracelets were only decorative, as most jewelry is."

"You must learn to look past your own assumptions," said Gathalia, reaching down and removing one of the bracelets from the chest. She gestured for Kareth to hold out her hands and placed a bracelet around each wrist. As Kareth traced her fingers over the cool metal, the image of a black dragon rose to the surface. It swam in a graceful circle around her wrist, arching its neck proudly, and Gathalia chuckled.

"Nerudian's signature," she said. "Well, he has earned the right to mark his work. I gave him the stone heart of a fallen meteorite and asked him to meld it with gold, thereby blending earth and sky. Not many dragons could perform such alchemy, but he managed it beautifully. He will make a wonderful advisor in the art of metallurgy."

Kareth nodded eagerly. She'd only heard stories of the ancient black dragon and was both honored and a little overwhelmed he would be attending her coronation.

Gathalia knelt beside the sofa and placed a hand on each of the bracelets.

"This gift is not merely the bracelets, although they are lovely, but also that of communication," she explained. The moonstone on her forehead began to glow, bathing her face in a milky white light. "We still have much to learn about how Cyphers can speak directly into each other's minds," she said, referring to the creatures that roamed the land and spoke with one another using strange telepathic abilities. "But one of them assisted Nerudian in creating the bracelets, and as a result, while wearing them, you shall be able to speak to your husband as they do—using only your mind."

Kareth's eyes widened, and she looked at the bracelets. "Schatten will have bracelets too? And we'll be able to speak . . . as we think?"

"Yes," replied Gathalia. "You will speak into each other's minds as easily as if you were conversing face-to-face, regardless of how far apart you are. Such an ability will serve you well in court, astounding those who seek to divide you, while at the same time making you appear united and wise. It will also have the far greater effect of strengthening your marriage so you will know each other as well as you know your own selves."

She closed her eyes, and when she opened them, they were as white as the moonstone on her forehead. Kareth felt a power course from the woman's hands into the bracelets, causing them to vibrate before they fell still around her wrists. Gathalia blinked, and her eyes returned to their usual warm brown as a sad smile crossed her face.

"I could not care for you more if you were related to me by blood, rather than by virtue of our shared profession," she said gently, her voice wrapping around Kareth like a familiar shawl. "You would have made a truly great **Princeps Shaman**, but now, rather than healing one patient at a time, you will heal an entire realm. There is no one better suited for the task."

Kareth thanked her, hoping she would one day believe the woman's words even though she had trouble accepting them now. Gathalia rose and moved to sit on the wide stone railing, her feet swinging freely beneath the embroidered hem of her long gown.

"Have you decided who your royal advisor will be?" she asked.

Kareth gave a decisive nod. "Yes. I'm assigning the position to Bartholomew."

Gathalia's eyebrows raised almost up to her circlet, and she considered this for a moment before dipping her head in acknowledgment.

"It is a wise move to include a Cypher . . . a being neither Astral nor Daeval," she finally said. "It will send a message that you value wisdom over blood, which is as it should be. And he is wise, make no mistake. He was the one who assisted Nerudian." She shook her head and sighed, then let out a surprised laugh. "I simply assumed the first royal advisor to the Felserpent Queen would be . . . well, I don't know who, but certainly not a bat."

"You must learn to look past your own assumptions," said Kareth, a mischievous grin pulling her rounded cheeks upwards. Gathalia laughed at hearing her own words used against her. Crooking the first two fingers of her right hand so they resembled the fangs of a snake, she pressed them against her heart and with a smile full of love, said, "Hail, Felserpent Queen."

31

SEBASTIAN

J lifted my head and blinked out into the cavern, listening to the sound of rustling fabric. Reaching for the dagger strapped to the leg of my nightstand, I readied myself to slip out of bed and confront the intruder until I remembered . . . the sound was coming from Kyra, who was probably just rolling over in her sleep.

I let my head fall back against my pillow. It was unnerving having anyone in my cavern, much less an Astral, and a woman, at that. The unusual circumstances no doubt explained the odd dream I'd just had, because there was absolutely no other explanation as to why I would imagine someone named Kareth, who looked exactly like the woman on my sofa, preparing to marry a Daeval with the name I'd given to myself in a previous dream.

That is not the only explanation, offered Batty. He was lying on his back on the far side of my bed, his wings folded over his protruding belly. I considered kicking at him and forcing him to move, but he'd only come back once I returned to sleep.

Of course it is, I replied. *Nothing else makes sense.*

Oh, well, if sense is what you are concerned with, then I suppose you are right, he agreed.

There was no supposing about it . . . even though I couldn't shake the unsettled feeling that had come over me, seeping beneath my skin and settling next to the fire in my blood. I looked down at the golden bracelet, wishing it would reveal some sort of answer, but it simply lay there, quiet and cool around my wrist. Rolling over onto my side, it was a long time before I fell back asleep.

Stretching my arms and legs against the soft sheets I'd spent an exorbitant amount of money on, I glanced over at the clock. One benefit of living in a cave was never being awakened by the unwanted glare of the sun intruding where it didn't belong. To my surprise, it was late at night, which meant Kyra and I had slept for over ten hours. My stomach growled loudly, followed by the sound of something falling and rolling along the floor from the part of the cave I used as a kitchen. That could only mean one thing—my Cypher had taken it upon himself to prepare food.

Pushing myself up into a sitting position, I winced at the soreness throbbing through my body, but all things considered, it wasn't a bad price to pay for being brought back to life. I turned the knobs on a few lanterns to illuminate the space, then shuffled into the living area just as Kyra sat up and yawned broadly. Her hair was tousled, and she gave me a smile that still bore the traces of sleep.

"Who is hungry?" called Batty, and Kyra's eyes lit up as she pushed aside the quilt and jumped to her feet. It was decidedly odd to see someone else wearing my clothes. They were still too large for her, even though she'd belted the tunic around her waist and rolled up the pant legs.

"I'm starving!" she said and fell into step beside me until we reached the table and she slid into a chair. The bat set down a plate of oatcakes, followed by a pitcher of syrup and a bowl of freshly cut fruit, assuring Kyra nothing he had prepared would compromise her planterian diet.

I only *just* resisted the urge to roll my eyes and instead focused on filling my empty stomach. After a few moments, Kyra put down her fork and looked at me. Her expression turned thoughtful, and a flicker of hesitation crossed her face.

"I want to tell you something—or ask you something—well, both, I suppose—but it's very personal."

My heart stuttered against my rib cage, and a roar filled my ears as flames danced inside my blood, ready to be summoned. What in the burning realm was she about to say? Forcing myself to breathe, I concentrated on chewing the bite I'd just taken, then gave a slow nod for her to continue.

"Back in the unicorn sanctuary, when I went into the pond after you, I was able to get a good sense of . . . your body." She ducked her head and dropped her eyes as her next words poured out. "Not because I was prying or exploring, but as a healer, when I touch someone for more than a few seconds, I can't help but learn about any illnesses or injuries they've ever had. When it comes to injuries, the body stores so much more information than we think—it actually assigns a trace memory, so there's always information available about when the wound was made, how it happened, and where it took place."

She finally brought her eyes back to mine. "You have a lot of injuries. They've all healed, and some of them you got as part of your *work*. But others . . . you have welts from being burned, on purpose. There are wounds on your arms where you were cut, on purpose. Your back is covered with scars where you were whipped. Some of the injuries, they've healed over more than once, which means you were reinjured . . . on purpose."

Fear and sadness and something else I couldn't quite place filled her eyes. "You were tortured, Sebastian. And every one of those injuries has a trace memory that says it happened in Rynstyn."

So many unspoken questions hung in the air between us, the tension expanded outwards to fill the entire cavern. I sat perfectly still, worried if I moved that everything around me would shatter, breaking into something that could never be fixed and changing everything I had worked so hard to establish.

Kyra tucked her hair behind her ear. "Is that how you knew it was possible for someone with silver blood to be in Aeles without setting off the Blood Alarm? Because you've been there before? Is that where you wore a suppressor medallion or something like it?"

This was it. I could lie or simply refuse to participate in the conversation, leaving Kyra with her questions and protecting my past. Or, I could tell her the truth, risk her disbelief—or worse, her pity—but also have a chance at enacting justice on the Astrals and the system that had harmed me.

Batty was surprisingly silent, perhaps knowing I'd be less inclined to do whatever he suggested. Finally, after a long silence, I made my decision.

"Yes," I said, choosing to tell Kyra the truth. "That's how I knew, and that's where they put a medallion on me."

"They?" she asked, although the uneasiness on her face said she already had a good idea of what I was going to say.

"The Astrals who imprisoned me."

Kyra's mouth fell open, but no sound came out. She glanced at her Cypher, then lowered her head into her hands, massaging her fingertips against her forehead.

I stared across the cavern at the lanterns interspersed between clusters of yellow and white quartz and chose my words carefully.

"Thirteen years ago, I was taken to a facility in the mountains of Rynstyn. It was run by Astrals conducting experiments on my kind. They wanted to see if they could change us. They started by trying to alter our blood, and when that didn't work, they turned to behavioral modification."

Kyra raised her head, and her eyes were wide. "Why did they want to change you?"

"Because most Astrals think my kind shouldn't exist," I shrugged. "If they can't kill us, I suppose they thought changing us was the next best thing."

"How did you end up there?" she asked, a look of horror unfurling across her face. "Did they come to Nocens and kidnap you?"

"No," I said, "at least, that's not how I got there. I'm not certain about the others; we weren't exactly encouraged to interact. I was given to them." As Kyra would no doubt have numerous questions about that statement, I added, "After my mother's death, my father didn't want anything to do with me, so giving me to Astrals who wanted to experiment on Daevals was a perfect solution for him."

Kyra's hands rose to her mouth, and her eyes filled with tears. Of course someone so sheltered would be unable to imagine a parent treating their child in such a terrible manner. At one time, I wouldn't have imagined it, either, but now it was so familiar it didn't conjure any feelings except a pervasive sense of fatigue.

"How old were you?" Kyra croaked hoarsely.

"Seven," I said. "I lived there for almost two years, and then I escaped."

"How?"

"My father didn't know I could make portals, so when the Astrals asked him if I had any special skills or abilities besides pyromancy, he said no. There were wards in place against portals, and other powers, too, but I tested them every single day I was there. One day, I got lucky. I don't know why the barriers were down, but that was all I needed."

Kyra shivered in her chair and wrapped her arms around herself. "Do you remember the names of any Astrals at the facility? Even a first name?"

I shook my head. "They didn't use their names in front of us. I might recognize a picture, but it was so long ago, I'm not sure."

Kyra drew a shaky inhale and bit down on her bottom lip, lost in her own thoughts. As much as I despised Astrals, even I could recognize this had to be difficult for her, hearing things about her kind she'd never imagined possible. Eventually, she shifted in her chair, appearing to have redirected her attention.

"In Vaneklus, you said your mother didn't just die . . . she was killed. Can you—" Kyra abruptly stopped, and judging by her conflicted expression, she was trying to decide whether it was appropriate to ask questions about my mother.

I fixed my gaze on the glazed ceramic plate in front of me. "Normally, I'd end any conversation about my mother right there," I admitted in a rare moment of brutal honesty, "but if I want you to ask Laycus about her, you're going to need information."

Kyra tilted her head to one side. "Did you hear the Shade Transporter introduce himself to me? I don't remember telling you his name . . . in fact, I'm certain I only referred to him as the Shade Transporter." She leaned forward slightly. "Did he speak to you before I found you or is there something else you aren't telling me?"

I shook my head, confused. "I didn't even see him before you arrived. Once you appeared, I could see the two of you speaking, but I couldn't hear anything. It was like the fog absorbed any sound, which seemed odd at first, but I didn't know what to expect, given where we were."

Of course, none of that explained how I knew the Shade Transporter's name, but then, it hit me.

"My dream," I said, which caused Kyra to startle slightly in her chair. "I had a dream last night," I explained, "and in it, a Recovrancer referred to the Shade Transporter as Laycus."

Kyra leaned forward. "What else happened in your dream?"

I drummed my fingers against the black and grey granite table top, not at all happy with the idea of telling Kyra I'd had a dream about a woman who looked exactly like her.

"If it helps," she added, "I had an odd dream last night too. I'm sure it's because we were so tired, our imaginations ran away with us."

I decided to go with the simplest explanation.

"In my dream, a woman was being given gold bracelets, like ours. She was a Recovrancer and when she mentioned the Shade Transporter, she referred to him as Laycus."

Kyra stared at me as if I'd suddenly grown the horns and tail her kind no doubt gave mine in Astral children's books. "That's impossible."

I stopped drumming my fingers. "Are you saying I'm lying?"

"No, I'm saying I don't understand," she said. "I had the same dream." She recounted what had occurred in her dream, and the more she spoke, the stranger I felt. Her eyes were bright as she rested her forearms against the table. "Have you ever heard of a Felserpent King or Queen before?"

"Not outside of my dreams," I replied.

"Dreams?" she repeated, noting my use of the plural form of the word.

"I had another one . . . about a warrior named Schatten."

Kyra held my gaze. "Was he able to control fire because of the Great Serpent's gift?"

I turned to Batty, who was sitting on the table near the bowl of fruit, eagerly watching my exchange with Kyra.

"Are we having the same dreams because of these?" I demanded, pointing to the bracelet.

"Well, you are connected to one another, so it seems reasonable you could share dreams," Batty said, taking a large bite out of a red and gold pear.

"But why would we dream about things we've never heard of before?" pressed Kyra. "I understand using your imagination *after* you've heard of someone, but we only became aware of Kareth and Schatten *during* our dreams."

"Perhaps you are simply reliving things," suggested the bat, "as opposed to imagining them."

Kyra gave me a quizzical look, and I was about to tell her to ignore the Cypher when I recalled what I'd seen studying the history of the bracelets. I shared what I'd witnessed and how the scenes fit with the two dreams we'd had, then added, "Nerudian did say he made the bracelets ages ago for a king and queen."

Excitement spread through Kyra's eyes. "He must have been talking about the Felserpent King and Queen! Perhaps they used the bracelets to record their memories and *that's* what we're seeing in our dreams! Although," her brow furrowed slightly, "in my dream, at least, Kareth looked quite a bit like me . . . and in the first dream, Schatten looked like you. Why would we be inserting ourselves into others' memories?"

I shrugged. "Even if the bracelets recorded their memories, we have no way of knowing what they looked like. It makes sense we'd use ourselves in their places."

Kyra nodded, and her mouth crept upwards into a smile. "That's true. It's not as if I know another Daeval who could stand in for Schatten."

For some reason, thinking about Kyra dreaming of someone who looked like me sent a tingling sensation across the base of my skull that wasn't entirely unpleasant. Nonplussed, I searched for a way to redirect the conversation.

"Well," I said, "if anyone can tell us more about the Felser-pent King and Queen, it's Nerudian."

Kyra nodded. "After we finish eating, can we go speak with him?" The excitement filling her eyes quickly faded, darkening to unhappiness bordering on anger. "If Kareth really was an Astral, I can only imagine what the Aelian government would do to erase someone like her from our history. She also mentioned being a Recovrancer, but unfortunately, I know from my own research she's not mentioned anywhere in the Aelian Archives."

"I *hate* to interrupt," Aurelius said in a voice that made it clear he didn't feel the least bit bad about interrupting, "but Halo just contacted me." He fixed an unhappy gaze on Kyra. "It seems Demitri needs to speak with you."

I recalled Kyra mentioning Demitri earlier and assumed Halo must be her Astral friend's Cypher.

Kyra's face paled, making her freckles stand out more than usual.

"Is it about my family?" she asked, worry filling her voice.

"No," said Aurelius, "it's something to do with Adonis. Apparently, he has more questions for you, or new questions for you —regardless, he wants to meet with you as soon as possible."

"That's odd." Kyra looked at me. "When Adonis interviewed me before, he used a captum. He could easily review our conversation."

"Unless this has to do with something else," said Aurelius darkly. "Such as recent events in the unicorn sanctuary."

Kyra and I both stared at him, and he quickly raised a paw.

"I'm not saying the two are related," clarified the lynx, "but I do think it's best to see what he wants."

"It could be a trap," I said, prompting Aurelius to roll his eyes as Kyra shook her head.

"No, Adonis wouldn't do that. I've known him since childhood. I trust him, and I agree with Aurelius—I should at least see what he wants."

The length of time you'd known someone was in no way related to how trustworthy they were, but I could see there would be no convincing Kyra of that.

"Shall I contact Alistair about using Caz's intersector?" asked Batty, swallowing the last of the pear.

"With the suppressor medallion, I can open a portal from here," I reminded him.

Kyra grimaced. "I think I'd prefer to use the medallion as little as possible, at least for now. I don't mind going to Caz's."

I nodded at Batty, who reached out to Alistair and soon informed us we were more than welcome to use the intersector.

"In fact," he added, fixing his beady eyes on me, "Caz is at his Diomhair Way office now and would like to discuss something with you. It seems Dunston will be involved as well."

As Batty led Kyra down a tunnel to change clothes, I ducked into my alcove and slipped on a clean tunic and breeches. Shoving my feet into my boots, I returned to the living area just as Kyra emerged from a passageway. She was wearing her now dry clothes and left mine in a neatly folded pile on the sofa.

I opened a portal to Vartox, praying to the Fates the doorway would cooperate and thanking them when it did. I still needed to talk to Kyra about going to LeBehr's, but that would have to wait until she returned.

We made it quickly to Caz's, as he had kindly decreased the distance his antiportal wards extended from his office. I appreciated that, as the more time Kyra and I spent walking around Nocens, the greater the likelihood another Daeval would recognize her golden blood and raise a fuss. I suspected, though, Caz would remind me of his "kindness" at some later date and make it clear I owed him.

Caz ushered us into his office, but was unusually preoccupied with a pile of papers on his desk, such that he did little more than wave goodbye to Kyra as she headed towards the intersector.

As Kyra strode onto the platinum plate, I couldn't keep from stepping forward.

"Be careful," I said, and although I'd intended to issue the words as a command, given that I needed the Recovrancer to come back quickly, there was something embarrassingly imploring about my tone . . . something that wasn't quite a request but might have been a wish. No doubt it had to do with our dream—spending so much time thinking about someone who looked exactly like Kyra was making me feel more concerned about the Astral than I otherwise would be.

A surprised but appreciative smile flickered across Kyra's face. "Thank you," she said. "Hopefully this won't take long, and I'll be back soon."

Aurelius scowled as he dematerialized, and Kyra gave me a quick wave before she was whisked back to Aeles, leaving me to see what Caz wanted.

32

KYRA

With my family gone, there was no need to use the intersector in the woods, so I held the coordinates to my parents' house in mind and arrived on their home intersector, stepping off the platinum plate onto the front porch. Racing inside the house, I retrieved my peerin and told Demitri to come over. Almost immediately, he appeared on the porch and let himself inside.

"Well, I must say, you don't look any worse for wear after being in Nocens," he sighed. When I'd first told him about my agreement with Sebastian, he'd alternated between being terrified I would be caught and shocked I was willing to break Astral laws; eventually, though, he'd agreed it was worth the risk, since Daevals clearly had resources our kind didn't, given how Astrals felt about Recovrancers.

"I'm fine," I assured him, hugging him tight. "Although I'm curious why Adonis is so insistent on seeing me."

Demitri leaned back against the staircase. "It must be serious if he reached out to me looking for you."

"Well," I said, "let's find out what he wants."

I contacted the Astral soldier, and within a few minutes, I heard the sound of heavy boots crossing the front porch . . . *two* pairs of heavy boots, which I hadn't expected.

Taking a deep breath, I opened the front door and then very nearly slammed it shut. Standing next to Adonis in a dark blue military uniform was the Astral guard who had sent Sebastian to his death in the unicorn sanctuary.

"May we come in?" asked Adonis politely, ignoring my rude behavior. Feeling as though everything was happening at a far slower speed than usual, I stepped aside and allowed the soldiers to enter. As introductions were made, my mind kept circling back to the only explanation for this unbelievable turn of events— Lieutenant Coran must have described the sanctuary intruders to Adonis, and my friend had recognized me from the description.

Demitri smiled from his place at my side. "Well, well, Adonis, fancy seeing you two times in one week. What can we do for you?"

Adonis glanced at Demitri, and an uncharacteristic frown settled across the soldier's wide mouth. "You can let Kyra tell me what she was doing in the unicorn sanctuary with the same Daeval who managed to break into Aeles a few days ago."

Anyone else would have been so caught off-guard by such a statement they would have either been rendered speechless or begun stammering incoherently. But Demitri wasn't anyone else, and his unflappable façade wasn't the slightest bit ruffled. "Well, since I don't make it a practice of speaking for Kyra, of course, let's hear what she has to say," he said smoothly.

He turned towards me, and even though his mouth was smiling, the expression didn't reach his eyes; he was obviously hurt I'd kept something from him and confused as to why. Pushing aside my guilt, I met Adonis's hard gaze.

"What do you want to know?" I asked.

Adonis continued to look at me but directed his question to the other soldier. "Is this her?"

"It's her, alright," replied Lieutenant Coran. I shifted my gaze to him, and his grey eyes snapped angrily. "Although I almost didn't recognize you without your Daeval *friend*."

I bit my tongue to keep from firing back a retort that would have done nothing beyond momentarily making me feel better.

The silence stretched on, until Adonis crossed his arms and shifted his stance.

"Tell me everything," he demanded.

I looked at Aurelius; it was a gamble, but it was also now or never. He sighed but nevertheless dipped his head, and I nodded in return. Then, turning back to Adonis, I said, "First, tell me what you know about the experiments Astrals have been conducting on Daevals in Rynstyn."

33

❦

SEBASTIAN

J settled into the chair across from Caz's desk as Dunston strode into the office and dropped into the seat beside me with a grunt. His Cypher, Wayah, materialized near his feet and gave Alistair a respectful nod, which she returned before settling herself onto a thick red and white carpet.

"Before we get started," Dunston said, turning towards me, "is this a good time to ask about the Astral woman Eslee saw you with recently here at Caz's?"

I wasn't surprised Eslee had mentioned the encounter to her father, as the two of them were incredibly close, but even so, I still wished she'd kept it to herself.

"Remember when I needed a way into Aeles?"

Dunston snorted. "As if I'd ever forget!"

I told him Kyra had accidentally come through my portal when I'd been escaping the Astral realm and I'd needed Caz's help to return her home.

Dunston's eyes widened. "It's a wonder she didn't raise the alarm herself when she saw you in her realm!" he exclaimed. "Good thing the Fates obviously had other plans for you."

"So it would seem," I agreed. "Interestingly enough, her father was Arakiss Valorian."

"That *is* interesting," replied Dunston politely before leaning towards me. "Eslee also happened to mention she was quite lovely. Friendly too. Are you, by chance, planning on staying in touch with her?"

Caz chuckled. "Really, Dunston, you hate everything about Astrals! Stop trying to play matchmaker between Sebastian and that fetching, intelligent, gifted young woman."

I scowled at Caz, and Dunston held up a finger.

"I don't hate everything about Astrals," he corrected his brother. "I love their money. And I'm not trying to play matchmaker . . . I'm simply asking a question based on an observation Eslee made outside this very office."

I certainly couldn't tell Dunston or Caz the real reason I was staying in contact with Kyra, but by not telling them, I was allowing them to believe I might be developing a romantic interest in the woman. That irritated me, but there was no way around it.

"I'll most likely see her again," I finally muttered.

Dunston responded by laughing and slapping a hand on the desk. "Then I insist you bring her with you when you come for dinner! It would be nice for Eslee to have a new friend, and it's time Devlin learned Daevals aren't alone in the universe. I promise everyone will be on their best behavior."

Caz wiggled his eyebrows. "I make no such promise about my behavior."

"I'm not certain when she's coming back, but thank you," I said stiffly, then quickly redirected the conversation to a safer subject. "Anyway, we're not here to talk about me. What do you need, Caz?"

Caz leaned forward and clasped his hands, resting them on top of the desk before speaking in a tone I'd only rarely heard him use. "I've asked you both here because I've been hearing some very unsettling rumors lately, and if anyone can confirm or deny them, it's you two." He paused, then tapped the knuckles of his still-clasped hands against the smooth wood. "I've heard Dae-val children have started going missing."

A faint chill ran down my spine, as if an icy finger had gently stroked my back. The flames stirred in response, as they always did when I felt unsettled, ready to be summoned.

"Missing?" repeated Dunston. "As in, kidnapped and held for ransom?"

"No," replied Caz. "At first, it was just a whisper here and there about some child who lived on the streets—they hadn't turned up at one of the charity meal handouts, or they weren't seen at a refuge for a few days. No one knew what happened to them, but no one really cared enough to do more than note it." He scratched his ear. "And then Wilhemina Stormburn's nephew, Gregor, went missing. The boy ran in the worst circles, to be sure, spending his time with pickpockets and petty thieves, but apparently one evening, he didn't return home for dinner. His Cypher did, though, with a story about how his young charge had been taken . . . by Astrals."

"Astrals?!" recoiled Dunston. "In Nocens?"

"It's not forbidden for them to be here," Caz pointed out. "They can easily enter by intersector. They simply choose not to."

This was likely because Daevals had historically done terrible things to any Astral who visited our realm without the express permission and protection of the Nocenian government. But I didn't correct Caz.

"I don't see why the boy's Cypher would lie," mused Dunston, fingering the large diamond pendant on the lapel of his coat.

I sat up a little straighter in my chair as an all-too-familiar feeling spread through me. It wasn't fear, exactly . . . more akin to dread. "Could our government have let the Astrals in? Or at least turned a blind eye to their being here?"

"It's possible," admitted Caz, "although even *I* have trouble imagining the money or favors it would take to let such a thing happen."

"Did Wilhemina believe her nephew's Cypher?" I asked.

"She did, but she had no idea where to start or whom to speak with," said Caz. "Fortunately, when Wilhemina doesn't know what to do, she equates doing more of anything with being successful. She made the rounds in the government and someone or other agreed to follow up. Nothing came of it until a few days later, when her nephew's body was found in an alley."

His expression darkened. "Perhaps the most important piece of information is what *wasn't* found . . . according to an autopsy, there wasn't a single drop of blood in Gregor's body."

Aside from my nostrils flaring, I was careful to keep my face as inscrutable as possible. Was it really possible Astrals were continuing the work they'd started on me over a decade ago?

"Was there anything else notable about the body?" I asked, keeping my voice level.

"Aside from some open wounds, no."

"So, other than the word of Gregor's Cypher, is there any *actual* evidence linking this to Astrals?" inquired Dunston.

"Not that I'm aware of," said Caz with a shake of his head.

"When they performed the autopsy, did they examine Gregor's injuries for trace memories?" I asked.

Caz scrunched up his face as he often did when thinking or gathering information from Alistair before turning his attention back to me. "What are trace memories?"

I shared what Kyra had told me about injuries, and both Daevals appeared impressed. "I do believe that woman is going to be the best *Princeps Shaman* Aeles has ever seen!" grinned Caz triumphantly, as if this somehow boded well for him. "I'll make some calls and see if our healers can uncover Gregor's trace memories. Hopefully that's not solely an Astral skill; otherwise, we might need to get Kyra involved."

I didn't necessarily like the idea of involving Kyra in anything beyond obtaining Rhannu, but if she was the only way to access Gregor's trace memories and incriminate the Astrals who'd harmed him . . . well, like any intelligent fighter, I would use whatever weapons were at my disposal, including the golden-blooded healer.

Caz's eyes burned feverishly. "If Gregor's body proves he received his injuries in Aeles . . ." his voice trailed off, but I knew what he was implying. The Nocenian government hadn't retaliated over what Astrals had done to me because I hadn't told anyone besides Dunston and Caz, but if the regents of my realm received proof of Astral experimentation, their vengeance would be swift and brutal.

"Wait a minute," interjected Dunston, "it's one thing to say Astrals came here and did something to one of ours to stir up trouble. It's something else *entirely* to say they kidnapped a Daeval and took him into their realm." He looked at me. "Do you think it's the same group who tortured you?"

"I don't know," I replied.

"This is terribly disconcerting," worried Caz. "So, I take it neither of you have heard anything about Gregor, or missing Daeval children, or Astrals being in Nocens?"

Dunston shook his head. "This is the first I'm hearing of any of it," he said.

"Me too," I nodded. "But if this involves the money and politics you suspect, Caz, there's no telling how deep it goes. Eventually, too many folks will be involved, and someone will slip up. That'll be our way in."

Of course, I wasn't going to just sit around and wait; I'd start my own reconnaissance as soon as I could. If that rehabilitation program I had survived was somehow still operating, there wasn't a moment to lose.

34

KYRA

*A*donis blinked at me, taken aback and obviously confused. "What experiments? What are you talking about?"

"I'm talking about how Astrals have done terrible things to Daevals somewhere in Rynstyn!"

Demitri gaped openly at me as Adonis and Lieutenant Coran looked at one another.

"Kyra," Adonis finally said, "if this is an attempt to avoid discussing why you were with a Daeval in the unicorn sanctuary, it's not a good idea." His voice held a warning note, and Demitri immediately stepped closer to me. While he wasn't intimidating in the manner of someone like Sebastian, there was no end to his loyalty to me, and such unwavering devotion could be daunting in its own way.

"The two subjects aren't mutually exclusive," he said, his voice cool as winter frost. "There's no reason we can't discuss both."

"Except that what Kyra's talking about doesn't exist, whereas we have proof of her being where she shouldn't have been with a Daeval!" snapped Adonis. The look he gave me was equal parts frustrated and condescending. "Let me guess—you heard about these supposed experiments being done on Daevals *from* a Daeval." He glanced at the other soldier. "Sebastian, you said his name was?"

Lieutenant Coran nodded, and I grimaced, wishing he hadn't heard me shout out Sebastian's identity.

"I did hear about it from Sebastian," I admitted. As Adonis rolled his eyes and ruffled his long hair, I added, "I didn't tell you and Senator Rex everything that happened when I fell through the portal. Sebastian assumed I was coming after him to hurt him, which didn't make sense, until he told me what other Astrals had done to him. He was tortured . . . locked up and used as an experiment. He let me examine the trace memories of his injuries, and they were all inflicted in Rynstyn. I told him I wanted to see the facility for myself, so he agreed to try and show me." I held the soldier's gaze, silently pleading for him to believe me. "You're a healer, too, Adonis . . . you know trace memories can't be faked or altered."

Adonis grunted unhappily and began pacing across the foyer, his boots thudding against the blue slate floor. Eventually, he made his way into the formal living room, where he sank down onto a sofa, knees splayed outwards.

"You're the best healer I know, Kyra," he said as we joined him. Lieutenant Coran took a wingback chair as Demitri and I settled onto the white loveseat opposite Adonis. "If you say that's how Sebastian received his injuries, I'm certain you truly believe it. But I'm also certain I don't trust Daevals, and there's more to this than we, or you, know."

"That's why we were in Rynstyn," I said, relieved to have hit upon a way to explain our being in the sanctuary. "I wanted to see the facility for myself. But Sebastian was only a child when he was taken there, so he didn't remember exactly where it was. We started in the unicorn sanctuary, because I'm at least familiar with it, and then we were going to expand our search."

"How did you manage to get him into Aeles in the first place?" asked Adonis. "Was he using a potion, like we suspected?"

"Yes," interjected Aurelius before I could speak. "Apparently he tinkered with whatever recipe he used the first time he entered Aeles and figured out how to make it last longer."

I cast a small, sorrowful smile at Aurelius, grateful for his help but sad he was having to lie to protect me.

Adonis frowned. "I'm still not convinced."

"How did you coordinate meeting with him?" asked Lieutenant Coran, scratching his head. "Peerins can't communicate across realms."

"No, but Cyphers can, and we met Sebastian's Cypher when we went through the portal," I said. Aurelius corroborated this, and both Demitri and the soldiers sat quietly for a moment, struggling to process my revelation about Cypher communication.

Finally, Adonis spoke.

"I can't condone what you did, Kyra . . . keeping this to yourself when Senator Rex and I questioned you earlier, sneaking around with a Daeval, and potentially endangering any unicorns you might have come across." Conflicting emotions warred across his face as he considered something known only to him. "But if there's any truth to Sebastian's story about being tortured . . ."

Worry filled his gaze, and he looked uncertainly at Lieutenant Coran before turning back to me.

"I want to help you, Kyra," he said. His eyes darted to Demitri before returning to mine. "Really, I do. I suppose . . . well, if you think it's worth looking into, I'll see what I can do."

"Thank you!" I exclaimed, relief exploding across the underside of my chest. "That's all I'm asking. That's all Sebastian wants too. He wasn't trying to get into Aeles to harm anyone."

The two soldiers exchanged disbelieving looks, but thankfully, neither elaborated. Next to me, Demitri ventured a smile at Adonis. "This is awfully nice of you. I'm not sure I can be of any assistance, but if you need help, don't hesitate to let me know."

Adonis gave him an appreciative smile in return. "Thank you. I might take you up on that."

Demitri draped his arm over my shoulders and gave me a squeeze, his grin turning downright cheeky. "That's the extent of my devotion to Kyra . . . I'm even willing to dig around in dusty old military records for her!"

Adonis's smile momentarily wobbled. No doubt he was imagining the repercussions of being caught looking through Astral military records for evidence our kind had engaged in torture. Not wanting him to change his mind, I quickly shared what I knew of Sebastian's time at the experimentation center. Although I didn't know much, Adonis listened closely, nodding every now and then. When I was done, he sighed and rose to his feet.

"It may take me a little while," he cautioned, "but I'll let you know if I find something."

I thanked him and rose, as well, followed by Demitri. Lieutenant Coran extended a hand towards me and gave me a tentative smile.

"No hard feelings, I hope?" he asked.

For a moment, I considered slapping away his hand and telling him exactly what his actions had done to Sebastian. But I couldn't very well get into that without explaining how I'd brought the Daeval back from Vaneklus, so I took the soldier's slightly sweaty hand and shook it. "No hard feelings, Lieutenant."

"Call me Nigel," he replied, his grin expanding. I had to admit, when he wasn't trying to drown Sebastian, there was something likable about him. "I've been partnered with Adonis here, so I'll probably be seeing a lot of you, at least until we sort this out."

"I've never known Adonis to work with a partner," frowned Demitri, his mood immediately shifting as he crossed his arms over his chest. "Usually he just oversees trainees and does . . . you know . . . other military things."

Adonis laughed. "Clearly I need to work harder to advance my career if that's all you think I do!" he said, and the tips of Demitri's ears reddened. Nigel grinned at Adonis, and I didn't miss the way my best friend's eyes narrowed at the easy give and take between the two men.

"Maybe Adonis's supervisors felt the same way as you, Demitri," suggested Nigel, his grey eyes sparkling, "and thought giving Adonis a partner might push him to step it up a little bit. After all, he only got, what was it, *three* awards at our last recognition banquet?"

Now it was Adonis's turn to blush. Rolling his eyes, he muttered, "It's not that important," then glanced at Demitri, who was glaring at the floor. An awkward silence descended over the room and rather than risk any more unpleasantness, I escorted the soldiers out to the porch and bid them goodbye. Closing the door behind them, I leaned my shoulders against the cool metal, then sank down until I was sitting on the ground. Demitri walked over, his annoyance at Nigel put aside, and crouched down in front of me. His eyebrows were raised, and his lips were pressed together in a thin line.

"I have some things to tell you," I said softly.

35

KYRA

Taking a deep breath, I told Demitri exactly what had occurred in the unicorn sanctuary, including Sebastian's death, my return to the realm of the dead, and my first shade recovery. By the time I finished, I had never seen my best friend's eyes so wide.

"So, what happens next?" he asked.

"Now that we have the unicorn horn, we can get the sword Sebastian wants from Vaneklus."

"And then you'll go your separate ways and never speak to each other again?" Demitri arched an eyebrow, and something about his tone suggested he wasn't certain I would give him the answer he hoped for.

I almost said yes, but stopped myself—there was still the matter of what had happened to Sebastian in Rynstyn.

"I suppose that depends on what Adonis discovers," I finally said.

Demitri's scowl deepened. "And what about your recovrancy abilities? Are you planning on saving any more shades? Spending *more* time in Vaneklus?"

I stared at him in surprise, not having expected him to be more distraught over me recovering a shade than sneaking around with a Daeval.

"Why are you so upset?" I asked.

"Because you're not even trying to keep what you can do a secret!" he exclaimed. "I know you didn't choose to be a Recov-rancer, but falling stars, you could choose not to use your abili-ties. Just because you *can* do something doesn't mean you *should*. Perhaps if you didn't keep going into Vaneklus, soon you wouldn't be able to anymore . . . and then things could go back to how they used to be, before this whole mess started!"

I started to speak, but Demitri continued.

"You know what happened to every other Recovrancer in our history . . . they were shunned or sent into exile or worse, they were *killed*! Killed, Kyra! Whether or not that was the right thing to do is beside the point. Being able to do what you can is a death sentence. You have to try to hide it, blend in, pretend you're no different from everyone else."

"But I *am* different from everyone else!" I retorted. "Why can't others just accept that? Why am I the one in the wrong? Why should I have to change?"

"Welcome to my life," he said coldly. "I used to wonder the same things. I'd lie in bed at night, shaking because I was so mad at how unfair things were. I would catalogue every single thing about our realm that needed to change, and I'd come up with argument after argument explaining why accepting those who are different was a good thing. Then, one night, I realized it was a waste of my time. I'm one Astral. I can't change laws and systems that have been in place longer than I've been alive." His face was so hard and still, it momentarily looked as if it had been carved from stone. "Sometimes we just have to accept things the way they are rather than wishing they were different."

His words were similar to the advice Aurelius had given me on numerous occasions, but this time, I didn't agree.

"Demitri, if everyone felt that way, nothing would ever

change. If I do become the *Princeps Shaman*, I'll be in a position where others will listen to me. I'll have the power to make things different, or at the very least, I'll be in a position to ask questions publicly and make Astrals think about things they haven't considered before."

"There's a reason they haven't considered those things before . . . they don't want to," Demitri replied with a sad shake of his head. "Unless it affects them personally, no one will care. They'll choose whatever option is the easiest and least disruptive to their daily lives." He fixed his eyes on mine, and they shone with unshed tears.

"Either the government will find out you're a Recovrancer and you'll never make it to being the *Princeps Shaman*, or you'll get the position and *then* they'll discover your secret and immediately remove you from office." His shoulders sank. "Your father wouldn't have wanted that."

"My father would have accepted me for exactly who I am," I said firmly. "I had hoped my best friend would do the same."

"I do accept you," Demitri said softly. "But you don't understand the repercussions of what you're doing. I don't want to lose you. Do you really want to start a fight you don't have a prayer of winning?"

Up until this point, I'd been so focused on learning about my recovrancy abilities for the sole purpose of retrieving Rhannu, I hadn't given much thought to what my life would look like afterwards. I'd given it *some* thought, of course, in the same way I'd thought about getting married and having children and growing old—the ideas were there, but everything was jumbled and hazy and not at all well-defined.

Did I really believe I could change the entire realm's perspective on Recovrancers? I didn't seem to be persuasive enough to change even my best friend's mind. Was I truly willing to subject myself to such public scrutiny? I'd already been hesitant about having folks speculate over me and my choices. Was trying to bring about change to benefit myself too selfish, given what it might mean for my family?

I closed my eyes, overwhelmed by my questions and afraid of both the answers I had and the answers I didn't. Suddenly, an image of Kareth staring up at the night sky filled my mind. She had been faced with incredibly difficult decisions and had ultimately forgone her chosen career to be one of the two most public figures in her realm. She hadn't shied away from making hard choices, even though they irreversibly changed the course of her entire life. I wished I knew more about her, the laws she'd passed, and the causes she'd championed, but what I knew was enough— if she could be strong without knowing how things would work out, so could I.

I opened my eyes and focused on Demitri.

"Place one pebble in a river and it might be washed away," I said. "But keep placing pebbles in a river and eventually, you'll change the course of the river."

"Your father said that in an Ash Festival speech," he recalled with a faint smile, and I nodded.

"I don't have everything figured out," I said, "but perhaps this happened to me because I'm going to be in a position to do something about it. Whatever the reason, I'm not going to let fear make my decisions for me."

"Perhaps you should," muttered Demitri, but the heat was gone from his voice. He reached out and pulled me into a hug. "Please be careful," he whispered. "I don't know what I'd do without you."

"Fortunately, you'll never have to find out," I assured him. We stayed like that for a few moments, drawing comfort from holding one another and being held, until Demitri eventually said he should be returning to work. I walked him to the intersector, waved as he left, then took the opportunity to call my family, assuring them I felt much better and was getting lots of rest. After saying goodbye, I was just about to reach out to Sebastian when my peerin gave off a pleasant ring.

I opened the hinged copper shell and was surprised to see Senator Rex's face on the chormorite disc. Swallowing hard to fight my surging anxiety, I pressed my fingertip against the lens and accepted the call.

"What luck!" exclaimed Senator Rex with a smile. "I was hoping to catch you. Am I interrupting?"

I told him he wasn't, and after a few pleasantries, his expression turned more serious.

"I debated whether to discuss this with you or your mother, but, in my heart, I believe you are the right choice. I apologize in advance if I was wrong. There is . . . the matter of your father's office." His eyes filled with a compassion that softened his words, although they still caused my heart to constrict. "After all your mother has been through, I didn't want to place another burden on her, although it hardly seems fair to place another on you, either."

I shook my head. "No, I'm glad you reached out to me. I hadn't really thought about it, but I suppose the office needs to be emptied to make room for the next *Princeps Shaman*." Aeles couldn't be expected to function for long without a high-level healer, and while I knew I wasn't ready to assume the position, it still felt wrong for anyone other than my father to have it. Trying to keep any bitterness out of my voice, I said, "May I ask who is being named to the position?"

Senator Rex sighed. "The Senate is still working out the details, but most likely, Healer Omnurion will be named acting *Princeps Shaman*. She's made it clear she doesn't want the assignment to be permanent, but she is willing to hold it until you've completed internship and further decisions can be made."

I expressed my appreciation, and Senator Rex momentarily dropped his gaze.

"It's certainly not personal, Kyra. If it were up to me, we'd leave your father's office exactly as is until you're ready to assume the position, but—"

"It's fine," I said. "I understand." Understanding, however, still didn't keep me from wishing things were different.

"I don't need you to do much," Senator Rex hurried to explain. "If you could just come and label things—I know there are personal mementos your family will like, and you might enjoy keeping some of the books—I'll ensure everything is sent to the proper place. That way Healer Omnurion can move her things in before the start of internship."

"I'll come now," I said, as this was a task I wanted to be done with sooner rather than later. Senator Rex thanked me and noted if his schedule allowed, he would stop by and say hello.

I contacted Sebastian, who handled the delay in recovering the sword better than I'd expected. In fact, it was clear his thoughts were elsewhere, but since I couldn't get a clear read on them, I simply said I'd let him know when I was ready to return to Nocens, then made my way to the intersector and headed off to Celenia.

36

KYRA

S tanding outside the door to my father's office, I glanced down at Aurelius as I fought off the exhaustion seeking to overwhelm me. I'd taken the intersector to the *Donec Medicinae*, hoping to slip in without drawing too much attention, but instead I'd been greeted with countless hugs and condolences from the well-meaning folks who had worked with my father. By the time I finally made it to his office, I was ready to return home and burst into tears.

Aurelius rubbed his head against my leg, and I braced myself, then slowly opened the dark wooden door before me. The clean smell of talc powder instantly filled my nose, followed by the citrus and sandalwood scent my father had worn on special occasions. Everything was exactly as I remembered it the last time I'd been here, before my father and I had gone to visit Marta. Floor-to-ceiling bookshelves made of reclaimed mahogany from the western part of Iscre matched the large desk positioned in front of the window. The saffron yellow curtains were drawn back, letting in the late afternoon sunlight glinting off the various vials and tools strewn across the desk.

Swallowing hard, I stepped inside and closed the door behind me. Pictures of my family lined the walls and shelves, and I stopped before one in particular. It had been taken last year outside our house, and although the professional image capturer had ultimately succeeded in getting a more posed picture, my father had always preferred this candid captum shot.

Deneb was hanging upside down from the porch railing next to his possum, as Enif perched on top of the railing, flapping his arms like they were wings, while Tiberius hooted loudly from his shoulder. The rest of us stood on the ground below—Seren was crouched down examining a flower, oblivious to everything else until Sappho flicked her tongue in my sister's ear, causing her to shout and leap to her feet. I was attempting to stand up straight and smile, with Aurelius positioned regally beside me, but then Flavius stuck his snout through the railing and licked my face, causing me to jump. My mother's Cypher, Dova, bounced up and down, calling out instructions to the image capturer while my parents stood in the middle of the chaos, gazing adoringly at one another as they laughed and shook their heads.

I reached out a shaky hand to touch the picture, attaching an *aleric* tag to the image. It would serve as an invisible label, appearing when someone else touched the picture and directing them to send it to the Valorian home. Then, wiping the tears from my eyes, I began to work my way through the office, attaching *aleric* tags to each book, picture, tool, and piece of furniture. Most of the books I labeled to be sent to my boardinghouse rooms in Celenia, but I directed a few to the family library as well. I had just labeled the last item, a lovely silver tuning fork I'd donated to the *Donec Medicinae*, when a soft rap on the door startled me.

"Come in," I said, my voice thick with pent-up emotion. I would have preferred not to speak with anyone else, but I didn't want to be rude. Senator Rex poked his head inside, then let out a loud exhale as he offered a tired smile.

"I was worried I had missed you!" he said. His cheeks were slightly flushed, as if he'd been running, and his chest rose and fell quickly beneath his gold and scarlet jacket.

"I'm just finishing up," I said, tucking my hair behind my ears before running a hand over my eyes.

"This must have been so difficult," he said gently.

"I just keep expecting my father to walk in," I half-whispered, unable to speak louder over the tightness in my throat. "I can't believe he's really gone."

Senator Rex sighed and stepped inside, leaning against the doorframe.

"I've only been a senator for a few years," he said. "I didn't work closely with your father, but I always admired him. I *did* have the good fortune of working with him on a project these last few months, and I'll always be grateful for the opportunity to learn from his wisdom."

I managed a smile. "He thought highly of you, too. He told my family numerous times how lucky Montem was to have you as one of our senators."

Senator Rex gave me a tight smile, and as his eyes filled with tears, I hurried to redirect the conversation. "What project were you working on with my father?"

The senator cleared his throat.

"We were studying Astral blood," he said. "You probably already know Astrals are superior to Daevals in every way, but you might not know there is one area where they, unfortunately, manage to outpace us—on average, those with silver blood tend to live longer than we do."

That was certainly news to me. How had he come into such information? He must have read the surprise in my eyes, because he added, "Your father participated in a diplomatic talk in Nocens a few months ago. While he was there, he exchanged information with a Daeval healer, just some general facts on average life expectancy, common illnesses, things like that. When I reviewed his role in the talk with him, he mentioned the difference between Astral and Daeval life expectancies, which, of course, caught my attention."

So, my father had visited Nocens, after all. While I'd known such a trip was at least a possibility since receiving Caz's flowers, hearing it confirmed by Senator Rex caused a deep ache to throb across my chest. I had always viewed myself as having an exceptionally close relationship with my father, closer than I had with my mother, although I loved her dearly. Why hadn't he shared something so important with me?

From the corner of my eye, I saw Aurelius twitch his ears. *Just because you didn't know everything about your father doesn't mean you didn't have a close relationship,* he said.

I know, I replied irritably, not wanting to let on how hurt I was. *I just hoped we might learn something about the suppressor medallion. Father going to Nocens still doesn't explain why he had one.*

Senator Rex appeared oblivious to the momentary lapse in my attention and as he continued, his eyes began to shine with excitement, rather than tears. "If there is a way to extend the lives of the citizens I am responsible for—to extend the lives of all Aelian citizens—that bears looking into. So, I arranged for your father to undertake a small study looking at the substantive properties of Astral blood. We had just begun to compare it to Daeval blood, but alas, with your father's passing, the project was placed on hold."

I blinked, desperately wishing I'd misheard the senator. "Where did you get Daeval blood from?"

He gave his head an apologetic shake. "I don't know. I believe it was given to your father by the Nocenian government."

That didn't make sense. Given what I'd learned about Daevals from Sebastian, they would never give something away without expecting something in return.

Senator Rex must have suspected I had additional questions,

because he quickly added, "Unfortunately, even though your father kept me updated on his progress, I wasn't involved in the actual research. I merely ensured he received the time and equipment he needed to perform the work. However," he seemed to choose his next words carefully, "after you settle into your internship with Healer Omnurion, I would be *most* interested in seeing you pick up where your father left off. I'm certain I could arrange it . . . if you're interested."

"I would love to be involved," I assured him as a cold dread stirred in my suddenly knotted stomach. Sebastian had been tortured thirteen years ago—surely my kind weren't still experimenting on Daevals! But how else would my father have acquired silver blood for his research?

There *was* another explanation, of course, and the same thoughts I'd had when Sebastian had told me about his time in Rynstyn rushed into my mind again, too strong for me to push away this time . . . had my father been one of the Astrals experimenting on Daevals? Was *that* why he'd had a suppressor medallion . . . because Daevals were still being brought into Aeles?

My head began to pound, and I apologized to Senator Rex, claiming to be overwhelmed by the process of sorting through my father's things, then excused myself and took my leave.

To my immense relief, I didn't encounter anyone else on my way to the intersector. I wasn't certain I could have managed even a simple conversation, given the questions exploding like miniature firecrackers in my mind and consuming my attention.

Back at my parents' house, I slammed the front door shut and kicked off my boots, leaving them where they landed in the entryway. My father *couldn't* have been involved in something as terrible as what Sebastian had endured. He would never have deliberately harmed any living creature, even those considered enemies by our kind. I marched up the stairs, offering additional assurances to myself with each step, running through memories of my father's kindness towards even the most challenging patients.

Try as I did, however, the words failed to calm the churning emotions trapped inside my rib cage.

This would all be so much easier if I could just ask *him what he was doing with a suppressor medallion and Daevalic blood!* I snapped as Aurelius and I walked into my bedroom. Sitting down on the edge of my bed, I dug my fingers into the soft purple coverlet, immediately feeling terrible for blaming my father for his inability to answer my questions. I also felt angry at being forced to ask such questions . . . and, if I was completely honest, a tiny part of me was afraid of the answers that might be waiting, should I delve deeper into my father's research. Aurelius hopped up beside me and rested his head on my shoulder. My lower lip quivered, and my throat began to burn. Hot tears streamed from my eyes, and, unable to maintain my composure any longer, I doubled over, pressed my face against a pillow, and sobbed.

I was awakened later by the feeling of something vibrating against my wrist. Groggily, I pressed my fingertips against the gold bracelet.

Hello? I croaked.

Are you ill? asked Sebastian. *You don't sound well.*

I just woke up, I explained, glancing at the clock beside my bed and realizing with a start it was early the following morning. I explained about sorting through my father's office, although I left out the part about his research comparing Astral and Daeval blood. I wasn't about to mention such a thing to Sebastian without having verifiable evidence.

Sebastian was silent for a moment, then said, *It seems like you were close to your father. That must have been difficult.*

I appreciated his unexpected sympathy and thanked him, then pushed myself into a sitting position. *Can we meet at Caz's office soon? I'd really like to come back and focus on other things for a while.*

Sebastian sighed. *Before you come back, there's something I need to tell you.*

37

SEBASTIAN

J sensed a shift in Kyra's emotions and heard the wariness
in her voice as she asked, *What is it?*

Rubbing the back of my neck, I explained my predicament.

I bought The Book of Recovrancy *from a bookstore owned by a
woman named LeBehr. She's always set aside books about recovrancy
for me, given its connection to Rhannu. The last time I was there . . . it's
a long story, but, I promised if I ever met a Recovrancer, I would introduce them to her. At the time, I thought it was impossible and obviously,
I was wrong, but . . . I still made a promise.*

Kyra remained silent, so I continued.

*In Nocens, there are aleric consequences to not keeping your prom-
ise.* I wasn't certain if things worked differently in Aeles, so it
seemed worth explaining. *You might feel ill and not be able to cast
strong spells. Or your abilities might weaken, like my pyromancy or the
way I can make portals.*

It's the same in Aeles, Kyra replied. *Which is why we take making
promises very seriously.*

I take them seriously too! I retorted. *I just never in my wildest
dreams thought I would meet a Recovrancer.*

So, what exactly are you asking me?

I huffed in frustration. *I'm asking you to go to LeBehr's with me when you come back, just for a moment, and let me introduce you so I can fulfill my promise.*

Kyra considered that. *But what will happen if someone in your realm knows there's a Recovrancer in Aeles again? I can't risk being found out.*

I've known LeBehr since I was a child, I said. *As much as I trust anyone to keep their mouth shut, I trust her. Besides, I think most of my kind would be thrilled to know there's a Recovrancer in Aeles again— they'd love how much it would upset your government. They'd also probably offer you more money than you can imagine to recover loved ones who died before their time. That's not necessarily a bad way to make a living, you know.*

Well, it's good to know if I'm exiled from Aeles, I can still make a living in Nocens! she replied before falling silent, and I soon heard two different but complementary sounds. They were muffled, though, as if I was listening to them with a wool cap over my ears or from under water.

Do you hear that? I asked.

Oh, I'm sorry, she said, and the sounds immediately stopped. *That was me. I was using my* sana *bracelet. You heard Glir and Tawazun . . . for clarity and balance.*

I wasn't able to hear other things happening around Kyra, so it was interesting I could hear her *sana* bracelet. Perhaps it simply demonstrated how connected she was to it, such that when she heard the beads in her mind, I heard them as well. At last, she asked, *What kind of aleric consequences have you been experiencing?*

What difference does that make? I snapped.

Potentially an important one, she replied. *Honestly, I think it would be great if your fighting skills were affected. It would probably also be good if your pyromancy abilities were diminished, too, since I'm sure you use those in your work.*

Anger swelled in my chest, and I let the fire rise to my palm, watching the flames shimmer in an attempt to keep myself under control.

Batty chuckled. *Perhaps she has been spending too much time with you. This seems like exactly the sort of thing you would do, if the situation was reversed.*

I clenched my teeth, and the flames flared brighter.

For your information, I finally growled to Kyra, *neither my fighting skills nor my pyromancy have been affected. It's my portals.*

Oh, she said, and I could hear the disappointment in her voice. I supposed she could argue I used portaling in my work, but she would also have to recognize I used it to bring her to my cave.

She let out a loud sigh. *Then, I suppose that's different.* She appeared to be deep in thought before saying, *I'll help you keep your promise if, while we're at the bookstore, we can ask the owner if she has any books on the Felserpent Queen and King. How's that?*

That's fine, I agreed. Most likely LeBehr had never heard of the rulers, and we'd be on our way. And if she did have something on the original wearers of the bracelets, well, there was no harm in learning more about them.

After checking with Alistair, I agreed to meet Kyra in a couple of hours at Caz's, as she said she needed to clean up. I ate dinner, finished fletching some arrows, and carefully bottled and labeled a sleeping potion I'd been brewing for a few days. When the time came to leave, I took a deep breath and willed a portal to open with all my might. It felt as if I was wrestling someone twice my size to force the gateway to cooperate, but eventually, it did, and I made my way to Caz's office. Kyra and Aurelius were waiting, having arrived a few minutes earlier.

I handed Kyra her shifter cloak, then found my eyes returning to her entirely of their own accord. She hadn't worn anything like these clothes before. She looked . . . different. Her reddish-brown boots gleamed with such polish, I could see my reflection on the toes. Her dark blue breeches were tucked into her boots, and the pants were soft and supple, clinging to the contours of her legs as she moved. Her long-sleeved tunic, a pale salmon color, grazed the tops of her thighs, and over it, she wore a fine covering of golden netting strung with pink and white pearls. Matching pearls dangled from her ears, and black kohl lined the upper lids of her eyes. I must have been staring because she cleared her throat, then dropped her eyes to her feet as her cheeks reddened.

"Since we're meeting someone you've known for so long, I wanted to look nice," she said, clutching her cloak to her chest.

"Oh," I said. Regardless of the occasion, I seldom varied from the black or grey tunics and suede breeches I favored.

"I don't know how women dress in your realm. Do you think this is alright?" she asked, looking at me with more concern than any decision involving clothes warranted.

"Women wear whatever they want in Nocens," I said. "Of course you look alright."

She nodded uncertainly, clearly not convinced; worried she might change her mind about going to LeBehr's, I added, "You look nice."

She did look nice, so it was odd that stating such a simple fact caused a sudden fluttering in my stomach. Perhaps it was because I didn't usually go around noticing what women wore and complimenting them on their clothing choices.

Kyra smiled and slipped into her shifter cloak. "Thank you," she said, sounding much happier. "I'm ready when you are."

I led the way out of the office. It was only a couple of hours before midnight, but Vartox was relatively quiet, which I appreciated, and we only saw a few palanquins and spelled carriages pass by until we reached a spot where I could open a portal. LeBehr's was all the way across the city, and I didn't want to walk and risk anyone recognizing Kyra's golden blood. Thankfully, as if it knew my destination, my portal opened easily this time, and we stepped through to arrive just outside the bookstore.

As usual, the lamps burned warmly in the dirty windows, and the front door was open, with Mischief guarding the threshold. I hoped she'd let Kyra pass, since it would be awkward to ask LeBehr to come outside to meet the Recovrancer.

I stepped over the black cat and was greeted with her customary hiss. I quickly turned and watched as Kyra hesitantly approached the Cypher. She carefully stepped over the cat and, to my relief, Mischief yowled loudly before hissing and flicking the tip of her tail. Kyra scuttled forward, apologizing to the Cypher, and came to a stop next to me.

"Now *this* is a treat!" boomed LeBehr's voice from behind a stack of books. She soon emerged and rested her hands on her broad hips. "Has my store become so famous it's being visited by citizens of Aeles now?" She smiled at Kyra, then winked at me. "It seems you found yourself an Astral. I'm impressed. Unfortunately, I haven't come across a book on how to revive long-lost abilities in someone with golden blood."

"You don't have to," I said, and although we were the only ones in the store, I kept my voice low. "This is Kyra, and she's a Recovrancer."

LeBehr's eyes widened, and she was silent for a moment before whispering, "Is it true?"

"I promised I'd introduce you if I ever met one," I reminded her, and Kyra nodded.

"Oh, my," the woman said, tears filling her eyes. "I never imagined I'd see the day." Rearranging the large scarf draped over her shoulders, she turned towards Kyra. "Grace—Sebastian's mother—was like a daughter to me. She and Sebastian were in here all the time when he was little. If anyone deserves this, it's him. Can you help him?"

I clenched my jaw as the fire surged inside my veins, wishing I could dematerialize like a Cypher. I'd *never* imagined LeBehr would embarrass me in such a way, even though I knew she missed my mother too. What was Kyra going to say? From the corner of my eye, I watched as the Astral reached forward and took one of the bookstore owner's hands between both of her own.

"I'm still learning what it means to be a Recovrancer," Kyra explained gently. "It's not exactly going to be welcomed by those in my realm, so it's a bit of a slow process. But I'll do everything in my power to recover Sebastian's mother." Still holding LeBehr's hand, her eyes found mine as she added, "I promise."

I stared at her, stunned. Why had she done such a thing? She knew how binding a promise was. It didn't make any sense, especially given how much she disliked me and what I did for a living.

LeBehr hugged Kyra so tight, I thought I might have heard the Recovrancer's spine crack. "Thank you!" said the bookseller. Releasing Kyra, she flashed me a broad smile. "Well, you kept your word, so that's done. Is there anything else I can do for you?"

I was still too confused over Kyra's promise to come up with a response, and she must have picked up on my inability to speak, because she said, "Actually, there is . . . we were hoping to find some information on a Felserpent King and Queen. Have you ever heard of them?"

One thing I'd always appreciated about LeBehr was that she never questioned why you wanted a book on a particular subject, and now was no exception. Tapping the tip of her nose with a finger, she squinted her eyes.

"Felserpent . . . Felserpent . . . where have I heard that name?"

"In the Myths and Legends section," came a scratchy voice from the doorway, and we all turned to look at Mischief. I had never heard the Cypher speak before. She blinked her different colored eyes. "In that book by Rainglass."

LeBehr threw her hands in the air. "Of course! How could I have forgotten?"

She bustled off, then quickly returned, holding a well-worn cloth-bound volume in her hand. The edges were fraying where the brown fabric was loose, and the binding creaked as she opened the cover. Flipping forward a few pages, she held out the book to Kyra, who took it and read:

It is said one of the earliest tales to feature both an Astral and a Daeval is that of the Felserpent King and Queen. According to legend, an Astral healer married a Daeval warrior and brought peace between those with gold and silver blood. A mural on a partially destroyed wall in Jaasfar, uncovered after a sandstorm, has been cited as confirmation of this monarchy, but no other evidence exists to corroborate this.

Kyra studied the page, then handed the book to me. I couldn't make out the faces of the two figures in the picture . . . the woman appeared to have black hair, although it could have been some sort of veil, and the man was pictured from behind, raising a large silver and gold sword in the air. I sighed, more disappointed than I'd anticipated, then blinked and brought the book closer to my face.

"That's Rhannu," I said, not entirely believing what I was seeing.

"What?" Kyra stepped closer to me and studied the picture again. "Are you sure?"

"Trust me," I said. "I would know that sword *anywhere*. It's Rhannu." I turned to LeBehr. "How much for the book?"

Back in the cave, I retrieved my other two recovrancy books and handed them to Kyra. She practically danced with excitement and immediately opened one, her eyes fastening eagerly onto the first page. I picked up the book I'd just purchased at LeBehr's and tapped my thumb against the fraying cover, not certain what was more jarring—the fact that Kyra and I had been dreaming about a king and queen who might actually have existed, or the fact that they seemed to have some connection to Rhannu. How had I missed this? I knew *everything* about that sword . . . or so I'd thought.

I looked at the picture of the mural in Jaasfar again, then turned to the beginning of the book and examined the rest of the pictures in the volume, one page at a time. Rhannu wasn't in any of them, so I scanned the index. Noting the pages that mentioned the sword, I flipped to each in turn, but quickly realized I was already familiar with the featured stories.

Scowling, I set the book back on my dining room table. Since there didn't seem to be anything else I could learn about the connection between Rhannu and the Felserpent monarchy, I might as well see what I could do with the information I'd learned from Caz.

"I need to go out for a while," I said to Kyra, "so I'll take you to Caz's office, and then you can let me know when you've read the books and are ready to come back."

"If it's all the same," replied Kyra, "would you mind if I stayed and read the books here? Taking them into my realm makes me so nervous. Reading them here feels . . . safer, somehow."

I had never expected anyone else to view my cave as a safe

place, but in this situation, it made sense. "That's fine. I don't know how long I'll be gone, but Batty will be here and can reach me if you need anything."

She nodded, but then her eyes flashed, as if she'd just realized something upsetting.

"Are you going out for *work?*" She asked the question as if I couldn't possibly be doing anything more offensive.

"No," I glowered at her in return. Then, remembering that I might need her help in this particular situation, I tried to temper my annoyance. "Daeval children have started going missing, and I want to look into it."

Kyra's ire immediately disappeared, and I told her what I'd learned from Caz.

"Do you think it's the same Astrals who tortured you?" she gasped.

"I can't imagine it would be; that happened over a decade ago. But even if it's not the same Astrals, it sounds like the same type of experiment. It'll probably turn out to be nothing, but I'd like to be sure."

Kyra nodded. "Well, in that case, good luck. Be careful, though, and may Acies guide you. She's the Astral Gifter of Wisdom," she added.

I blinked at her. When was the last time someone had cared enough about what I was doing to remind me to be careful? I couldn't even remember.

"I'm always careful," I replied. "And, just so you know, in Nocens we don't have Gifters. We have Fates." I'd meant to simply explain a fact about my realm Kyra likely didn't know, but my words came out more like a snide lecture than an invitation for conversation . . . probably because I didn't really engage in conversation outside of work or at dinner with the Dekarais, and even then, they did most of the talking.

Luckily, Kyra's attention was elsewhere, and she didn't comment on my rudeness.

"I've never heard about Nocenian deities before!" she exclaimed, her eyes lighting up. "Do you have a Fate of Wisdom or Protection?"

"We have three Fates," I explained. "Rhide is the Inflexible and brings about things that can't be changed. They're often associated with the past. Dayewis is the Choice-Bringer and allows us to set our own course. They're usually associated with the future. And Ga'lie is Possibility, usually in the present . . . things could happen as ordered by Rhide or come about through choices offered by Dayewis."

"You say 'they' like each Fate is plural," Kyra noted, tilting her head to one side.

"We refer to each one as 'they' because it would be offensive to use incorrect terminology," I explained. "The earliest texts to mention them don't state whether they were male or female, and it doesn't matter. They don't need labels. They're the Fates. Now, if you need anything while I'm gone," I pointed to where Batty was hanging from the chandelier over the kitchen table, "just let him know."

"Alright," Kyra agreed. She started to walk towards my sofa, then paused and turned back to face me. "It sounds like Rhide might not be the most helpful Fate in this situation, so may Dayewis and Ga'lie look favorably upon you." She said each name slowly, making an obvious effort at the correct pronunciation, and then offered me a shy smile.

I dipped my head in acknowledgment as a warmth that had nothing to do with the fire in my veins tickled the underside of my collarbones.

38

KYRA

$\mathcal{J}$ mulled over Sebastian's words as he disappeared through a portal before making my way to the sofa. I'd never heard of such things before, and I felt as if a window had been opened in a dark room—a window I hadn't even known existed—and a sliver of light had shone inside. In Aeles, everything was viewed as a duality: men and women, male and female, masculine and feminine. They were categories, not spectrums, and they certainly weren't optional labels whose application was subject to choice.

I wondered if Daevals claimed the latitude they allowed the Fates for themselves, forgoing classifications in favor of simply existing. It was certainly an intriguing possibility, and for the briefest moment, I wished Demitri had been born a Daeval . . . then he wouldn't be forced to hide parts of himself that didn't conform to others' definitions and could love whomever he wanted.

Why do you think we're so quick to label things in Aeles? I asked Aurelius as I sat down on the sofa. Pausing, I studied the lynx. *Now that I think about it, you've never said certain behaviors are exclusive to men or women. You've always just encouraged me to be me . . . well, aside from saying I ask too many questions sometimes.*

Time offers the clearest perspective of all, Aurelius replied, padding over and hopping up next to me. *Once you've lived as long as I have, you realize everyone is the same when it comes to certain fundamental things. All Astrals feel the same emotions, even if they deny it, and they are all capable of the same good or bad actions, even if they pretend otherwise. Similarities are far more important than differences.*

That's surprisingly open-minded, I said.

Perhaps because I am a Cypher and not an Astral, yawned the lynx.

What about Daevals? I asked. *Do you think they're the same as Astrals when it comes to certain fundamental things?*

I'm not certain I'd go that far, he responded stiffly.

When it comes to disliking Daevals, you're more of an Astral than I am, I said. *Is that because you've been paired with my kind for so long or do you have others reasons?*

Aurelius crossed his front paws and rested his head on them, but as I waited for a reply, Batty materialized on the coffee table nearby.

"It is a good thing you do not shed," he said, eyeing Aurelius, "as fond as you have become of that sofa."

Aurelius glared at him, then closed his eyes. I settled down next to the lynx and carefully opened one of Sebastian's books. The pages were thick and smelled of clean, dry parchment, a smell guaranteed to make me smile. Batty caught my eye, then happily clapped his wings as I patted my lap and waved him over.

A while later, I had finished the two books, and my mind was so full I felt as if the words I'd read were leaking out of my ears. Massaging my forehead, I closed my eyes.

While I'd certainly learned a great deal from the only three books about recovrancy I would likely ever come across, I still had so many questions. It was going to be almost impossible to find answers, though, given that much of the art of recovrancy had apparently been passed down orally from a senior Recovrancer to her protégé. But since there *were* no others Recovrancers, and *The Book of Recovrancy* would only divulge additional information as it saw fit, how was I going to learn what I needed to use my gift?

There was someone who might be able to help me . . . someone who had at least known other Recovrancers. Someone who had seen them work and had likely overheard them using certain spells, who had probably even watched them train their successors to navigate Vaneklus. The question was, would Laycus be willing to share what he knew? Part of me dared to hope he would, but the rest of me cautioned such generosity was highly unlikely—after all, there was no benefit to him if I fully understood my powers. If anything, he stood to lose the most if I became a competent Recovrancer.

Well, there was only one way to know for sure. Scooping Batty off my lap, I placed the sleeping bat beside Aurelius and pushed myself off the couch, then walked out into the open space of the cavern. The first time I'd gone into Vaneklus, I'd come out with soaking wet clothes. The second time, I'd ended up in the hot springs, so whether my clothes had gotten wet in the realm of the dead hadn't mattered. But I didn't want to risk getting Sebastian's sofa wet, so moving to where there was nothing but rock seemed safer.

"Sit down," instructed Aurelius, opening one eye. "Remember what happened last time. I don't want you falling and hitting your head."

"Me neither," I agreed, lowering myself into a cross-legged position on the ground.

Aurelius watched me closely as Batty let out a loud snore,

and I said the increasingly familiar spell: *"Bidh mi a 'dol a-steach!"*

The rushing sound wasn't as loud this time, or perhaps I was simply becoming more accustomed to it. I arrived in a slightly crouched position and as I stood, a haze of fog and shadows enveloped me. I remained where I was, allowing it to swirl over me as the river gently slapped my knees. I had the unnerving sense of being inspected, scrutinized down to my shade to determine who I was and whether I belonged here. I shivered, imagining some terrible creature leaping up from the water through the veil of fog to eat me even as I reminded myself I had every right to be here. Whatever had been examining me must have agreed, because the fog slowly dispersed until it disappeared altogether.

At first, the only sound was the river swirling around me, but then, I heard the splash of oars. I took a deep breath and forced myself to stand up straight, even though part of me wanted to duck my head and make myself as small of a target as possible. Simply because I had spoken with Laycus before didn't mean I felt comfortable around him. He was still a frightful spectacle to behold, and I sensed that, like Sebastian, he could be very dangerous if crossed.

The prow of the Shade Transporter's boat made its way towards me, and I bowed at the hooded figure standing at the front, peering out intently.

"Exactly how often are you planning on visiting me?" Laycus asked, a smile playing at the corners of his thin, pale lips. "Perhaps we should establish some standing appointments so I can prepare myself."

"I'm sorry if I interrupted," I said. "If there's a way to let you know I'm coming, I'm happy to do so in the future."

Laycus traced a spiral pattern on the surface of the water with the tip of his wooden staff. "Well, given the short span of your mortal life, I suppose you must act when you can. What a pity all of your experiences are so finite." He shook his head as if I both saddened and disgusted him.

"If you're not mortal, are you similar to a Cypher?" I asked, as my curiosity leaped ahead of the questions I'd originally planned on asking. "Does doing something helpful, like ferrying shades, make you immortal?"

"I am not like a Cypher," he shook his head. "And while ferrying shades is indeed helpful, whether I *choose* to do so is another question."

There was clearly more to the story, but as Laycus didn't seem inclined to share it, I tried a different approach.

"Are you in any way related to Gifters or Fates?" I asked.

He chuckled. "Those are terms used by Astrals and Daevals to make sense of things otherwise incomprehensible to them. I existed long before the need for such names, and I shall continue to exist long after new ones are used."

I nodded and worked to gather my thoughts, returning to the real reason I'd sought out the Shade Transporter.

"I finished reading all of Sebastian's recovrancy books," I started. "It seems a more senior Recovrancer used to mentor a junior one to take her place before she retired. She taught her protégé about Vaneklus and how to recover shades and how to know if they'd died at their appointed time or not. Unfortunately, that option isn't available to me. *The Book of Recovrancy* will supposedly share more information as I need it, but I don't know when that will be. There isn't anything else I can read, so I was hoping—" I momentarily faltered, then forced the words out: "I was hoping *you* could help me. As best you can, of course."

Laycus's eyes flickered in surprise. "That's awfully bold, considering our roles are at complete cross purposes."

"Not exactly," I countered, emboldened by the fact he hadn't refused me outright. "I only want to recover shades that die before their time. If it is their time, I want to ensure they go on to . . . well, whatever comes next."

"What sorts of things did you wish to learn?" he asked, tapping his long fingers against the black shroud covering his chest.

"How do I know when a shade has crossed into Vaneklus? Do I have to actually watch someone die or can I know it's happened even if they're hundreds of miles away? How do I know if it was their appointed time, or if they died prematurely? And, is it possible to communicate with shades that passed on under your care weeks or months or even years ago?"

"Hmm," replied Laycus. "I have never attempted to teach anyone such things. I'm not entirely certain I can . . ." His voice trailed off, and he was silent for a moment. I held my breath, waiting. "But," he continued, "as you have no other options, I am willing to try." I let out a relieved exhale as the Shade Transporter smirked. "Who knows—it might even be entertaining. First things first, though." He gestured towards my arm. "Tell me, how are you enjoying wearing the bracelet of the Felserpent Queen?"

My heart lurched inside my chest.

"You know that name?" I asked, and as Laycus nodded, excitement raced through my arms and legs. "That means . . . you're saying the Felserpent Queen was *real*?"

"Kareth was as real as you and I," replied Laycus.

"Sebastian and I think she and Schatten stored their memories in these bracelets," I said, thrilled to discuss this with someone who had actual knowledge of the topic. "We've been seeing their memories when we dream, but I only know bits and pieces about her. In the last dream we had, she mentioned being a Recovrancer. She also mentioned coming here to talk to you."

Laycus smiled fondly and nodded, then gazed at something far down the river, losing himself in his own thoughts.

After a moment, I asked, "What was she like?"

The Shade Transporter stared at my face for so long I began to think he either hadn't heard my question or simply wasn't going to answer. Finally, he said, "She was remarkable. An unusual balance of tender-hearted and fierce. Folks often underestimated her because she was kind, which frustrated her to no end until she learned how to use their short-sightedness to her advantage. She was everything to Schatten, and when she died . . ." he stopped and gazed out over the water. It was a while before he spoke again, and when he did, his voice was heavy with a pain it was clear time hadn't softened. "When she died, everyone who knew her wept. Including myself."

I stared down at the ripples eddying around my feet. She must have been an extraordinary woman to have prompted such devotion, especially from Laycus. Would I ever leave behind such a legacy? I desperately hoped so, and for a moment, I felt such an intense longing I could hardly breathe.

Laycus sighed and gave me a wry smile. "Of course, Kareth is also the reason why every Recovrancer who came after her was killed."

I jerked my head up.

"What?" I sputtered. "Why? Because she was so powerful?"

The Shade Transporter studied me, then said quietly, "That is a story for another time."

"What was the Felserpent King like?" I asked, changing the subject in the hopes Laycus would keep talking.

The Shade Transporter snorted and tossed his head inside his cowl. "He was the most brilliant military strategist I've ever encountered," he admitted. "However, his social skills were sorely lacking, and he preferred to fight first and speak second. He was a wise ruler, but much of that I attribute to Kareth—she was the only one he listened to, and he never made a move without consulting her."

"So, were our dreams true—was Kareth an Astral and Schatten a Daeval and their marriage brought peace to the realms?"

"Yes," said Laycus.

I looked down at the golden bracelet. "Do you know how they stored their memories in here?" I asked. I was certainly familiar with enchanting objects, but I'd never heard of storing memories in them.

Laycus appeared to be considering something, but his attention was quickly captured by the arrival of a woman on the wooden dock.

Turning back to me, he grinned wolfishly.

"I'm afraid duty calls, Recovancer. But the next time you return, we shall start working on how to determine if a shade has crossed over before its appointed time . . . although, I fear I shall be depriving myself of a great deal of fun as a result."

"One more thing, please!" I entreated, remembering my promise to Sebastian. "Sebastian's mother was killed thirteen years ago. Her name was Grace. I'm not certain if you remember her or—"

"I remember every shade I ferry!" Laycus declared indignantly.

I bowed my head in apology, then continued as quickly as I could.

"I was always taught Astrals go one of two places when they die—to Karnis for rebirth or Ceelum for rest. I don't know if it works the same for Daevals, but do you know where Sebastian's mother went? I promised him I would try to recover her, but if she chose rebirth, it may not be possible."

Laycus shifted his staff from one hand to the other.

"It is the same for Daevals, although they call Karnis *Ath-Braith* and Ceelum *Gabfarr*. I remember Grace Sayre. She chose rest rather than rebirth, although that might have changed since I ferried her."

My heart sank. "You mean, you can't tell where she is right now?"

"I don't waste my time keeping up with shades once they've left my care," huffed Laycus. "All I know is, thirteen years ago, she chose rest, and I haven't seen her since."

His boat began to pull away, and I stepped forward, grabbing the side and holding the vessel in place against the insistent oars.

"Can shades be recovered from Ceelum?" I asked, leaning back and digging my heels into the riverbed.

"That depends," replied Laycus. The oars rowed harder, and the boat jerked away. I lost my balance and nearly fell face-first into the river, but, stumbling forward a few steps, I managed to right myself.

"Depends on what?" I asked, wringing water from the front of my tunic.

"On whether or not they died at the appointed time," replied Laycus. He pointed one end of his staff at me. "Do not touch my boat again, Recovrancer." Scowling, he angled the craft towards the dock and began to move away.

I reached down and ran a finger over Rheolath, imagining thick ropes of *alera* tethering the boat to my bracelet. "*Bana sevap verakessin*," I murmured, summoning all the power of the red carnelian bead known as The Controller. The boat lurched to a sudden stop, and Laycus whirled around to glare at me. I inhaled slowly, fearful of breaking the connection. I could sense everything about the boat, the pattern of each grain of wood, the carefully carved notches where the planks fitted together, and every curve of the long-handled oars. The entire craft was completely under my control.

I could have directed the spell at Laycus himself, but the idea of using my *alera* to control a living being, as opposed to an inanimate object, frightened me. Rheolath was powerful and enjoyed being used; she always wanted more, and desired absolute control over everything around her. I usually paired her with another bead to temper her appetite, but this was worth the effort it took to wield her by herself.

"I have always *hated* that bracelet!" growled Laycus.

He raised his left hand in the air, and a wicked-looking pale green light began to swarm around his fingers.

"Did Sebastian's mother die at her appointed time?" I asked, heart thudding loudly as I concentrated on holding the boat in place.

"No," Laycus hissed. "She died before her time. Now, release the boat!"

"Then, if she's still in Ceelum, is it possible to recover her?"

Laycus glanced at the shade on the dock, then back to me. "I suppose it might be . . . but not even Kareth ever attempted such a thing!"

I lowered my hand and dropped my finger from the bracelet. Laycus's boat rocked from side to side before steadying itself. He gave me a final glare, then muttered something and shot the light from his hand into the river. The water between us rippled and, suddenly, a large wave rose before me, taller than my head. Crashing down, it swept over me with such force I was knocked off my feet and tossed over backwards. Coughing and sputtering, I floundered in the water for a moment, grateful it wasn't deep, then managed to push myself up.

I suppose I deserved that, I said unhappily to Aurelius, before quickly saying the words to leave Vaneklus. I felt myself squeezed in on all sides, although it wasn't as pronounced as before, which was nice. Opening my eyes, I looked around from my seated position in Sebastian's cave. A ring of water surrounded me, spreading outwards across the stone floor, and I grimaced at the feel of wet clothes against my skin.

"I have to learn if there's a way to stay dry in Vaneklus," I said to the nearby Cyphers, getting to my feet as water ran down my arms and legs. My hair was plastered to my face, and I combed it back as best I could with my fingers. "Otherwise, I'm going to need some waterproof clothing."

The air before me suddenly shimmered, and a portal crackled into view. Sebastian stepped through and gave me a long look, likely wondering why I was standing there in soaking wet clothes, dripping water onto his floor.

"I was talking to Laycus," I explained. "Since I don't have an Astral mentor who can teach me about recovrancy, he agreed to help me." I wasn't certain if he would still be so inclined after I'd taken control of his boat, but I would apologize the next time I saw him. "I also learned more about the Felserpent Queen and King!" I said, and told Sebastian what the Shade Transporter had shared.

He listened closely, then traced a finger along the edge of his bracelet. "Nerudian's gone to visit his family in Breagha for a few days, but when he returns, we'll talk to him. I want to hear what he knows about the Felserpent King's connection with Rhannu."

I nodded and wrapped my arms around myself. "I also asked Laycus about your mother," I said gently.

Sebastian froze, becoming so still I doubted he was even breathing. More emotions than I could name crossed his face, but I felt each one deeply, thanks to our connection. I recounted what Laycus had told me, and when I was done, Sebastian ran a hand through his hair.

"I can't believe it," he finally said. "It really wasn't her time."

I probably would have responded to similar news by crying or storming around the cavern ranting about my loss, but perhaps he was simply too shocked to do more than stand there, working to believe my words.

"It wasn't her time," I agreed. "If there's any way to go into Ceelum, or Gabfarr, I'll find it. And if your mother is there, I'll find her."

Sebastian shifted his weight and studied me. I'd never seen such vulnerability in his dark eyes, and I could sense how unsettled he was at lowering his ever-present guard.

"Why did you make that promise at LeBehr's?" he asked. "This goes beyond anything we agreed to. I don't have any more books to give you. If you want money—"

I quickly shook my head.

"I don't want money. I . . ." It was time for me to be vulnerable as well. "When I recovered you after the unicorn sanctuary, I asked Laycus about my father, and whether it had been his time to die." I swallowed over the lump suddenly filling my throat. "He said my father died at his appointed time."

Tears rose to my eyes, and one slid down my cheek before I could wipe it away. "I *hate* knowing there was nothing I could do, even though it's also a bit of a relief. But if things were different . . . if he'd died before his time and there was a chance someone could bring him back . . ." I gazed up at Sebastian as two hot tears streaked down my face. "I would give anything to see him again. So, if I can do that for someone else, I will."

"Even for me?" asked Sebastian, disbelief filling his eyes. "Someone with silver blood and a profession you hate?"

"Even for you," I said.

He stared across the cavern a moment. "You know, you could have said the only way you'd try to bring my mother back was if I found a different career. There's a good chance I would have agreed. You don't think about things like that, do you—how to use information to your advantage?"

I shook my head.

"No, I don't." Recalling how different Sebastian's childhood had been from mine, I added, "I've never *had* to think that way . . . seeing all the angles and trying to get the best deal for myself. I've never had to look out for myself—not like you."

"I don't like accepting help," admitted Sebastian. "I'd rather bargain with someone or pay for what I want."

I tried to explain my position in a way he might understand. "I feel like, if I can do something that will help someone, then it's my duty to do it. Not because they owe me, or I owe them, but because I choose to do it, to make them happy or make their life a little easier." I held his gaze. "And as much as I hate what you do, I would never want you to close your business because I forced you. You've been forced to do enough things by Astrals."

Sebastian ran a hand over the caramel-colored stubble coating his jaw.

"Then," he finally said, "I suppose the only thing I can say is, thank you." He sounded almost disappointed in himself for accepting my help.

"You're welcome," I replied. "Now, if you don't mind, I'm going to have Aurelius fetch me some dry clothes, and then we ought to discuss recovering Rhannu. I can go in and out of Vaneklus whenever I want now, so once we have a plan, I'm ready to retrieve the sword."

The uncertainty in Sebastian's eyes was immediately replaced by enthusiasm, and an expression that reminded me of when he'd watched the unicorns flitted across his mouth.

"I'll get some things we need to review while you change," he said, then hurried down a tunnel. Aurelius rolled his eyes, but nevertheless dematerialized to retrieve dry clothes for me from back home.

39

SEBASTIAN

Snatching a few parchments from my weapons vault, I quickly made my way back to the living area. My heart-beats pulsed in almost the same fast-paced rhythm as my boots pounding against the stone floor, and I couldn't help feeling as if each step was carrying me closer to my destiny. Normally I wasn't given to such melodrama, but I'd also never been so close to acquiring the object I had spent my entire life searching for. Rhannu's connection to the Felserpent King was an interesting development, and even though I wasn't certain what to make of it, I had no doubt it was important. More would be revealed when we found the sword, and I was more certain than ever we *would* find the sword.

I stepped out of the tunnel just as Batty placed a heaping plate of steamed rice and vegetables on the table and waved Kyra over. There was nothing in my kitchen a planterian would eat besides bread, so I supposed it was good he'd gotten food for her. For a second, though, I wished I'd thought of it myself.

Putting the matter aside, I set the sheets of parchment on the table.

"In a perfect realm, we could hand over the unicorn horn, get the sword in exchange, and be done with it," I began, "but I don't think it will work that way." A small part of me worried what I was about to share would frighten Kyra so much, she might change her mind about helping me. But she needed to know what we were up against. And, given what I'd learned of her so far, most of me was certain she would keep her word to find the sword, even if she was frightened. "Hopefully Laycus can tell us more, but it looks like we're going to have to pass three sets of tests or challenges."

"Alright," Kyra nodded around a mouthful of food. "What are they?"

"That's the problem," I grimaced. "I don't know. The most I've been able to learn is that they exist." I pointed to a piece of parchment. "I copied this from a reference book in an artifact preservation center."

Rhannu, it is said, is one of the most difficult items to recover. This is likely because of the triplet of challenges awaiting any who seek the sword.

"And then there's this," I said, pointing to the last legible sentence on another piece of parchment before the rest of the page was torn away:

The recovery of the weapon is said to involve three elements: bone, mind, and blood.

Kyra's face paled, and she rested her fork on her nearly empty plate. "I don't like the sound of that. Do you think bone could be referring to the unicorn horn?"

"I don't know. It would certainly be nice."

"*Mind* could mean we have to solve some sort of problem. I hope it doesn't involve calculations," she winced. "Mathematics was never a strong subject for me. Now, if it's a problem involving anatomy, physiology, or biology, we should be fine."

"I can handle calculations," I assured her.

She picked up her fork again. "Was that your favorite subject in school—mathematics?"

I shook my head. "History. I liked learning about different wars and the decisions made by military commanders." I wasn't used to talking about myself so much and tried to redirect the conversation, tapping a finger against the parchment. "Now, the third element mentioned here is bl—"

"I can definitely see you liking anything to do with fighting," Kyra interrupted with a smile. "Were there any subjects you didn't like?"

I had actually graduated at the top of my class, although I hadn't attended graduation or given the expected speech. I hadn't seen the point, since I wouldn't have had family there to see me. But I didn't want to sound like a know-it-all, so after a moment, I replied, "I hated anything involving groups. My lowest marks were when I had to collaborate with others."

Kyra nodded and swallowed the large bite she'd just taken. "I still prefer to practice new spells or write essays alone. I understand the value of working with others, of course, but it's not my preference."

"Really?" Given how easily she interacted with others, I hadn't expected that, and Kyra noticed my reaction.

"You seem surprised," she said.

"I just assumed you enjoyed being social," I replied. "From what I've seen, you're friendly, a good conversationalist, and easy enough to get along with, especially for an Astral . . ." My voice trailed off, and I focused on Kyra's plate, suddenly embarrassed at how I'd listed off her personality traits as if I'd been purposefully cataloging them. It wasn't my fault I noticed even seemingly insignificant details about others; in fact, that's what made me so skilled at my work. The fact that some part of me had unconsciously been studying Kyra didn't mean anything out of the ordinary or have anything to do with *her*—I was simply doing what came naturally.

I shrugged, trying to appear nonchalant. "I just assumed, that's all."

"You must learn to look past your own assumptions," she said with a slight smirk, repeating the words Kareth had said in our dream.

I had absolutely no idea how to respond, but thankfully Kyra reached forward and picked up *The Book of Recovrancy.*

"Since we don't know how the third challenge involves blood, there's no point frightening ourselves," she said, making it clear she'd been paying attention to the parchments I'd shown her, "but maybe something's changed in here since I last went to Vaneklus." I waited as she flipped through a few pages, her eyes skimming the text. Suddenly, she stopped and leaned closer to the page, her mouth silently forming words until she finally lifted her head.

"We may have a problem," she said, then began to read out loud:

Time is something that must always be considered in the realm of Vaneklus. When attempting to recover an object, rather than a shade, a Recovrancer must not only take into account the payment necessary to retrieve the object, but the time the payment was obtained. Unicorn horns are a good example of this—when a horn is obtained, the stage of the moon must be noted in the realm where the horn was given. If the horn is not presented to the Shade Transporter before the moon moves into the next stage, the horn will disintegrate and be rendered useless. To determine lunar cycles, please refer to the appropriate almanac for each realm at the end of the book.

I felt as if someone had struck my chest and knocked the air from my lungs. This couldn't be happening—not *now*, when we were so close to the sword! I was torn between racing to my weapons vault to make sure the unicorn horn was still where I'd stored it and staying put to see what else the book revealed. After a few agonizing beats, I decided to stay put and watched as Kyra flipped to the back of the book. The moon had been full when we'd obtained the horn . . . but given the time differences between the realms, I wasn't certain if it had already begun to wane.

"This is incredible," Kyra said, getting to her feet and coming to stand next to me, placing the book between us. It was nice this section of text wasn't something only she could see, and I gazed in fascination as lunar charts appeared on a page under the heading, "Moon Cycles of Aeles."

Kyra ran her finger down the page. "It was evening on Gwener, Astral time, when we found the horn. The moon was full, which means now the visible portion will start to decrease. The next phase will be a waning gibbous moon, and that should occur . . ." she inhaled sharply and looked at me. "Tonight."

"Are you sure?" I demanded. "Are you certain we still have time?"

Kyra nodded with a confidence I was glad one of us felt. "Yes. It's currently late afternoon on Sul in Aeles, around three o'clock. The moon won't enter the waning gibbous phase until after midnight, so we have about eight or nine hours until that happens . . . probably eight or less, just to be safe."

I ran a hand through my hair, accepting Kyra's words and letting them slow my pounding heart. "All right." While part of me wanted to grab the horn and take it to Vaneklus that instant, I also knew Kyra and I needed to be as alert as possible when we next entered the realm of the dead. "We should try to get a few hours of rest, then, before heading out."

Kyra nodded, and I studied her from the corner of my eye, uncertain how to proceed. Logically, it made the most sense for her to stay here, rather than going to Aeles for a few hours and then coming back, but I didn't want to offend her by suggesting she stay or worse, somehow imply *I* wanted her to stay.

Kyra shared a long look with Aurelius, briefly catching the inside of her cheek between her teeth before turning to me. A faint blush blossomed behind her freckles. "I can go back home, if you like, or . . . I'm also fine staying here, but I don't want to intrude."

Batty spoke before I could. "You are not intruding!" he assured her. "Besides, it is a much more efficient use of our time for you to remain here." He turned to me and batted his eyelashes as he flashed an overly bright smile that set my teeth on edge. "*Logically*, that makes the most sense, wouldn't you say?"

I glared at him, hating when he listened to my thoughts and then used them against me, even though in this instance he was technically correct. At least Kyra was waiting for me to verbally give my consent, which I appreciated, rather than taking the bat at his word and encouraging him to think he made any decisions for me.

"It's fine if you stay," I said to her, and no sooner had I uttered the words than Batty snapped his claws, and the tunic and breeches I'd lent Kyra before suddenly appeared on the table. The sight of them stirred something inside of me that wasn't just the fire in my veins, which made absolutely no sense. It wasn't as if she was staying with me because we enjoyed being around one another . . . she was simply remaining here until we left for Vaneklus to complete our business agreement. And what I'd just felt had been the first workings of the adrenaline that filled me before a fight, nothing more.

Kyra smiled at me, then scooped up the clothes, and followed a happily chatting Batty down a tunnel to change. I used her absence to change into my own sleeping clothes and had just crawled into bed when she returned and settled herself onto the sofa.

"Sleep well, Sebastian," she said, her voice easily carrying across the cavern. "Perhaps we'll have another dream about the Felserpent King and Queen!"

"Perhaps," I replied, although truth be told, I wasn't nearly as enthusiastic about such a possibility. Dreams had the disturbing tendency to affect emotions, as I well knew, and the feelings that arose in dreams had a way of persisting during waking life. Having another dream about someone who looked like the Recovrancer currently on my sofa might make it more difficult to be around Kyra . . . or *not* be around her, which was more problematic, since we'd never see one another again after recovering the sword.

I rearranged my pillows as Batty dimmed the lights, then materialized on the handle of my wardrobe, flipping upside down and wrapping his wings around himself. He would wait there until I fell asleep, then move onto the bed. Rolling over onto my side, I closed my eyes, and to my surprise, sleep found me quickly.

40

S chatten glanced around the meadow. Stars twinkled overhead, and the full moon cast a silvery light on the trees. Torches ringed the perimeter of the grove, and the scents of burning cedar and damp earth filled the air.

Glancing down, he admired his new cloak. The Uchel Doeth had fashioned the sheet of scales shed by the Great Serpent into a beautiful cape that trailed all the way down to his feet. It was trimmed with the black fur shed by pine martens in the summer and fitted with a silver clasp shaped like a four-legged serpent.

Movement up ahead made him raise his head, instinct after so many years spent as a warrior, and he immediately sensed the presence of Astral blood. A tall woman came into view, and as she strode confidently across the grove, a barely perceptible smile rested at the edges of her mouth. Soft lines that spoke of a full life were strewn across her face, and her long auburn hair was shot through with thick streaks of white. She wore a thin copper circlet around her forehead, set with a large moonstone giving off a milky white light.

Stopping a few feet away, the woman gave a deep bow.

"I am Gathalia, the Princeps Shaman of Aeles."

Schatten returned the bow, and the Shaman gestured for him to follow her. As he stepped after her, something inside him shifted. This was it. His feet were set upon the path to kingship, and there was no going back to being merely a soldier ever again.

Gathalia led the way along a winding path that twisted deep into the forest. After a while, the trees were replaced by rocks and, eventually, they arrived at the entrance to a large canyon. The walls on either side were little more than overlapping slabs of granite, jutting upwards through fallen shale, likely formed during a past upheaval of the land. A narrow crevice created a doorway in one of the walls, and torches were fastened to the rock, burning bright against the mottled stone.

Gathalia stopped near the doorway, and a small wooden chest appeared near her feet.

"Your Uchel Doeth chose wisely," she said, looking at Schatten approvingly. "However, the decision to accept such a choice was yours, and you have made both your ancestors and your descendants proud by the responsibility you are assuming, Schatten."

She leaned down and touched the lock of the wooden chest. Slowly, the lid raised. Inside lay two heavy cuffs of bright, shining gold.

Gathalia explained the purpose of the bracelets as she fastened them around Schatten's wrists. He nodded solemnly, ready to use any tool that would make him a strong king while also improving his relationship with his wife.

His wife. The fact that he was getting married was almost more difficult to comprehend than his being named king. Orphaned at a young age, the Daeval military had become the only home he'd ever known, and there, under the guidance of battle-hardened soldiers, he had honed his gifts to become the most feared warrior Aeles-Nocens had ever seen. While he was gaining more than he'd ever imagined, he also realized certain gains required specific losses. He would miss the focus fighting brought, the simplicity of having a single objective, and the satisfied exhaustion that came from directing all his might to accomplishing it. He wondered what his soon-to-be wife was giving up to become queen. What was she grieving? She likely wouldn't understand his love of combat, given that she visited the realm of the dead to recover those who died before their time, but perhaps she would understand the sense of loss, nonetheless.

Gathalia stepped back and smiled at him. "In three days' time, a crown will be set upon your head. But for now, be free from such cares."

Schatten nodded. "I must confess, I never imagined meeting my bride or spending the first nights of my wedding ceremony in a cave."

Gathalia smiled understandingly. "As you know, whoever rules Aeles-Nocens is uniquely connected to the realm. A wise, just ruler makes for a thriving land with plentiful food and resources. At this time, it is important for you and Kareth to be as close to the land as possible, since your relationship will directly influence the very earth, waters, and air upon which all living things depend."

Schatten nodded again, and Gathalia bowed low as he squared his shoulders, then walked purposefully between the torches.

With each step, questions rose and fought for space with the doubts filling his mind. Had the woman who would be his queen even seen a Daeval before? Was she excited to be named half of the new monarchy or did she resent being chosen? And, what, exactly, was she going to expect of him tonight? Schatten certainly hoped he would grow to love the woman he had been paired with and, feeling the fire within him stir, he even imagined the possibility of them knowing one another intimately . . . but she certainly wouldn't expect such a thing on the night of their first meeting, would she?

The tunnel wound deeper into the cave, then ended in a large open space that had been thoughtfully decorated. Thick carpets covered the stone floor, woven in shades of burgundy, gold, and green, and ornate tapestries hung from the walls, imparting a softness to the otherwise cold rock. Food and drink appeared to be plentifully stocked, and cushioned ottomans had been arranged around a low table. A reclining sofa was *piled high with blankets and pillows, and since it was clearly meant for two, his heart began to beat faster. When his eyes landed on the woman standing before a tapestry, however, he was certain his heart stopped altogether.*

His intended wife must have heard him, because she turned around, her blue eyes large beneath long dark lashes. Spelled lanterns provided ample illumination, and he studied her as closely as she studied him. Kareth was small, but there was nothing frail about her. Straight black hair hung well past her collarbones, framing an oval face scattered with freckles. Her softly rounded chin hinted at stubbornness, but the corners of her mouth turned upwards slightly, even when she wasn't smiling, although he suspected that was something she did frequently. She looked kind, Schatten decided, like someone who genuinely cared for others. He felt silly admitting it, but he hadn't expected a Recovrancer to be so full of life.

Kareth must have found his appearance to her liking, or at least acceptable, because she smiled broadly and bowed her head towards him. "How fares the Felserpent King?"

Schatten felt as if his first words to the woman he was marrying ought to be brilliant, or witty, or at least memorable. But, running a hand through his hair, he replied, "I still can't believe I'm really here."

Kareth laughed and stepped towards him. She was wearing a dark blue dress with black ribbons crossing over the bodice and gold embroidery on the hem and sleeves. While it fit her well, it was her cloak that caught Schatten's eye. The garment was made of thick blue velvet colored with sprays of indigo, pink, and purple; spatters of silver strewn across it made him think of stardust. There was something about the garment he couldn't quite put his finger on, then, to his surprise, the colors suddenly shifted, turning black and grey and arranging themselves into the same pattern as the scales on his own cloak.

"That's a shifter cloak!" he exclaimed. "I've read about them, but I've never seen one."

Kareth nodded and touched her fingers to the silver clasp, fashioned into a four-legged serpent.

"Nerudian sent it to me," she said. By the tone of her voice, Schatten could tell she felt a similar awe towards the ancient creature who had created their bracelets. "The note he sent with it said the clasp was fashioned to resemble the Great Serpent himself." Kareth's eyes ran over Schatten's cloak, her gaze a mixture of wonder and sadness. "I heard your victory over him was hard-won and well-deserved."

"It was a legendary battle," nodded Schatten, "and by that I mean, I made up the entire story." He told Kareth the truth about the Great Serpent's passing, and she laughed, appearing both impressed and relieved.

"I wouldn't have expected a warrior to feel bad about killing something," she admitted.

"Animals are different," he replied, then wondered if she would think him weak for such a remark.

A gentle respect began to unfold in Kareth's eyes.

"After I agreed to be queen, I asked Gathalia to tell me something about you," she said, "something to reassure me I wasn't making a mistake marrying a Daeval. She told me you once put men under your command in the stocks because you caught them being cruel to an injured pangolin."

"There's nothing reassuring about that," said Schatten, confused. "And certainly nothing romantic."

Kareth tossed her hair over one shoulder.

"I beg to differ. Standing up for a creature that's being treated badly is incredibly king-like. And doing something that might not be popular because you believe it's the right thing to do . . ." She gave him a smile *that made him feel warm all over.* "That's the kind of man I want to rule a kingdom with . . . and build a life with."

Schatten swallowed hard, some part of him unnerved, the rest of him wondering how to get Kareth to smile at him like that again. He walked over to the table, sat down on an ottoman, and poured two glasses of fruit-filled wine. Kareth joined him, popping an olive from an overflowing fruit tray into her mouth as she sat down.

"Did you ask anyone anything about me?" she asked.

"Yes," Schatten admitted, worrying Kareth might not like what he'd asked.

"And?" she prompted, leaning forward.

"I asked the Uchel Doeth—the Daeval equivalent of your Princeps Shaman—if you were intelligent," he said.

"Before you asked what I looked like?" exclaimed Kareth, clearly taken aback.

Schatten nodded. "I don't need a pretty queen. You're not going to be a decoration in the castle . . . you're going to be ruling alongside me. I need you to be intelligent because I need your help. Every decision we make will set a precedent. The laws we pass will affect everyone who lives in the realm. I don't take that lightly, and I could never be paired with someone who did." He was somewhat surprised at his own frankness, but he'd meant every word.

Kareth grabbed another olive. "So, what did the Uchel Doeth say about me?"

"He had me speak to the Shade Transporter."

"You spoke to Laycus?" Kareth nearly fell off her seat. "How?"

"Apparently he's able to come into our realm at certain times or for certain reasons, although I have no idea how that's determined," said Schatten. "I had to stand in the Bera River to meet with him, and even then, he couldn't stay long."

Kareth groaned and covered her face with her hands before returning them to her lap.

"Why Laycus?" she asked. "He hates me. I'm constantly fighting with him over shades, and he despises me being a Recovrancer."

"He doesn't hate you," said Schatten, "but he is the closest thing you have to an enemy. You can learn a lot about someone from their friends, but you can learn more from their enemies. The Uchel Doeth knew I'd listen to whatever Laycus had to say."

"I can't even imagine what he told you," muttered Kareth.

Schatten leaned towards her until she brought her gaze back up to his.

"He said it was impossible to talk you out of whatever you believed was right. He said you constantly pushed the boundaries of Vaneklus to recover shades. He said you were relentlessly curious, incessantly talkative, and annoyingly optimistic." Schatten smiled, hoping to ease the horrified expression creeping over Kareth's face. "He also said you put your healing and recovrancy duties before yourself, and that I would be the realm's biggest fool not to marry you."

Kareth's expression softened, and her eyes filled with a tenderness Schatten wasn't entirely sure the Shade Transporter deserved, regardless of his compliments. "He said that?" she asked softly.

Schatten nodded. "He also told me he had a special place reserved for me in Vaneklus if I ever hurt you."

A disbelieving laugh leapt out of Kareth's mouth. "I'll have to thank him for his glowing endorsement the next time I see him."

A slow, teasing smile made its way over Schatten's mouth. "After I learned all of that, then I asked what you looked like."

Kareth raised her eyebrows. "And?" Her voice was cool, but her expression made it obvious she was quite interested in his answer.

"He nearly took my head off with his staff and told me I would be lucky to have someone as lovely as you so much as glance in my direction." He swallowed, feeling the edges of his cheeks burn. "He was right."

Kareth rolled her eyes but smiled as she did. She then took a drink from the heavy crystal wine glass and said, "Even though I'm looking forward to being queen, I'm going to miss being a healer and Recovrancer. I'll still do both, of course, but neither will be my primary occupation anymore." She gave him a searching look. "Will you miss fighting and being a soldier?"

"Yes," replied Schatten without hesitation. "The Daeval military is really all I've ever known. Both of my parents died when I was young."

Kareth's expression softened, and she reached forward and tentatively laced her fingers through his.

"Well, then, we'll have to make a new home . . . together," she said, a hopeful smile tugging at the corners of her mouth. "My mother was certain I would never wear the wedding dress she's been working on since I was born, so she can't wait to meet my husband."

"Do you have any brothers or sisters?" asked Schatten, enjoying the way her hand fit against his.

"I have an older brother," she said, her entire countenance lighting up. "Donovan. He's three years older than me, and he and his husband recently adopted a little girl, so I'm an aunt!" She grinned wickedly as her eyes danced. "I'm going to spoil his daughter so much! He has no idea what he's in for."

Schatten had never found it so easy to converse with someone for so long. "What else do you like to do? When you aren't plotting to spoil your niece?"

"Well," she said, "I love to read. I'm afraid my books may take up most of the castle library. I can't draw or paint anything recognizable, but I like playing the harp. I love being outdoors, and I spend a lot of time in the water, swimming or exploring in my kadac." She lowered her *eyes to the table and tilted her head so her long hair partially obscured a smile that was both embarrassed and proud.* "And, I've made friends with a few Cyphers."

"Really?" *Schatten asked eagerly. He'd always been fascinated by the creatures who could appear and disappear at will and spoke to one another using only their minds. He gestured to one of the golden bracelets without letting go of Kareth's hand.* "Gathalia told me these would allow us to speak with one another like Cyphers. Did one of them help Nerudian make the bracelets?"

Kareth nodded, clearly pleased at his excitement.

"Bartholomew helped him, although I didn't know he was going to be involved. I can't wait for you to meet him! He's a fruit bat, just so you aren't surprised, and I know he was very pleased with how the bracelets turned out."

She pressed her fingers against one of the gold bands and appeared to be concentrating as a small black dragon appeared and circled the bracelet. Suddenly, Schatten heard her voice in his mind.

Hello? *she asked.* Can you hear me?

I can! *he replied, limiting his response to telepathy, even though he felt his mouth twitch, not used to being left out of communicating.* Say something else.

Kareth grinned at him.

Is it true you've been involved with building the castle? *she asked.* I can't wait to see what it looks like, even though it'll be fun to be surprised.

Yes, *he replied.* I like building things and figuring out how to make things work. If I hadn't been in the military, I probably would have studied engineering or architecture . . . anything that let me use my hands.

Staring down at where their fingers were intertwined, his stomach tightened. His comment could have been interpreted as more suggestive than he'd intended. Was it too early to be saying such things to his wife?

Fortunately, Kareth didn't seem bothered.

"I'm glad we have this time together," she said, speaking out loud again, her voice soft. "To start getting to know one another. I . . . I wasn't sure what tonight, or the next few nights, were going to be like."

"Me neither," agreed Schatten. "I didn't want to disappoint you."

Kareth squeezed his hand, and Schatten silently vowed he would never do anything to dim the hopeful trust that shone from his wife's eyes.

"I'm not disappointed," Kareth said. "In fact, I'm more convinced than ever I made the right choice to become the Felserpent Queen." A smile crept over her mouth, and she leaned forward. "Also . . . I have so many questions I'd love to ask you about Daevals!"

41

❧

SEBASTIAN

I couldn't recall ever waking up from a dream *smiling*, much less feeling genuinely happy. I raised my right arm and stared at the bracelet. Exactly how many memories did these things contain? I pushed myself into a sitting position and looked at Batty, perched on the footboard of my bed. He smirked as if he was savoring a secret, then dematerialized.

Glancing at the clock on the nightstand, I reached over and switched off the alarm I'd set. It was due to go off soon, so there was no point in trying to go back to sleep. Swinging my legs over the edge of the bed, I shuffled quietly to my dresser. I would take a shower, get dressed, then wake Kyra. It was going to be difficult to work with her without thinking back to that absurd dream, but there was no way around it.

An unexpected voice suddenly broke the silence: "I guess neither of us could sleep very well."

I wheeled around, my eyes quickly landing on the sofa. Kyra was peering over the back of it, watching me.

"I'm sorry," she said. "I woke up a little while ago and couldn't go back to sleep. I was just waiting for you to wake up."

I nodded and said the spell to illuminate the lanterns around the cavern. "If you're hungry, Batty can get you something to eat while I clean up. Then you can get ready."

She nodded, then said, "That was quite a dream."

I swallowed instead of replying, but Kyra held my gaze, intent on gauging my reaction and refusing to pretend as if nothing had happened. Sighing, I leaned back against my dresser and crossed my arms.

"Yes, it was quite a dream," I finally admitted, although I had *no* desire to discuss the particulars of what had transpired during my sleep.

"I wonder if Kareth and Schatten had any idea how much they would eventually love one another," mused Kyra, who obviously had no qualms about revisiting the dream. "Laycus made it sound as if they had quite a relationship."

"I don't know," I replied. "It seemed like they were both at least open to the possibility of . . . being together." As if my mouth had suddenly acquired a will of its own entirely separate from my control, I found myself asking, "Do you have someone like that . . . in Aeles?"

Kyra blinked, likely surprised to hear me ask such a thing, and I didn't blame her. I was surprised too. While she and I had shared some very personal information, this was entirely new territory. Why in the realm would I ask such a thing? It would have no bearing on me or my life, even if I was inexplicably interested in her response.

"No," she finally said. "I've been really focused on school and learning to be a healer. Courting someone has never been that important. I mean, I *want* to," she clarified, "it just hasn't been a priority up to this point." She shifted on the sofa, and a troubled expression flitted over her face. "I also recently learned that, if I become the *Princeps Shaman*, most of Aeles expects me to make a match that's *politically advantageous*." She rolled her eyes and shook her head.

"I take it you have other ideas," I surmised.

"I'll live alone—well, with Aurelius, of course—before I marry someone I don't love," she said, her voice deepening with the strength of her conviction.

I didn't blame her. I would disappear and start a new life in the furthest reaches of the realm before I ever let myself be forced into a marriage that wasn't of my choosing.

Kyra crossed her arms over the back of the sofa and propped her chin on them. "How about you?" she ventured. "Do you have someone?"

I made a snorting noise in the back of my throat and was about to toss off a flippant response, but then, I paused. Judging by her expression, Kyra didn't seem to be teasing . . . in fact, she appeared genuinely interested in my answer.

"No," I said cautiously, still not used to freely sharing information about myself. "After school, I was mainly focused on establishing my business. Once it started doing well and I had more time . . ." I shrugged. "Given what my childhood was like, it's hard to find common ground or shared life experiences with others. It's easier to just not talk about it than to keep explaining things over and over again."

I'd also feared being in a relationship would reveal me to be more like my father than I wanted to admit. I couldn't imagine harming someone I claimed to love, but I'd seen him do it on numerous occasions. It frightened me on a level I rarely acknowledged to think that, simply because I was his son, I might be capable of something similar.

That was too personal to share, though, so instead I said, "But, I'm not opposed to courting someone. I like my privacy, and I like doing what I want, when I want, but . . . I can see how it could be nice to be in a relationship."

Kyra smiled at me, and for a brief, purely self-indulgent moment, I imagined being in a relationship with *her*. She was smart, which was a requirement for anyone I courted, and I appreciated how quickly she could think on her feet, as she'd done in the unicorn sanctuary. I liked her smile. I also liked the way her eyes lit up, like the ocean struck by the noontime sun, when she was excited about something.

Perhaps more than that, though, I liked how comfortable I felt interacting with her. I wasn't certain whether it was because she gave me her full attention and treated what I said as important, or because she was simply a skilled conversationalist who managed to smooth over my deficits in that area. While none of those things were likely enough to establish a relationship, there was no denying I had become accustomed to having Kyra around. And for me, that was something.

Glancing down, I tugged on the gold bracelet. To my complete surprise, I'd started to become accustomed to it, too. In fact, I liked being able to speak with Kyra whenever I wanted.

Correctly sensing the direction of my thoughts, Kyra said, "I suppose Nerudian will take the bracelets off when he returns. It's funny, because . . . sometimes I forget I'm wearing it."

She sounded almost wistful, and I raised my head to meet her gaze. "There's no reason Nerudian has to remove them," I said, trying to sound more nonchalant than eager, as if I was just casually tossing off a suggestion. "I mean, we don't have to do it right when he comes back. There's no rush."

Kyra stared at me, and I felt a surge of emotions sweep through her—curiosity, hope, excitement—followed by a wave of fear so powerful, it dampened everything else. She turned to stare at something across the cavern, breaking our gaze, and I dropped my eyes to the floor beneath my bare feet. She was right to be afraid . . . not of me, as I hadn't sensed that, but of what might happen as a result of our staying in touch.

It was simply too dangerous, given the animosity between

our kinds. And it went without saying that if we couldn't speak with one another, we certainly couldn't engage in a courtship. I scowled, annoyed I'd even considered such a thing, and made my way down a tunnel, reviewing all the reasons a relationship with the Astral woman was impossible.

Kyra was slated to become the *Princeps Shaman* of Aeles. She needed a partner who was comfortable in the light of public scrutiny, something I would never be, even if my blood hadn't been an issue . . . which, of course, it was. I was forbidden from entering her realm, and even if we used the suppressor medallion to sneak me in again, I could only *imagine* what her family would say about me. With the combination of her personality and how pretty she was, she could easily have any Astral man she wanted, and she would want someone who made her life easier rather than complicating it.

On top of that, she despised the business I'd built for myself, and I had no interest in finding another career, as I'd worked hard for what I'd created and was proud of my reputation. I didn't want to argue with my partner every time I left my cave, having to justify where I was going and why. And while my kind might not banish or imprison me for courting an Astral, I also didn't want the attention that would come from being the first Daeval to court someone from Aeles since . . . well, probably since Schatten and Kareth.

A romantic relationship with Kyra would never work, and it was best to accept that now and focus on retrieving Rhannu. Afterwards, we would go our separate ways like we'd originally planned. Unlike Schatten, I wasn't destined to bring peace between Astrals and Daevals, so my time was better spent reviewing which weapons I would bring with me to Vaneklus.

42

KYRA

I watched Sebastian stalk out of the cavern, lantern light glinting on his blonde hair before he disappeared down a tunnel. I could sense the anger roiling inside of him, but I couldn't pinpoint exactly what he was upset about—was it my enthusiasm for keeping the bracelets on indefinitely? My fear over the consequences we'd both likely experience if we were caught communicating with one another? Or—and far more embarrassing to consider—when we'd spoken of courting, had he glimpsed the thoughts I'd had imagining myself courting *him*?

I don't understand why in the realm *you would waste time imagining such a thing!* huffed Aurelius.

I tossed my hair over my shoulder. *Perhaps he's grown on me.*

The same might be said of a barnacle on a ship, scoffed the lynx. *My dear, I'm not surprised if being around him feels familiar, given what you've been through together. I wouldn't even begrudge you feeling sympathetic towards him, given his past. And those dreams are clearly affecting your emotions, which is understandable. But to care about him beyond that—*the lynx pinned his ears back against his head—*there is simply no reason.*

I like talking with him, I countered, sensing Aurelius's surprise when I continued the conversation rather than changing the subject or falling silent. *He's obviously smart. The Daevals who know* him, at least the few I've met, are clearly fond of him, and no one would feel kindly towards him if he was thoroughly evil. Guessing what Aurelius was about to say, I held up a hand. And while I absolutely do not condone his career choice, even you have to admit it says something about his character that he didn't just give up after everything he's been through—losing his mother, being given away by his father, being tortured . . . he overcame things I can't even imagine and took care of himself, by himself.

I also found it strangely endearing how he constantly seemed to be fighting with his hair, brushing it back off his forehead, but there was no need to mention that observation.

Aurelius shifted to look directly at me, reassessing our conversation and taking it more seriously than he had initially.

I have always supported your desire to marry for love, he said, *rather than for prestige or political gain or simply because some paid professional believes it would a good match. At the same time, I would hate to see you choose a partner because you feel you need to prove something, to show all of Aeles you make your own decisions without regard for what others think or say. That could leave you just as miserable as being with someone simply because you've been told you must.* He held my gaze and added, *I only want you to be with someone you love, who loves you, and works every day to deserve you.*

I reached over and rubbed his head.

Thank you for always wanting the best for me, I said. *But there are some choices I'm going to have to make for myself, and if I make a wrong one, I'll learn a lesson and move on. You can't protect me from everything, Aurelius.*

His thick silver whiskers drooped.

I know, he said softly. *You've just been through so much. I don't want to see you hurt again.*

I have no desire to be hurt again, either, I agreed, *but I also don't want to be so afraid I stop trying things or limit myself.*

Batty kindly produced a plate piled with fruit and hot slices of toast covered in a sticky orange jam, and I ate in silence, dwelling on my last conversation with Sebastian, until movement at the mouth of a tunnel caught my eye. Sebastian emerged, hair damp from showering, and I noticed the stubble I'd seen on his jaw the night before was gone.

He tossed a towel and the clothes he'd slept in into a laundry basket before shoving his hands in his back pockets.

"If you want to clean up, Batty can show you the way. Then we can get going."

"Alright," I agreed, grabbing my clothes from where I'd draped them over the arm of the sofa before following the bat down a passageway I hadn't been in before. At the end of the tunnel, he proudly showed me how Sebastian had fashioned a shower using pipes and pulleys to direct water from an underground river. As I enjoyed the fruits of Sebastian's labor, I couldn't help comparing him to Schatten; like the Felserpent King, the assassin would also be quite good at a career involving engineering or mechanical design. Aurelius sighed loudly at my thoughts but refrained from commenting on them.

Drying off with a thick towel Batty kindly provided, I put on the clothes Aurelius had retrieved for me, my brown breeches and one of my favorite tunics, a deep blue shirt trimmed in gold thread and decorated with small embroidered gold stars. I managed to work my fingers through my hair well enough to style it into a tight braid, which would keep it out of the way in Vaneklus.

When I returned to the living area, Sebastian was waiting near the sofa. In addition to his black breeches and tunic, he was wearing a low-slung belt fitted with knives, a rope, numerous small vials, and two leather pouches. He also wore a scabbard buckled across his chest, and while it currently only held one sword, there was a sheath for a second. I was surprised to see he'd pinned the suppressor medallion to the front of his shirt, and he noticed my reaction.

"Daeval children are going missing," he reminded me, "and these types of medallions are the only way I know of for someone with silver blood to be in Aeles without setting off the Blood Alarm. I want to know if there's a way to track the medallions or even counteract them. Given how long Laycus has been around and everything he's seen, I thought he might know something."

"We certainly can't ask anyone else," I agreed, "and Laycus said he remembers every shade he's ever ferried. If anyone would have more information, it would definitely be him."

Sebastian nodded and held up the box with the unicorn horn in it, signaling he was ready to go, so I grabbed my cloak from the back of the sofa and slipped it over my shoulders. It hadn't escaped my notice that, in our last dream, Kareth had worn a shifter cloak identical to how mine had first looked when Nerudian gave it to me, which was yet another thing I'd be discussing with the dragon when he returned. Thinking it might be good luck, I pressed my hand against the fabric, changing it back to the blue velvet covered in whirling pastel nebulas before walking towards Sebastian.

"We should sit down," I explained, "so our bodies don't topple over when our shades leave."

He nodded and sat down cross-legged away from any furniture. I wasn't certain where to sit but directly across from him seemed odd, so I lowered myself down next to him, accidentally bumping my knee against his.

"Are you ready?" I asked. He nodded, so I reached over and took his hand in mine. Before I could say the spell to take us to

Vaneklus, however, the bracelet vibrated roughly against my wrist. I glanced at it, wondering why Sebastian hadn't just spoken out loud, but before I could ask, the cavern began to flicker in and out of view. Sebastian startled and gripped my hand, and I gasped as images filled my eyes, pulling me into a dream even though I was very much awake.

43

「*Thank you for letting us use your cave,*」 Kareth said, smiling at Nerudian.

The large black dragon gave her a toothy grin in response. "Of course, Your Majesty." He glanced over at Schatten, who was leaning back against a boulder with an unhappy expression on his face. "You are both always welcome here."

Schatten dipped his head in thanks, although his scowl remained.

"We need to take Rhannu to Laycus," he said to Kareth. "If Tallus gets his hands on it, he'll be invincible."

Kareth narrowed her eyes. "We will ensure the sword is safe after I bind our shades together. I'm much more concerned about never finding you again than I am about that sword."

Schatten ran a hand through his hair, but didn't disagree, since he knew better than to try and sway Kareth once her mind was made up. And, in his heart, he, too, valued his and his wife's shared destiny more than the sword.

Nerudian sighed, and a veritable gust of wind swept through the cavern.

"I still cannot believe Tallus divided the realm," he said sadly. "Without you two to care for it, I fear for all who live on both sides of the divide."

"What do you think might happen?" asked Schatten. Kareth heard *the pain in his voice and knew how much he cared for every inch of their kingdom.*

The dragon's powerful shoulders drooped.

"Floods," he replied. "Famine. Earthquakes. Avalanches. Things that haven't been seen since before the Great Serpent."

Kareth unrolled the Pelagian Scroll and took a deep breath.

"It's so complicated," she said, her voice tight with worry. "I have to use different combinations of the sana *beads at different times. And I have to take us in and out of Vaneklus." She smiled briefly. "At least Laycus agreed not to interfere."*

"What did he say when you told him what you were planning?" asked Schatten.

Kareth couldn't hide the fear in her eyes, even as she busied herself smoothing out the edges of the parchment.

"He said there's no more difficult enchantment to apply and only a few folks every millennia manage to get it right."

Schatten leaned forward and tucked her hair behind her ear. "That's us," he said, the tone of his voice leaving no room for argument. "We will get it right, and then we'll go back to Laycus, together, and show him there's nothing we can't do."

Kareth covered his hand with hers and drew his palm so it was cupping her cheek. She leaned her face against the callused skin she knew better than her own and closed her eyes.

"You're right," she whispered before settling her gaze on Schatten. "Thank you."

He nodded, and she pushed back the sleeve of her tunic, giving herself easy access to the sana *bracelet on her left wrist.*

"We will return, Schatten," she said, running a finger over Rheolath, The Controller. "We will come back in another time, in a place that will likely bear little resemblance to the realm as we know it now.

We'll come back, we will find one another, and we will reunite the realms."

"However many lives I live until that happens," said Schatten, "know I will never stop looking for you. Not until I find you."

Kareth leaned forward and pressed her lips against his. Then, placing her hand against his heart, she began the spell for binding their shades.

44

KYRA

The vision disappeared, and I gaped at Sebastian, who appeared every bit as astounded as I felt.

"How did that happen?" he demanded. "We weren't even asleep!"

I shook my head. "I don't know." Looking around, Batty was nowhere to be seen, although Aurelius was watching us with wide eyes.

"It doesn't make sense!" insisted Sebastian. "Rhannu was stolen by Astrals, not hidden in Vaneklus by some Felserpent King and Queen! I don't understand." He looked at me as if I might have an explanation for why everything he'd been taught his entire life was now being called into question.

"I don't know," I repeated. "I've never heard of a spell for binding two shades together." I glanced down at the gold bracelet. "I wonder if they succeeded . . . and if they ever came back."

As I spoke, a twinge tickled the back of my mind, like I was forgetting something important, but I couldn't remember what.

"What was that about the realms being divided?" wondered Sebastian. "They've always been separate . . . haven't they? And who was Tallus?"

"I really don't know," I said, wishing I had a different answer to give. "I feel like I don't know anything anymore."

We both fell silent, lost in our thoughts. Was it truly possible to bind two shades together? Was the Pelagian Scroll somewhere in the Aelian Archives? But most importantly, had Kareth succeeded? Between the bracelets, my cloak, and our dreams, I felt intimately connected to the former ruler and found myself deeply invested in what had become of her.

Sebastian shifted beside me, drawing my thoughts back to the cavern. "We're not going to get any answers by sitting here," he said. "We need to give Laycus the horn before it's too late."

I nodded and tightened my grip on his hand, then said the words to take us to the realm of the dead. The usual roaring filled my ears, and I felt myself tossed forward and hurtled out of my body. Concentrating, I pictured myself landing on my feet with my boots in the river, and when I opened my eyes, for the first time since I'd begun visiting Vaneklus, I found myself standing upright in the familiar grey river. Sebastian was standing next to me, and his eyes were wary as he surveyed our surroundings. I squeezed his hand before letting it go, trying to reassure him, since I had no doubt it was unnerving to be back in the place he'd gone after dying.

"Now we wait," I said, but no sooner had I spoken than the sound of rowing oars broke the silence. The fog before us parted, and there, at the front of his wooden boat, was the Shade Transporter. He gave an exasperated sigh but dipped his head in welcome as his eyes met mine. When he turned to Sebastian, however, his expression hardened.

"Recovrancers are the only living beings I suffer to enter my realm," he hissed. "Unless Kyra has tired of you and decided to hand you over to me."

"Sebastian is here with me," I said firmly, refocusing Laycus's attention. "We've brought you something, and we also need your help."

Curiosity flared in the Shade Transporter's garnet eyes. Sebastian held out the box containing the horn, and Laycus eagerly snatched it from his hand and ran it under his nose. A slow smile spread across his face.

"You have come for Rhannu," he said.

"How did you know?" I asked. From the corner of my eye, I saw Sebastian's mouth open in surprise.

Laycus slipped the box up the sleeve of his cloak, where it disappeared.

"Because that sword is the only thing here worth something as valuable as a unicorn horn," he said. "When the Felserpent King and Queen left it with me, they wanted to make it as difficult to recover as possible. There are only one or two things more difficult to obtain than a unicorn horn that has been freely given."

"So, it's true, then?" asked Sebastian. His dark eyes filled with astonishment. "The Felserpent King and Queen brought Rhannu to you? I was always taught Astrals stole it from my kind and hid it here!"

"That was the story that was spread, yes," nodded Laycus. "It allowed Kareth and Schatten to be removed from history, while also adding to the antagonism between those with silver and gold blood." He sighed. "A calculated move on Tallus's part, since he desperately wanted the sword but was unable to retrieve it."

"Who was Tallus?" asked Sebastian.

"An Astral who never accepted his kind could live in harmony with Daevals," replied Laycus. "He was the one who orchestrated the coup overthrowing the kingdom . . . who ultimately divided the realms."

"But, in school we learned Aeles and Nocens have always been separate," I said, feeling as if I was grasping at something not meant to be held, even though I desperately wanted to. As silly as it was, I couldn't just immediately abandon something I'd been told all my life.

"And everything you learned in school has proven to be correct?" sneered Laycus.

I thought back over recent events—my expectations about Nocens, my views on Daevals, and my understanding of Cypher communication—and slowly shook my head. It was as if some integral part of me was starting to unravel as I admitted at least some of my foundational beliefs were wrong.

"Why did Tallus want Rhannu so badly?" asked Sebastian, still more concerned with the sword than anything else. "I've read it makes whoever wields it invincible in battle, but now, I don't know what to believe."

"It does make you impervious to injury," said Laycus, "among other things, but Tallus wanted it for another reason—combined with the right incantation, it has the power to reunite the realms. He wanted to ensure that never happened."

My mind was reeling, working to keep up with so much new information, but I managed to ask, "So, is that why Astrals killed all the Recovrancers after Kareth and then outlawed recovrancy . . . so no one would be able to recover the sword?"

"I think, deep down, Tallus knew it was incredibly unlikely anyone besides the Felserpent King and Queen could ever recover that sword," replied Laycus. "The *real* reason recovrancy was outlawed was to prevent Kareth's return." He glanced at Sebastian, and a frown flashed across his face. "And Schatten's, too, I suppose."

"Because if they returned, they would recover the sword and use it to reunite the realms," Sebastian concluded.

Laycus nodded. "For all his faults, Tallus was quite skilled at planning ahead. He knew Kareth and Schatten would try to return and undo what he'd done, so he did everything he could to prevent it. Anyone who possessed recovrancy abilities might turn out to be Kareth, coming back to start the process of reclaiming her kingdom." His red eyes held my gaze. "Ensuring she never returned was the most effective way to prevent the Felserpent monarchy from being reestablished."

"I wonder if any of the Recovrancers I read about in the Archives were really Kareth, coming back," I said, looking out over the water. Then, fixing my gaze on Laycus, I added, "I know you said you don't keep up with shades after they leave your care, but do you have *any* idea where she might be right now? Is there a way to know if she's in Karnis or Ceelum or if she returned and is alive somewhere?"

"Oh, I know exactly where she is," replied the Shade Transporter. Then, to my surprise, he raised his fingers to his lips and whistled a complex series of notes. I gasped as Batty suddenly appeared on the edge of his boat.

"But . . . Cyphers can't come to Vaneklus!" I stammered, even though my own eyes told me otherwise. "How are you here?"

Batty smiled at me. "Let us say I am simply *unique*."

Sebastian stared at his Cypher as if he'd never seen the creature before. The bat looked up at Laycus, who gestured towards us.

"They are here for the sword, which means it is time," he said.

Batty nodded, then cleared his throat. "While my full name is too long for everyday use, perhaps today we shall make an exception. While both of you know me as Batty . . . I am pleased to be Bartholomew, your humble servant."

I stared at him, unable to form a response.

"No," said Sebastian after a long stretch of silence, shaking his head. "It's not possible. You can't be. You're not . . ." His voice trailed off as he searched for the words to express himself.

"Not old enough?" offered the bat. "I told you I was older than Nerudian, but you did not believe me."

My mind was spinning as a tremor of excitement rushed all the way to my fingers and toes. "You knew Kareth and Schatten!" I said, stepping closer to the bat. "You served as the first royal advisor. You helped Nerudian create the bracelets."

He nodded.

"What happened to them?" I asked, anxiety sloshing in my stomach. "Did they ever return?"

"Yes," said the bat, "they each returned many times trying to find the other, but it is only now they have returned, *together*." He swept a wing across his body and bowed low. "Welcome back, your Majesties."

I felt as I had in the forest, when I'd first seen Sebastian. For a moment, I couldn't speak or swallow or even so much as breathe. The only thing I was aware of was Batty staring at me. It was too preposterous to believe . . . yet somehow, in a way I couldn't explain, I also felt as if part of me had known all along and had simply been waiting for the rest of me to realize the truth.

Even so, trying to comprehend this newest development was like trying to force the north poles of two magnets together—my mind repelled it, pushing it away and refusing to allow it to join harmoniously with the rest of who I knew myself to be.

The struggle must have shown on my face because Batty grimaced and wrung his wings together. "This is very difficult for you, I am certain, especially since shades do not usually remember anything from a previous life. Oh, they might enjoy the same food, or meet someone and feel as if they know them without understanding why, but beyond that, memories are not typically maintained across life cycles."

A slow grin spread across his black furred face. "Then again, most shades are not bound across multiple life cycles. Your bond appears to have kept your memories intact."

"What are you talking about?" exclaimed Sebastian. "We

don't have memories like what you're suggesting. We've seen *others'* memories in our dreams since you put these bracelets on us, but . . ." He paused, awareness dawning across his face. "Are you saying the memories in our dreams *aren't* coming from the bracelets? They're coming from . . . us?"

Batty nodded. "I had hoped Nerudian's gift would help you remember your pasts, given how powerful the bracelets are and what a part of your lives they used to be. I am confident your memories would have eventually returned without their assistance, but there seemed to be no harm in helping things along."

"But why don't we remember making those memories?" I asked. "And surely we made more . . . why are we only remembering certain ones?"

"That I do not have an answer to," replied the bat. "This is unprecedented, so I have no idea what to expect. You made those memories in other bodies, which means the bodies your shades currently inhabit don't have even trace memories to drawn upon. It is likely easier to perceive them as belonging to others than to yourselves. I believe all of your memories, including the knowledge you made them, will return when you are ready, but that is based off very limited evidence and a great deal of speculation."

"I don't believe it," I managed to choke out, my voice hoarse with shock.

Suddenly, I heard Aurelius in my head.

Remember, Kyra, there is a difference between choosing not to believe something because it is nonsensical and choosing not to believe it because it is distressing.

Is Batty right? I asked. *Do you believe him, Aurelius?*

The lynx was silent for a moment, then said, *I do.*

I turned to Sebastian, almost more taken aback by my

Cypher's admission than by Batty's revelations. "Aurelius be-lieves him."

Sebastian momentarily covered his face with both hands, then ran them through his hair. He turned to face me, his fore-head creasing. "That means . . . you and I . . . we were . . ." He clamped his mouth shut and swallowed hard, but I heard him finish the thought in his mind: *We were in love.*

I could tell by the warmth in my cheeks I was blushing furi-ously, so I settled for pressing my lips together and remaining silent.

Sebastian frowned at his bat. "So, my interest in finding the sword . . . that wasn't me? I was only chasing after something that used to be important to someone else?"

"It belonged to *you*," corrected Batty, "simply a past version of you. And you wanted it because some part of you knows it is yours."

Laycus cleared his throat.

"It's highly unusual you both look as you did before and have so many of the traits you used to possess," he said, studying me from beneath his cowl. "I agree with Bartholomew, in that I suspect it has to do with your binding spell . . . more things were kept intact than is usual. But," he swung his gaze to Sebastian, "while some aspects of you may be identical to your past selves, each life cycle is different, and you are no exception. There are things about each of you, now, that will be different from who you were before. I can assure you it's all still *you*, but it will take time to discover both the differences and the similarities."

Before either of us could respond, Laycus held up a bony hand.

"I am certain you have more questions, and we shall answer them as best we can," he said. "But, aside from Recovrancers, the living cannot be in Vaneklus for long periods of time without suffering ill effects." He cast a meaningful look at Sebastian. "I suggest you recover your sword. Your unicorn horn has fulfilled the test of bone." Holding his staff over the water, he spoke a language I didn't understand, and lights appeared beneath the surface, forming a bright trail beckoning us onwards.

I glanced at Batty. "Can you come with us?"

He shook his head. "Alas, my Queen, I cannot. This is one thing you must do on your own." He flew towards me, hugging my neck tightly and encouraging me to be careful. He then waved at Sebastian and dematerialized, saying he would meet us back at the cave.

"Good luck, Felserpent Queen," said Laycus, a soft smile spreading across the lower half of his face. Sighing loudly, he added, "You, too, Felserpent King." His boat began to move away from us when Sebastian suddenly exclaimed, "Wait!"

The Shade Transporter's eyes flared a brighter red than usual, but he paused, nonetheless.

Sebastian gestured to the suppressor medallion pinned to his tunic. "What can you tell me about this? Do you know who invented it? How does it work? Can it be rendered ineffective?"

The Shade Transporter stiffened at being addressed in such a way, so I quickly added, "I'm sure it's a terrible hazard of your occupation, Laycus, but the fact is, you're the only one who has information about certain things."

"I am the only one you can safely *ask* about certain things," corrected Laycus, but my comment must have appeased him because he peered intently at the medallion before shaking his head.

"There is no time for details, so I shall leave you with this— seven such medallions exist, including this one, and they are some of the most carefully guarded items in all of Aeles, since no living Astral knows how to make more of them. They are very old objects, and the secret of their manufacture died with the Astral who requested their creation."

And with that, Laycus's boat slipped behind a bank of fog, and I found myself alone with Sebastian. My thoughts were racing almost too quickly for me to process—why had my father, of all Astrals, been entrusted with such a precious object? Given what Laycus had said, would Sebastian begin to question the story I'd told him about accidentally finding the medallion in a box intended for storage? Who was the Astral who had requested the creation of the medallions, and, perhaps most important, who had been the actual creator?

Sebastian and I looked at each other, and I could tell he had just as many questions as I did.

"Everything Batty and Laycus told us," I said, "about our pasts and the medallions . . . it's too much for me to process right now. I don't know what to think, but I feel like the best thing to do is focus on recovering the sword. Once we get back to your cave, we can work on sorting everything else out."

"I agree," nodded Sebastian.

Stepping carefully through the river, we followed the trail of lights until, all of a sudden, the water in front of us began to swirl, forming a whirlpool that extended farther and farther outwards. The swirling vortex parted with a loud sucking noise, and two walls of water shot upwards, exposing the dry ground of the riverbed. To my surprise, the ground formed a wide pathway that spiraled downwards, and although I squinted, there was no end in sight. Sebastian reached back into his scabbard and unsheathed his sword before cautiously stepping forward. I followed close behind, conjuring an orb of light to guide us as the path twisted deeper beneath the towering walls of water.

45

❧

KYRA

We made our way downward until the trail turned into stone steps, which we carefully descended. Although they looked worn with time, thankfully, they felt sturdy beneath my boots, and I soon stepped off the last stair and stopped next to Sebastian. Torches flared to life, illuminating the space around us, revealing us to be in a small room. The staircase was behind us, but there was nowhere else to go . . . lichen-encrusted stone walls hemmed us in on all sides, and there were no doors to be seen. I swallowed hard as fear pulsed at the back of my mind, ready to flood the rest of my body at the slightest provocation.

The bracelet on my wrist vibrated, and I quickly touched it. *Listen*, said Sebastian, and I held my breath to hear better. While it was faint at first, a staccato pounding sound quickly drew closer.

Something's running, Sebastian said, cocking his head. *More than one something.*

I was about to reply when the silence was broken by a chorus of snarls and growls, and I pressed myself against Sebastian's side. Three creatures suddenly leapt out of the dank rock walls, and I screamed as Sebastian raised his sword and stepped in front of me. The clanging of metal against stone rang out, and when Sebastian didn't leap into action, I peeked around him and let out a sigh of relief—each creature was tethered to a different wall by a thick metal chain.

"What are they?" I asked, moving to stand next to Sebastian again.

"Barghests," he replied, and I glanced at him just in time to see his lips press together in an unhappy line. The creatures resembled dogs, although they were closer to the size of horses, and while their bodies were muscular, they didn't appear entirely solid—their slick black coats rippled and shimmered, reminding me of the air when Sebastian conjured a portal. Their white eyes were especially unnerving, as were the long claws sticking out from each of their four paws.

As we studied the Barghests, a door appeared in the wall behind each creature, decorated with ornate designs and fitted with smooth handles that appeared to be made of bone. My worry of how to get past the Barghests was suddenly replaced by uncertainty over which door we should go through.

"Difficult, isn't it?" came a voice from the center of the room.

Sebastian leveled his sword at where the voice had come from, and slowly, a woman appeared. Her dark skin gleamed and when she opened her eyes, I wished she hadn't—they were identical to the Barghests'. She smiled, but there was nothing friendly about the expression. I couldn't sense either gold or silver blood in the woman, but then it dawned on me.

She's an enchantment! I said to Sebastian through my bracelet with no small amount of surprise.

Yes, but that doesn't mean she can't harm us, he replied. *She was placed here for a purpose, and she'll perform her duties, even if she's only a spell. If Laycus is to be believed, we probably placed her here to protect the sword, so don't underestimate her.*

"I hope you came prepared," said the woman in a low, lilting voice. "You're going to need all of your wits to get past my guards."

This must be the challenge involving the mind, I said to Sebastian, and he nodded without taking his eyes off the figure before us.

"Here is how this will work," said the white-eyed woman. "I will ask you three riddles. If you answer the first one correctly, the Barghest and the door it is attached to will vanish. If you answer the second one correctly, the same thing will happen. If you answer the third riddle correctly, the Barghest will disappear, but the door will remain, and it will be clear which way you must go. If you answer one of my riddles *incorrectly*—" she paused and raised an eyebrow. "I shall simply say the consequences will be most dire and leave it at that. Do you understand?"

Sebastian and I nodded.

"Riddle number one." The woman turned to the animal on her right, and as the creature spoke, its words hung in the air in red flowery script:

Who makes it has no need of it.
Who buys it has no use for it.
Who uses it can neither see nor feel it.
What is it?

Sebastian's response was immediate and confident: "A coffin."

I was astounded to see his words hang in bold, silver letters in front of him as he spoke. I was certainly glad he'd understood the question, as I'd never been fond of riddles or guessing games.

The woman nodded. "Correct."

With a wave of her hand, the Barghest slunk back into the wall until it disappeared. Sebastian's two words floated across the room and pressed themselves against the door, which vanished from sight.

"Riddle number two," said the woman, turning to the creature on her left. As it spoke, words floated outwards in green, slanted letters:

As I was going to the Mount of Druthers
I met a man with seven brothers
Each man did have two wives
And each wife had seven knives
Each knife had eighteen marks
From preparing food for the hearths—
Marks, knives, wives, and brothers
How many objects were heading towards Druthers?

My mind scrambled to do the calculations, and I desperately wished it hadn't been a question where being off by even a single digit would mean a deadly creature rushing towards us. I was still counting knives when I heard Sebastian say, "One."

My mouth fell open, and I braced myself for the sound of a chain being undone.

Instead, I heard the spelled apparition say, "Correct."

The Barghest faded from view and Sebastian's single, silver word touched the second door and caused it to disappear.

How did you know that? I asked, both relieved and impressed.

He glanced at me. *If the man going to the Mount of Druthers met someone, they'd be headed in the opposite direction. It's a common riddle in Nocens. You've never heard it before?*

I shook my head. *It's definitely not something we say in Aeles.*

It was now obvious which door we were supposed to go through; all we had to do was answer one more riddle. My heart began to beat faster, and I saw Sebastian shift his weight from one foot to the other, the only outward indication he, too, was nervous.

"Third and final riddle," said the woman, moving slightly to her left so we could better see the creature chained to the wall behind her. The last Barghest opened its mouth, and words issued forth in bright yellow block letters:

At night they come without being fetched.

By day they are lost without being stolen.

What are they?

I inwardly breathed a sigh of relief. I had actually heard that one before and remembered the first time Seren had proudly told it at the dinner table. I held my breath and waited for Sebastian to reply . . . except, he didn't say anything.

I glanced at him expectantly. Was he pausing for dramatic effect?

Still, he remained silent.

His shoulders began to rise and fall faster. Slowly, he turned his head and as he looked directly at me, I saw the panic rising in his eyes. Reaching over to grab his free hand, I said in a clear voice, "Stars. The answer is stars."

The spelled woman nodded. "That is correct."

At a snap of her fingers, the third Barghest retreated into the wall. My words floated in golden cursive letters towards the remaining door, and as they pressed against the wood, the handle turned, and the door swung open.

"Congratulations," said the enchanted woman, inclining her head at us before she, too, disappeared.

Sebastian and I looked at one another, and he squeezed my hand.

"I'm glad you knew the answer to that last one," he said. "I'd never heard it before."

"It's lucky we had each other," I said, even though I suspected luck had little to do with it, given that this entire recovery process had been planned out by the two of us ages ago.

I tightened my grip on Sebastian's hand, enjoying the way his long fingers interlaced with mine. "But, if we'd had to face a Barghest, couldn't you have fought it?"

Sebastian shook his head.

"Barghests usually appear in Daeval children's stories where a child didn't do as they were told and got eaten as a result. But I've also heard whoever kills a Barghest is haunted by it for the rest of their life. I've read Daevals ended up killing themselves because they couldn't stand decades of being tormented by the creature."

I shuddered, even more thankful we'd answered the riddles correctly.

"Are you ready to keep going?" asked Sebastian.

I nodded, and together, hand in hand, we stepped forward through the open door.

46

KYRA

*W*e emerged in another small room, empty except for a wooden table. Moonstones embedded in the rock walls around us began to glow, and thanks to the illumination, I could now see two copper bowls sitting on the table . . . next to two daggers with long shiny blades. Sebastian and I stopped in front of the table, where an inscription had been burned into the wood: "Blood of the Queen, Blood of the King."

Sebastian and I shared a long look.

"Well," he said, "I suppose this will prove if everything Laycus and Batty told us was true." I nodded, then let go of his hand and pushed up the sleeve of my tunic as I positioned myself in front of the first bowl.

Sebastian quickly sheathed his sword and grabbed my wrist as I reached for one of the daggers.

"I should go first," he said. "In case something goes wrong."

I pointed to the inscription. "It mentions the Queen before the King. I think I ought to go first, just so we're following instructions as closely as possible."

Sebastian scowled but begrudgingly relented. Picking up the knife in my right hand, I made an incision along my left forearm, wincing as the blade sliced through my skin. At least I could heal myself afterwards. As golden blood rose to the surface, I held my arm over the copper bowl and let a few drops fall. There was an inch or so of water in the bowl, and my blood dispersed quickly throughout the still liquid.

"How much do you think we need?" I asked, but before Sebastian could respond, the stone wall behind the table groaned. Slowly, the rectangular stones began to rearrange themselves, moving outwards from the center towards the left and right, like two bulky curtains being pulled back one brick at a time. As they shifted, they revealed an opening roughly the size of a large window. And there in the opening, secured to the wall by metal rods, was Rhannu.

"Do you know what this means?" whispered Sebastian, staring ahead as if he couldn't believe his eyes. I'd never seen him so shaken.

I nodded, for once in my life completely at a loss for words.

Sebastian turned towards me. "It means . . . you were . . . you *are* . . . the Felserpent Queen."

I inhaled slowly, looking from Sebastian to the sword, then back at Sebastian again.

"Our dreams, what Batty and Laycus told us . . . it's all true," I said. I likely would have continued to stare ahead in disbelief, unaware of little else, but the pain in my arm reminded me I was still bleeding, so I quickly pressed my fingers near the cut and applied a healing spell.

Sebastian nodded, then turned to face me. His nostrils flared as he inhaled deeply.

"This has become about so much more than you learning to be a Recovrancer and me owning Rhannu, Kyra. When we agreed to work together, I *never* imagined anything like this happening."

"You couldn't have known," I said. "Besides, apparently I was the one who bound our shades together." My cheeks might as well have been on fire, and I suddenly felt shy, standing next to a man I had once been happily married to.

"What I'm saying," continued Sebastian, "is you didn't agree to this." He hesitated, then said in a low voice, "You kept your word and did what you promised, but . . . if you want to leave the sword here, I'm willing to discuss it."

I blinked at him, certain I'd misunderstood. "I'm sorry, what are you saying?"

He frowned as he gestured towards the sword.

"We hid Rhannu here for a reason. If we take it, who knows what will happen? We might set things in motion we're unable to stop. Your life is going to be difficult enough being a Recovrancer, and . . . I don't want to add to that."

"Leaving the sword here won't change who we are," I pointed out.

"No, it won't," he agreed. "But it might be easier—not to mention safer—than finding out any more about who we used to be."

"You've wanted this sword your entire life. It means everything to you, and now you're saying you would give it up . . . for me?" I asked softly.

He nodded.

I stepped closer to him. "I told you before, you don't owe me anything for recovering your shade," I began, but he interrupted.

"It's not about owing you," he said. "It's about doing something for you because I *choose* to do it . . . to make you happy, and to make your life a little easier."

My mouth fell open, and it was a few beats before I had the presence of mind to close it.

"You . . . remembered what I said," I stammered, thinking back to my words when I'd spoken of recovering his mother.

He nodded again. "It's up to you. We can leave the sword here, go our separate ways, and forget we ever heard of the Felserpent King and Queen. Or, we can take Rhannu, see what happens, and rediscover who we used to be . . . together."

My heart threatened to beat out of my chest as I clenched the edges of my cloak in my hands to stop them from shaking.

What do you want? I asked, unable to say the words out loud.

He dropped his gaze to his feet, and two streaks of red appeared along his sharp cheekbones.

I want my sword back, he admitted, then slowly raised his head. *But I also want answers. And . . . I don't want us to go our separate ways.*

I want answers, too, I said, *and I want to get them with* you.

His eyes widened, and I felt a pang of hopeful excitement flash through him before he quickly locked it aside and turned towards the table, singularly focused on the task at hand. Picking up the other dagger, he made a swift cut along his right wrist, studying where the drops of blood beaded on his skin.

"My blood looks different here," he noted. "It's so pale; usually, the silver is brighter. It must have something to do with being in Vaneklus."

I made an acknowledging noise, not having come across anything in my reading about how Vaneklus affected blood, even as something inside me insisted Sebastian's observation was important. And then, I realized—the medallion! Sebastian was still wearing it, which meant it was suppressing his blood.

"Wait!" I said, but it was too late . . . Sebastian held his arm over the second copper bowl, and a few drops of blood splattered into the water below.

"What?" he asked, turning towards me, his eyes filling with apprehension.

"The medallion," I cringed. "I think that's why your blood looks different . . . the silver part is being suppressed."

We both looked at the sword, waiting for the metal rods pinning it in place to unfold at the recognition of Sebastian's blood. Instead, the floor beneath us lurched, and I gasped as Sebastian reached out to steady me, then took the opportunity to apply a healing spell to his arm.

"Something's wrong," he said. The entire room trembled, and dirt sifted down from the low earthen ceiling. I cast a panicked glance around the small space as the walls on either side of us wavered.

"Stay here!" ordered Sebastian. Summoning the fire to his hands, he darted around the table and pressed his palms against the metal rods trapping the sword. At first, they simply glowed as they absorbed the heat, but they soon began melting beneath his flames, turning into a thick liquid that spattered down onto the floor. Sebastian grabbed the sword as it came free and rushed back to my side, slipping Rhannu into the second sheath of his scabbard.

"This entire place is going to collapse!" he shouted, and the ground rolled wildly, as if to prove his point, causing us to sway on our feet.

"How do we get out?" I cried. Was it possible to die in Vaneklus? I didn't want to die . . . I couldn't leave my family or Demitri, and I certainly didn't want to die after just discovering who I used to be and finding the man I'd been married to.

"*Fosgail!*" Sebastian shouted, and to my relief, a portal snapped open. He shoved me through, then almost landed on top of me as he dove in after me. We crashed into the river, splashing loudly as we struggled to our feet, and Sebastian closed the portal just as the room we'd been standing in collapsed on itself. We stood in the river, gasping for breath, and I looked around for Laycus. He must have been occupied with a shade, because I didn't hear his boat heading towards us; instead, the only sound disturbing the stillness was our rapid breathing and the water dripping from our wet clothes.

"Are you alright?" panted Sebastian, and I gave a relieved

nod, momentarily resting my face in my palms. We'd made it out. We had the sword. Now all that remained was for me to take us home. Knowing I needed to do something filled me with renewed strength, and I closed my eyes, ready to say the words to leave Vaneklus . . . then found myself shoved backwards so hard, I nearly lost my balance. I opened my eyes and managed to steady myself as Sebastian unsheathed Rhannu and pointed it at where the water was churning a few feet ahead of us. A figure slowly rose from the small whirlpool, immediately followed by two more behind it.

"What are they?" I asked, wiping water from my eyes and pushing back the hair that had come undone from my braid.

"Formari," replied Sebastian, his voice filled with a concern I wasn't used to hearing from him. "They're spelled creatures created to protect specific locations or items. They're incredibly difficult to create, but I probably placed them here when we hid Rhannu . . . a last measure to keep anyone but us from leaving with the sword."

"If I'd realized sooner about the medallion, your blood would have been recognized, and they wouldn't have appeared!" I groaned.

"You had no way of knowing that would matter here!" Sebastian said, tightening his grip around Rhannu.

The three creatures had risen all the way out of the water, and they were hideous to behold, taller than Sebastian, with skin like mangled red leather. The one closest to us extended a pair of wings and beat them against the air, snapping its pointed jaws as it let out an ear-piercing shriek. Saliva dripped off sharp teeth, sizzling loudly as it fell into the water.

Their saliva is poisonous, said Sebastian. *I'm going to engage them while you make a run for shore.*

Alright, I gulped. *Be careful!*

Sebastian summoned his fire to his hands and threw a ball of it at one of the Formari, causing it to cry out in pain as the flames settled onto its skin. I'd only seen him summon a small flame to his hands before, and I slowed my retreat, eyes fixed on him, marveling at his control of such a dangerous substance. He ran towards the other two creatures, ducking and diving and slashing with Rhannu as if the weapon had always belonged to him . . . which, I supposed, it had. Realizing I needed to move, I made my way to the shore and sprinted towards a cluster of large rocks. Breathing heavily, I watched as Sebastian ran his sword through the chest of one monster, causing it to shriek as black blood spurted from the wound. The creature collapsed into the river, sending up sprays of water, and then, with a loud sizzle, it disappeared.

I'd never been supportive of what Sebastian did for a living, but in this moment, I was exceedingly grateful for his fighting abilities. He moved gracefully, with the ease of a dancer, as if wielding the sword was no more difficult than walking down the street in Vartox. I crouched low next to the boulders as he turned to the two remaining Formari . . . and then, suddenly, I felt as if my shoulder was on fire.

It burned like nothing I had ever experienced before, a thousand times worse than a sunburn and even worse than when I'd accidentally touched a hot pan on the cookstove at home.

Twisting my neck for a better look, I didn't expect to see large drops of something resembling black tar on my shoulder. The substance spread quickly, eating through my tunic and making contact with my skin. Looking up, I shrieked in terror at the monstrous Formari that had appeared behind me. Where had it come from? Saliva poured out of its gaping mouth as it reached for me, and I screamed again.

"Sebastian, help!"

47

※

SEBASTIAN

At Kyra's scream, my body turned of its own accord.

A Formari was dragging her away. It must have been spelled to materialize on the shore, rather than in the water with the others, and while I appreciated my tactical foresight, I also wished I hadn't made retrieving my sword so difficult.

The other two Formari moved to block my path, one of them still fighting the flames even the river couldn't quench. I kicked that one in the stomach as I plunged Rhannu into the chest of the other. Drawing my arm back, I elbowed the burning creature in the mouth. Teeth and bones cracked, and the monster howled in pain, grabbing its broken jaw. Almost simultaneously, I sliced Rhannu in a downward arc across the other Formari's chest. It screeched as blood gushed out and swiped at me with long black claws.

The bleeding monster lunged at me, and I stepped behind the second Formari, still burning and holding its jaw. Timing it so the creatures were facing each another, I rammed Rhannu through both of them at the same time. The one farthest away reared back a few steps, and I sliced off the head of the Formari immediately in front of me. It fell to the ground, flames rising upwards, just as the other creature leapt towards me with an ear-splitting roar. I threw myself into a front flip and used the momentum to separate the Formari's head from its body. The head landed with a thud in the water just as my feet touched down.

Kyra screamed my name again and I ran towards her, letting the fire in my veins flow freely. Flames rose upwards from my hands, enveloping the sword and illuminating strange symbols carved into the blade.

I had wondered how Rhannu could make someone unbeatable in battle, but now I was experiencing it firsthand—when I used the weapon, time very nearly stood still. I wasn't certain if my opponents actually became slower or if I became faster, but either way, I felt as if I could anticipate every move the Formari made.

The last surviving creature had his arms wrapped around Kyra so her back was pressed against his scarred red torso. Black acid was pouring from between his pointed teeth, running down thick lips and dripping onto her neck and shoulder. It had already eaten away part of her tunic, and I knew it had to be burning her skin.

"Let her go," I demanded, summoning the fire mask to my face.

The Formari laughed, a wet, gurgling chortle. "She will die here, as will you!"

Moving the sword from my left to my right hand, I pulled a dagger from my belt. Exhaling half of the air in my lungs, I let the blade fly. As it sped through the air, I ran past it to stand directly behind the Formari. The creature, seeming to move at half-speed, began to lean out of the knife's path. As it moved sideways, it did exactly what I'd hoped it would do and let go of Kyra. Before the monster could shift more than an inch or so to one side, I leaned around the creature and used Rhannu to stop the dagger, catching it by the handle. With my left hand, I plunged the blade up through the Formari's rib cage, piercing the creature's heart.

With my right, I drove the sword through the creature's neck before separating his head from his body. The lifeless monster crumpled to the ground, and I kicked it sideways so it wouldn't fall near Kyra, who was lying in a heap. Her legs must have given out when the Formari released her, and I quickly sheathed Rhannu and dropped to my knees at her side.

In some places where the saliva had fallen, her skin was red and festering, but in others, the skin had been burned so badly I could see muscle tissue and possibly bone. There were long claw marks on her rib cage, visible through her tattered shirt, and while they didn't seem terribly deep, golden blood shimmered from the wounds.

I hoped she could remain conscious long enough to use a healing spell, but as I turned her over, her eyes rolled back in her head. Her face contorted into a mask of pain, and she screamed, rearing up off the ground as if her body had been shocked with an electrum stick. I picked her up, trying to avoid her injuries as much as possible, when a splash rang out behind me.

I whipped around to see Laycus's boat pulling up to the shore. His red eyes blazed at me, and his skull-like face was contorted with rage.

"I *told* you before I had a special place in Vaneklus for you if you ever hurt her!" he bellowed.

We can heal her! shouted Batty inside my head. *If you can bring her shade back to her body, I know how to heal her!*

"Batty—Bartholomew—can heal her!" I shouted. "Send us back to my realm so I can save her!"

Laycus stared at me, then gave his head a sharp nod. He said something in a strange language and made a flicking motion with his skeletal fingers, and as the water around my feet began to churn, I felt myself squeezed in on all sides. The rushing sound I'd heard before filled my ears, and I felt as if I'd been thrown backwards, spinning end over end. I gripped Kyra with all my might, terrified she would be ripped from my arms. Without warning, I suddenly found myself falling forward, and as I opened my eyes, I quickly threw out my hands, back in my physical body and only just managing to keep my face from slamming into the stone floor of my cave. Next to me, Kyra's body slumped to the ground, and she groaned in pain.

"What do I do?" I hollered at Batty as I moved to Kyra's side. At least we weren't soaking wet like Kyra had been the last time she'd returned from Vaneklus; I didn't need my movements hindered by sodden clothes. Aurelius sprinted over, fur on end.

"You will need to work with an Astral healer," said the bat.

"She's the only Astral I know!" I shouted, my voice ragged.

"Adonis has some skill with healing," offered Aurelius. "No one in Aeles can match Kyra, but he is strong."

"And what am I supposed to do, talk him into coming to Nocens?" I asked, becoming more panicked by the second.

Then, I remembered—the medallion!

"I can portal her directly to Aeles!" I said to Aurelius. "Where should I take her?"

Aurelius shared the coordinates to Kyra's home with me, then said, "I'll contact Adonis, and Demitri as well."

I nodded and gathered Kyra into my arms. The poison was visible beneath her skin, long black lines that resembled ink-colored snakes slithering outwards from her shoulder. It was moving slowly, but it was still moving, hungry to consume all of her. She whimpered, and without thinking, I pressed my lips against her forehead.

"You're going to be fine," I assured her.

Rising to my feet, I held the coordinates in mind and opened a portal. Stepping through it, I found myself outside of a large, two-story wood and stucco house. Spelled lanterns hung from the corners of the roof and dotted the sweeping front porch, a bright contrast to the night sky overhead. Thunder rumbled in the distance, and a few stray drops of rain fell on my face. An Astral man suddenly appeared on the porch where I assumed there was an intersector, then raced towards me, taking the porch steps two at a time. Since he wasn't the Astral I'd seen in the Tryllet Forest, he had to be Demitri.

"No, no, no," I could hear him muttering under his breath as he drew near. His eyes met mine, and I was surprised at the depth of fear they contained. "Is she—"

"She's alive," I interrupted, "but she needs help. Where's Adonis?"

"Aurelius was going to get him," replied Demitri, his eyes widening as Batty flew through the portal and landed on my shoulder. I quickly closed the doorway, and Demitri turned his gaze back to me. "How are you here without setting off the Blood Alarm?"

Kyra moaned, and rather than waiting for my reply, Demitri ushered me into the house. As I looked around for a place to set Kyra, I couldn't helping noticing the space was exactly how I would have imagined her childhood home—elegant, yet welcoming, clean, bright, and filled with smiling family pictures.

I turned to ask Demitri when he thought Adonis would arrive, but the other man held up his hand. The fear in his light blue eyes had been replaced by anger, and he looked as if he hoped to watch me die by whatever method would be the slowest and most painful.

"If anything happens to her because of you—" he hissed between almost clenched teeth, then stopped as Aurelius materialized next to me.

"Adonis is on his way," the lynx said, and no sooner had the words left his mouth than I heard heavy footsteps running across the porch. The door flung open just as a flash of light-ning streaked across the sky and outlined the figure of the As-tral soldier I'd seen in the forest. Demitri's jaw dropped, and I couldn't necessarily blame him; it had been a rather impressive entrance.

Adonis stepped inside as Kyra stiffened and began shaking in my arms. She made a choking noise as her legs and torso spasmed, and I immediately lowered to my knees, lest I drop her, placing her gently on the slate floor.

"What do we do?" I shouted at Batty, as Kyra cried out and then went limp. The bat hopped from my shoulder to the floor and gazed up at me.

"You have to burn the poison out," he said. "With your fire."

"With your *what?*" exclaimed Demitri, looking at me as if I might suddenly explode before his very eyes. I ignored him and shook my head at Batty's instructions.

"That will kill her—" I began, but the bat interrupted.

"No," he said, before pointing a wing at Adonis. "He will use his healing abilities to protect her while you destroy the poison."

"It will never work!" I exclaimed, digging my fingers into my scalp in frustration.

Batty reached out and placed a clawed wing on my knee.

"It will work," he said, his shiny eyes fixed intently on mine. "I have seen it done before . . . by a long-forgotten king and queen, a Pyromancer and a healer, who worked together to save a young boy's life."

I stared at him, and he nodded ever so slightly.

You have done this before, he assured me.

The fire inside me flared to life, and I could see the flames dancing just beneath my skin. I placed one hand against Kyra's collarbone, the other on her forearm. Adonis knelt down across from me on the other side of her.

"Use all the healing *alera* you have," I said. "I don't want the fire in her a second longer than it has to be."

Adonis held his hands about chest high, palms facing upwards. He closed his eyes and muttered a spell I wasn't familiar with, raising his arms slowly above his head as he did. When his arms were almost fully extended, he opened his eyes, and golden beams of *alera* began wrapping themselves around his hands and wrists. He let them sink into his skin and, when he'd finished absorbing them, he lowered his glowing hands towards Kyra.

"No!" roared Demitri, pounding his fists against his thighs. "Don't help him! He's going to roast my best friend alive!" He stared fearfully at Adonis's *alera*-filled hands, then clenched his jaw and stepped forward to stop the soldier. Aurelius suddenly leaped over Kyra, launched himself at Demitri, and knocked the Astral to the ground. I'd never seen a Cypher interfere in such a manner, but I was grateful he cared enough about Kyra to do so.

"Let them do this, Demitri," the lynx said in a commanding voice. "I don't like it any more than you, but it's the only chance she has." He looked back from where his paws rested on Demitri's chest, pinning the man to the ground, and gave me a single nod.

I summoned all the fire inside of me and willed the flames to find and destroy the poison with every ounce of my might. Adonis grunted and pressed his hands against Kyra, sweat forming on his brow at the effort it was taking to counteract the fire. I watched as Kyra's skin began to glow from within, a reddish light spreading outwards from my hands, quickly catching up to the black poison claiming her shoulder and crawling up her neck.

As I watched, fighting for Kyra's life, the fire finally reached the poison. The black lines writhed angrily, struggling, but they were no match for my flames, and slowly, the poison began to fade, growing dimmer and weaker until it vanished completely. I immediately lifted my hands while Adonis continued to pour healing *alera* into Kyra, and her skin soon returned to its usual shade of brown. Cuts and bruises vanished, and two spots of color spread across her cheeks.

And then, she opened her eyes.

48

SEBASTIAN

J couldn't help myself . . . without thinking, I leaned forward and gathered Kyra into my arms.

I thought I'd lost you, I whispered, and I could sense her smiling.

You could never lose me, she replied. *Apparently we're bound together.*

I lowered my arms as Kyra shifted into a more comfortable sitting position. Running a hand over my face, I was surprised to find myself shaking. Batty scurried forward, wings extended, and Kyra smiled and hugged him to her chest.

"Thank the Gifters!" cried Aurelius, jumping into Kyra's lap as if he was a domesticated house cat and licking her face with his tongue, forcing Batty to dematerialize and reappear on the back of a nearby chair.

"What happened?" Kyra asked, and Aurelius explained all that had occurred since she'd lost consciousness. When he reached the part about how Adonis and I had worked together to heal her, she reached over and squeezed the soldier's hand. "Thank you," she said. "I hope this didn't interrupt something important."

Adonis grinned. "I was at home, doing laundry, so obviously my evening needed a little excitement. I'm glad I could help."

Kyra smiled in return and appeared about to respond, but then her eyes fell on Demitri. He had gotten to his feet and was standing a little distance away, arms wrapped around himself, eyes brimming with tears.

Kyra quickly rose and hurried towards him.

"Everything's alright. I'm fine," she assured him, as Adonis and I also got to our feet.

Demitri shook his head and a tear splashed against his cheek.

"But you almost weren't, and it's all my fault!" he said, his voice strained. "I was so afraid they'd hurt you, I told them not to touch you. If Aurelius hadn't—" his voice broke, and Kyra quickly wrapped her arms around him. I pushed down the plume of jealousy that flared at the sight of the woman I cared about embracing another man. Demitri was her best friend, and there was nothing wrong with her comforting him. Still, I found it easier to breathe when she released him.

As she did, Demitri studied me as if seeing me for the first time. His eyes narrowed. "Exactly *how* did Kyra become poisoned in the first place?"

Kyra and I looked at each other, then she cast an uncertain glance towards Adonis. He grinned and stuck his hands into the front pockets of his breeches.

"You probably don't know this," he said, "but I'm quite skilled at keeping secrets."

"You aren't going to tell the military about this?" asked Kyra. "Or try to arrest Sebastian?"

Adonis shook his head. "No," he said. "In fact, I'm going to need Sebastian's help." He turned towards me. "You were right about the experimentation center in Rynstyn. I've had to be careful about digging around in the military archives, but I found some records, from fifteen to twenty years ago, and . . ." he swallowed hard. "I never thought Astrals were capable of such things."

"From what I've heard recently in Nocens," I said, "it's possible Astrals are still doing those types of things."

Adonis's face paled as Kyra moved to stand at my side, quietly slipping her hand into mine. I didn't miss the way Demitri's face momentarily contorted in anger, but he quickly assumed a more neutral expression before anyone else noticed.

"While that's certainly tragic," he said, "I'd still like to know how Kyra was poisoned."

"She was helping me with something," I said, which earned me a snort in response.

"Oh, I have no doubt," Demitri replied. "However—"

"You know, I had *no* idea healing was so exhausting!" exclaimed Adonis. He cast a lingering glance at where my fingers were interlaced with Kyra's, and a look I couldn't decipher passed over his face. I expected him to make a fuss, but instead, he stepped towards Demitri. "I'd love a glass of water, and maybe something to eat, but I'm not sure I remember where the kitchen is."

I could tell Demitri was about to point him in the direction of the kitchen, then return to the topic of his best friend being poisoned, when Kyra spoke.

"That's really common after healing," she said. "Sometimes you feel tired or even light-headed. I almost fainted once." She smiled at Demitri. "Perhaps you should go with Adonis to the kitchen, just to make sure he's alright."

Demitri gave her an imploring look as Adonis added, "Please, Demitri? I'd never live it down if I passed out in Kyra's hallway and knocked myself unconscious."

The tips of Demitri's ears turned a furious shade of red, but he nevertheless began walking toward the kitchen, waving for Adonis to follow him.

Adonis flashed a wide grin at Kyra and dipped his head towards me before striding after Demitri. I tugged on Kyra's hand and pointed to the open front door; she nodded and led the way outside.

As we stepped onto the porch, I closed the door behind me, then turned to face Kyra. To my surprise, she stepped towards me, slid her arms beneath mine, and rested her head against my chest.

"Thank you for saving me," she said, hugging me tightly.

I carefully wrapped my arms around her, not wanting to squeeze too hard, and hugged her back.

"You've done the same for me," I said, and she chuckled in response.

"I suppose we're even, then." She raised her head and looked up at me. "What about Rhannu?"

"It's safe," I assured her, enjoying the familiar weight of the weapon between my shoulder blades.

We both lowered our arms, although we continued to stand near one another.

"So, what do we do now?" I asked.

"Well," she said, "I'd love a long bath and a good night's sleep, and then I have some questions for Batty and Nerudian. I'm certain Batty, in particular, will have a few thoughts about what we should do next." Her expression darkened. "There's also the issue of the medallions. I have to find out where they came from and what *exactly* they've been used for." Her voice was urgent, but her gaze turned sad, as if some part of her knew discovering the truth would be painful, further calling into question everything she'd been taught to believe.

I didn't disagree with the things she wanted to do, but none of them were my most pressing concern, and I swallowed hard, afraid to ask the question balanced precariously on the tip of my tongue. It had been years since anything had truly frightened me, but then again, what I was about to ask had the potential to change the rest of my life.

"What about *us?*" I asked, studying Kyra's face for any hint of a response. Simply because I had a past with this woman didn't guarantee me a future with her.

She was silent for a moment, staring at the door behind me, before bringing her gaze back to mine. A smile—part disbelieving, part excited—made its way across her mouth before reaching all the way up to her eyes.

"I like you, Sebastian. Not just who you were in another life, but who you are now. And I'd like to get to know you better. I'm not certain how to handle what you do for a living—although after Vaneklus, I certainly have a new appreciation for your fighting skills—but, we don't have to solve every problem tonight."

Her gaze filled with a determination I was fast becoming familiar with and suspected I'd been well acquainted with in the past, and she continued.

"At one time, I loved you enough to bind my shade to yours . . . to ensure we would always find one another. It's confusing, because we're different than we were then, and it's not as easy as just picking up where we left off."

I nodded. It *was* confusing, having memories I knew were my own but didn't remember making.

She hesitated, then said, "I might need some time to get to know you . . . again . . . but I want to. I want to know why I loved you so much."

"I want that, too," I said. "Just based off the few memories we've seen, you were everything to me. I don't know what it's like to feel that way about someone, but . . . I'm willing to learn." Without thinking, I reached over and tucked her hair behind her ear. The gesture felt so familiar, it took me a moment to realize I'd never done it before, at least not in this body.

Kyra caught my hand and pressed her cheek against my palm. She closed her eyes and inhaled slowly, and I could sense the emotions swirling through her, changing as quickly as I could identify them. She blinked her eyes open, and I felt as I had when I'd first seen her in the Tryllet Forest . . . frozen in time, pinned in place, aware of only her.

She rose onto her tiptoes, and I tilted my head, bringing my mouth against hers. As our lips met, it was as if a dam suddenly burst inside my mind, and a flood of memories overwhelmed my senses, pulling me into them, carrying me along, piecing things together to form an entire lifetime—my lifetime. I gasped as Kyra pulled back and stared at me. Her eyes were wide and her cheeks were red and she pressed her fingertips against her lips.

"Did you . . ." she said, then stopped as if she couldn't find the words. She didn't need to; I knew what she'd been about to say.

"Yes," I said, gazing down at her as a smile crept over my face while memories swirled through my mind. "I remember."

EPILOGUE

*W*hen Kyra pulled back from kissing Sebastian and pressed her hand to her mouth, Aurelius flattened his ears against his head.

"If he somehow burns her—" he growled, but Batty merely chuckled.

"They have finally recovered the rest of their memories," he said, gazing happily out the large window. "I knew they would find them when they were ready." He smirked at the lynx. "It appears they were ready."

Aurelius let out an annoyed sigh and shook his head. "I still cannot believe this is happening. If Sebastian hadn't somehow ended up in the Tryllet Forest when he was trying to get to Rynstyn, things would be *completely* different!"

"That is not true," argued the bat. "They would have found each other eventually, no matter how long it took. *However*," he clasped his wings behind his back, "I have never been good at waiting, which is why I interfered with Caz's intersector and ensured the two of them met."

Aurelius's eyes widened with surprise. "You *what?*"

"I have been watching her ever since she first went into Vaneklus," Batty admitted. "A fact, it seems, you were not aware of." Aurelius snarled a warning, but the bat continued. "After she accidentally entered the realm of the dead, Laycus sent me a message. He wasn't certain, but he had a strong suspicion Kareth had returned."

"Her name is Kyra," snapped Aurelius, "and I don't care who

she used to be. In this life, she is *my* responsibility, and I don't look kindly on your meddling!" His scowl deepened. "It's bad enough she's a Recovrancer . . . now she's going to be involved with a Daeval? It's unheard of!"

"It won't be unheard of for long," said the bat. An unexpectedly serious expression came over his face, and his oblong ears pointed straight up. "Theirs will not be an easy path, I fear. Change is difficult, even when it is welcome. When it is not . . ." His voice trailed off, and he shook his head.

"Exactly what sort of change do you have in mind?" demanded Aurelius.

"Well, the first step was for them to find one another. Then, they had to remember who they are," explained Batty. "Since they've accomplished that, they can now fulfill their other reason for returning." He grinned broadly. "Reuniting the realms."

Aurelius's mouth fell open.

"You cannot be serious!"

"I am quite serious," Batty assured him. "That was their pact when they bound their shades. They would return, together, when the time was right to reclaim what had been taken from them."

"I will not let you turn Kyra into some upstart revolutionary simply to fulfill your own purposes!" hissed Aurelius.

"I am not turning her into anything," corrected Batty. "I shall merely offer guidance as she continues down the path she set herself upon lifetimes ago. We must move quickly, though."

"And why is that?" asked the lynx, everything inside of him suddenly dreading the bat's response.

Batty's dark eyes filled with a worry Aurelius had never seen him display before.

"Because," the bat said softly, "they are not the only ones who have returned."

Acknowledgments

Ever since I can remember, I've wanted to be a writer. Whether it was done for pleasure or academic publication, writing has been one of the few constants in my life, a refuge I can escape to when reality is too painful or overwhelming, as well as a place I can go where it's okay to be different and where I'm never alone, judged, or misunderstood.

The books I read as a young adult without question shaped who I am today, and it is truly a privilege to share my work with readers. So, my first thank-you goes out to you, dear reader, for taking a chance on this book and sharing your time with Kyra, Sebastian, and those in their realms. I hope you realize you are stronger than you think, and when you feel like no one understands you, know that my characters are always there for you.

Thank you to my publishers at SparkPress, particularly Brooke Warner and Samantha Strom, for giving this book a chance to live in the physical world and not just on my computer. Thank you to Julie Metz for such a beautiful cover design; you not only embraced the vision I had for the cover, you improved it, and I couldn't be happier. To my amazing team at BookSparks—Crystal Patriarche, Hanna Lindsley, and Sabrina Kenoun—thank you for your tireless efforts and incredible initiatives to promote this book and for making me feel like a "real" author.

Thank you to my incredible editor, AR Capetta, who saw the gem buried deep within the original manuscript I sent them and helped me to tell the absolute best story I could.

Sarah Bills and Isabella Taormina, you have both supported me since I very first mentioned I was working on a novel, and I will always appreciate our book conversations over lunch in the hospital cafeteria. Thank you for believing in me, for reading early drafts of my work, and for loving my characters when they were little more than ideas in my head.

Dad, thank you for always keeping our house filled with books and even building additional bookshelves when needed.

Mom, thank you for all the trips to the library, for believing in my writing abilities, and for always encouraging me to go after my dreams.

To my amazing sister, Dondi, thank you for supporting this book when I was at one of the lowest points in my life. The text stories you sent about my characters kept me going in ways you will never truly understand and brought laughter to a time filled with tears. Thank you for believing in me, for loving me whether I turn out to be a successful author or not, and for inspiring me with your strength every single day.

Dante, you were my best friend and the love of my life for almost 11 years, and you were truly the best dog to ever exist. You listened to me read whatever I was working on out loud, and I will always remember you sleeping at my feet, snoring and grunting in your dreams, while I wrote on my laptop. I wish you were here to see this book in print; you were, and always will be, my Cypher.

To my incredible husband, Cameron, thank you for always seeing me as a writer. Thank you for supporting me as I navigated the process of bringing this book to life and for calming me down every time my Capricornian fears surfaced and resulted in a panic. I never imagined I would share this part of myself with anyone, but you've made me feel safe enough to bare my deepest hopes, dreams, and vulnerabilities with you. I truly could not have a better partner, and I'm so incredibly lucky.

To all the other friends and family members who have offered encouragement and support in ways big and small, thank you. Writing is a solitary process, but you all constantly remind me I'm not alone, and I'm forever grateful for your social media shares and word-of-mouth recommendations.

And finally, to paraphrase a certain rapper, I'd like to thank myself, specifically my creative muse. Thank you for always showing up, for pushing me forward even when I can't see the path, and for having so much to share. As Garth Nix wrote in *Sabriel*, "Does the walker choose the path, or the path the walker?" I am immensely fortunate we chose each other.

About the Author

Photo credit: Cameron Bowman

KATIE KERIDAN made her literary debut at ten years of age when she won a writing contest by crafting a tale about her favorite childhood hero, Hank the Cowdog. After that, Katie continued to write, through college and graduate school and during her career as a pediatric neuropsychologist. While Katie enjoyed being a doctor, scientific research didn't bring her nearly as much joy as did creating her own characters and worlds, so she slowly left the medical world behind to focus exclusively on writing. In 2018 she self-published a poetry book, *Once Upon a Girl*, and her work has been featured in *Highlights Hello Magazine*, *The Blue Nib*, *Youth Imagination Magazine*, *Red Fez*, *The Red Penguin Review*, *Sand Canyon Review*, and *Every Day Fiction*, to name a few. She loves sharing her writing with others who feel different, misunderstood, or alone. Katie lives in Northern California with her husband and two very demanding cats.

SELECTED TITLES FROM SPARKPRESS

SparkPress is an independent boutique publisher delivering high-quality, entertaining, and engaging content that enhances readers' lives, with a special focus on female-driven work. www.gosparkpress.com

The Goddess Twins: A Novel, Yodassa Williams. $16.95, 978-1-68463-032-5. Days before their eighteenth birthday, Arden and Aurora's mother goes missing and they discover they belong to a family of Caribbean deities. Can these goddess twins uncover their evil grandfather's plot in time to save their mother, themselves, and the free world?

Above the Star: The 8th Island Trilogy, Book 1, Alexis Chute. $16.95, 978-1-943006-56-4. *Above the Star* is an epic fantasy adventure experienced through the eyes of three unlikely heroes transported to a new world: senior citizen Archie; his daughter-in-law, Tessa; and his fourteen-year-old granddaughter, Ella. In this otherworldly realm, all interests are at war, all love is unrequited, and everyone is left to unravel the truth of who they really are.

Red Sun: The Legends of Orkney, Book 1, Alane Adams. $17, 978-1-940716-24-4. After learning that his mom is a witch and his missing father is a true Son of Odin, 12-year-old Sam Baron must travel through a stonefire to the magical realm of Orkney on a quest to find his missing friends and stop an ancient curse.

Kalifus Rising: The Legends of Orkney, Book 2, Alane Adams. $16.95, 978-1-940716-84-8. Sam Baron's attempt to free his father brought war to Orkney. Now captured by the Volgrim witches, Sam's only hope lies with his friends—but treachery shadows their every step.

Blonde Eskimo: A Novel, Kristen Hunt. $17, 978-1-940716-62-6. Neiva Ellis is caught between worlds—Alaska and the lower forty-eight, white and Eskimo, youth and adulthood, myth and tradition, good and evil, the seen and unseen. Just initiated into one side of the family's Eskimo culture, she must harness all her resources to fight an evil and ancient foe.